OATHBOUND

Silverlands Book Two

DONNA MAREE HANSON

AUTHOR NOTE

Please note:
British/Australian spelling conventions are used in this book.

For example, color spelled colour, recognize spelled recognise, traveling spelled travelling and other variations and so on

Copyright Information

First published by Aust Spec Fiction (Donna Maree Hanson) in 2017.

Copyright © Donna Maree Hanson 2017.

The moral right of the author has been asserted.

Print on Demand format ISBN: 978-0-9757217-7-3

Ebook format ISBN: 978-0-9757217-8-0

Edited by Kaaren Sutcliffe

Cover by Croco Designs

Map by Russell Kirkpatrick

To report a typographical error, please email donnamareehanson@gmail.com

 Created with Vellum

To Taamati, Shireen (Beans) and Erana. I am proud of you all. Please keep on pursuing your dreams.

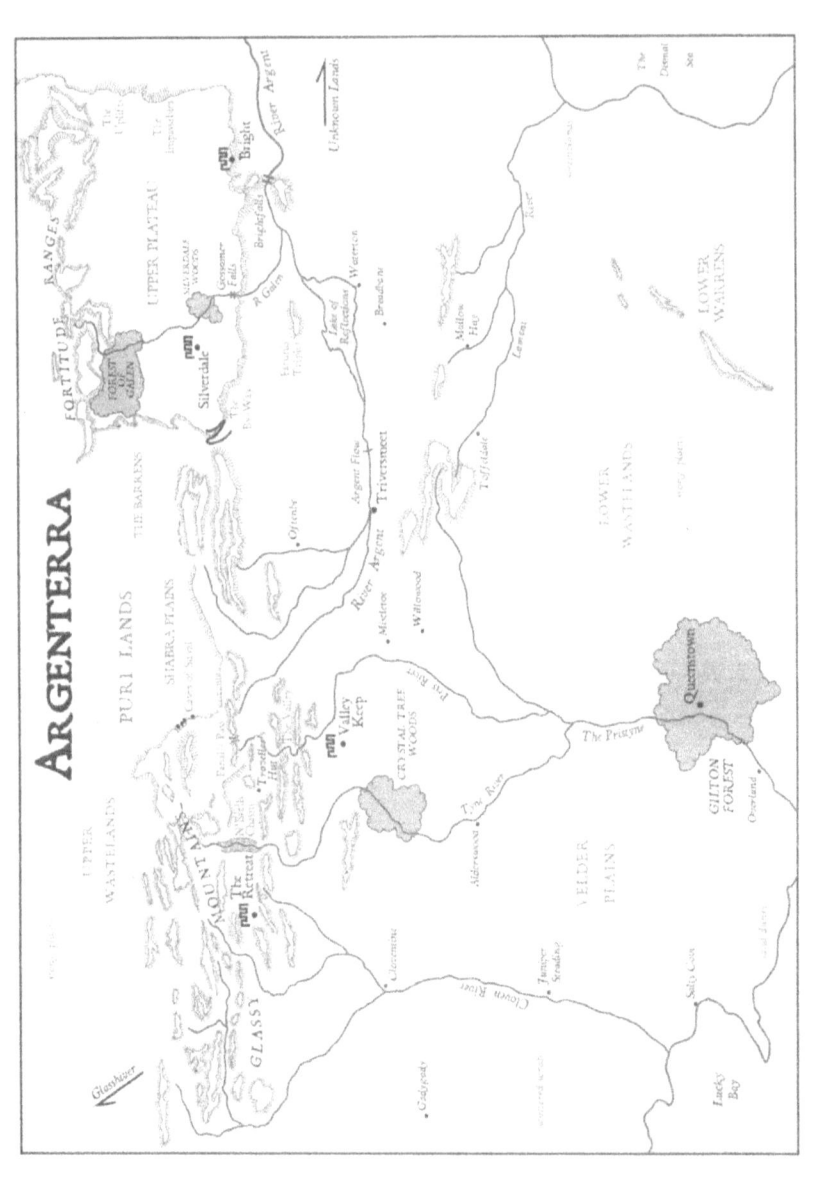

TO THE VALLEY

The sound of baby Gillcress's hungry wail pierced the haze of Oakheart's dream, bringing him to wakefulness. He heard Lillia stir as she went to tend the child, whispering soft words that calmed his shrilling demands for food. Oakheart breathed deeply, trying to ignore how Gilly's cries sounded like heartbreak and abandonment, the very feelings that churned within him as he lay there, hoping for a moment of oblivious sleep. Horror ebbed from his mind as the tendrils of the dream receded like the fading aftertaste of too much wine.

Camped in a wooded hollow as they fled from the warrens back towards Valley Keep, they huddled against the cold and the threat of pursuit. Sentries periodically whistled an 'all is well'. Oakheart counted the signals and relaxed the tension in his neck and arms. Wearily, he opened his eyes, and groaned as the recollection of events came flooding in with uncalled-for clarity. They had saved Aria's and Dellbright's son, Gillcress, but he had lost Sophy, his oathbound bride, to Rufus and his dark enchantment. He grimaced at how he had let Sophy spring the trap set by Rufus—baby Gilly in exchange for herself.

Oakheart tried to understand what the being Rufus had done to Sophy. The leaf from the Crystal Tree had been growing within her, that much he had witnessed. But a total transformation? How had Rufus bound her in that crystal shape? What effect did it have on her —and on Argenterra? While he did not know the full of it, deep in his gut he knew it portended ill. Something was very wrong, not only with Sophy but also with Argenterra.

Knuckling sleep from his eyes, he squinted at the sky, still dark with night's cloak. Lifting his head, he saw faint wisps of dawn creeping up the horizon. Still an hour or so short of daylight, not enough time to go back to sleep before they had to pack up and leave again.

A yawn seized him and he stretched out his aching limbs. By the *given*, he was tired. Even after many nights, he was not accustomed to the repeated nocturnal waking of the babe. Lillia was constantly feeding him and the little boy's body was now well-rounded and his cheeks chubby and pink. That the child was safe and thriving was all the comfort he had for the moment. Again, his mind was brought back to the scene in Rufus's cave, the churning noise of the warren beasts as they clawed the stone floor and ground their teeth together in anticipation of blood. His blood.

Within that memory was Sophy, tall and proud, willing herself forwards into the trap prepared for her. Oakheart had detected the power of the golden ring as it twisted and bound Sophy. Her metamorphosis dragged at his senses. Being oathbound allowed him to feel her edges hardening as she was wrenched and bent into that unnatural state. Even now, they were tethered by their oathbond that remained alive and strong between them, fixed in blood and deed. He sighed. It kept him going, knowing that she lived still within that gem.

"That child has a lusty appetite," Fern commented, his words muffled by his blankets. Oakheart heard his friend shuffle and turn on his side. In the dim starlight, Fern was a dark mound. "Are you sure he is not your close kin for he eats as much as you do?"

Oakheart chuckled quietly, glad that Fern's light banter helped dispel his morose thoughts. His cousin, Fern, was a fine warrior and natural commander and had saved them from certain death, arriving with help just in time as they were surrounded by Rufus's screavers and beasts. Now that Rufus had Sophy, he wanted Oakheart dead.

"No, not so close in blood as his appetite would lead you to believe. I wonder how Lillia bears it," Oakheart said, and then placed his hands behind his head to stare at the deep, purple sky and watch the stars fade.

"Oh, but she does not bear it well. She nearly knifed me yesterday when I commented on how well she looked."

Oakheart smiled in the dark and shook his head. Fern would never change. His mouth caused angst wherever he went, unless of course there was a pretty maid to be lured away for a cuddle or a kiss.

A frown of annoyance marred his features when he remembered how Fern's acid tongue had flayed poor Sophy, for days, even weeks, on end. In fact, Fern pointing out all of Sophy's faults had only led Oakheart to think well of her and to focus on her good points.

A sound of scratching interrupted his musing. Oakheart's hand closed upon his dagger, and he listened intently. The scrabbling noise grew louder and a man-shaped shadow rose up and then hunkered next to him. Oakheart tensed.

"Oakheart?" Mellow whispered urgently.

Oakheart tried to slow his heart rate; it was only Lillia's mate. "What it is it? The child?" Oakheart hissed, flinging off his blanket and fearing some threat to his charge.

Mellow's shadow rose, a dark shape blocking out the stars. "No, fear not. The child is hale. It is of Lillia I come to speak."

"Lillia?" Oakheart braced himself and repressed a groan. He had been expecting Mellow's entreaty for some time.

Mellow leant in closer and lowered his voice. "Yes. She has served you well, excellency..." As he hesitated, Oakheart could hear Mellow breathing. "Is it not time to free her from her duty when the child is returned to the valley?"

Oakheart closed his eyes for a second, opened them and tried to look Lillia's husband in the eye. It was difficult. Mellow's eyes appeared like dark holes in his head. Daylight spread thin fingers into the sky but the forest man was cloaked in grey gloom. Oakheart softened his voice. "Mellow, good friend, your mate has served me well. But she does not do my bidding. I cannot influence her where you cannot."

Mellow's breath grated in his throat. "But she is with child..."

Oakheart let the air sigh out of him. He knew about the pregnancy because Sophy had whispered it to him as he held her in the night. The memory of his oathbound came tantalising and pure. Her soft flesh pressed against his and the burning warmth of her love. "And…"

Mellow edged closer and spoke urgently in Oakheart's ear, keeping his voice low so he could not be overhead. "She cannot continue to feed the babe and fight off attacks and keep her…our…unborn child. Surely you see it. Daily she weakens."

Oakheart reached for Mellow's hand, now grasped tight to Oakheart's blanket, and squeezed it companionably. "My heart goes out to you both. Soon we will be in the valley. The task of feeding Gilly will pass from her. There you must decide what path you will take. Lillia would be affronted if I tried to dictate her duty. She would not even listen to Sophy…"

He thought he heard Mellow sniff and then noticed him wipe his arm across his face. "I cannot shake her from this path. Never has she been so stubborn. She will not even speak about the matter with me."

Fern chose that moment to speak from his bed. "Best you disarm her before you try…"

Oakheart rolled his eyes as Mellow swung round, still crouched. "Be still…" Mellow hissed. "I will knife you myself if you speak against her. She is the mother of my children, a warrior in her heart, the love of my life since we were children. We drank from the same breasts. We climbed our first tree together. We dived from Fell Falls to the pools below, our first feat of daring. Our breath and our life are in the Gilton Forest."

Pausing to draw in a breath, Mellow faced Oakheart again. "How do I get her to return? What sway does your oathbound wife have on her?" Mellow's voice was plaintive.

Oakheart did sympathise, but there was nothing he could do. He had tried on many occasions to dissuade Lillia, to send her home. Making an enemy of the forest maiden was not wise, and nor did he want to for she was dear to him. She would become a bitter foe if he persisted or stood between her and her desire to serve. He could not help but be glad of her aid.

He ran his hand through his hair. "I cannot answer for her, my friend. You must bare your heart to Lillia...only she can tell you what you wish to know. Lillia is a forest maiden, a warrior; that much you have always understood. I know Sophy touched her heart somehow... since they first met she warmed to her."

Mellow's inarticulate expression of defeat sounded in the quiet of the night.

"Very well...I will make the attempt at Valley Keep, even though every day I am away from Gilton Forest I feel less of a man and more like a ghost. I do not feel whole without the spirit of the trees, or the smell of the damp earth, or my tree home surrounding me. I miss the sounds of the children...I miss her."

Oakheart sighed. "Aye...I understand your need. Your help on this quest has been valuable. If it is any comfort to you, your presence has made Lillia happier."

Mellow slunk away, disturbing the loose soil and rocks with his feet as he headed back to his blankets. Oakheart did not think his words had comforted the man. Biting his lip, he realised that he understood Mellow's situation all too well. Sophy, too, was headstrong and independent.

☙❧

NEXT MORNING, AFTER CRESTING A SLIGHT HILL, OAKHEART pulled his mount to a halt next to Fern. His friend had sent scouts out and was peering into the distance, his face creased with concern.

"What is it?" Oakheart asked.

The wood was open, thinning to haphazard groupings of trees. A few hillocks in the distance could hide an ambush. He recalled that there were a few farmsteads in the area, though they were isolated from each other and the main road linking Silverdale and the valley. If they rode hard, they could reach Valley Keep by moonrise. An uneasiness crawled up his spine. Something did not seem right. Mist lay in shallow depressions in the fields, clinging to trees and floating above a small pond.

Ahead, the exposed grassland appeared white with frost. Unease, like a knife's edge, dug into his gut. Oakheart's breath curled in the air as he exhaled. Steam rose from the flanks of Fern's horse. His disquiet grew in the still morning atmosphere. Oakheart's eyes slid sideways as the guards nocked arrows. Expectation filled the air.

The sound of distant hoof beats thumping the ground alerted him to the lone scout riding hard towards them. Clods of damp earth flew up behind the rider, churned by the horse's hooves. His men bristled with tension as they waited for the rider to draw closer. A few horses shook their heads, jingling bridles and bits. Fern signalled for four men to angle around to the right and another four to the left. His gaze never left the approaching scout.

Without looking behind him Fern spoke. "Lillia, take the child to the rocky outcrop behind us. Make your position defensible." Fern spared Oakheart a quick glance. "You best stay by me for the present. But be ready."

"Of course." Oakheart watched as Lillia slid from her saddle and scurried to where there was a cleft between two boulders. She crouched and backed into the gap with Gilly fast asleep in her arms. Mellow took the horse behind the outcrop and returned with an armful of branches. After disguising the horse's hoof prints, he also backed into the cleft, sheltering Lillia and the child with his body and holding the branches in front of him to disguise their presence. His dark and angry gaze peered out, knife at the ready. The other forest folk, Illart and Raven, crouched in the shadows on either side of the outcrop, ready to provide protection.

Oakheart could not believe danger lurked so close to the valley. For many years he had travelled along these trails free from harm. Dellbright talked of the occasional skirmish with Puri raiders, but they were not fraught with danger and evil. Surely whatever surrounded them was sourced in Rufus and his hate.

The scout rode up, his red face clenched with worry and fright. He was young and his brown hair flew about, loose from its tie. "I found a farmstead burnt-out. There were no signs of inhabitants, dead or alive. Something stalks these parts, though. I heard it, saw traces. I came to give warning as soon as I could."

Fern chewed his lip as his grey eyes surveyed the ground ahead. Another scout hove into view, galloping from the opposite direction.

Behind him followed a riderless horse with what looked to be a body draped over the saddle. Another look and Oakheart saw the leading rein. A whispering spread through the men. Oakheart waited, his heart beating a rapid time while the scout drew nearer.

When the scout rode up on his foam-flecked mount, Fern leapt from his horse and rushed to him. Oakheart eased himself out of the saddle, all his senses on alert. Fern grasped the rein of the second horse. By the clothes, the body appeared to be a dead farmer. The scout held the reins while Fern jerked the body free of the ties binding it to the horse and eased it to the ground.

Oakheart's gaze roamed about the countryside warily. He eyed the mist, which seemed to move and shape by itself. It distracted him.

"Oakheart, look at this," Fern called from beside the body.

Shaking off his disquiet, Oakheart strode to where Fern was leaning over the body. Oakheart crouched and took in the farmer's blood-stained clothes and the face stretched by death. The stench of wrong emanating from the body almost knocked him over. Murder; another death taken in hate and anger. Oakheart kept his expression bland but knew he had failed. His jaw clenched. He did not like what he was seeing or feeling. All these happenings spoke of dire portents, he thought as his heart iced over.

"There is a dagger." Fern pulled it out, with the sound of a squelch, and held it up to the light. He stared at the handle, rotating it slowly in his bloody fingers. "Look, 'tis a Puri blade."

Oakheart's attention flew to the hilt. The dark handle was etched with silver swirls. It was a familiar pattern and definitely of Puri manufacture. "Yes," he said, taking it into his own hand. He examined the pattern closely. "Nasheen's markings." He stared at it, not believing the evidence of his own eyes. Nasheen was a Puri troublemaker, leader of a relatively small tribe. Oakheart knew him from his travels through the wastelands. He thought he understood Nasheen and his ways. This knife seemed out of place, not only in Argenterra but also in the back of some innocent farmer.

Fern stared at him expectantly and Oakheart met his unspoken query.

"Puri do not kill like this, nor would they leave a dagger behind. It is too precious an item. They steal goods and people. 'Tis not their way to...take life like this. They are bound by the binding oath as are we. I have met Nasheen many times...trickery, theft, maybe, but I cannot believe him capable of cold-blooded murder."

Oakheart near spat the word—murder. It was a word to scare children, an unknown bogey man that lurked in the legends of old, the time before Vorn brought them to this land. A time of war and death and suffering. A time of the Ancient Evil.

To take a life was to break the binding oath. Oakheart's heart sank at the thought of it. He did not want to accept that the time Vorn feared was nigh upon them. He did not want Argenterra to lose the *given*. It was part of them, part of who they were. This had to be Rufus's doing. Did that evil, alien creature's deeds undo the oath? That was Oakheart's single vestige of hope. That Rufus was not oathbound and therefore his actions did not harm the relationship with the land.

The sparkle in Fern's eyes died quickly. "Yes, but they do say the Puri know how to bend an oath." Fern glowered at the body, shaking his head. "Mostly to do with taking wives though."

"Perhaps. But there is no reason to harm in this way, risking the oath and all that means. I cannot credit it." Oakheart inspected the body closely, searching for evidence that would reveal the truth as to why this poor farmer had been killed. The man was not that long dead. A sense of alarm troubled Oakheart. Convinced that he saw movement out of the corner of his eye, he leapt up. Alert and tense, he moved to a fighting crouch. Surely that slight alteration in the shadows signalled movement.

Fern also bolted upright. Wiping his hands on his breeches, his head swivelled left and right. "The mist moves stealthily. Strange..."

The mist! Oakheart understood—the mist had crept furtively, oozing from branch to branch while their attention was on the remains of the farmer. Fear jabbed into his belly. There was purpose in its stealth.

Movement and a grunt beside him surprised Oakheart and the knife was ripped from his hand. He looked down at the crouching corpse, waving the knife like a serpent's head. Fern's throaty yell brought the others, who circled warily. The dead thing lunged for

Oakheart. He kept his gaze riveted on the hand that clenched the deadly blade, circling out and away. The eyes flashed red in the dead farmer's face. Wrong rippled from the walking corpse like rotting effluent. *Rufus!*

His men were hesitant, uncertain. Oakheart caught a glimpse of the fear and revulsion in their faces. Such an unnatural act was beyond their ken. Perhaps it was better, no one underfoot to hamper his defence.

Oakheart backed away, all his senses riveted to the animated corpse. The blade thrust forwards again. He sucked in his breath, and stomach, away from the tip of the blade. Too close! Sweat dripped into his eyes. His breath was short and painful in his throat. *Fear.* He was afraid of this thing, afraid of death and all that it meant. Afraid of failing Sophy. If only he had an extra second or two to pull his own knife free. How did one kill something that was already dead?

The eyes hungered for him, for his death. To look at them for any length of time was to lose one's soul. Another cut severed the air to his right as he bounded left. The farmer's face grimaced in a sickly parody of a smile. Rufus's control was not complete. The automaton was clumsy and it had lost the element of surprise. Oakheart sensed there was a chance to evade it, maybe destroy it.

A yell from behind distracted him. Oakheart rotated to see the guard, Duen, smothered by mist. "Ware, Fern. The mist is..." He saw Fern move to assist Duen as he turned his attention back to the corpse.

The knife swished close to his thigh. He winced as the blade found flesh. Oakheart darted backwards, his cut spraying blood onto the dirt. The corpse did not follow. Finally, enough distance to retrieve his own dagger from his boot. Grasping it, he circled the corpse, all the while his mind raging: How do you fight the dead? The thought that Rufus inhabited this body, that it danced to his tune, made Oakheart shiver. The binding oath must truly be broken for a travesty like this to assail him. Or Rufus was more powerful than any of them, including the most learned of the adepts, had ever estimated.

Oakheart circled. When the corpse lunged, Oakheart kicked the dagger free from its grip. Unperturbed, the corpse advanced with bare hands outstretched, fingers clawed ready to grasp him. Oakheart threw his knife and caught the body in the chest. It faltered for a heartbeat, only to step more purposefully towards him.

Out of the corner of his eye, he saw Lillia approach. He began to think of the child she protected when he saw she held his sword. He angled towards her, hand held ready for the toss. The corpse hissed and threw itself forwards. The sword flew in the air, arcing towards him. Oakheart stepped back and reached up. In one movement, he caught the hilt, which settled like an old friend into his palm, and swung the blade, still full of momentum, to sever the head from the corpse. The head landed with a wet thunk and rolled, mouth stretched in a feral grin and the eyes smoking holes. The headless body took a few faltering steps and fell jerkily to the ground. Oakheart, filled with revulsion and what he hoped was not hate, staggered over and thrust the sword through the corpse's back into its heart, anchoring it to the ground.

The mist dissolved with a drawn-out sibilant hiss. Rufus's presence fled, but the sense of unease and defilement remained. The stench of the corpse mired their resting place. Oakheart pulled a kerchief from his pocket and held it to his nose. His eyes met Lillia's. The forest maiden staggered from the stench, her hand clasped tightly over her face. He nodded his thanks to her.

Fern stepped up and kicked the corpse, spilling more gore. His face was pale. "We should bury it," he said, his grey eyes now storm-dark. "If it will not defile the soil of Argenterra."

Oakheart nodded, too weary to disagree and too ready to weep. "Yes, bury it. 'Tis not the farmer's fault that his body was thus corrupted. But hurry, I do not think I can bear to remain here any longer." Gilly cried and squirmed in Mellow's embrace. "'Tis not good for the babe to be so exposed to Rufus's influence."

Mellow succeeded in soothing the child, a sight that seemed contrary to the man's general air of anger and command. Yet, that was the way of the forest folk. Fern signalled to three guards and, after standing stunned for a few moments, they grabbed small shovels from their packs and began to dig a grave. Soon they had dug a sizeable hole.

In their eagerness and relief, they worked hard. They too did not wish to linger.

The corpse fascinated Oakheart. He backed away, his heart still beating wildly with the realisation of how close the encounter had been. The next time he might not be so fortunate. He shared a look with Lillia and nodded to Mellow. His heart was heavy as he walked away to distance himself from the stench, from the memory of that unnatural thing.

Lillia found somewhere to sit and began to suckle the babe with Mellow standing over her, eyes alert to any threat. Sunlight bathed them clean and pure, transforming the clearing, making it superficially look like Argenterra again. As he watched, Oakheart could see normalcy returning. The men joked. Duen, the guard that had nearly been smothered by the mist, looked pale but there was a smile there. Oakheart sighed. He wondered if it was resilience in the face of adversity or just blindness to the situation. It seemed so strange to experience what they had and then to move on with things as if it had never happened.

Leaning on a rock, he bound his leg wound and watched the burial proceedings only to turn his mind again to what he feared most. That the time of prophecy was at hand and if that were so, worse was yet to come—Vorn's dark vision and a future so desolate that he could not bear to dwell upon it.

✼ 2 ✼

THE BITTER KEEP

A s they rounded a curve in the road, past a long stretch of woods, Oakheart caught sight of Valley Keep's white spires, the tips burnished red by the setting sun. His heart lifted; soon the child would be safe and his promise would be fulfilled.

Although tired, when the rest of the party saw the pristine valley and its keep, they put on a final burst of speed, hoping to reach its confines before night fell. The pall of fear that had hung over them since Rufus's assault sloughed off as the wind caressed their cloaks and the walls of the valley rose up to embrace them.

Passing through the small town that served the keep, Oakheart saw the pinched and frightened faces of the inhabitants peering out at them from half-shuttered windows and closing doors. None raised a hand in greeting or would meet his eye.

Where were the laughing children waving and calling out their greetings? It was not yet full night but even the young ones were hidden away as if frightened of the shadowed spaces between the buildings. Surely Rufus's influence had not spread this far and so quickly. Shaking his head, he cast away that thought. Perhaps it was his own morose thinking that led him down that train of thought.

When they entered the bailey none of the usual ostlers and stable hands came to assist them with the horses and unloading. That dark nervous feeling that had begun in the village crept up anew. When Willow did not emerge to greet them, nor Dellbright, he clenched his reins.

Fear, that unseen predator, made his heart skip a beat. His sense of unease was overwhelming. Never had he thought he would hesitate to enter Valley Keep. He signalled to some of the men to dismount and take their horses. All remained quiet. Perhaps there was some other reason for this lack of reception. A feast? Sickness?

Oakheart eased his clenched jaw and surveyed the bailey as he dismounted. Fern threw him a concerned look as he jumped down and headed to the stables. Fern paused. With his back to Oakheart, he shrugged and then tied his reins to a pole while giving orders for his second to see to the horses and men. Fern then came to stand beside Oakheart, his hand on the pommel of his axe. "I will wait with you," he said with a nod and a look that brooked no argument.

Lillia's worried glance darted from shadowed corner to shadowed corner as Mellow helped her and the babe dismount. Oakheart could say nothing to ease their concern as he took Gilly into his arms. He dared not voice his troubled thoughts. The babe smiled at him, the smattering of ginger curls now long and framing his face. Oakheart smiled back and smoothed the hair from the babe's little white brow. The bonny child cheered him. Gilly laughed and reached his little hands up to Oakheart. The tang of soap teased his nostrils as he held the freshly bathed child, in contrast with his own sweat and dirt gained from weeks in the saddle. Oakheart thought he would never be able to scrape his chin clean of the beard again. He was becoming rather accustomed to it.

With a grin, he anticipated the joy the return of this child would bring to his parents and indeed the whole of the valley. Still no one had come to offer greetings so he nodded to the others to follow him and headed for the door.

There was no one in the vestibule. On entering the great hall, Oakheart's step faltered. The corners of the once bright room were unlit, leaving a dull gloom to linger over its fine walls and floor. Shafts of late evening light entered from one unshuttered window, revealing air thick with dust motes. He stepped further in and all about was evidence of leftover meals and smears of dirt. As the light faded, the gloom grew.

The stale smell was an insult to his senses and the hallowed memory of this place. The whole building felt subdued, quivering in revulsion at its own defilement. Anger began to burn in his blood but then his eyes widened when they fell upon Dellbright sitting in a raised chair. His cousin was changed, his posture sagging and desolate. Willow, hollow-eyed, stood next to him, mouth fixed in a stern line, with his white robes now stained with grey smears. Oakheart inhaled the air filled with tension and fear.

Oakheart instinctively relied on his ambassador skills and experience. He hid his disquiet behind a neutral facial expression and filled his voice with charm.

"Dellbright, I bring you greetings," Oakheart said to his cousin, keeping his gaze riveted. Young Gilly had dropped off to sleep peacefully cradled against Oakheart's chest, a smile on his chubby face. The thought of what the child was returning to squeezed the blood from Oakheart's veins. This was not the moment of joy he had thought it was going to be.

Dellbright raised dull, brown eyes, no hint of welcome in them. "Have you brought my son?" Dellbright said, his voice barely above a whisper. Dark smudges smeared the skin under his eyes and dulled cheeks. Then his eyes widened when they landed upon his son in Oakheart's arms. "Gilly!" Dellbright was thinner, face haggard, with blotchy skin around his neck, but that was nothing to the sneering expression on his face.

Oakheart held the child closer to his chest. "Yes, he is well. But what of you and your people?" Oakheart looked around, seeing no one else in the room. "Please tell me, cousin, what ails you? What has happened here? Where is Princess Aria?"

"Give him to me," Dellbright demanded, rising out of his seat, his shrill voice echoing and amplifying in the hall. Balanced on the arm of his chair, he wavered. Willow dropped back, almost cringing from his master. Dellbright did not take a step towards him, which Oakheart thought was even stranger. Why would he not race over to embrace the child? Why was Willow so afraid? Where was the joy, the welcome? What had happened here?

This scene was more unnerving and strange than encountering an animated corpse wielding a knife.

Oakheart's sense of disquiet grew as he drew himself to his full height and placed his feet slightly apart. Fern stiffened too, taking his cue from Oakheart. "I made a vow to place him in the hands of his mother. Is Aria not here to take him from me?"

Dellbright's expression soured and grew wary. Resentment seemed to make his sneer worse, curling his lips evilly. His eyes darted left and right until after a heartbeat he nodded to Willow, who then scurried out. "A vow, you say?"

The dark eyes of the prince were once again on Oakheart and the child he carried. Dellbright's expression lightened when he lifted a thoughtful eyebrow, a hint of a smile on his lips, but then it vanished. Cunning was not something Oakheart had associated with his cousin until that moment. "Do you speak of a vow to that ungrateful wretch, Sophy, or to her friend, Aria?"

Oakheart frowned. Something pulsed within Dellbright and it was not something light. He shared a sideways look with Fern. Already his offsider was assessing the situation, discreetly sending his men to surreptitiously secure the hall. "Aria did request a vow from Sophy and Sophy in turn requested one from me. She sacrificed her freedom, risked her life, to win the child back from Rufus's hand. Even now her life hangs in the balance."

Dellbright sat back and rested on the edge of his seat, eyebrow raised condescendingly. "Oh? Not dead then, as she should be for all she has wrought?"

Dellbright's callous manner made Oakheart flinch. "Do not speak of Sophy in that way. She has brought no ill on you and yours." His neck muscles tightened as he bit down on the words he wanted to say. After all that Sophy had done, to be slighted in such as way wounded him deeply.

"No ill?" Dellbright lifted his face and yowled to the ceiling, like some beast badly wounded in a hunt. Oakheart tensed and Lillia flinched while Mellow brooded, brows lowering over his dark eyes. Fern's mouth was a straight line as he watched as the prince lurched out of his seat, with fists clenched and his eyes flashing. "My mother is dead." He forced the words out through clenched teeth. "Her blood seeps into the very fabric of this keep and you say Sophy has brought no ill?"

Oakheart projected an air of calm, even though his cousin's behaviour and words provoked him. "Aye, I do say it. She is my oathbound wife. Best you keep your poisoned words to yourself. Sophy had no part in what happened here, although I am heart sore to hear of your sorrow."

Dellbright straightened and his gaze ranged over Fern, Lillia and the rest of the gathered men to once again centre on Oakheart. "Do you tell me that you wed her without my permission?"

"I do. We were to seek your permission 'ere we formalised our vows, but our mission to rescue your son took priority." Oakheart kept his gaze on Dellbright, trying to assess what had befallen him. Surely grief alone could not account for this change in his cousin. Could Rufus reach this far into the heart of pure men?

"Do you tell me that that evil dame is to be the next high queen? That she has married you, the high prince? What a cunning wench she is."

Oakheart's jaw clenched. "Sophy does not know what the oathbonding entails. Aria thought it best to keep the knowledge of my lineage from her."

Dellbright's mirthless laugh echoed around the hall. "It cannot be so," Dellbright said at last, though he looked near hysterical "Someone has told her. She has ensnared you and will be the end of us all. Worry not, for I would strangle the life out of her before that comes into play."

"I believe she was still ignorant of it. Nevertheless—"

Princess Aria came bursting through the double doors. Straightaway he saw something was not right with her also, although she was not laced through with inner rot, as her husband appeared to be. She was thin, her clothes hung off her body and her flesh was flaccid. Her eyes were sunken with hurt and sadness.

"Princess?" He began to walk towards her when her eyes alighted on the child in his arms.

"Gilly!" She rushed forwards. The tremulous smile overshadowed the evidence of hurt in her face. Tears fell down her cheeks as she touched the baby's face, his hair.

Oakheart eased the sleeping child into his mother's arms and rested his hand on the child's head. The pressure of his oath eased as it was fulfilled. *Now I am free. 'Tis done.*

Aria's tear-laden eyes stared up at him. "Oh, thank you, Oakheart. Good friend." She wept as she held the child, tears dropping on her son's cheek. Gilly stirred, wriggling free of his blanket.

Aria appeared to be soothed by holding her child, easing the tension lines around her mouth. Her breathing calmed, and she looked around the room taking in the travel-stained array of people in the hall. Her brows furrowed. "Where's Sophy?"

Before he could answer, Dellbright bellowed, "Give the child to me." Dellbright's look was thunderous as he swooped on her.

Aria flinched, instinctively hugging the child closer, and stepped back. "No, please. Let me hold him."

Her husband continued to stalk her. "You will not taint it with your weakness," Dellbright sneered at his wife. "Give him to me."

Oakheart was hard-pressed to believe his own ears and eyes. What had happened to his once besotted cousin? Incredulous, he watched as a change came over Aria. Instead of rebuking her husband for such an unwarranted comment, she seemed to freeze as if he had struck her. Aria, eyes downcast, stepped closer to Dellbright and handed over Gilly. The look of pain on her face gripped Oakheart's stomach.

With his lips twisted in spite, Dellbright took the child from her and without a backward glance marched back over to his dais and seated himself.

Oakheart heard Aria's sharp intake of breath. He turned to see sadness etched into her beautiful face as her green eyes, red-rimmed from weeping, tracked her husband while he walked away from her. Hesitantly, Aria's glance passed over Oakheart's and what he saw in that look froze his innards.

Dellbright stared at Gilly in rapture and then his face twisted in pain as a sob escaped him. Clutching the child close he wept the words, "My son. I never thought to see you again."

Oakheart narrowed his eyes. Everyone else was quiet. Oakheart could see Aria shake with repressed sobs. A certain light in her eyes while she watched Dellbright gave Oakheart pause. Was it hope or hate that tainted her gaze?

Dellbright shook once and regained his composure. The dark eyes he anchored on Oakheart were part misery and part something else. It was like a hollow opening where no light escaped. "I thank you, cousin. What can I do to repay you?"

Oakheart stepped forwards, sensing some normalcy in Dellbright's thanks. "I seek your aid, even though I see that all is not well in the valley. Though I have brought back your son, a high price was paid. I seek your aid to return to the Lower Warrens to rescue Sophy from Rufus."

Aria came to stand beside Oakheart, adding her support. "Yes... please help her."

Dellbright did not acknowledge his wife. Cheeks crimson, he said, "You dare ask me aid to free her when all she has done is create havoc? She is the Ancient Evil incarnate. Can you not see it?"

"No!" Aria shouted. "She is not. Your grief distorts your thinking. You said if she rescued your son, you would forgive her anything. Where is that forgiveness now? She gave herself to free him. We must aid her in turn."

"Shut your mouth, Aria. Dare you speak to me? You, who were in league with her to bring about this happening. You brought that thing, that *ungiven* female, into our midst and nothing but treachery and death walk in her wake. I see how you work. You sent Rae off to the Puri and now they attack us. This time with a vengeance do they visit us. Your friend, your *creature* has even beguiled my cousin and set herself up to rule by his side. As high queen she will heap evil on us all. There is no end to the ways in which she can subvert the land.

"I would stand by and watch Sophy carved open and bled dry, like she did to my mother. Nay, I would order it done. Better still, I would do it myself and watch the life drain from her eyes." Dellbright turned to glare at Oakheart with an expression as near to loathing that he had ever seen on anyone.

Chilled, Oakheart squeezed his fist. Dellbright was not himself. To speak such about Sophy was absurd. It was not possible that Dellbright could do this thing, let alone utter the words.

"Dellbright?"

Dellbright's dark eyes glittered as they settled on him. "Cousin, you have sworn your oath mistakenly, as I have. You will see in time what misery she will bring you. I can spare you nothing—all I have I need to defend Valley Keep and my people. Already we are less than we once were."

Oakheart nodded, realising that it was futile at this time to ask for anything. With a swallow, he held back the dismay in his chest. He must tread carefully. "My heart is saddened by your words, but more so by what I see in your heart. You speak truth when you say that you are less than you were. It breaks my heart to witness what I have seen this day. How can I aid you?"

Dellbright paled, the anger appearing to bleed away with Oakheart's words. Perhaps his cousin was at once himself again, but that thought was quickly dismissed. Anger blazed out of Dellbright's eyes, his mouth becoming a grim line as he clutched the babe to him. Gilly cried a protest but Dellbright was deaf to it.

"Bring back my mother...undo the deeds that have been done. Send these so-called Gifts of the Crystal Tree Woods back to whence they came." He headed for the door, stopping to spit on Aria. The princess casually stepped back, escaping the globule. Dellbright stopped and regarded Oakheart. "Only then will I be happy."

Willow slunk after Dellbright, head down. His cousin spoke before he left without looking at them. "Willow, see to their needs and fetch me a wet nurse for the child." Dellbright left the hall, the door shutting quickly behind him. Gilly wailed as he was taken away.

Silence fell as the last of Dellbright's words died and the sounds of Gilly's distress could no longer be heard. For the first time in his life, Oakheart had no words to counter what had just been said.

Aria rushed to the door to follow Gilly but met doors shut tight. Dellbright must have ordered the guards to hold them closed. She hung her head, shoulders hunched with weeping, and leant her head against the carved wood. "Gilly," she moaned. "My Gilly!"

⚜

DELLBRIGHT HELD THE CHILD TO HIS BREAST, NOT ABLE TO articulate what he felt. He had expected never to see the child again. It went against everything, all the possibilities that had churned through his mind since the day the babe had been taken. He knew then that Sophy had been the cause of it all. Even before that fateful night, he had known it through the months of Aria's pregnancy, how she always came between him and his wife. Even when absent she had a hold on Aria. Despite his efforts to separate them, Aria kept defying him. Now rage seized him. Sophy had managed to bed Oakheart. *Impossible.* Such a bonding could not be allowed—he would find a way to end it. The binding oath was already broken so what was one more death? It would do no more damage. Sophy would die at his hand. He pictured his hands around her neck, squeezing, squeezing until her face was purple and her eyes bulged, and then he would drop her lifeless to the ground and laugh. Yes, he would laugh.

In the months during Aria's pregnancy, Aurore had tried to soothe him, but he had paid her no mind. What did she know of friendship? She had no friends. Her life was an empty shell, with nothing but him to fill the dark, empty spaces of her life. It was her fault his father had left them. Stale, frigid woman she was, never letting his father near her. He may have been young, but even then he knew his father's sadness, the empty bed he slept in. If Aurore had been more of a woman, she would not have let Mara, that whore, steal Daken away from the valley, away from him.

Dellbright hated the very thought of his father. That man had left him. *Left him!* How could a father do such a thing to a deserving child? Now that Aurore was dead, Gillcress was his only kin. Aria, the betraying wife, was his possession. Did not that voice in the dark tell him so? Yes, he remembered rightly. Aria was to be punished for her crimes. She was unworthy as a wife — weak, manipulative and evil. It was she who had allowed his son to be taken. The voice told him of the faked nightmares and of how they had worked together, she and Sophy, to break the binding oath, right here in the keep. Those outlanders schemed of the deepest and bitterest betrayal.

At first, it had not occurred to him until he had gone to that room where Aurore was killed. Kneeling in the blood stains, he had sensed something. While he wept that voice came and insinuated itself into his heart and mind, twisting the threads of suspicion, ripening them with the fruit of anger.

Right now, Dellbright hated everything and everyone. He revelled in that feeling, soared with it. Gillcress cried out and squirmed in his grip. "Except you, my son. I could never hate you."

Aria needed to suffer. Only then would he be happy again. Laughter and joy would fill him up. He had never thought Oakheart would betray him and speak so disrespectfully. Well, he could do without Silverdale too. He could do without Oakheart in his life. They had not come to his aid when the Puri raided his lands. He was better off without them. Much better. Condescending they always were.

Noise at the door made him swing around. Willow entered with a young woman. A wet nurse, he supposed, from the fullness of her breasts. He watched as Gillcress was fed, bathed and changed. The child did not need Aria. He fed hungrily from the wet nurse's breasts, caring not who was at the other end of them.

Watching over the child in its crib, Dellbright waited until he slept, then stroked the fine head of red curls. His lips twisted. The hair was like hers, not his. The child was cursed with outlander blood. His breathing quickened and he stepped back from the child. Would her blood overshadow his? Would his son become a weapon to destroy them all?

Panic flamed across his senses. His thoughts scurried. Was it right to love the child, one so tainted with bad blood? Then the thought came to him that the hair would darken with age and as the child grew he would become more like him, more like the Prince of Valley Keep. Then he sighed as his fear seeped deeper inside of him.

3

THE HEART OF THE MATTER

Oakheart ached to go to Aria as she stood there with her forehead resting on the door that had been shut with such finality. Willow returned through the door to the kitchens, snaring his attention.

Willow did not bother to bow as was his usual custom. "I am afraid that I can only offer you accommodation in the barracks. The rooms above stairs are not in use since..." he grimaced, "the unfortunate event."

"Very well," Oakheart said. "Fern, see to it. I wish to have a private moment with the princess."

Fern nodded, but his eyes lingered on Aria's face. The man's expression of bewildered admiration worried him, but he could not entertain any further complications at this moment.

"Come, show us the way," Fern said and gestured for Willow to precede him. Aria stepped back. Fern bowed elegantly to her and then stood behind the chamberlain. Willow called out a command and the doors opened, and closed swiftly once he passed through with Fern close behind.

Again Aria tried to leave the room but the doors were shut against her. She stood there staring at them.

"My lady?" Oakheart called to her softly. He thought at first she had not heard him because she did not respond. After a few more moments, she pushed away from the doors.

The sound of approaching footsteps prevented her speaking. Dela, Willow's wife, entered from the kitchen, accompanied by a maid, who brought food and laid it on the tables. It was wine, bread and cheese, nothing hot to fill and warm their stomachs; a lean and miserable welcome. The urge to weep too came upon Oakheart when he thought of what he had witnessed this day.

Lillia, ramrod straight, stayed by his side. Mellow lingered behind them like a dark shadow. With a distracted wipe of her face with a hand, Aria turned and walked towards the table. "Come and eat something," Aria said, leading them to sit. Somehow, even with all that she had obviously suffered, she had the poise to act with care.

"Princess..." Oakheart began.

Her sad, red-rimmed eyes met his and lowered. "Best you not call me by that title. Dellbright has taken it from me." Her face, though pale, held strength. Her lips trembled.

Lillia reached out and held Aria's hand, stroking it soothingly. Aria smiled wanly and squeezed the forest maiden's hand in return. "Please sit. It's not much, but it's better than nothing. More than I expected he would allow."

Oakheart placed his hand on her shoulder. "He cannot take away your grace. You were meant to be a princess from the day you were born." His fingers brushed against her tear-stained cheek.

Aria lifted her hand to pat his and sighed. "You were always a good friend to me, Oakheart. But what happened to Sophy? How do you plan to get her back?"

Oakheart let out a pent-up breath. He could hardly look at her. He had failed both of them, but then again it was Sophy's oath to Aria that was responsible for their predicament. "Even if I travelled to the Lower Warrens, I could not help her. I do not know how to free her from Rufus's snare. I must seek help from the adepts for she is transformed."

Aria's eyes widened and she sat down heavily and wrung her hands.

"Transformed? Into what?" She did not look him in the eye, but instead focussed on her hands, clenching and unclenching.

Oakheart sat next to her. "'Tis hard to believe or explain. When we reached Rufus's abode, she bargained for the child and bound me with oaths beforehand to prevent me from aiding her. Somehow she was changed into a gem, as large as she was, but cut and faceted. The crystal pulses dark blue with her life force. It all happened so quickly..."

"Are you sure?" Aria asked, as she poured him some wine. "How do you know she's alive?"

"I feel our oathbond. I sense that she is alive."

Aria turned to him and put her trembling hands over his. "Oh thank god for that. There's more, tell me." Now her bright green eyes didn't leave his face. He knew in his heart that she understood his feelings for her friend.

"Well...either she *is* the jewel or she is trapped within, frozen but alive. How to free her is the problem. It is beyond my knowledge and I feel so helpless..."

Aria sucked in a breath and her eyes never left his face. Oakheart made a shape of a circle with his hands. "Rufus had constructed a ring of gold for her to enter into...like this, and when she did she was enclosed by blue flame and when it dissipated a crystal was in her place."

Aria covered her face with her hands. "Oh god, no." She rocked back and forth. When Oakheart patted her head, she looked up. "'Are you absolutely sure she is not dead?" Aria's voice was hoarse.

Oakheart clasped her hand and squeezed. "Yes. She lives. For now."

"Truly?" Her face held some disbelief, then for the first time he saw a ghost of a smile around her lips. "How did you accomplish an oathbond with Sophy? I thought..."

He shrugged and shared a look with Lillia. "'Tis a long story. But she is my oathbound wife and..."

Aria's face became horror stricken. "And Dellbright will never permit it. He has come to hate her, and me, too. What is to be done?"

Oakheart thought she was near to hysteria. He patted her back, soothed her with sure, firm strokes, and she calmed. "He has refused his consent, made threats on Sophy's life. He is not himself. Dellbright's words and actions mean we no longer need formal permission from him. Instead, I will petition the high king. Fear not, for all will be well."

"But Sophy...She's so independent...I..." Her brows furrowed. "Did you tell her about being the high king's heir?"

Oakheart shrugged, not quite able to explain his heart or his motives easily. "No. I believe she still does not know. Lillia has not told her. But that is beside the point." He let out a sigh. "It was expedient to bind her to me. I would not shame her and our relationship had progressed beyond friendship." His face heated and he drew a stray hair away from his eyes. "This may sound coarse but bedding her was the only way to have peace between us. And I must admit that to keep her safe, keeping her close to me was the only way."

"Aye to that," Lillia added, joining them at the table, spearing some cheese with her dagger. "Their feuding drove us all mad. He loves her though he admits it not. It is all oaths to him, so Sophy told me. For him to trick her as he did it must be from the heart."

"You tricked her?" Aria said, a flush stealing up her neck. Then she looked at him, narrowing her eyelids. "Oakheart?"

He lowered his gaze, unable to hide his shame. "Lillia, you put a different slant on happenings than I would, though in essence you are right. Sophy always fascinated me from the first, but I was not free to...ah well." Oakheart drew in a breath. "As heir I have duties and as a prince I must make alliances. Veld is stubborn and holds onto old grievances. I could not convince him to make a politically astute alliance, bound with a marriage to Hanal's sister."

Lillia frowned. "Then you would have married Lyant?"

Oakheart gritted his teeth and then nodded. "If Veld would have permitted it. But he would not. For that I was sent away when first you arrived in Silverdale. In order to avoid bringing attention to Sophy, you were also ignored until Hanal had departed. Forgive my father, Lillia. He meant no disrespect to you or the queen."

Aria's face was furrowed. "But if you couldn't marry this Lyant, how could you bind Sophy to you without his consent?"

Lillia's blue eyes flashed with sudden insight. "Veld consented, did he not?"

Oakheart shrugged. "In essence, yes. Veld saw advantages to the match as Sophy was one of the Gifts of Crystal Tree Woods. I was undecided, confused. At the Lake of Reflections, I saw Sophy, the real Sophy that only that lake can reveal. I realised many things but sifting through those realisations took time...and Sophy was difficult.

"You see, I was hidden from Sophy's eyes also. At the Lake of Reflections she saw my true face. It scared her, I believe. It brought home to her all the enchantments and danger that had surrounded her since her arrival. It was hard to believe that I, too, was hidden from her eyes. Then I began to think about why. Why could Sophy not see me as I am, as others see me?"

"Why was that, do you think?" Aria asked.

"By disguising us from each other, we did not fall for one another as perhaps we might have done at the first..."

Lillia leant forwards. "If Sophy and you had not been enchanted you would have. I am sure of it." She shrugged. "Who knows what would have happened had you been united from the start?"

"Yes," Oakheart agreed. "I realised I was meant for her, from the very beginning—as much as I dislike so-called fate or destiny, I knew then that Rufus had tried to keep us apart. It was part of his plan, part of what the Ancient Evil designed for Argenterra. Now we see the outcome. Sophy in that crystal form is draining the *given* from the land, weakening it, weakening us."

Aria nodded. "He has caused us all great harm."

He squeezed her hand gently, and she continued. "It has a certain kind of logic, but I can't understand how Sophy would marry anyone." Aria held Lillia's and Oakheart's gaze in turn. "The Sophy I knew would not trust marriage. Her mother left her for a lover. Abandoned her. Before that, Sophy had seen how destructive a marriage can get when her father and mother were together. It affected her deeply."

Oakheart lowered his head, unable to meet her eye. "Sophy did not understand the import of the vow when she gave it. She did soon after...she says that she loves me, so perhaps that exonerates me a little. Yet it shames me that I did not tell her..."

"About being Veld's son and heir?" Aria asked.

"Yes, I let her believe I was only his ambassador."

"She has no idea that she will be the high queen when you inherit the throne? How she will hate the thought of it." Aria covered her mouth and then after a few calming breaths dropped her hands to her lap. "Well, I'm sure she won't mind...much," Aria said doubtfully, though her expression appeared preoccupied. "Was she happy to be wed to you, Oakheart? I mean really..."

"Aye, she was," Lillia answered. "She loves him. Many times she did show it through the risk of her life. It is no fault of hers that she is cursed."

"Cursed? She isn't cursed. She's just different." Aria glowered at the forest maiden and stood up from the table. "How I hate it when people say that. Sophy is...interesting...and loyal..."

Lillia sat back. "But she was cursed. First with her looks, the accidents and then the loss of her child."

Aria paled. "Sophy was pregnant?" Her hand pressed to her abdomen, perhaps in sympathy.

Oakheart lowered his head. Lillia spoke when he did not respond. "Aye, that she was, but it was a strange business. It was like a hand took that child from her."

A tear trickled down Aria's cheek. "Poor Sophy."

There was a pause and Oakheart took the moment to change the subject. "Aria, what has happened here? The keep feels strange as if the pulse of life is..." Oakheart struggled for the word, "out of tune with the surroundings. And Dellbright has changed so much. There is more to this situation than has been told so far."

Haunted emerald eyes stared directly at him. Fear and hurt lurked in their depths. "If you have finished eating I will show you, Oakheart. For only then will you see..."

Oakheart stood, food no longer important to him. With a nod, she beckoned for Oakheart to follow. Mellow held Lillia back as she tried to leave her seat and after a moment's hesitation, she sat back down.

This time, the door opened when Aria pushed at it; the guards no longer held it shut. Oakheart followed her out, seeing that the guards were still there but no longer under orders to keep their princess within. Oakheart could not hold back the glare he levelled at them. One turned his head away, face flushing.

Aria headed for the stairs and took each step gingerly as if something would leap from the shadows to slay her. It was dark, for all windows were covered, leaving the once airy and bright passageway looking like one of Rufus's tunnels. He went back a few steps to grab a firestick from its holder and then he hastened to keep pace with Aria.

"Where are we going?" he asked.

"To Aurore's room. It was where she and the nursemaid were murdered. You will see before we reach it."

He held the firestick higher and as her steps slowed, he saw it. Dark tendrils spread through the white stone of the keep, along the floor and up the walls and even to the ceiling. It felt so wrong, like a canker or a rot, destroying the floor and walls of the keep. Gingerly, he stepped on a thread and that wrong crawled up through his boots into his legs. He hesitated. It was like a force was seeking out his life and drawing it out. Breathing deep, he centred the *given* in his body and stepped on the stain again. He continued on and pushed open Aurore's door. The smell of death hit him, a ripe, putrid smell of rotting carcasses. "Why did you not have it cleaned?" he asked, his voice hoarse with horror.

"We did clean it thoroughly many times. I scrubbed it myself, even though it made me heave with revulsion. But it will not be cleaned off. The blood has seeped into the stone and spread."

"No," Oakheart said with more force than he meant. "It is not the blood, but the deed. Murder!" What he sensed was beyond description. He could feel this stain making his bones ache. Revulsion curled his innards as he surveyed the damage. His fist clenched in futile anger. "This cannot be happening. Not to this keep." He turned to Aria. "We must clean it."

"I told you we did."

"No soap and water will help this. We must clean it before it reaches the heart of this place."

"The heart?" Aria's brows furrowed. "You mean the bonding chamber, don't you?"

"That I do."

29

"Come on then. We better check that rot is not already there." Aria led the way out, her feet skipping along the ground in her haste to leave the stench of murder behind. Down through the lower levels she led him as he held the firestick high. The bonding chamber was not decorated as it had been on his last visit and the dark pool in the centre was still. Oakheart sighed as he entered the darkened chamber.

"It has not reached here. Praise Vorn."

"It feels so strange down here," Aria commented as she looked around her.

Oakheart's gaze flew to her face, matching green eyes to green eyes. "What do you feel when you are here? Please describe it to me."

Aria edged around, touching the walls tentatively, almost reverently. "If feels alive. It pulses with life, though there is a tremor there that I have not noticed before. What lies here, Oakheart? There is something. I know it."

Oakheart knelt in one of the niches along the rim of the bonding pool, placing one aching knee after the other onto the stone ledge. He had been in the saddle for a long time and his body let him know it. His gaze lingered in the pool. "Not many know this. I doubt that even Dellbright does as the keep passed into his family's charge many generations ago." He glanced towards Aria as she lingered nearby. "This is Vorn's resting place. He is buried under this pool."

"It's a tomb?" Aria gasped as she rushed to stand beside him. "But people live here. I don't understand."

"'Tis no tomb...but a mausoleum, a place of reverence for a great man. The adepts built it in his honour and his essence has joined with it. 'Tis meet that people live here and make it flow with life. That is what Vorn would have wanted. In many ways, he is the land." He turned to face Aria. "There has been a debate for many years about whether it was Vorn who was inherently gifted so that he wrought the *given* from his own hand and that his vow bound his power to the land. The other side of the argument says it is the land itself that holds the *given* and gave it in response to Vorn's binding oath."

"Oh my god. Either way it doesn't matter, does it? When that blood reaches here it will have the same effect? I mean, it's so, so... dark. Surely it will destroy this place, quench the life that is here."

He searched her beautiful face. "You understand." So much sorrow and yet she could care for this keep that must be alien to her. Care for something where so many horrible things had happened. Where she found love and had it turn sour. "We could try to prevent it, remove it. I think you can work the *given* sufficiently to help me. If I leave here with nothing but the cleansing of this place, the removal of this stain of murder, I will be happy."

Aria's eyes were round with shock. "You want me to help you, wielding the *given*? But I am weak...useless. Dellbright says..."

"I care not to hear what Dellbright says to you. Forgive my abruptness. I can see that he has hurt you greatly, oppressed you with his words and deeds. But I have tasted enough of his bitterness for one day.

"Anyone can see that he is no longer what he was. I only pray that his good sense will return after his grief has passed. I sense in you the ability to use the *given*. While I travelled with Sophy, I came to realise that you should not have been separated and that you, too, should have gone to Glassy Mountain Retreat. Not to solve a riddle, but to receive training as an adept."

"What?" Aria's voice quavered. "An adept? I wouldn't have chosen such a path for myself. I thought only that I could use it to make cloth and repair wilted flowers."

He stared at her, touched her chin and smiled. "I think you would have once you had been there for a while. Look at what you achieved with little or no training. Most Argenterrans learn to use the *given* from childhood. To achieve what you did in a week, maybe two, showed great promise. I am surprised Dellbright never told you so. When you said that Rufus...forgive me for reminding you of those terrible events...when you said he would not have taken Gilly if you were with him, I understood what you meant. You have talent in working the *given* and he dared not risk a confrontation with you. So, she who doubts herself, will you help me?"

"I would aid you even if I had no skill. Thank you for believing in me." She leant forwards to hug him, and he returned it. Her warmth comforted him and he knew instinctively that her heart ached for what she had suffered, and for Sophy.

"First we must test the pool to see if the *given* will respond. I mentioned before that since Sophy's transformation the *given* has been hard to work and less comes when called. I wish the events were not linked, but I am afraid they are. If you will take my hand we shall start."

"What will my hand do?" Aria asked as she placed her petite, pretty hand in his.

He smiled and squeezed it gently. "It comforts me. More importantly, it provides a connection between us."

Smiling slightly, she nodded, though her eyes were dark and serious.

Oakheart did not seek to invoke the Crystal Tree as Adage had done during Aria's bonding ceremony. He thought he could possibly do that, but he wanted a lesser show of strength. He needed to draw some *given* from the pond to take away with him. Holding Aria's hand was a comfort, but she, too, could store the *given* within herself to share with him when they were at their task.

With his free hand in the pool, the water quickly numbed it. He willed warmth to his fingers and breathed through knife-edged pain as the cold seeped in and travelled up his arm. He sent more warmth into his flesh and more still into the pond. He came close to drawing his arm out, for the chill was almost impossible to bear. The cold reached into his heart, snagging his breath. What kind of fool was he to risk the power within the pond?

A pulse of his thought was tugged into the pond. He did not understand why that had happened. It came from him unbidden. While he struggled to draw breath, a flash of white surrounded them and a vision sprang into his mind. Vorn, in all his glory, blared to life in front of him. Pinpricks of power freeze-burned his skin. Fear leaked like liquid down his throat. He could not form words.

The powerful vision etched across his mind. Tall and full-bodied, Vorn towered over him; those green eyes so like his own bore down on his. "Why do you disturb me, blood of my blood, seed of my seed?" Vorn's voice reverberated within Oakheart's bones.

Awe sang through his blood. Vorn, First Comer and High King, was speaking to him and what would he say? He swallowed with a throat dry and tight. "I need strength from the *given* to cleanse this keep. A murder most foul has stained its very fabric and the stench of death threatens to reach this very pool, your resting place."

The eyes glowed molten green within the fire, and white flames warmed Oakheart's face and the chamber. Oakheart, out of the corner of his eye, saw that Aria, too, witnessed the vision, as her face was stretched with fear and wonder. "Murder?" Vorn's voice vibrated with anger and was laced with fear. Oakheart thought the great man's heart was breaking. "No," Vorn said. "The worst of my dreams comes to life. The Ancient Evil has stretched her hand and tainted this place, our haven. What about the jewel? Have you the jewel?"

Oakheart frowned. His heart beat solidly in his chest, though his breath seemed to want to burst him open. "No. We have no jewel." Oakheart bit his lips as the thought burst free of his mind. "Could you mean Sophy, the Gift of Crystal Tree Woods who has been transformed into a jewel?"

Vorn swelled, his figure towering above them. "Crystal Metamorphosis? Yes, I dreamed of the change. Only one who has a true heart can free her, or can wield her. I surrender to you what power I can. But I fear the binding oath is broken and, if so, its unravelling will affect everything near and far..."

With a rush of blood to his ears, the numbing cold that had almost reached his brain turned to heat. He screamed at the rush of power and pain. Aria clung with a death grip to his hand while the force issuing from the pond battered her. An ear-splitting scream emitted from her mouth and then died slowly away.

Oakheart blinked. He was lying flat on the ground and Aria lay draped across his chest. He took a tentative breath, certain that the attempt would hurt. His lungs worked freely. Only the memory of agony left an aftertaste on his tongue and skin.

With the rise of his chest, Aria stirred. Her eyelids flickered and she recognised him.

"Did that..." she began, her voice full of awe. She drew in a shuddering breath. "Was that...*the* Vorn?"

Oakheart put an elbow beneath himself to gain leverage so he could talk. "I have only seen his picture. But, yes, it appears that it was. Here, let me look at you. Are you hurt?" His eyes travelled down her body as she unsteadily climbed to her feet. She appeared whole, though her hair seemed to have a life of its own as it rippled with the after-effects of power.

"I'm all right. But tell me, is it usual to have visions like that? I thought this was a bonding chamber, not some means to communicate with the dead."

Oakheart sat with his knees bent and held close to his chest, taking breaths in and out slowly. The bonding chamber throbbed around him, but he was not sure whether the effect was from the chamber or him. How much *given* did he hold?

He reached for Aria's hand. "I think not. I have never heard of it, but then again I have never dared such before." He struggled to stand, letting go the brief contact with Aria. He took a few tentative steps as his strength returned. "Come, we must see to this cleaning now."

When he stood and regarded her, his mouth fell open. "You are throbbing with the *given*," he said as he took in her glowing skin and sparkling eyes. She was still thin and worn but power glowed within her.

Backing away from him, she stared nervously at the pool and then at him. "I don't know how to describe you, then. You look ready to burst, like the sun rising over the horizon in midsummer."

Oakheart wavered. His hair had somehow come loose and was draped over his shoulders. His clothes, once travel stained, were clean. He looked at his hand, flexed it and tensed. It was as if his hand held a thousand bees, each sting pricking his flesh. He looked within and stopped. Every fibre of his being pulsed with the *given*, as if it was barely contained within the barrier of his flesh.

"Bursting," he said with a smile. Vorn had filled him with incredible power. He only hoped it was enough. "Let us tarry not. I would see the keep, at least, back to its old self. Perhaps that will aid Dellbright's healing."

They hurried up the steps and slowed as they neared the creeping stain in the hallway. "Show me the exact place it happened. It would be best to start at the centre."

She trembled. "I would prefer to start at the edge. I lack courage."

He frowned. "It is frightening to be sure. Your fear is justified, but..."

Aria lifted her chin. "You're right, though. It must be fed by the centre, the place where the murder took place."

"That is my conjecture."

"Very well." She took his hand in her small one, squeezed once and gently tugged him along. A fleeting remembrance of Sophy was drawn from his memory. Her small hand in his. What was he feeling? He did not know and dared not look into his heart to find out. What if Sophy could never be freed? No, he could not contemplate that. He would free her no matter what.

Aria trod warily. Each foot as she placed it on the stained floor was lifted quickly. Oakheart, too, felt it, like a rot, as he stepped on the fouled substance of Valley Keep. Aria halted by Aurore's door, her hand trembling. He leant forwards and pushed it open for her. The wrongness hit him like a wave. He rocked back, and Aria whimpered. "It's too strong," she wailed. "It has grown more powerful."

"No, not more powerful. 'Tis afeared. That is why it assails us. There is a consciousness here, an awareness that seeks to shake us from this path. Let it not touch you. Think of Vorn in the vision. Perhaps that will help you focus."

He pushed past her and drew her along behind him. The stench of death pervaded his senses to the extent that he became disoriented. The stain of decay writhed and shifted like a muddy whirlpool.

"Aria, where did it happen? I cannot see." He could barely get the words out as the wrongness crawled up his leg. He had to keep moving. Tugging on Aria's hand, he drew her to face him. Terror relived was in her eyes and he hated to force her to endure more. "Aria, listen. You must show me. Point, for it swirls and convulses so that I cannot see its source."

A trembling hand stretched out towards the wall behind him. Blood still stained it high above his head. How could such a thing have been accomplished? All around him, smears of blood eddied and flowed. It was like swimming upstream. Sweat broke out on his brow and his back. He leant towards it, dragging Aria along with him. She did not pull back, nor did she use her strength to surge forwards.

Putting forth his hand, his finger touched the wall. The *given* leapt out upon contact, an invisible battle. Pouring what he could of himself into his hand and beyond, he leant against the wall. He remembered the keep as it was, the pulse and beauty of it. "Aria," he grated through clenched teeth. "Help me. Try to remember the keep, the pulse of life you once experienced. Use that memory to guide you."

Her jaw set at a determined angle, she nodded and stood beside him, placing her hand on his arm. Her eyes closed, and the heat of the *given* emanated from her. She was strong. He dragged her hand forwards and placed her hand full on the wall. Side by side, they sent the *given* within back into the keep.

A few moments later, the walls rocked and the floor shuddered. Frightened cries from below filtered up to them as their work continued. The wrongness waned but it was not completely banished. They had to do more.

The last of the stored *given* slid out of him like a final exhalation. He was not yet done so he drew on his own life force, his blood fire, and sent this energy into the keep. The beating of his heart resisted the last tug against his life force. It *thumped, thumped* painfully. *Just a little more. Please!*

Oakheart didn't know if he'd lost consciousness but he found himself kneeling on the floor, his body supported by the wall, his faced pressed hard against the cool stone. He blinked a few times, reached out with his drained perception and noticed that the wall pulsed with life and energy. Pure and clean energy that throbbed with the *given*. Vorn was safe. A sigh escaped him as exhaustion made him slump to the floor. He was dimly aware of Aria beside him. Opening his eyes, he saw that she was breathing shallowly and her skin was whiter than white. They had done it, at great cost to themselves. Before he could smile at their triumph, the angle of the wall appeared to shift and he passed out.

4

A TOUCH OF WISDOM

Aria awoke in her room. Through the open window a breeze fluttered the translucent curtains. It must be morning. Bird song floated on the air, heralding the arrival of spring. Her eyes closed and then snapped open. She was back in her room because the stain of death was gone from the keep.

Memories of what Oakheart had achieved rushed to greet her. It was lovely to have the keep back, to be back in her room. Then her eyebrows furrowed. Something wasn't quite right. She propped herself up and looked around. Dellbright's things were not there. The room was hers alone. She sighed heavily. It was better this way; the souring of Dellbright's spirit was more than she could bear. That he focussed all that disappointment and bitterness on her was a bane to her existence. His need of her was also his undoing. She could not satisfy his desire for security and, now that his mother was dead, he was bereft. Now that his son was back, perhaps he would heal.

"Gilly," she breathed. Throwing back the bed covers, she threw her legs over the side and reached for a gown. She caught her reflection in the mirror and stilled. *Is this what I've come to?* Dark smudges surrounded her eyes. Her cheeks were drawn and her hair, lord, her hair was a disaster.

"I cannot go out looking like this." She stepped into the washroom to bathe and put some order into her wayward locks. Gilly was safe and although she ached to touch and hold him, she knew that Dellbright would not let her. It had gone too far for that. The minute she had let Dellbright drug her and remove Gilly from her care, she had let the bond of motherhood sever. She couldn't undo that deed and, even though she had tried with all of her will and strength to defend her child, she had lost. Now Dellbright had changed and she doubted she could recover any lost ground with him.

As the last of the bath water sank into the drain, she thought of Gilly. He would give joy to Dellbright. Perhaps his son would heal him more than anything else. But the Dellbright that once was had been erased. There didn't seem to be a place for her in his life anymore. Yet, the day was yet young and Oakheart's cleansing of the keep may well have worked some good on her husband. There was a small chance she could save the marriage, overlook the harm he had done her and, perhaps, dispel the hate for Sophy anchored so deeply in his breast.

Her gowns were arrayed in her closet. The green, once so loved, she passed over. A mauve gown, worked with the *given* and gold, caught her eye. She didn't remember ever wearing or seeing it before. But Aurore had forever added to her gowns with love and exquisite taste. Perhaps this was the last dress she had placed there before...before her death.

Unbidden, the memories flooded back. Biting her lip, she willed herself to be calm and centred so that memories of the painful past would recede. Like the passage of a storm, the memories left devastation in their wake. Her hands shook as she drew on the gown. Over by the mirror, she picked up the comb and re-tidied her hair, soothing herself as she arranged her ringlets and curls to fall negligently down her back. She grasped the tiara that Dellbright had presented to her and fitted it over her head. He may have taken her right to use the word 'princess' but he had not taken back her bride gift. Let him snatch it from her cold, dead hands.

Her morose thoughts were hard to shake off. Not a good way to charm a prince. She tried smiling. The image in the mirror mesmerised her. The gown fitted well, even though it was a little loose due to her weight loss. The colour almost clashed with her hair and yet it did not. Her skin had regained its creamy glow and somehow it blended the hair and the dress to make her feel sensual. The tiara may be a bit overdone for everyday wear but she needed something to give her an edge—facing Dellbright was a daunting prospect. Maybe Dellbright would see it as a peace offering, that she wore her bride gift with pride. She touched it lightly with her fingertips. It made her feel confident; perhaps that was enough.

Her toilette complete, she marched up to the door and pulled on the handle. It didn't move. She tried again. Still it did not move. It was locked. "No!" Surprised at first, tears pricked her eyes until anger overrode them. She called out, rattled the handle, but no one came. Was there another way out? She raced through Dellbright's dressing room, but that door was locked also.

Obviously, Gilly's return had not placated her husband. She sat down and stared at the door, thinking hard. Oakheart wouldn't leave her here, of that she was sure. She only had to be patient.

Pacing the room, she tried to think, but everything was a bundle of pain, so tight and fraught she might lose herself in it if she but tugged a thread loose. Hunger stirred. Dellbright wouldn't starve her. He could not. Curling herself into a ball on the bed, she waited.

She didn't realise she had fallen asleep until Dellbright stood in the doorway. She gasped at the look in his eyes. Once passion, desire and love had filled them; now there was only distrust and hate.

"Come with me." His voice devoid of warmth, he turned his back on her, expecting immediate compliance.

"Gilly?" she asked breathlessly. She ran her fingers through her hair and straightened the gown. Luckily, the way she had reclined on the bed had preserved her appearance.

He turned back abruptly, dark curls falling over his face and ears. "You will not see him," he said harshly, fist clenched. Then blinking, his expression changed subtly and he softened his tone. "For the moment, at least. He sleeps peacefully now. There are others that wish to see you...and I will allow you to meet with them."

He turned, his back stiff and unbending. She glared at him as she followed him out of her door. There was no need to ask why he had locked the door. Then eyes forwards, head held high, she glided down the steps and into the great hall, heart thudding so hard she wondered how she could still appear calm.

The colours in the room seemed to leap out at her: flowers on the side table, the rich brown of the furniture, the bright pennon hanging above the hearth. The keep was back to normal. Oakheart's bright green eyes latched onto her as she walked in. She nodded to him and noticed his jaw unclench and his fist uncurl. After his amazing feat of driving the stain from the fabric of the keep, he looked well and unharmed.

The echoes of tense words lay like dust motes in the air. Why had they been arguing? Was she only here because Oakheart demanded to see her? Movement at the end of the room drew her attention to a man in brown and blue robes.

An adept had come. Lillia and Mellow were talking with him in soft undertones. Aria's chest tightened. *An adept!* Maybe some sense could be made of this mess. Surely Dellbright would listen to a learned adept from Glassy Mountain Retreat. Soon this nightmare would end. She let out a sigh. Dellbright would return to normal. Her fingers unclenched. Sophy would be safe. Her mood lifted at the thought. Aria could forgive him and they would be a happy family. A smile widened her mouth. Then she saw Dellbright's expression and the smile died.

Dellbright arranged himself on his raised seat. He had never bothered with such trappings of princehood before. It was a new position for a new Dellbright, she thought stormily. Perhaps it would help to soothe his insecurity. If it did, she would keep quiet about it and not poke fun at him. Not that she ever poked fun at her husband, but he used to be able to smile and act with gentleness.

Oakheart walked up and touched her hand. "My lady, you are well? I was worried when Dellbright said you would not see us."

"Not see you?" She blinked and lowered her gaze. "Yes, I am well, thank you. Now that I am free of my room. He lock—"

"Aria," Dellbright called out, interrupting her.

She shut her mouth and willed Oakheart to understand her, to know that she had been kept prisoner.

"Dellbright?" Oakheart whispered to her, raising his eyebrow in surprise, then dropped her hand before turning to his cousin.

"Oakheart! You see my wife is well," Dellbright said. "I grow weary of this endless debate. The adept has arrived. The keep is whole. I know not what prevents you from your quest. You have perhaps lost this fancy for that evil outlander and have changed your mind about rescuing her?"

The adept rose from his seat. He was a young man and when Lillia and Mellow withdrew from his side she straightaway saw the likeness. This adept was of the forest folk and close kin to Lillia and Mellow.

He strode forwards but his eyes were strange. The otherness in them was like that of Adage, whom she had met before.

"Princess Aria," he said, sounding relieved. He bowed his head in her direction.

Dellbright stood and shouted, gesturing widely in the adept's direction. "I told you not to call her that. She is no princess, just a curse inflicted upon us from a land beyond our own."

Oakheart shouted back in denial, but the adept kept his gaze on her as if nothing but polite conversation passed around them. "I am called Brookfell Treesinger. But with me I bring the thoughts and words of Adage, whom you have met. He asks me to ask you..."

Oakheart stood close and picked up her hand, squeezing it gently. His friend Fern stood at his shoulder. Fern's grey eyes were troubled as they gazed at her. She tried to smile at him but couldn't quite manage it.

"Fear not, my lady," Oakheart said and her eyes found his. "Brook is a good friend. I know it may seem strange that Adage can speak to him from such a distance. At first I was unbelieving but Brook has told me things that only Adage could know. So, if you would revere Brook as you would Adage, I would be ever grateful."

"Of course. What does Adage ask of me? I fear that you are all ahead of me. I don't know what's going on as I have been secluded in my room all morning. The keep feels restored. Is it so?"

"Yes," Brook replied. "All is as it should be. However, without the bounds of the keep the land is in much need. Oakheart must travel back to the Lower Warrens and free the Lady Sophy as soon as may be."

"I understand that. I will go with him."

Dellbright stood up suddenly, snagging her attention. "You will not." He frowned and latched his gaze onto her. "You belong to me and they cannot ask you to go with them unless I give them leave. I will not. There is much to resolve between us."

Aria's anger swelled. She tried to calm it, to temper it. "Belong to you? I do not. Anyway, you do not want me! And can't stop me," her voice rang out.

"Shut your mouth or I will stop it for you."

A gasp escaped her. Eyes wide, she watched as he continued.

"You will not disrespect your husband in his own hall—or anywhere else."

Aria closed her eyes, knowing she could not stop the rage building inside. If she did not stand up to him now, he would dominate her forever. She would lose what she had left of her self-respect. She stepped around Brook and faced Dellbright, who had sat back down, not bothering to hide the anger seething within. "I will not shut up. You have denied me my freedom. Without cause, you locked me in a room. You have denied me my son, as you have denied me food." She was shaking now. "You have withdrawn your love from me. No more. I decide my own path."

Dellbright's eyes glittered with fury. "You cannot leave this keep without my say-so. I allow you to listen and participate now because of Oakheart's request. My cousin's stubbornness allows you this much. But he will leave within the hour, or sooner, if we can finish this ridiculous audience. Then you will do as you are told. You will do as I say."

Brook spread his arms wide. "Please, calm yourselves. This is not courtly behaviour. I expected better from the inhabitants of Valley Keep." Aria wondered if that was Brookfell speaking or Adage. The adept's gaze, filled with otherness, then settled on Aria. "Oakheart has told us of his bond with the Lady Sophy and the vow she exacted from him to return your child to you. Adage asks if you made any vow to Sophy?"

Aria's eyes lowered as she thought. "We often promised things to each other before we came here. I...recall...when we argued about my marriage...I said I would always come for her. Yes, that is it. I would come for her and that is what I must do. I can save her."

"Perhaps," Brook replied with his eyes lowered, but he could not disguise the otherness to them.

"You would come with me then, Lady Aria, and help me save Sophy?" Oakheart asked, reverting to her pre-marriage honorific but with relief evident in his voice. The cleansing of the keep had built a stronger accord between them.

Turning her back on Dellbright, she said, "Of course I would, Oakheart."

Brook shuddered once and his eyes glowed eerily blue. Adage's voice emitted from his mouth, making Aria's skin crawl. "Danger. The crystal must be destroyed or reverted into Sophy's form as soon as may be, for while it exists in this land there is danger. Alien it is. Drawing the *given,* sucking the land's power with each pulse. A tool is being forged by Rufus, the agent of the Ancient Evil, and it will be used to destroy us. Hurry. You must hurry."

Chilled by Adage's words, Aria stepped back. Brook shook himself, and the bright blue glow faded from his irises, leaving them dark brown. He smiled, the skin around his eyes crinkling. "Forgive me. Adage needed to speak and I could not prevent him. We will depart now. Adage has bade me to serve him further. I am to travel with you."

Oakheart tensed. He seemed ready to ride out and was only held back by some vague uncertainty. Lillia surged forth with Mellow dragging on her clothes. "My son, you travel with Oakheart? We hoped that you would return with us to Gilton Forest. We are in need of your woodsinging skills."

Brook turned, arms outstretched. Lillia rushed to embrace him. As he stroked her hair, he spoke softly. "Mother, dearest mother, I know that the Gilton Forest is in need. But if I do not follow Adage's request and accompany Oakheart, then there will be no Gilton Forest. Not as you know it. Every day that the Lady Sophy exists in this crystal form is another day less in the life of this land. We fear the binding oath is undone and with the crystal pulsing and drawing in the *given,* it can only hasten the end. You must choose your path, mother. I have chosen mine."

Lillia looked up into his face; tears rolled down her cheek and her nose ran. "I know you have chosen, my son. The day you left us I knew how it would be." She turned back to Mellow. "Come, husband, I must speak with you. We have much to decide." To Oakheart she said, "I will meet you in the bailey 'ere you depart."

Oakheart nodded, but he lowered his eyes as Mellow passed him by. Aria thought he looked uncertain, afraid even. Her eyes surveyed the hall. Oakheart's men and Fern stood rigidly lined up behind him, ready to defend him with their lives. Brook took a few steps and stood behind Oakheart and waited.

There she was standing between her husband and Oakheart. What had happened to simple choices? Just then Dela brought in a crying Gilly. She took a step in his direction but Dellbright was there before her, preventing her approach. Dela showed no sympathy as she held Gilly in her arms. Aria was wounded that their friendship had not survived the events at Valley Keep.

"You wish to touch him?" Dellbright asked, holding the baby out invitingly. "Come, he is your son, is he not? Why do you hold back?"

She trembled. Dellbright was playing with her. Oakheart's eyes were on her. She shook her head imperceptibly, knowing that she was being manipulated but unable to fight the bait held out to her. This was her child, her flesh. The love she had for him had been screwed tight inside her. Afraid of loss, afraid she would never see him again. Then Dellbright, so fierce, so disregarding of her right to be a mother. She walked up, hand outstretched to stroke the child's cheek and then she took him in her arms. Dellbright's hand encircled her wrist and dragged her to him. "Come, my sweet wife. We must farewell Oakheart and his men on their journey. Then we can continue being a happy family."

"No," she said as she struggled against him. "You do not mean this. It is a trick. Don't do this. Please."

Dellbright leant in close to her ear, aimed his words directly to her. "You could not go with them. How would you survive? They have no time to pamper you and you are afraid of your own shadow. Yes, my little mouse, so fearful and yet so sweet." His hand forced her chin around to face him. She wanted to slap him. His dark eyes bored into hers. She would not struggle against him. He knew that she wouldn't. She could see it in the smile that slipped onto his face for a bare second. He poked at her weaknesses and laughed at them. There was something evil growing behind those once-loved eyes.

Aria twisted and Dellbright's hand dropped away. At a sharp word from Dellbright, Dela took Gilly into her arms. Aria's gaze riveted to Oakheart's face; her anguish made it hard to breathe. Oakheart's jaw clenched. She knew he understood her dilemma. She could not deny Dellbright. Dellbright knew how to lever her emotions, knew the price of her loyalty. Gilly. Her son.

"Tell them," he whispered in her ear. "Tell them you will stay or I will never let you see your son again."

"No," she moaned. She was lost. He had her and would not let up.

Oakheart tensed and made to step in their direction. "Do it," Dellbright hissed. Gilly chose to wail at that moment, sealing her fate.

Aria stood straight. Dellbright loosened his hold, confident she would do his bidding. "I will stay with my husband, Oakheart. Please forgive me." She lowered her head. When she raised her eyes, the assembled party was gone. She was alone with her husband.

Dellbright grabbed her by the shoulders and threw her to the ground. "Weak, you are, so weak. Oakheart will thank me for keeping you out of his way. Willow," he bellowed. "Willow."

Willow burst through the doors, robes flowing out behind him. Aria struggled to stand. Willow did not even look at her. She could feel the hate rolling off him, worse than Dellbright. "Take her back to her room and lock her in."

Willow's hard fingers gouged into her upper arms as he tugged her to him. "No. No," she protested. "You said I would be with Gilly."

Dellbright's face, distorted by anger, loomed in front of her. "Hah! As if I would let my son be tainted by you."

Aria was pulled inexorably to the door. She struggled in Willow's grasp and her dress tore. "Don't do this. I haven't eaten. You cannot think to starve me as well as deny me my son."

"Oh, I will feed you soon enough. Just wait and I will serve you a sumptuous feast, full of meat you will find difficult to swallow." His voice dripped venom.

Willow dragged her up the stairs as she struggled and wept. Oakheart and the others had gone, thinking that she had deserted them. *Fool! You must think clearer than this.* Willow shoved her through the door. She landed in a sprawl and the lock turned.

"Willow? Please." She could not keep the pleading from her voice.

Then she heard him whisper through the door. "My lady, my wife will bring you food. Never fear." She listened, straining to hear over the sound of her thudding heart, and heard Willow's retreating steps. She was shaking with anger and remorse. Oakheart must feel betrayed, but what of Sophy? How had Sophy felt when she abandoned her to marry Dellbright? How right she had been to preach caution!

Striding from one end of the room to the other, she had time to lay the blame for all that had happened at her own feet. Her actions had set things in motion. Her abandonment of self in Dellbright's embrace and her thoughts of love. Sophy! How utterly alone she must have been, cast alone in this world and bereft of friendship. Sophy had found friends in Oakheart and Lillia but her one true friend, she, Aria, had cast her off.

Aria was done with self-pity. Sloughed off were those childish thoughts and memories of laughter and love in Dellbright's arms. Oakheart had shown her an inkling of what she was capable of. She could not allow Dellbright to sway her from her path. Her husband was manipulating her, now. As she thought back, she realised he had always done so. Subtly, at first, but more overtly as time revealed her weakness. She had blinded herself to it, made excuses, because she could not admit her mistake.

From the bailey, she heard the sounds of Oakheart's departure. She raced over to the window to see the last of the horses depart. "Goodbye Oakheart. You are a true friend. Sophy is lucky to have you," she said to the breeze as he had no hope of hearing her. "We will meet again."

5

QUEST BOUND

Oakheart left Valley Keep behind, and even though the sun shone it could not lift the dark mood that lay upon him like a cloak of despair. It was wrong to leave Aria. A dark premonition troubled him and he knew in his heart that they would all be tainted by what would follow.

The cracks in his cousin's personality had erupted like fissures, forever disfiguring him. Oakheart did not know how husbands treated their wives. He only knew what guided him and his own sense of right said that everything he had witnessed boded ill for Aria. Could he have done more, fought for her freedom? But this mission to save Sophy was urgent, as the very land was in peril. He had what he had lacked before, an adept, who could free Sophy from her unnatural bonds.

Had Dellbright been physically aggressive towards Aria before? That would explain the timid way she behaved when they arrived. How could such a beautiful love turn so bitter? Oakheart reeled at the enormity of it. Was this linked to the fate of the land, to Adage's dire warnings? Would he be able to stop the loss of the *given?* He could only hope he was wrong about Aria and Dellbright. To think otherwise threatened to unravel him.

When Dellbright had said it would be unnatural for a mother to abandon her child, Oakheart could not disagree. It was a wound that was ever sore in his heart. His own mother's abandonment had near ruined him as a child. She had abandoned him for the love of another, and he had never understood it.

Forcing Aria from Valley Keep and the child was beyond his power. Yet deep down, he knew Aria was the key to Sophy's freedom. They were bound, not only by oaths, but by something else, perhaps some strange force from the world they were born into. And he had witnessed her power. Her subtle and brilliant manipulation of the *given*. That could only assist them. Oakheart was tempted to turn back, to halt his horse and go back on foot and beg her to change her mind. Yet he knew that Dellbright would not let him in. What a strange pass that the bonds of friendship and kinship were so easily severed. That thought alone kept Oakheart going, his chest so tight he could barely breathe. A casual glance at the others and he could tell that their minds were similarly engaged.

Fern's shoulders sagged. Aria's beauty and plight had touched him. Oakheart closed his eyes as they plodded along, shutting out the view of the adept's robes fluttering in the breeze, Fern's pouting gaze and the solemn expressions of his men. It chilled him to know what Dellbright had become. How easily his cousin had fallen prey to bitterness and anger. And what of himself? Would he, too, fall prey to such negative emotions? He shuddered, hoping he had more strength than that.

Unease itched between Oakheart's shoulder blades as they passed abandoned houses and travelled along the empty streets of Valley Keep's small village. The people who had huddled there when they had passed through had now slunk away. He felt someone's gaze and turned. Fern's grey eyes were storm-tossed.

"Speak your mind, Fern."

"How could you do it?"

He glanced ruefully at his friend. "He is her husband. I cannot come between them, unless she bade me to do so. You heard what she said."

"Yes, but it was wrenched from her unwillingly. He held the child as ransom."

"And she chose…"

"But you know…he has kept her locked up and half starved. He will not let her near her own son…you know that."

"I do not know it…but I fear it."

"Then why do we not return…"

"We cannot, Fern."

"But Oakheart…"

"Fern…"

"Is this why we travel so slowly…so you have time for your conscience to recover?"

"Enough. By the *given* I am torn, Fern. I must hurry to Sophy's aid, yet the thought of Aria and her fate…I would stay. Such choices are not for me…"

The adept slowed his horse until he was abreast of Oakheart. "You made the right decision," Brook added, his voice tinged with strangeness and with his irises haloed in blue. "The destruction, or freedom, of Sophy is what takes precedence."

"Destruction?" Oakheart could not keep the horror from his face as he gazed at Brook. "You cannot think to…she lives within that gem." His fist clenched his reins and his horse began to prance.

"Easy, Oakheart." It was Brook's own voice, his eyes once again plain brown. "What if you cannot change her back? What if you cannot save her? What then? Will you doom us all? Would you let Argenterra become less than it is?"

Oakheart gave vent to his fear and outrage. "This cannot be happening! Why does this choice come to me?"

Adage's voice now issued from Brook's lips. "Take heart, my friend. Your oathbonding causes you to have these choices and it has been our saving. I cannot see what the future will bring. Even now, Rufus is forging his tool but he cannot wield it. Your bonding with Sophy has flawed his gem…but I do not know if you can free her." Oakheart nodded agreement. He had considered his oathbond an obstacle for Rufus, hence the savagery the foul beast had unleashed to kill him. "From this distance I cannot see a way for it to be done."

Oakheart calmed his frantic heart and let his fear die down. "Aria may not be needed to free Sophy?"

Adage looked out at him from Brook's face. "That I cannot say. Like you, I theorise that they are bound in a way that I cannot understand."

Despair shrouded Oakheart as he returned the adept's gaze. "'For the first time in my life, Adage, your words do not comfort me."

The adept glanced over his shoulder to look back at Valley Keep, then he sighed as he returned his gaze to Oakheart. "I know," said Adage's voice from Brook's lips. The glow in Brook's eyes faded as Adage's essence dissipated. Brook shrugged and said in his own voice, "I am truly sorry, Oakheart."

"Thank you, Brook," he replied. "It cannot be comfortable to have Adage speak through you."

Brook lowered his gaze. "It is not."

Fern's pout had disappeared, only to be replaced with a frown of worry and concern. "Brook, how does that feel when he...you know, takes you over? Do you hear and see us?"

Brook glowered at Fern and swallowed once before answering. "It is like being seized by a creeping numbness, which paralyses my legs, my arms, my torso, my head, my mouth in turn. I can see and hear but I am muffled. Adage is...how can I say this...an awesome presence. His will is strong, forged over hundreds of years to a purpose."

Fern chewed his lips. "Sounds disgusting to me." He nudged his horse forwards and Oakheart saw him shake himself.

Oakheart regarded Brook for a while and then by unspoken mutual consent they spurred their mounts and caught up with the others. He shuddered once, realising that Adage was practising what must be a deeply held secret of the retreat, perhaps never before accomplished. Argenterra's need must indeed be great.

※

ARIA RUMMAGED THROUGH ALL OF THE CHESTS. MOSTLY GOWNS AND underclothes filled them, but she searched for something suitable for travel. Dellbright's chest stood next to his side of the bed. She wondered if any of his things still remained. Reluctantly she threw the lid open while she kept an ear out for anyone's approach. Surely they would guess she meant to escape. Her hand trembled as she knew she couldn't escape soon enough.

There were a few cloaks on the top, but underneath she found a pair of breeches and a jerkin. She lifted them out and surveyed them. They appeared a little large but the ties could be adjusted. She rolled them hastily and looked for a place to hide them.

Her gaze fell upon the bed. She rushed over and stuffed them beneath the mattress. Now she needed to find shoes. She had nothing sturdy enough for outdoors and for walking on foot. Unless she reinforced them with the *given*.

Time was ticking away. He would come. It was as inevitable as the sun setting and the moons rising. He would come to punish her, to purge her of her weakness, of her love for him.

She found a pair of soft, high-ankled boots with laces that secured both sides. Frowning, she inspected them. They had flimsy satin soles. She remembered how Aurore showed her to reinforce cloth. Concentrating, she bent her will to the boots. She breathed out with effort and gazed at the thin soles. Nothing had changed. Her attempt had failed. She tried again, peering into the weave, pushing herself into it. There was a slight change. She kept at it, pushing and prodding with the *given* in small amounts, so lost in the task that she lost all sense of time and place.

The door swung open, crashing against the wall. Startled, she dropped the slippers. She stood and turned slowly to face him. He smiled at her, and her breath caught. It was almost his old smile and then she caught the look, the gaze tinged with bitterness.

While he grasped the door to shut it behind him, his eyebrow quirked mockingly and he said, "So there you are playing with your clothes. Do you hope to tempt me with your dainty feet?"

"Dellbright..." Her voice was near to pleading.

"Do not speak. When you open your mouth it will be to say the words I want to hear."

She shut her mouth. Her stomach pounded with hunger and fear. Foreboding hung in the air; she could taste it on her tongue.

"I will not ask you to take off your gown. I will take it from you myself when I am ready." He paced catlike around her, slowly closing in. "You will only take what is passed to you from my hand...whether it be food or clothes or love."

Aria clamped her mouth shut. Her instinct was to stay quiet. There was no use in provoking him. Yet if she didn't stand up for herself, how would she ever be free? *Oh no!* She could never be free of him. She was bound to her oath, bound until death. She could only pray that he would return to his old self, but she knew in her heart that it could not be. He may improve over time, but he would never be the Dellbright she had met and married. The cracks were too deep for that.

"Tell me that you agree to these terms. Promise me on the life of your child."

Shaken by his words, she exclaimed, "No, not that. Don't ask me...I can't swear or promise you anything, especially not on the life of our child."

His hand swung and connected with her cheek. "You deny me?" he roared.

Her face smarted; her nose stung and her eyes watered. "I deny you nothing. I cannot swear to you, that is all."

"All? You are my wife, bonded to me through the power of the Crystal Tree. How can you deny me?"

Aria searched for an escape. Why did he twist everything? "I have denied you nothing, except the giving of a promise on the life of our child. I know not if the promise alone is binding, but I cannot, must not, make it."

"Why?"

"Because I gave you an oath to be your wife and you have denied me. There can be no more oaths between us. There is already one too many."

He lunged. Her beautiful gown tore as he sundered it with one hand. The other hand held her by the hair. "You are mine, Aria. You cannot deny that. Can you?"

Great tremors ran through her body. She looked down at the remains of her bodice. Dellbright let go of her gown and his hand cupped her breast and squeezed. His other hand, grasping her hair, shook her head. "Can you?"

Her lips clenched shut. The hand on her breast squeezed and she cried out, trying to wrench free. "Answer me." Dellbright had his face next to hers. She could see his eyes filled with rage. He jerked her back and forth. Stunned, she wavered when he let go. She didn't even see the punch coming, nor the next, but she felt them bruise her face, her ribs. Then he stopped, panting heavily. "Well?"

"No," she breathed through swollen and cut lips. Let him figure out what she was saying. His eyes widened, questioning. Something broke inside her. With all her might, she swung up her fist and hit him in the side of the head. It was a mistake. He anticipated her. Bending her fist back, he nudged her backwards until she hit the bed with the back of her knees.

With a shove, she was down. Blood leaked down the back of her throat. She swallowed and tried to cover herself but his hands were there before hers. The rest of her gown and underclothes were ripped to shreds as Dellbright erased the last of her dignity.

"Oh," Dellbright said in mock surprise. "You offer yourself to me as a feast. How I hunger for you...Do you like the meat I offer you in return?"

❦

Cloaked in a cape and laden with misery, Aria edged out to the gates in the dead of night. She limped and each breath hurt as she sucked in the cool air. She shifted her pack, easing it over her bruised neck. It contained the one meal that Dela had given her and a change of clothes. Nothing else.

She shivered with trepidation, sliding into shadows at every sound. Peering out, she watched a lone guard pace, stop at the edge of his round and turn. Her frightened eyes glanced left and right and she darted forth, keeping to the shadows.

Thoughts of Sophy's bravado came to mind. How she missed her friend, especially now. Aria had no skill at braving the night, at skulking in shadows, at climbing out windows...until now.

A footstep sounded behind her. She froze as her heart leapt into her mouth, blood pounding in her ears. She eased back against the wall and waited. Hoping that whoever it was would not hear her erratic heartbeat and her gulping for breath.

It was quiet. The sound did not repeat. She headed towards the wood, certain that no one would look there first. She tried to recollect the lay of the land and whether the wood met the road out of the valley. Why hadn't she paid attention?

A wince stretched her features as pain shot up her back. She shifted her pack and eased it to the other side. The scent of roses was gone from the garden. She skirted the wall and kept going. Her feet hurried, driven on by the fear of pursuit.

Hunger pushed up into her throat, but she couldn't stop to eat yet. She hadn't eaten before she fled. Could not eat...

There were rumours that bounty abounded aplenty in the valley. Perhaps later, when she could stomach food, she would find something to supplement the loaf of bread and quarter of cheese that sat in her pack.

If she had stayed, Dellbright would have had her begging for mercy within a week, maybe even a day. To stop him, she would have pledged anything. That was too horrible to even contemplate. She shuddered, closing her mind to thoughts of him. There was too much...

Increasing her pace, she skirted the keep and entered the wood. Overhead, large branches loomed like hovering dark claws reaching to the sky.

Once inside the cover of the trees, she relaxed. Edging behind a large tree, she peered back the way she had come. She searched the practice ground and the path from the garden. There was no movement. Closing her eyes, she laid her forehead on the tree trunk carefully, saying a silent prayer. Not followed. A sense of peace grew within her like a flickering candle flame.

With one last look at the keep, she turned and stepped deeper into the wood. It was dark. She couldn't see well but there was a well-worn path to follow. Soon the sun would rise and she needed to get away from the valley but also needed to hide. Daylight would bring pursuit. Dellbright would not give up his revenge that easily.

The wood was larger than she expected, although a faint doubt about her direction made her worry that she was lost and going round in circles. After a couple of hours the gloom lifted. It was so eerie and still. She glanced up. The sky was pale and grey. Yet daylight was growing stronger with each step.

The other side of the wood was close. Light silhouetted the dark trunks of trees, revealing open space beyond. Hope rose and she sped up, crunching twigs under her feet. Another sound made her start. As the sun continued to rise, the wood around her came alive with blurs of green and brown. An arm circled her neck and a knife flashed and was then pressed to her neck. Suddenly, nothing mattered anymore. She was caught. Her mind went red, like the blood stains on her sheets. Her knees bent, and she fainted.

⚜

ARIA'S EYES OPENED. AT FIRST, EVERYTHING WAS A BLUR, THEN SHE made out a grey overcast sky. She struggled to sit up, wedging her elbows underneath her. Squatting around her were the faces of the forest folk.

Mellow's dark gaze lowered. "Forgive me, my lady...I meant you no harm."

Aria's hand rubbed her bruised neck. "I'm sure you didn't...what are you doing here?" Her voice was scratchy, barely recognisable as her own. She swallowed. "I thought you were headed in the other direction back to the Gilton Forest."

Lillia darted out of the bushes. She looked flushed and sweaty but still ready for a fight. "What has happened?" Her eyes took in Illart, Raven and Mellow, then they rested on Aria. "By the trees, what has happened to you? Mellow, tell me that you did not do this."

Mellow's haunted expression lifted and then his eyes narrowed. He edged closer and flicked Aria's cape back, revealing dark bruises and cuts to her neck, face and chest.

"Have a care, woman. I held her by force, but I did not do that."

A wail left Lillia's lips as she fell to her knees. "I have failed you, my lady. I have failed in every way."

Lillia's emotion almost moved Aria to tears. "No. You didn't."

Stifling a sob, Lillia gently reached out and touched Aria's hair. "Sophy will not forgive me for abandoning you."

Aria swallowed again and looked at the faces of the people surrounding her. "I don't understand. You haven't failed me."

"Your face...He beat you..."

Aria lowered her gaze. "I'm here now. That is a good thing."

"Of course it is but—by the trees, Dellbright has wronged you."

Aria shrugged off her backpack, wincing as the straps brushed her bruised back. "Yes, it shames me to admit it. By the look on your faces the bruising must be bad."

"How can you be shamed?" Lillia knelt beside her. Placing her hand on Aria's head, she stroked her hair. "The deed is not yours...violence like this...is not...it happens occasionally...rarely...but it is not condoned. In the Gilton Forest such acts are held to be contrary to the oath. Mellow," Lillia said gently. "We will camp here for now. I must tend Aria. Please make us a shelter that is well camouflaged."

There was a sound of an impact as Mellow slapped his hand against his thigh. All eyes centred on him. "Then what happens?" Mellow hissed, shoulders hunched as if ready to fight. "Oh, do not tell me, for my heart breaks with the knowing of it. You will go with Aria to join Oakheart's quest. I see it clearly."

Lillia pursed her lips before raising her eyes to her husband's face. "I must...please forgive me, my husband." She paused, evidently thinking. "It is not by chance you found Aria. In her condition she cannot go on alone. I cannot turn away from this."

Mellow nodded stiffly. His dark gaze travelled over Aria. "I never thought I would witness such a deed." He smacked his chest. "It wounds me. Makes me feel less a man." He went away to find branches to make a shelter, his shoulders sagging and an air of defeat following.

Lillia touched Aria's shoulder tentatively. "My lady, can you ride a horse?"

Roused from considering her many aches, she said, "No, not really. But I'm sure to learn soon enough." Aria frowned, realising that Lillia meant physically able to ride, and then shrugged.

Mellow returned, dragging two large branches with him into the clearing. Illart and Raven helped to bind them to make support for a tent. Before he headed back into the forest in search of more wood, Lillia spoke to him.

"Aria may be fit to ride. After I have tended to her wounds, I will ride with her and deliver her to Oakheart. I will stay by her side until the quest is done. You and the others may follow on foot or return home. Either way, our paths separate this night." They locked gazes. "Forgive me."

Mellow moved closer and the fierceness left his expression. "There is nothing to forgive." His eyes softened and he touched her forearm lightly. It was a small, yet powerful gesture. To Aria it spoke volumes about their love and friendship. It filled her with a pang of regret and even envy.

"You remind me of why I love you: your warrior-maiden heart. You risk everything, even me, to do what you see is your duty, to do what is right," Mellow said quietly, a look of resignation settling on his face. He shrugged. "Here I was thinking I was to be happy to be here amongst the trees. It is not home but, for a short time, it comforted me."

"I am sorry," Lillia said, with a shake of her head and tears trailing across a smiling cheek. "You honour me."

"I will follow on foot, but I will not be able to catch you. Not for a while, at least."

The other forest folk added their pledges to follow. "Look for our signs," Mellow said. "Perhaps when you need us we will be close."

Lillia looked to Raven and Illart, who had finished draping a blanket over the branches and pegged the edges to the ground. They nodded their agreement as they stepped away from the makeshift tent. "Come then, my lady," Lillia said, easing Aria to her feet. "Let us see what can be done to ease your discomfort."

Illart, Raven and Mellow darted into the forest again to retrieve branches and leaves. Very quickly the shelter blended in with the surroundings. Even though it was not a complete camouflage it was sufficient to shield them from casual observers.

Lillia led her inside. The entrance was covered by branches with leaves and more twigs. Aria could see that it had been made over two large roots, which grew like folds out of the soil to create a cradle.

There was enough room for two people to lie down to sleep and at least to stand if bent over double. A blanket spread on the ground looked inviting. Fatigued, Aria wished for nothing but to be free of fear. The forest folks' presence eased her anxiety.

"Sit down, my lady; my things are here."

Aria eased herself down to sit, stifling whimpers at the pain even that small movement produced.

Lillia rummaged through her pack. "Take off your cloak and other clothes," she said gently, while she pulled some clay pots and cloth bundles out and placed them by her feet. Very quickly she had lit a small fire under a little metal cauldron.

Aria began to comply, when Lillia asked, "Tell me what happened, my lady." Aria froze.

Meeting her gaze, the forest maiden said, "It will ease your burden if you do."

Aria's face heated and she kept her eyes downcast. "I don't want to tell you...I have forgotten it." She tugged on the laces of her jerkin, while Lillia edged closer to take her cape and fold it.

When the older woman didn't speak, Aria glanced up. Lillia's gaze roamed over Aria's face, her mouth pensive. "I see..." She turned to her little cauldron and broke herbs into it, shoving dry twigs underneath to feed the fire. The smoke mingled with the air. It was but a small flame. Aria pushed down her anxiety. This small flame would not lead to her capture. She had to believe that.

Aria winced again when she tried to undress. Seeing her discomfort, the forest maiden helped to tug off the jerkin and then turned to her breeches. The older woman's face became more and more severe. Blood stuck to the crotch of Aria's breeches. Aria looked down at the bruises in the shape of hands up her thighs; nail marks raked across her belly, and bruised nipples framed by bite marks contracted in the cold air.

Wordlessly Lillia turned her around and ran her fingers lightly down her back. "You do not...speak of it, my lady," she said brokenly. "For...it is plain...to see."

Aria's lips trembled, the empathy undid her. A soundless scream issued from her lips; a voiceless sorrow that knew no bounds wrenched away the ties of love that bound her tongue. Sobs rose, choking her breathing, as she let her grief pour out. The memories of Dellbright's hands on her, the torment that knew no end replayed. She let it come from that dark well that had started with a cruel word here, a cutting look there, and culminated in a savage rape and brutal beating.

With sudden clarity, she realised then how close she had come to death at the hands of Dellbright. She pitied him, even though she could not love him anymore. It made her angry, too, that she could not love him ever again. He had made himself unworthy of her love—and for that she grieved.

"I escaped after..." she began. "I had planned to. I knew what would happen but I could not escape in time...I tied the sheets, though they were not long enough. I was so numb, full of desolation, that I cared not where I fell. I didn't think I could do it alone. I'm not brave like Sophy...I'm so glad I found you."

"Yes," Lillia replied, tears streaking her face. She sniffed and wiped them with the back of her hand. "I am glad you found me, too. And Aria...you are very brave...Sophy would be proud of you."

Lillia tipped the liquid from the small cauldron into a cup. "Now drink this. I think we need healing bark. Some of your injuries will not travel well. I will see if Mellow has some handy. I thought perhaps he had prevailed upon Master Willow for some."

Lillia eased out of the shelter while Aria sipped the brew. It slid down her bruised throat, soothing her hurts. She sat and stared, feeling so deadened. It was as if her life had disappeared and she remained as a ghost to float in life, not quite dead and not quite alive.

LILLIA SOUGHT OUT MELLOW. HIS DARK EYES MOVED TO HERS instinctively. She ran the last few steps and flung herself into his embrace. "Oh Mel...you do not know...you cannot know what has befallen that child. How glad I am that I am yours and you are mine. I hope we never live to see such violence enacted again..."

Mellow brushed a kiss across her forehead. "I know, Lil. Her pain cries out from beneath her clothes. Such a wrong cannot be still or quiet. It screams its outrage to all those who would hear it. Dellbright is less of a man for this deed, but she is no less a woman."

"I need the healing bark, Mel. Her injuries...she cannot ride, not like that. I do not know how she lived through it. I do not think there is a part of her left untouched." She cried into Mel's shoulder, a hopeless sobbing that summed up what she felt. If there had been good in the world, surely it was departing. She feared for her people, for the Gilton Forest, and she feared for herself. What was coming would change her, and Mel, too, if they lived.

Mel drew the healing bark from his waist pouch and handed it to her. He closed her fingers around it and kissed her. "Keep her quiet. Men are on the rim of the forest, searching. If they come near, we will lead them away. When dark comes make your way out. I hid the horse in a copse on the edge of the forest, near the road. Pray they do not find it, or you will have to double back and steal another."

"Farewell, beloved. I will get her to sleep first. Then we will leave. Keep sharp to the lookout." She smiled and rested a hand against her abdomen. "I hope to be at home when this child comes and with you there to greet him."

Mel drew her to him, hugged her tight and released her. The memory of his body on hers stirred her, soothed her hurt. She stepped away and wiped her tears. Mel melted into the wood; Raven and Illart sank back, too, waving farewell. Lillia went back to the shelter to tend Aria.

❦ 6 ❦

THE CAVES OF SUVAL

Rae trod up the path leading to the Puri's main water source. Fed by an underground spring, the small lake sat in the centre of connected caves. A flurry of laughter stilled as she passed by a group of gossiping women. They turned their backs to her. Rae bit down on her sadness, trying to ignore the shunning. She rubbed her belly where her child grew, and drew comfort from its existence. With a sigh, she adjusted the water jug on her hip and kept walking. Being outcast hurt her pride, although she tried not to dwell on it.

This close to the lake dampness filled the air and moistened the earth as she neared the edge. Even the walls of the cave glittered slickly in torch light. Water dripped from the rocks above. She heard the drops plop and splash, echoing into the dark. She wondered why she could hear it so clearly when the caves were full of Hanal's clan. Only that morning Hanal had been raining curses down on his kinsman Nasheen's head. Hanal liked it not when his orders were disobeyed, and Nasheen was meant to bring tidings of Argenterra. Hanal grew more distracted every day that Nasheen failed to join up with the clan in the Caves of Suval. Rae ached to ease her beloved Hanal's worries.

Kneeling on the bank, she daydreamed of Hanal's joy when she would tell him of the child growing within her. The dark water bled into the neck of the jug. She lifted it, spilling some back into the lake. The baby stirred within her, like a light flutter of butterfly wings. She smiled to herself until the sound of whispering behind her disturbed her thoughts and soured her expression. She edged around to gaze behind. A group of women pointed at her and talked behind their hands. It was as if they suspected about the babe, about what Umri had done to her.

Rae positioned the jug on her hip and stood to leave, letting water drip down the leg of her Puri tunic and trousers. She swung her head, sending her colourful headpiece over her shoulder to fall down her back. Straightening her spine, she strode past.

"Shame on you," one of them hissed.

"He will cast you out for sure, now," another said.

"Yes, for who has fathered it? It could be anyone, you hussy," said another voice. Then their laughter chimed in, and Rae hurried her step, biting her lip.

Her heart beat like thunder. She prayed that they were wrong. Surely Hanal would not do such a thing. He was an honourable man, or so she thought. She was not convinced, though. For many months now he had shared his bed with her, taking what she had to give, but offering nothing, other than his household to live in.

Panting, she headed back to Hanal's chamber. The curtain yielded easily as she pushed through. Hanal stood alone, back to the entrance. On the rug by his foot his tea mug steamed vapour into the air.

"Rae?" he said without turning.

She slid the urn full of water to the floor and shifted it out of the way. Bowing low, she knelt and pressed her face to the matting, and said, "I am here, Hanal."

When she looked up, he was there before her, robe still swaying from his quick steps. "Is it true?"

Rae pushed herself up to a sitting position but kept her head bowed. "Is what true?"

"Do not play games with me, Rae. I see from your expression you know of what I speak. Do you carry a child within you?"

Rae's face heated and tears pricked her eyes. Her throat closed up, so she nodded.

"Is it mine?"

Again she nodded, appalled by the loaded question. Who else would have fathered the child if not he?

"No!" Hanal exploded, hitting his fist into the palm of his other hand.

At the sound of the impact her head shot up, eyes searching his face. "You are not pleased?" Rae asked, trembling. Blood crashed in her ears, making her head spin.

His expression was furious. "Pleased? Are you out of your mind?" he hissed at her. "You know what precautions I took. You please me, Rae, but you are not to be the mother of my children." He turned and walked away, then came back to her in two quick steps. "How did it happen? I kept my seed from you. Have you lain with another?" His voice was quick and urgent.

Rae climbed to her feet, affront making her brave. With fists clenched, she said, "No. I did not. You know I did not. I have been little from your side since we first lay together."

His piercing gaze delved into her, searching out her secrets, and Rae could not meet it, so she looked away, flushing.

"Oh...There is more to this, I see. You will tell me all."

Rae stepped back, shaking her head. "There is nothing to tell. Your seed is in me and a child grows as a result."

"Look at me," he said seductively, softly, as he stepped closer.

Rae could smell his spicy scent and the damp chill of the cave made her shiver. His hand touched her chin, made her look up and meet those startling eyes of his. Rae could not breathe. It was as if her chest would explode for the want of air. And then he let her go.

He watched her silently and then spoke quietly. "You will leave my household. I will not have a liar close to me. You cannot be trusted." He turned his back on her and sat down on the mat next to his tea. His shoulders were back, his spine straight, and then he looked at her. Those eyes of his washed over her body as her heart sank to her feet.

Rae sagged to the floor. "Do not send me away. I could not bear it. Already, I am shunned. How would it be without your protection? And what about the babe?" She fell onto her hands, nose pressed into the rug.

The cup chinked as he lifted it to sip the tea. He placed it down again, calmly, deliberately. "You speak of being shunned as if I am to blame. But you chose to seduce me. I could have married you off nicely to another man but you chose to bed me instead. From the beginning, I offered you nothing, just as you could offer me nothing. What do I care for a child I do not want? What could you be thinking to keep it? Surely Umri would have assisted you to lose it. She has the herb lore."

Rae's eyes lifted to his. She heard his words and could not understand them. This was not the Hanal she knew, or wanted to know. "Umri..." she whispered, as if in a trance. How had her dreams come to this? What kind of manipulation was she involved in? Her eyes watered.

Hanal's eyes nailed her when she spoke Umri's name. "I see. You did go to Umri but not to rid yourself of the child. Why did you go to her?"

Rae wiped her eyes with the edge of her headdress. "I fear to tell you. I fear your anger."

"At this moment, nothing you could say would make me angrier. Speak, or leave and never come back. Your future in my household depends on what you say next. Make sure it is the truth."

Brokenly, she told him of Umri's questions and her instructions. He sucked in a breath when she told him of how Umri had placed his seed inside of her. "I see. Wait here. I will summon Umri."

Rae tried to calm herself while Hanal went to send someone to fetch his seer. Dread threatened to overwhelm her.

There were other options, even though they involved a wretched broken heart and endless shame. She could go home to Kushlan. He would not turn her away. Yet would Hanal let her take his child? Despite his words, she thought not. And she was not about to part from it.

The curtain behind her swished open. Hanal stepped past, not sparing a glance at her. Rae wanted so much for him to forgive her. Next she heard softer footfalls. Umri stepped through and knelt beside her, bending her neck so her head touched her chest. Rae looked sideways and thought she saw Umri tremble.

Hanal stood, hands on hips and feet spread wide. "Speak, Umri, before I cast you out of this clan."

Umri raised her eyes. "Of what do you wish me to speak? I have done naught to warrant such treatment. I have served only your interests in all that I have done."

Hanal barked a laugh that was cold and deadly. "Really?" he said, his gaze raking over Umri. "I think corrupting this child, preying on her capacity for wild tales and then filling her womb with my child serves only *your* interests and *your* revenge."

Umri's expression showed no emotion. Rae was alert—something she never realised before was becoming clear. Her lips parted, but Hanal spoke before she could. "Oh, little sister. You wonder about what I speak. You see, Umri was my lover, secret lover, a few years ago. Like you, she gave herself to me willingly. She wanted to leave her clan, wanted power, wanted me. As with you, I took what she offered, giving no vow.

"Umri despaired, often begging me to wed her. I grew tired of her in many ways and gave her to my brother, Tarkel. If he suspected our relationship I do not know, but he took her, used as she was, without question. The medicine woman of her clan told me that she suspected that Umri used the herb lore to avoid getting with child, either that or she was barren. I suspect she uses her arts to deny my brother an heir."

"You stupid, insipid, Argenterran weakling girl," Umri spat at her. "What lies have you told him?" Turning back to Hanal, she said, "Do not be taken in by her guile. She appears innocent but she is not. She used me to get to you."

Alarmed, Rae turned her pleading gaze to Hanal. "No," Rae protested before turning back to Umri. "You used me. All the time, I thought you wanted to help me, and all the time you wanted to get even with him, to hurt him and me along with it." Rae turned her face to Hanal. "I love you, Hanal. With all my being, I am yours. I will stay with you if you let me. Serve you in any way I can. If you cast me out, I will die."

Umri's hands were clenched, her expression dismissive. "Will you fall for that? She knew what she was doing…"

"Enough. Umri, you will stay out of my household. If I need to consult you, I will convene a council. I suggest you use your talents to get yourself with child. If you are not with my brother's child by the end of the year I will cast you out. For good."

"You cannot mean that," she almost howled. Then she pulled all her despair into herself and funnelled it out like a snake spitting venom. "You cannot do this to me. I am your seer. I neither want nor need a child. You need me. Without me, you are nothing."

"Hah. Next you will say that this child Rae bears will be my heir, a great leader and ruler of all Argenterra and the wider lands. What I fool I was for listening to you," Hanal said, signalling for her to depart with an indifferent wave of his hand. "Use your vast array of talents to help yourself. I would that my brother had a better deal and a son to follow after him."

Umri screeched and thrashed about. Hanal watched her calmly as if he had seen a performance like this many times before. After a few minutes while she continued to writhe, he put his hands on his hips. "Shut up, Umri, and get out before I call your husband. Then he can decide your fate."

Suddenly silenced, Umri staggered to her feet, sent a menacing glower at Rae and stomped from the chamber, leaving the curtains trembling in her wake.

Rae watched her leave, realising that she was now truly friendless. Tentatively, she glanced at Hanal. Some of the anger had left him. She could see it in how he relaxed his shoulders and slowed his breathing. He sat down again, crossing his legs and then leaning back on a cushion. "Come here, Rae."

Rae shuffled forwards on her knees, confused by his summons and soft tone of voice. She felt like a child, but knew she had to be a woman now. She had to be smart because she had no one to guide her. Umri had led her down this path and yet it was not in her to hate the other woman. All hope was not lost. "Yes, Hanal."

"Little sister," he said sweetly, reaching for her, brushing his forefinger along her chin. "You love me. Only love would have led you to do this. I understand your feeling and I only hope you will be content with your lot."

Rae kissed his dark lips tenderly and breathed in his scent. "I am content as long as I am near you."

He tugged off her headdress, stroked her hair, trailing his hand down her back to cup her buttocks. "I hope you will not regret it. Tu Raenal, daughter of Kushlan Silvertongue, because it can only grow worse for you. I will not marry you. I gain nothing from such an alliance. If I am to give up my freedom, it will be to better the lot of my people."

"I care not as long as you are near me," Rae said and surrendered to his touch.

7

A BREATH OF HEART AND A TOUCH OF SOUL

"Ware," Fern hissed as he rode up from the rear. "Someone comes behind us. Fast." Oakheart glanced around, looking for a place to hide. The shadows were lengthening as the sun set behind the hill. Everywhere the men scattered to hide, pushing horses back amongst trees. Oakheart bounded ahead and slid off his mount. This place was as good as any to face an attack, though not quite good enough to stage an ambush.

Behind a wide tree, he hid, waiting. It was not long before he heard the sound of hooves thumping against the ground, muffled by clumps of grass. Whoever approached was not using the road. The tread slowed and the horse snorted. From his vantage point, he could see a few of his men, though Fern was hidden from view. Oakheart eased out and tried to catch a glimpse of the rider. He pulled back. There were two riders, with cloaks hiding their faces and hair.

There was a whistle, a signal. He thought for a moment that it was a trick and then, nearly bursting with relief, he stepped out. "Lillia?"

The lead rider drew back her hood and Lillia's short-cropped hair and fierce blue eyes greeted him. "Well met, Oakheart. We caught you sooner than I expected."

"Who is with you?" The cloaked figure slouched down. It was too small to be Mellow.

A pale hand reached up and tentatively drew back the hood. Ginger ringlets spilled out and a swollen and bruised face smiled shyly at him.

It took a moment for him to comprehend. "Aria?" He rushed to take her hand and help her down. His emotions were in a whirl. She was here but the condition she was in! He could barely stop his hands from shaking.

Fern took a few steps towards the horse, grabbing the reins as Oakheart reached up to lift her down.

"Careful…" Lillia warned. "She is injured. We have ridden as hard as we could to find you."

With trembling hands, he lowered Aria and as he drew her down, he sat on the ground and placed her across his legs to cradle her like a baby. She grimaced. Her legs moved stiffly but there were other injuries. Her hurts were not hidden from him. Pain blazoned from her as if it was borne in his own skin. Since they had cleaned the rotting blood eating into the fabric of Valley Keep, he had felt a closeness to Aria, a bond strengthened, he believed, by the *given*. He did not know he was crying until Aria placed a finger on his lips to quieten him, a tear slipping silently from her pain-filled eyes.

"Shhh. It's not your fault. I shouldn't have let him blackmail me with Gilly. I'm sorry I let you go without me."

"See, I told you," Fern said, though his voice only held pain and remorse. Fist balled, he paced, then much affected, he sniffed. "He has harmed her. For that alone I would kill him."

Lillia's eyes flashed. "Enough…does violence breed violence? Is the binding oath foresworn by everyone? Listen to what you say. Murder most dire caused this. Dellbright was once a good man, now something eats at his heart. For you to even utter those words taints you with this deed."

Fern flinched as if the words hit him like darts, then he stood transfixed as the enormity of her words sank in. He fell to his knees and bowed his head. "Forgive me. You speak true. But I have never heard of, or seen, such a deed as this." He gestured to Aria. "Oakheart has the better sight, but I can feel her pain from where I stand. Yet..." he could speak no more.

Aria turned her head towards Fern. "I thank you for your concern, Lord Fern. I'm well, believe me. The worst is treated with healing bark. It is only the horseback riding that has me so laid out. I'm not used to it, but Lillia helped me. I was never brave enough to go alone. I'm not as fearless as Sophy."

Her eyes slid from Fern to Oakheart. "You miss her, don't you?" she asked.

"Yes...I did not know it would ache this much, but it does."

Aria smiled, her split lip paining her for a moment. "I'm glad that Sophy finally saw who you are, Oakheart, and that you could finally see her."

Oakheart stroked Aria's hair, soothing her while he thought through their situation. There was no point in continuing; it was late and Aria could not travel any farther.

"Everyone, make camp. Fern, set the watch. Rufus still wants me dead so best we be wary."

Lillia began unsaddling her horse and unstrapping her packs. Over Aria's head, he asked Lillia, "Is there anything you can do for her? Can my men set up a tent, cook some food? Can I do anything?"

Lillia dropped two packs on the ground and then tugged on her bed roll. "Rest and food for the moment. I have not been able to get her to eat. She sickens at the sight of food."

Oakheart nodded, and continued to run his fingers over Aria's scalp. Her eyes were closed and he could feel her breath slow and deepen. Soon she was sleeping in his arms. When a tent for the women had been set, Oakheart placed Aria inside. The beaten outlander maid stirred out of sleep and eyed him dazedly. "Oakheart?"

Oakheart knelt by her. "Now, young woman, you will take some of Lillia's broth. For if you are to free Sophy, you will need your strength."

Her eyes sparkled in her pale face. He brought the bowl to her mouth and helped her sip. She swallowed, and he could see that each mouthful hurt her throat. The bruising on her neck was still coming out. She took small sips and gazed at him with her sorrowful green eyes. He handed her some bread, broken into little pieces, which she chewed slowly, eating methodically, her eyes never leaving his. After the meal, she drifted off to sleep, her pain beaming out of her like a beacon. Oakheart shuddered.

Lillia spoke softly to him as he made his way out of the tent. "Thank you, Oakheart. You have coaxed her to eat. She will not speak of what happened but the evidence of abuse is everywhere..."

"I know. It radiates like the rot of murder in the fabric of the keep. Yet it does not consume her. I think she will conquer it in time. Physically, at least. Now," he said, taking Lillia's hand, "what am I to do with you? Where is your mate?"

Lillia squeezed his hand and smiled. Her belly was full with child. Not enough as yet to make her body unwieldy. "Mellow follows with Raven and Illart. They would not like you to slow your pace, yet they can defend our backs. I will meet my mate in the Gilton Forest at the time of the birth, if we do not meet before then. His heart is with me. He was shocked by what had befallen Aria...and he could not prevent me pursuing my duty. Indeed, he was so appalled that he honoured me for it."

Oakheart nodded, relieved. He did not wish to be the cause of a rift between Lillia and her mate. Now, with his own parting from Sophy, some of Mellow's angst made sense to him.

"I will let you sleep, and thank you." He paused before stepping away. Lillia's expression invited further confidence. "In my heart, I hoped Aria could join us. We travelled at a slow pace just in case." He brushed a loose chunk of hair out of his face. "It sounds strange, I suppose, yet I felt that each step away from the keep without her I drew no closer to Sophy."

"I think I understand." She slapped him on the shoulder and she turned to squeeze through the tent flap. "Good rest. I will see you in the morning."

He smiled a small smile. "You too. See you in the morning."

Oakheart drew in a lungful of air and let it out slowly. The night sounds surrounded him. With a quick glance at the rising moon, he went to find his blankets. Fern was already rolled up, but awake. "The watch is set," he said as Oakheart unravelled his blankets and slid in between them. "And I sleep with an eye open."

Something in Fern's tone warmed him. His mood improved all of a sudden. Aria was here with them. There was more hope now that their mission would succeed. "That is good, as long as you do not sleep with your mouth open."

Fern raised himself up on his elbows, flinging off his blanket. Oakheart thought he would come back with a retort, or a laugh, but Fern surprised him. "I shamed myself today, Oakheart. Forgive me. I do not know what came over me. Something about her moves me...but even if that were not so...the violence done to her ..."

"I know, my friend, I know. I can see your heart is true. Do not surrender to vengeful thoughts otherwise Rufus has already won."

Fern settled back down into his blankets. "Thank you for understanding me. You have a forgiving heart lately. I never suspected that of you."

Oakheart let out a chuckle. "Nor I of me. Good night and good rest."

Curling himself into his blanket, Oakheart recalled thoughts of Sophy's body pressed close to his and the tinkle of her laugh in his ears. Then the slow creep of sleep took him down to oblivion.

۞

"RISE. RISE!" CAME THE WARNING.

Oakheart threw off his blankets and jumped to his feet, sword at the ready. With knees slightly bent, he balanced on the balls of his feet, ready to move. It was early morning. Sunlight peeked through the ripe grey clouds. Shaking off sleep and senses alert, Oakheart took in the situation. Fern was up and racing to the perimeter, his axe at the ready.

"Attack ho!" yelled the outer sentry. "Attack—" His voice was cut off abruptly.

Riders approached, their hooves pounding like thunder. Diverted by that sound, he did not realise it was a feint until their adversary was amongst them. Slipping off their mounts to put their knives and swords to the necks of the men who were too slow to leave their blankets, the invaders in flowing robes took control of the camp. Brook stepped forwards. No Puri attempted to restrain him. An unconscious sentry was dropped unceremoniously in front of Oakheart. The colourful robes of the Puri floated on the breeze as a small, middle-aged man slipped off his mount and yelled orders to his men. He placed his sword point against the downed sentry's stomach.

Oakheart eyed the invaders, anger seething. He fought for calm, remembering his training in diplomacy. Oakheart stepped forwards. "Nasheen," he greeted the Puri leader with the traditional bow. "Why are you attacking us?"

Fern was dragged along the ground, cursing as he fought his captor. Nasheen's black eyes widened when they saw Oakheart and the carefully executed bow. He did not return the bow and kept the sword poised above the sentry's torso. "You? What do you do here?"

Oakheart pointed south. "I am on a mission from the high king. We travel to the Lower Warrens with great urgency. We mean to pass in peace."

Nasheen grunted. "In peace? When my warriors are slaughtered, our homes attacked. I think not."

Fern burst out. "Liar. It is you who slaughtered one of our own."

Nasheen signalled and Fern was dealt a stunning blow.

"You say your warriors were attacked?" Oakheart could not hide the surprise in his voice. "Not by us."

"Do not bother to try to hoax me with one of your speeches, excellency. I am immune." Nasheen's teeth flashed in a savage grin.

"One moment." Hands held high in a gesture to assure Nasheen that he meant no trickery, he turned to Fern, who was climbing to his feet. "Fern, show him the dagger..."

Fern's guard sought permission from Nasheen. The Puri leader lifted his chin and Fern was free to move. The Puri warriors were wary and watched everyone closely.

Nasheen's dark eyes followed Fern's movement as he went to his pack and dug out the dagger retrieved from the dead farmer. He did not let up the pressure of the sword digging painfully into the sentry's midsection. The sentry was conscious now, his eyes wide as he took in his predicament.

Fern walked up warily, his eyes assessing the number of Puri with each step. He passed the dagger, hilt first, to Oakheart.

Oakheart took it and raised it where Nasheen and the other Puri could see it. "I found this...in the body of a farmer. Since when do the Puri take the life of innocent men?"

Nasheen's eyes narrowed when he saw the blade; his expression bespoke recognition. "It was stolen three weeks past. We murdered no one."

Oakheart pressed his advantage. "You deny the Puri are attacking the people of the valley?"

Nasheen withdrew the sword and strode towards them. "No, I do not deny it. Yet we act in retaliation. We have not shed blood and have only taken goods and captives to compensate for Dellbright's attacks against us." His eyes assessed Oakheart and roamed over their camp, settling on the tent. Lillia and Aria had not moved or made a sound since the attack had started.

"Who is in the tent?" Nasheen looked at the tent and frowned. "Tell me!" The Puri leader took a step in their direction.

Oakheart moved to block his path. He would die before he let the Puri touch either Lillia or Aria. Before they could resolve the standoff, the forest maiden stepped out of the tent, hands at her sides and her weapons not in evidence. Close behind was Aria, walking stiffly. The tent flap fluttered noisily in the breeze now that it was unsecured.

One of the Puri men ducked inside to check it was empty. Coming out again, he signalled an all clear to Nasheen.

"So you travel with women as well as an adept." He walked towards Aria, his eyes roving over her from head to foot. His mouth held tight. "What has happened to this woman? I feel pain so strong I can taste it. Has anyone here harmed you, my lady?" he said, surprising everyone with his gentle expression.

Aria smiled and bowed her head. "No, they protect me from harm, honourable Nasheen."

"Who are you?" Nasheen asked.

Aria's gaze flicked to Oakheart. He shook his head slightly, but she shrugged. "I am Aria, wife of Dellbright, Prince of Valley Keep."

Nasheen's gaze became penetrating, his demeanour calculating. "Where is your husband, my lady...how has he let this hurt be done to you?"

Oakheart saw Aria's chin tremble. Nasheen's gaze travelled between Oakheart and Fern and Aria. Oakheart made to move towards her, but was stopped by Nasheen's warning look.

In the silence everyone waited to hear what Aria would say. "It was he, my husband. Dellbright did this. His heart is tainted by the murder of Aurore. The binding oath is undone."

Nasheen flinched as if she was a knife-wielding fighter. "No? Aurore murdered? But...she was my kin. You are my kin." He swung around to face Oakheart. "Is what she says true? All of it?"

"Yes. Aurore is dead. Murdered at Valley Keep, along with a wet nurse."

Nasheen's dark complexion greyed. "Is the binding oath undone?"

Brook strode amongst them, unrestrained by the Puri. In fact, they appeared to shy away from him as if he was tainted. "We fear it is so."

Nasheen's expression paled further as he stepped back. "Great Adept? You walk the land..."

"Yes."

Oakheart thought that Adage was speaking and somehow the Puri leader knew it. He lifted an eyebrow in wonderment. The Puri had an uneasy relationship with Glassy Mountain Retreat. They did not become adepts as far as he knew, yet it was clear some Puri had deep knowledge of the *given* lore. Now was not the time to ponder on why there was a rift.

Nasheen found his backbone and shook himself. The colour seeped back into his face. "My people heed you not. We have no respect for Glassy Mountain Retreat."

Brook's glowing blue eyes took in the Puri raiders holding Oakheart's men by sword and knife point. "Yes, I see that it is so. But what has happened in Valley Keep has affected you, too. Your ancestors were bound by the oath, as are we. You have been defying the oath."

Nasheen's face flushed with anger. "No, we have spilled no blood, taken no lives. Even though we were sorely tempted when our own blood was spilled."

Brook's eyes ranged over the gathered Puri. The otherness came over him and his eyes glowed full blue. In Adage's voice he said, "He speaks true. They have not the taint of murder. Some other entity seeks to create a war between the Puri and the people of Argenterra."

Nasheen appeared taken appalled by Adage's possession of Brook. He stepped back. "And who is this other?" Nasheen asked, eyes keen like the edge of a knife.

Oakheart sighed in relief. If the man was asking questions then that meant he was willing to listen. Oakheart spoke for them all. "The one we seek. The one who dwells in the Lower Warrens...Rufus. He is an agent of the Ancient Evil."

Nasheen did not look surprised. "I know him. He has visited amongst us. I am ashamed to say he was welcomed in my tent." His eyes narrowed. "You can prove he is an agent of the Ancient Evil?"

Oakheart shook his head. "Not irrefutably."

Brook lifted his head, arms outstretched. "The time of Vorn's vision is here. It is the work of the Ancient Evil."

Nasheen turned back to Oakheart as Adage's presence faded from Brook. "Interesting times. Hanal will be anxious to hear your news."

"Rufus holds Sophy, Gift of Crystal Tree Woods. We seek to rescue her and bring her back." He did not add that she was his oathbound wife as he did not wish to tell all to Hanal's kinsman.

Nasheen's eyes ranged over their group, assessing them, his mind calculating. "Hanal told me about her. He told me also of how you and Veld tricked him into believing she was of no importance and how you hid when by right of honour you should have wed Lyant, Hanal's sister. Even now, Hanal gathers in the Caves of Suval, our winter home, calling in all the clans. Already I am late in joining him."

Lillia stepped forwards, anger evident in every muscle of her body. "We do not keep you," she said, eyes bright. "Oakheart is oathbound to Sophy. He is no value to you as a prize; he cannot wed Lyant."

Nasheen's jaw clenched and released. "Speak not to me, woman. I do not converse with a woman who wields weapons. I do not trust this little scene. I must send word to Hanal, and I warn you that he will not sit idle...Yet I see the evidence of harm to this kinswoman of mine." He gestured to Aria. "I, and one other, will accompany you to the Lower Warrens. The rest of my men will ride to the Caves of Suval and take word of these happenings to Hanal. We do not accept the adept's presence but we will tolerate it, for now..."

He nodded to one of his men, the rest dispersed like the wind had blown them away.

The tension had not left Oakheart's men. Nasheen moved towards him and held out his hand. Oakheart looked at it and placed the dagger into the other man's palm.

Perhaps it was better to have your enemy near than on your trail, Oakheart thought. He caught Fern's eye. His friend looked grim, his brows drawn into a frown, but he nodded, silently agreeing to Oakheart's acceptance of the Puri men amongst them.

𝕤 8 𝕤

A FOE IS A FICKLE FRIEND

They had stopped to make camp. Aria helped Lillia by
gathering wood as the others set the guard, put up the tents
and prepared a meal. She sensed someone looking at her and
turned around. Nasheen's dark eyes widened when he realised he had
been noticed and then he moved closer to talk to her.

"Here, let me help you carry those," he said, taking the dead tree
branches from her.

"You are very kind, thank you," Aria replied, feeling curious and
embarrassed at the same time.

Nasheen headed back to camp in a flurry of robes. She followed
behind and observed as he squatted to stack the branches with the logs
and kindling near the fire.

"Are you well, kinswoman?" he asked.

"Yes, I am much better, thank you."

He stood there poised, appearing relaxed. He indicated a half-
buried boulder, partially sheltered by an overhanging branch, and
gestured for her to sit. Aria sat down and drew her wayward hair away
from her face.

"Forgive me if I am being rude in asking this, but something you said before puzzles me...you said that the Puri and the adepts don't get along, why is that?"

He dusted off his hands, staring at the fire for a moment before speaking. He shrugged once, setting his cloak rippling. "It's an old history, but the hurt still runs deep."

"Oh, I see." Aria chewed on her lip, wondering how to keep the conversation going. Nasheen glanced at her and then turned to walk away.

"Please, it would be an honour to hear your story. Rae told me so many."

"Rae?" he said, turning back with puzzlement crinkling his face. "Oh...daughter of Kushlan, whore of Hanal..."

At her sharp intake of breath, he added, "Forgive my directness. I am like the old women to gossip so. Yet, her audacity, her lack of shame, is famous amongst the clans. That she wooed Hanal to her bed is one thing, easily hidden. That she stayed in it is another thing entirely. It cannot be ignored."

Aria's face heated as she thought about Rae. The young Argenterran girl would be embarrassed by such talk. Aria could not help but wonder at the turn of events and pity her young friend. "But she wanted to marry him, had her heart set on it. I find it hard to believe. She was a sweet and lovely girl and deserves so much better. Dellbright hurt her, too. The Puri were all she had left. That is where her hopes and dreams lay."

Nasheen looked around him. None of the others were close enough to hear but he dropped his voice a level. "Well, she is happy enough with my kin and underneath Hanal. While they shun her, they do not evict her, as they should, for Hanal would not allow it.

"You asked me the story of why we Puri do not trust the adepts living in the retreat. Long ago, even before Vorn died, our ancestors populated the wasteland. We are descendants of Shabra and Lilt of the Blue Eyes and those who followed them. Vorn's kin have never trusted us. We have always been separated by our culture and the colour of our skin. I am descended from both Tineal and Shareal, daughters of Shabra. Many times has their blood been woven through my line."

Aria thought his words through. "Then you are not related to Goslien as is Hanal?"

"No, thank the waters that flow with the *given,* I am not Vorn's spawn." The Puri warrior looked ready to spit and spoke rather loudly, attracting attention.

Fern stopped mending a bridle and strode over. "Hold your tongue," Fern said, his grey eyes storm-tossed. "You should not speak so of Vorn. Not here. Not in Argenterra. This is his place and you are outside."

Nasheen swung round, dagger whipped out of the folds of his gown to sit in his palm. He waved it menacingly. "I was not speaking to you, pawn of Veld, but to my kinswoman. Now leave us or you will be sorry for it."

Aria stood up and put her hand on Fern's sleeve. "Please, it's all right."

He turned to her. "My lady?" Fern asked, eyes darkening.

"We're just talking, Lord Fern. It will be all right. Please, do not worry for me."

With a reluctant nod, Fern moved off, sending Nasheen angry looks as he went to talk with Oakheart. Aria could tell that although they pretended to be absorbed in cleaning horse tack, they were intent on listening in and intervening if they saw the need. She shook off her annoyance, realising that love and care for her motivated their concern.

The Puri leader looked at her again and bowed slightly. "Forgive my ire. I do not like to ride with these folk. I trust not their ways."

"Why? It's all connected, isn't it?"

"Yes, I suppose it is. It stems from the fact that the retreat continues to endorse Vorn's successor. Shabra's kin have equal rights. Some say it was Shabra and not Vorn who led the First Comers through the gate and found the *given.*"

"And this is why you fight with each other?"

"We do not always fight but we do not mix well. We do not trust as the resentment runs deep, except in the bedding of their women. The fairness of their skin is prized by us."

Aria swallowed. "I see. Wasn't Lilt of the Blue Eyes a bit devious or something? I thought I heard that she schemed to—"

Nasheen pulled himself up to full height. "Ware of which tales you repeat and to whom you repeat them. Lilt was misunderstood; no more will I say of her. Our attempts to marry into Vorn's line have ended in failure. Only Heer' Panal was successful, though he achieved it by stealth. His ways were not the ways of Silverdale."

Aria sighed. "Yes, Goslien of the Valley. A romantic tale." Nasheen's expression became thoughtful so she added hastily, "Thank you for sharing your history with me, Nasheen. I will treasure it."

He didn't smile as he turned away, but the tension seemed to ease out of his shoulders. Aria watched him walk away to tend his own horse and rearrange his possessions. Occasionally, he talked to his kinsman in a low voice. Aria hoped her comment about Goslien's tale being romantic didn't imply that she would like to be kidnapped herself.

❧

NEXT DAY THE PARTY PASSED THROUGH A SPARSE FOREST WITH TREES spiny and tortured.

"Come, we will rest here," Oakheart called. "The horses need to rest and we need to eat."

Nasheen pulled up his horse and stared at them. "Are all men from Silverdale as weak as you lot?" he said as he unwrapped his headdress and let his long plaits fall down to his waist. He grunted as he dismounted.

Oakheart laughed out loud. "'Twas for your sake we stopped, venerable Nasheen. I thought our pace may be taxing you."

Nasheen drew up to his full height, perhaps onto his toes, and pushed out his chest. "We Puri can ride till we drop."

"Yes, and after your horse is dead you will ride no farther. We have a ways to go and we must be hardy when we arrive. We will stop now, if it pleases you." Oakheart was doing his best to keep his tone light.

"Very well," Nasheen said. "I agree that we should rest our mounts." He moved stiffly as he went to tend his horse.

Later as they ate their meal, Lillia look perturbed. Nasheen and Jeloh, the other Puri, kept staring at the trees in expectation.

"What is it?" Aria asked. The air did feel strange to her but her lingering pain masked everything.

Fern stopped chatting. Oakheart stood and turned full circle, surveying the trees.

The forest maiden moved closer to Aria. "I know not," Lillia said. "Something wrong is happening."

"Wrong?"

Nasheen leapt to his feet, his large form proving rather agile as he frantically surveyed their camp. "Down!" he shouted, and dived on top of Aria. Instinctively, she threw herself down before he covered her with his body. Aria smelt spice and sweat, then fire.

A *whoosh* bounded through the camp accompanied by the sound of stampeding horses. Lillia yelled, and there were shouts of men and the screaming of their various mounts

Someone, Oakheart, pulled Nasheen from her. His white-blond hair was singed and his clothes and skin were burnt in places. Around them, the trees were aflame, some half blown apart at the roots.

Lillia rolled on the ground in a foetal position, wailing as if it was her own skin that was on fire. Nasheen stood by Aria although he wobbled on his feet as if he would faint. Flame and smoke drifted up from his back. Fern doused his cloak with a pail of water that had been set for one of the horses. Nasheen acknowledged the favour and proceeded to pluck bits of cloth off his back and throw them on the ground. His once colourful cloak was in tatters.

"What is this treachery?" he said, sneering and wincing at the same time. He appeared to be in shock, not quite grasping what had happened. Aria was relatively unscathed. Her knees and elbows were scraped from hitting the ground and that was the extent of her injuries.

Fern dumped more water on Nasheen from a pail. "You are burnt across your back, Nasheen. Water will cool the skin."

"Leave me, you fool. I will not be indebted to Veld through you. What happened? What foul trickery is at work? Is this the scheming of the retreat?"

Oakheart checked Aria for injuries. "Not the retreat."

Lillia was still crying and writhing on the ground. No one dared approach her as her distress was too great. She had already kicked one of Oakheart's men who had tried to touch her. Oakheart stepped away from Aria towards Lillia.

"Thank you for your warning, Nasheen. You felt it coming. But you can see that it must be Rufus that has killed these trees," Oakheart said from where he tried to tend the forest maiden. "Lillia is deeply affected as she is one of the forest folk and was born amongst the trees."

Lillia quietened somewhat and Oakheart knelt beside her, talking quietly as if to a child. Other than the anguish she seemed to be suffering, she seemed unharmed. She responded to Oakheart and stopped rolling about in the dirt and sat up. When she saw the trees still aflame, she began to whimper and chew on her hand.

"Rufus, you say?" Nasheen said. "I detected something coming by a strange keening in my bones and in my teeth. A sense of wrong."

"Where is the adept?" Nasheen asked.

Fern spun round to search their camp. "There," he said, bolting to the horizontal figure of the adept. Brook, too, was of the forest folk. Fern roused him with a wet cloth. After a few moments Brook cried out, then sat up, looking morosely around at the trees, as if it was the end of the world.

"I am well, Fern," Brook said as he pushed away the wet cloth. The adept climbed shakily to his feet. "I thank you." He nodded to Oakheart, and then checked himself for injury. The edges of his blue robe were singed and there were patches on the cloth where burning leaves had dropped, leaving soot stains in their wake. "It is only that I was overwhelmed by the distress of the trees," Brook commented breathlessly.

A guard came back to the circle of smoke and flames. Aria had not seen him leave.

"Two of the horses are dead. The others have fled. It will take time to round them up."

"Do it," Fern said. "We may as well camp here for the night. There are no more trees to kill. We will need to redistribute supplies now we have fewer horses."

"Fern," Oakheart called. "Assist the women."

After a glance at Lillia, Fern shrugged and came to kneel down next to Aria. He moved a lock of her hair from her face. "My lady?" he asked in a soft, tender voice. "Are you well? Can I help you? Set up your tent?"

Aria was still stunned. She coughed from the smoke that lingered in the clearing. The ring of burning and burnt trees was a stark reminder that lives hung in the balance and that hers was one of them. "Fern," she said quietly, not wishing to injure him, but not quite ready for his gallantry. "Don't..." She edged away from him, trying to maintain her personal space.

"What have I done?"

"Nothing...thank you." He assisted her to stand by placing a hand on her elbow. She didn't dare look at Nasheen, but her impulse was to pull away.

Her caution was justified. "Take your hand from her," the Puri leader growled.

Aria's blood grew cold. It was a strange reaction. Nasheen's voice was pitched in anger and that triggered something. Fear. Stress. Flashback?

Fern clasped her hand tighter. "No."

Aria tried to free herself but Fern held her firm. Panic was climbing up her throat. She thought she might scream.

"She is my kinswoman. It is not meet that you sniff after her, always hanging around."

Aria's heart raced. The aggression and anger reminded her of Dellbright. She began to sweat and her head began to spin. Please, stop, she thought at them, too timid to voice her protest.

Fern did not hide his disgust of the Puri leader. "It is my business what I do. She was under Oakheart's protection before you decided to follow along. Your claim to kinship is weak. You are no more related to her through blood than I am."

"Please stop," she managed to say in a soft voice. Either they didn't hear or they ignored her plea.

Nasheen did not back away. Instead he drew closer, facing off against Fern. "Nevertheless, I like you not."

Fern smiled and tugged Aria away, bringing her behind them. "That is fine by me, Puri scum. I like you not."

Nasheen's dagger glinted in the light. She had to fight this fear. She had to act. Make it stop. Only she could do that.

Aria whirled, snatching her arm out from Fern's grip. "Stop!" she cried. "Stop it right now." She eyed them both in turn. Her heart rate was high, her breath tight in her chest. Fear made her gut churn and she fought the urge to vomit. "This is ridiculous. I am oathbound to Dellbright. To him I am bound until I die. Unless you wish to end my life now with that dagger there is no point to this argument. My honour is safe regardless of who assists me."

"She speaks true," Oakheart said as he walked up and put his hands on her shoulders. "Come, Aria, Lillia needs you. I know not how to help her."

He nodded to Nasheen and Fern. "You two had best join the search for horses. You waste your energy fighting. Best you learn to trust each other. You may need it before our task is done."

⚜

ARIA TRIED TO UNBEND LILLIA'S CLAWED HANDS. "LILLIA? TAKE this tea. Come on. Let me help you, though I don't know how. Let me tend you as you have me. Please."

Lillia's frightened eyes settled on her. There was some recognition there. Aria held the cup of tea to her lips and Lillia sipped. She drank a quarter of the cup before she drifted off to sleep. Aria warmed some water and bathed the soot from the forest woman's face and hands. Then she herself sought sleep in her blankets.

Aria woke to the sound of weeping. "Lillia?" She edged closer and stroked the woman's back.

"The trees...you should have heard their agony. I could not voice it and could do naught to stop it. Nothing afears a tree like fire, but a fire from within placed there unnaturally by Rufus's hand was as if the trees' lives had been undone." She turned misery-laden eyes on Aria.

"How can such a thing happen? I worry so for the Gilton Forest and my people. If he has this power he only has to stretch out his hand and attack us where we are most vulnerable. If only one tree suffers that fate, it would cripple my people. I do not know how I have the strength to carry on. My only comfort is that Mellow did not see it or experience it."

"I'm sorry. I feel that it is my fault somehow."

"No, not your fault. Though you do sound like Sophy. She would blame herself if she could. It must be the breaking of the oath. As the *given* fades from the land, Rufus can send his power farther and stronger. He can do the unthings."

"Unthings?" The word sent chills up Aria's spine.

"Yes, when the First Comers fled they left behind the unthings. Deeds that undid creation. I am not certain because the stories are old, but in my heart this is what an unthing is—a tree exploded from the inside."

The sounds of movement and packing up reached them. "You must eat something, Lillia. We are on the move again."

"Yes, perhaps we will reach the Lower Warrens tomorrow or the next. I must build up my hope, forget this tragedy so I can fight for Sophy. What horrors must await us there! How I wish it was not so..."

❧ 9 ❧

A FLAW UNRAVELS

Three days later the Lower Warrens appeared as shadows on the horizon early in the morning. Fear rose in Aria's throat. She had sent Sophy to this place, when she should have come herself. She tried to swallow and then dry-retched into the dirt. Oakheart, riding ahead of her, did not notice.

"My lady?" asked Lillia from beside her.

"I'm fine. Really. Just a bit nauseated this morning."

"I have a tonic that might settle your stomach." When Aria shared a look with the forest maiden, she swore the woman knew what was wrong with her. She could see her fear. Aria was ashamed to have it known. She was certain Sophy did not fear so much that she was sick to her toes. Right then she envied her friend's bravery.

Aria nodded and took the proffered vial. Lillia watched her take it and commented, "I would take it too, but as I am carrying I cannot."

Aria managed a smile after coughing. The spirit seared the soft tissues of her throat, but she was grateful for the implied solidarity. Her gaze rested on the other woman. Lillia's eyes were hard glints when she looked away from the Lower Warrens. The older woman had been there before; she knew what waited for them. Aria was not comforted by what she saw in the other woman's eyes.

The high king's guards murmured nervously amongst themselves as the cave-ridden ridge grew increasingly visible. They were not veterans of the previous skirmish to save Gilly.

Oakheart slowed his mount and brought it alongside Aria's. "I am sorry to take you so close to Rufus's domain, my lady, but I fear you might be needed for Sophy's sake."

Worried in case he saw her fear, she avoided looking at him. "Sophy is in that place and the only way to get her out is to go in there."

He reached out and squeezed her hand gently. "Thank you." His voice was heavy with emotion. With that touch, she lifted her head and met his gaze, finally finding the courage to rise above the terror that had been plaguing her all morning. "I haven't met Rufus in the flesh, but his presence has been with me for a long time now. I feel I know him well, too well, and I don't want Sophy with him one more minute than necessary."

Oakheart nodded and then his gaze ranged over the ridge. "On that topic, we are in agreement. But what about strategy? I know not yet how to release Sophy."

The adept rode up next to them. Aria had noticed that Brook had been quiet in the presence of the Puri. "Adage feels that the oath you have with Sophy impedes Rufus's progress. He will kill you as soon as you are near. We need a way to distract him until we can release Sophy. Failing that, you must use what you can of the *given* and this axe to smash the crystal..." Brook held up an axe, with one edge a fine pick.

Oakheart eyed the implement, unable to keep the distaste from his face. "But what will happen to Sophy if I do that?"

Brook looked sad. "I know not."

Aria let out a gasp, appalled at the adept's inelegant strategy. "I will distract Rufus," she said.

Oakheart let out an inarticulate sound of protest and turned in his saddle to face her. "But he has no interest in you now he has Sophy."

"Really? Then why does he plague my dreams? Why does he infiltrate Dellbright and fill him with hate? I'm not as ignorant as you think. Until he stole Gilly and killed Aurore, he was afraid to act."

"But he may kill you outright," Oakheart said. "You endanger yourself needlessly."

"If we are saving Sophy then it isn't needless, is it? He may have no interest in me, now that my purpose had ended." Aria was angry now. Her dreams had been shattered and she was close to admitting that he could take the rest of her life too, because what was left wasn't worth living.

But she couldn't acknowledge her own despair. Sophy needed her and, despite everything, she had hope. Her mother had repeatedly said there was always a way, you just had to keep looking and never give up hope. Why had she thought of her mother suddenly? Because her mother had always been strong. Aria needed that strength now. She lifted her chin. "I can give as good as I get. He has a lot to answer for." Aria was proud of how she sounded, sure and steady.

The adept kept his gaze on her, a thoughtful expression on his face. "It may work. It is a start at least."

Oakheart glared at the adept, anger wafting off him in waves. Voice echoing with resentment, he said, "Have you nothing better to offer?" He lifted the axe and waved it. "Is this the best the retreat can do?"

Brook faced Oakheart calmly. "Your anger is misplaced. Do you think this is written down? That we were left instructions in how to deal with is? We have a record of Vorn's dream. We have some documented interpretation of that dream and some vague histories compiled from the recollections of the First Comers. I have faith we will find a way. You must have faith, too, and take an opportunity when you see one. All depends on this."

Fern spoke up. "The axe will be useful against the warren beasts or other creatures he may have at the ready."

"That is true." Oakheart took a few deep breaths and calm settled over him. He glanced to the ridge. "We will stop here and plan our attack. Fern, place sentries."

They all dismounted and secured and fed the horses. Aria did not think their mounts would be needed until after...She didn't want to think about after. She didn't seem to be able to conjure up a thought about what lay beyond. There was only this steady, looming wall of caves and Sophy's destiny, all their destinies, tied to this act.

Fern called them all over to discuss tactics. Oakheart started first.

"Fern, you will stay here with the Puri. Aria and I go in alone, perhaps..."

Fern's face grew dark and before he could say anything, Lillia interrupted him. "No. I will go, too, as will Brook."

Oakheart sighed. "I hoped the adept would come, although he has no idea what to expect or how to counter it." He turned to Fern and, seeing his expression, said, "What?"

"I would come with you. I may be able to help. Guard your back."

'Thank you, my friend, but 'tis not my back I am worried about. Rufus will try to kill me for certain, but he will do it head-on. He has enough power for that. With you outside you can prevent a force being sent in behind us."

"But what of Lady Aria if you fall? I could be there to protect her."

Nasheen squatted near them, his robe gently rippling in the light breeze. He began to chuckle. Aria found it very annoying. Surprisingly, Oakheart was gentle when he addressed the Puri raider.

"Very well. Nasheen, what are your thoughts?"

The Puri stood up from his squat, walked slowly around them and shook his head. The Argenterrans topped him by a head but it made no difference to his confident stride. "This is your tactic? This is the best you can do?"

Oakheart stood up and pushed out his chest. Fern stood also, scowling. "It worked before."

Nasheen studied him. "Really? Is that not why we are here, because your first attempt ended in this disaster? If this is the cream of Argenterran strategy, I wonder why it is the Puri who are confined to the upper wastelands and not you."

Fern pushed past Oakheart. "I have had enough—"

"Hold, Fern. I would hear what he has to say," Oakheart said with his hand against Fern's chest. With a nod to Nasheen, he asked, "What do you suggest?"

Nasheen's dark gaze swept over them all. "You have been here before. Can you recall the layout of the warrens? Is there more than one entry?"

Oakheart nodded, knelt and began to trace what he remembered of the warrens' layout. Lillia added to the drawing, based on her recollection.

"So you do not know the location of the other openings? You went in the same way you came out?"

Oakheart and Lillia agreed that was the case. Aria watched the Puri man and saw that he was serious, rather than mocking, in his attempt to get them thinking. "We should send a scout to find the other openings."

"Risky," Oakheart commented. "I would not waste a life."

"Jeloh." Nasheen called to his man and gave him instructions. Jeloh ran off. "We wait for him to return. If there is another way in there, he will find it."

Fern swallowed, losing his hard edge of anger at the Puri man. "What do you propose? A diversion?"

Nasheen nodded. "Now you are thinking like soldiers instead of sacrifices. It may not solve all our problems, but from what you say it could lessen the numbers of beasts inside the caves and provide a distraction, divide Rufus's power."

"He will not leave Sophy unprotected," Oakheart said with certainty.

"I did not say he would, but a dual-pronged attack will weaken his defence, keep him guessing. He will wait for you to come to him, I suspect. He wants you dead, yes?"

Oakheart nodded, his mouth turned down into a frown.

"Then we must not let him succeed." Nasheen grinned.

Brook walked up, Adage's blue shining from his eyes. "The Puri has a sound strategy. I endorse it."

Fern chuckled, then smiled for the first time at the Puri leader. "I would say it is the only strategy and a darn good one too."

Nasheen grunted. Fern turned away and called the high king's guards to him. He selected six men and began to discuss who was going to be positioned where.

Oakheart stood rubbing his chin. "Nasheen."

"Yes, Oakheart?" answered the Puri leader, lifting his chin with pride. "What is your wish?"

"Nasheen of Puri," Oakheart said formally and then bowed in the

Puri manner. "You have given me hope that we may win through. For this I thank you. I said before we would need to cultivate trust between us and so I have a favour to ask of you. In doing so I put my life and the lives of these others into your care."

"I understand the need for trust. What is your desire?" Nasheen drew himself up to his full height, which was somewhere near Oakheart's shoulder, and carefully arranged the front of his robe so that it fell elegantly and showed the darker colour of his inner tunic.

"If you will guard our backs and prevent other beasts from coming against us, I will be grateful. However, I must ask another boon. If none of us return, enter into the warrens and shatter the large, blue crystal which was once Sophy. Rid us of Rufus if you can. If you do not do this deed then we are all lost for Rufus will have free access to Sophy's power. Already the *given* weakens in this land and if we fail, then we fail Argenterra and all those who depend upon the *given*."

Nasheen bowed his head. "I swear to do this on my life and that of my kin. May the water that flows with *given* be with you."

Oakheart nodded and performed the Puri bow. Fern walked up and said under his breath, though all nearby heard him clearly, "Do not betray us."

⚜

Jeloh returned before nightfall with news that there was an alternative entry point. Fern instructed the six men to camp near that entrance. At moonrise, they would make their move. Lefro was to head the diversionary force. Two men were to remain with Nasheen to guard their backs and to keep the path of retreat clear.

As night fell, they shared a cold meal and Aria rolled herself into her blankets and tried to rest. She must have fallen into a deep sleep as soon as she closed her eyes because it seemed too short a time when Lillia came for her. Aria had been dreaming, though, dreaming of a possible future with Gilly running to her with his smiling face and head full of ginger curls. Every part of his face was embedded into her mind. The shape of his forehead, the curve of his ears, the fullness of his lips were all drawn with clarity in her memory. Also, she dreamed of the feel of him, the particular pattern of the *given* that flowed through his body. She would know him anywhere.

⌘

THE LOWER WARRENS REMINDED ARIA OF THE TUNNELS UNDER Castle Crioch. The air was fetid, close and damp as she edged in behind Oakheart. Brook and Fern followed closely with Lillia bringing up the rear. It was quiet. The sound of pebbles dislodged by their feet tickled her ears. It grew darker as they edged further in. Aria couldn't stop her hands from shaking so she clutched the fabric of her breeches.

Oakheart ignited a firestick with a quick word and turned down a passageway. The sound of skittering feet surprised them and they held still. The pitch black beyond their meagre light made seeing anything impossible.

In the dimness, she saw Oakheart's shoulders clench and then he shook himself. The adept was so still and quiet she had to look back to see if he was still with them. Her gaze met Fern's. His face, pinched with concern, eased into a smile of reassurance. The sound of creatures lurking in the dark did not repeat so she turned back and stepped after Oakheart. They followed the main passageway. Ahead she could see a dim glow, growing slowly wider as they approached the large cavern.

It was empty. Grey walls roughly gouged from the earth rose up around them. A few torches shed some smoky and poor light. It was squalid and rank. Aria covered her nose, trying not to gag.

Oakheart seemed tense as his eyes ranged, looking for Rufus. He took a few more tentative steps. Aria stuck close behind.

A portion of rock reflected a blue light. Edging further around, Aria hissed out a breath when she beheld the dark blue jewel locked tight in a round, golden ring sitting on a dais. The gem pulsed, giving off a blue-tinged light, almost the same pattern as a heartbeat. Aria went to lunge ahead but Oakheart's hand on her shoulder stopped her. She glanced up at him, a question framing the arch in her eyebrows. "It's Sophy."

He stood mesmerised, a thousand painful thoughts etched across his features. "Something is not right. The diversion would not have emptied this place." He held her by the shoulder and stepped in front of her. "Sophy," he breathed. Without warning, he bounded towards the jewel in large strides. Aria, startled into action, ran close on his heels, panting when she reached him.

Oakheart stood with a hand raised, ready to caress the jewel. Aria eased next to him to take a closer look. At the top, through the centre, was a dark cord, a flaw in the crystal. Fascinated, Aria drew closer. It looked like it was woven, two threads intertwined. Strands of red angled through the flaw. It reminded her of blood and Rufus. This was where he was trying to reach Sophy and control her. How could Sophy exist inside that gem? How could she breathe?

"Is that the flaw Brook or Adage spoke about?" she whispered to Oakheart.

Silence. Aria turned to look at Oakheart, but he was looking all around him, tension writ on every muscle. Their eyes met and he tugged Aria back, bringing her smack up against him.

A groan echoed around them. Then a choking laugh that sounded half mad, but familiar. "Rufus." Oakheart exhaled the word.

Aria tensed. All the fear that had accumulated in her rose up, smothering her, filling her ears with blood, stopping her will. The foul being who had taunted her dreams leapt out from behind the jewel, ragged bat wings rippling and a shaft of power emerging from his clawed hands. Rufus tossed it between his hands negligently. He saw their expressions, and the creature's lips drew up in a grotesque parody of a smile.

Aria couldn't help drawing back into herself, withdrawing from the horror. Rufus was even more hideous in the flesh than in her dreams. Flesh hung from him as if he hadn't eaten for weeks. His red eyes seemed so much larger in his mouse-like face, and his stench was like rancid bacon. His knees bent backwards as he pranced around on his dais, sneering at them as his thin and torn wings quivered in apparent delight.

Oakheart dragged her back another step and thrust her roughly behind him. Fern's hands guided her away and out of reach. Aria took her gaze from Rufus and focussed on Fern. He smiled at her, a grim lift of the lips that spoke of regret, then he leapt to guard Oakheart's back.

Aria had to get a hold of herself. She was next to useless cowering in this way. Sophy needed her. Oakheart needed her. For herself Aria needed to wash away the shame, wash away Dellbright's words and deeds. She needed to find the core of herself and face her greatest fear.

Oakheart's sword was out. He circled, crouching and readying himself to thrust. Fern had his axe out, twirling it in his hand as he watched with his stormy eyes. Brook stood calmly impervious to Rufus's malice, and Lillia's eyes ranged all around searching for treachery, her mouth like a cut. The outrage suffered by the trees had remained with the forest maiden and an expression of dread was etched upon her face.

"So you are here at last, Oakheart." Rufus's voice sounded like snake scales grinding over rock. He lifted himself higher, throwing out his chest. "Your diversion was welcome and expected. But you knew I would not leave my most precious jewel unguarded. She is fair rippling with power, filling up with the *given*, sucking it out of the land."

The power between his hands continued to sizzle. Aria thought she recognised the smell of ozone. Rufus took another step. "Come smite me. I would see what power you hide. I would know how you ensorcelled Sophy and bound her to you. Despite all that I had done to hide her from you. Soon Argenterra will be the *Ungiven* Land and there will be nothing to stop Unesta coming. She will have all of you Vorn spawn; she will feed on you, feed on your hate until you are used up."

Brook stepped into position, his eyes those of Adage. Rufus's red eyes slanted to the adept, his mouth curled up into a sneer. Aria shook, feeling power start to crackle in the air.

"Leave this place, Rufus, 'ere you die by my hand." The adept raised a fist but Rufus's power, so casually tossed between his hands, shot out and blasted Brook. The adept's body twisted and buckled as it was thrown against the back of the cave. Brook fell in a crumpled heap, landing with his head at an angle. Lillia's cry was urgent as she scuttled across the ground to tend him. The forest maiden crouched before the adept, dagger at the ready, eyeing the darkened corner for the beasts, which they could hear now, growing ever louder.

Aria stood transfixed. Rufus had just casually slain an adept. *Adage*. The retreat's most powerful adept. What chance did Oakheart or she have against such power? Oakheart's neck muscles rippled. Rufus's actions were dividing his loyalties. Oakheart struggled to speak, his gaze returning again and again to Sophy's gem, continually shifting between her and Rufus's menacing approach.

Aria sensed something, a connection to the gem. She stared at it, puzzling out the significance of what she was feeling. She not only saw the pulsing light, she tasted the power within it, growing steadily stronger. The power was resonating in her.

Rufus snarled at Oakheart, his wings rippling softly, exultingly. "What? No power at the ready to thwart me? And here I was taking my time to see what you would do. Yet you come powerless before me. Hah!"

Rufus's laugh echoed hollowly around them. He drew on more of his dark power. To Aria it was like an ache in her teeth. She tensed, anticipating Rufus's attack. He struck Oakheart full in the chest. Oakheart's green eyes widened in surprise, then his mouth grew firm. With a strange gesture of his hand, Rufus increased the force he sent against Oakheart.

Aria willed Oakheart to fight but he didn't seem able to. Then she reached out with her senses and realised he was fighting. The *given* residing in him was resisting Rufus. But would it be enough? There was nothing left of the power they had drawn from the pool deep within Valley Keep. A moan pierced through Oakheart's throat as he fell slowly backwards to the ground.

Aria yelled, "No. Oakheart, fight him."

"Sophy!" The anguish in his voice and face was too much for Aria to bear. He *couldn't* be losing or giving up—he was Oakheart, dependable, strong. Then his eyelids fluttered and while she watched, he shut them finally. Aria looked to the gem and saw the dark chord of the flaw unravelling, fading as Oakheart faded.

"No! It can't be." Fist clenched, she tried to control her fear.

Rufus's laughter was everywhere, in her ears, in her bones and under her skin. It sickened her, made her cringe. Tears streaked her face. Fern's cry distracted her. He swung his axe but Rufus tossed him negligently aside with a flick of a wrist, sending him to crash against the wall as he had Brook.

Rufus strutted up to the gem and used his blackened tongue to lick the spot where Oakheart's oath was fading. Aria screwed up her face, disgusted by the ugly creature. Was he really trying to suck power from Sophy?

"Come, little one," he whispered in a sad mockery of intimacy. "Let me in. Let me plunder you utterly. Oakheart's death will deliver you to me. There will be no oath, no prior promise, between us. Just me and your power, the power of Argenterra."

A moan from Oakheart reverberated around the cavern. His chest heaved as if he was breathing through broken ribs. Rufus attacked him again, blue flame issuing from his hands. Small licks of fire like matchsticks clung to his fingers.

"No," Aria yelled. "I won't let you do this to her." She crouched next to Oakheart, screamed at him. "Fight! Fight it! You can! You have so much more power and skill than me."

Oakheart opened a bloodshot eye, his life spark fading. "I cannot. I do not know how..." His eyes closed and Aria saw the life leak out of him.

"No!" she screamed at him, grasping his clothes. But he didn't move. With resolution, Aria stood, clenched her fists and edged out her chin as she faced Rufus.

Rufus turned away from Oakheart, dismissing him from his mind. Ignoring Aria, he rubbed his hand over the jewel, his claws edging into the flaw as if to work his way inside.

"I said you cannot do this," she said forcefully, her voice carrying in the large space. "Stand away from her or you will suffer."

"Hah! You can do nothing. You are pathetic," Rufus replied, not even bothering to glance at her. "You are as impotent as Oakheart, dying in the dirt. When she surrenders her soul to me, you will die next to him, nameless in the filth of this land."

"I don't think so." Aria couldn't believe how sure and deadly she sounded. The connection she had to Sophy sprang up, true and firm. She could feel her friend's presence.

Rufus turned slowly, red eyes glowing maliciously, as if he detected something in her voice, an undercurrent of power. "You sound so confident, you, the insignificant one, so useless and weak. That makes me curious. Like watching an insect struggle as I pull its wings one by one and then the legs..."

When he moved aside from the gem, she saw that a flaw still existed within it. Finer and paler now that Oakheart's bond was fading. She reached out to it. Yes, it was there, the sinuous link to Sophy and the power of the crystal.

Rufus must have sensed it because he shot back around to stare at the gem, wing rigid in outrage. "No. It cannot be. I did not see it before. It was hidden behind his."

"Yes! I am bound by an oath to Sophy. I said I would come for her and I have." She reached out for Sophy's power. Cold blue and encompassing, she let it flow through her as she had allowed the *given*. The potency nearly overwhelmed her, but she cordoned it off, so it wouldn't overflow and disintegrate her. Rufus aimed his force at her, but she reflected it back on him as casually as if swatting a fly. So much for insects.

He staggered back. "No, no," he gasped as pain gripped him. Then gathering his strength, he channelled more power and tightened the focus, narrowing it down to a beam. When it hit her, she rocked back on her heels. His attack leaked through her defence, like through holes in a sieve.

She reached out again to Sophy. "Please, Sophy, give me more," she begged under her breath.

Like a storm cloud releasing its load, power burst from her in a thunderous roar and struck Rufus. Blue fire dissolved his substance. He began to leak red-tinged smoke as his body transformed into a ghostly apparition. The cloud of blood-red wisps swirled and then fled through the roof of the cavern into the minute cracks in the rocks.

Aria panted and let the power seep from her as she sagged to her knees. Taking a few deep breaths, she turned around. Lillia was weeping over Oakheart, who lay like one dead on the ground. His blond hair flared out around his head like a halo, his handsome chin relaxed. Fern was propped up next to Brook; both were conscious but badly shaken. Relief flooded into her—she thought Brook had been killed.

Sophy still pulsed in the gem, an erratic flame flickering within. Aria staggered over to her and stared into the facets, trying to think of a way to release her. She put her hand on the flaw, dug her nails in and tried to prise it open. With a grunt, she gave up and leant against the stone.

"Sophy, come on. I have come to fulfil my oath." There was no response. Her fist came down, smacked against the stone. "Come. To. Me!" she yelled in desperation, clenching her teeth as she forced her will into the substance of the jewel.

There was a flutter in her mind, a stirring of consciousness. She could feel Sophy's bond, feel Sophy. "Now," she yelled and let whatever strength she had flow out of her hands and into the jewel. A flash of blue exploded, blinding her. The force made her stumble back and she had to cover her eyes. When she lowered her arm and blinked away the stars blurring her vision, Sophy stood there, dressed in her blue velvet gown, as beautiful and whole as she had been before they had come to this place.

Aria caught Sophy's elbow before she fell. Dazed, Sophy only fumbled, unable to speak.

"My lady," Lillia called brokenly from besides Oakheart. "He fades."

Aria swung around, her curls standing on end from residual power. She dragged Sophy after her and crouched down next to Oakheart. "My son is dead, my lady." Lillia's voice quavered. "Do not let Oakheart die too." Aria looked to where Fern sat against the wall. Brook was still, his eyes opened, face ashen. So the adept was dead, but she had seen movement. There was no time to think on Lillia's pain.

Oakheart wheezed another breath. Aria's tears blurred her vision.

"Oakheart?" Sophy mumbled, reaching out. "Oakheart." Sophy appeared dazed, barely sensible to anything but Oakheart.

Aria sighed, overwhelmed by sadness. She touched Oakheart's chest. Then she thumped down hard.

Lillia cried out. "What are you doing?"

"I'm trying to save him." She thumped again and then leant over to listen. It wasn't the best CPR. She knelt next to him and pushed down on his chest.

"Can you not use the *given*?" Lillia asked. "You are full of it."

"Oakheart?" Sophy said, looking around her blindly.

Aria studied her hands. She had helped Oakheart clean the keep from the evil stain. Even now she could feel her bond to him, feathery light and fading. Could she? Oakheart was not breathing. She thumped his chest again and this time she spiked her blow with the *given*. She struck again and again.

Live, damn you!

Oakheart hauled in a breath, and coughed.

"Spirit of the trees, you have kept him here! Oh, that you could have done so for my Brook."

Aria looked at Lillia's grief-torn face. "I didn't know it would actually work. Is he going to be all right?"

Sophy lay next to Oakheart with power oozing out of her. Aria could feel it. Tempted, Aria reached for it, like she and Oakheart had reached for the *given* in the bonding pool. It tingled her skin.

"He lives," Lillia said and then broke down. Oakheart was unconscious, but breathing.

"Yes, he does."

Sophy was limp and unseeing. Aria supposed she was traumatised.

"How are we going to get them out of here?" Aria stood shakily. Lillia's outstretched hand steadied her, but it was Fern who lifted her, gathering her under the knees. Too dazed to protest, Aria lay quietly in his arms, trying to think. Lillia took Sophy's hand, drawing her up and hugging her close.

Fern's embrace was warm. "My lady," he breathed into her ear.

"Put me down. I can walk, but we have to move the others."

Fern placed her on her feet and then she saw the blood in his hair. "I am well," he said. "A slight headache." His hands were also bleeding.

"Are you sure?"

Fern nodded, then his eyes fell on Oakheart's inert form. He fell to his knees and took her hand and kissed it. "Thank you for Oakheart's life."

Lillia managed to sit Sophy down on the edge of Rufus's dais.

Sophy sat there complacently so Lillia went to her son's body. Aria watched, her eyes burning with tears, as Lillia kissed Brook's forehead. He moaned softly, startling the forest maiden, who jumped back. The adept's vacant eyes closed and then opened—they were no longer brown, but blue.

"It's Adage..." Aria said quietly.

Aria climbed to her feet, feeling a bit steadier, and went towards Brook and Lillia, conscious of Fern following her. To her amazement, Brook climbed to his feet, using the wall to assist him. When he reached his full height he shook his head, feeling his face with his hands tentatively only to gaze at his fingers wonderingly.

The forest maiden was beside herself. "Give me back my son!" Lillia screamed at Adage. "Give him back!" Then the forest maiden struck her chest with a thunk, and struggled for control of her grief.

"I cannot," Adage said, using Brook's voice.

"What happened, Adage?" Aria asked. She cast a nervous glance in Lillia's direction, not sure whether the forest maiden would kill what was inhabiting her son's body or go mad with grief.

The adept inclined his head and then he had to use a hand to steady it. "Brook is dead, Lillia of the Quick Bow. Rufus's power killed his spirit. That is not all. The power reached far even unto the retreat. I am severed from my body. I would that it were not so, but at the time of the strike we were joined. I did not anticipate Rufus's strength, nor Brook's weakness."

"No," Lillia screamed, falling to her knees. She hugged her abdomen as sobs controlled her. "No."

"You complain of your loss. What was Brook, except for this flesh?" Adage indicated the body he was in. "I am trapped within his body. I did not take it from him."

They all stared at the adept. Then something seemed to move there under the surface. "Forgive me," Adage said to Lillia. "Your son loved you and your people deeply. He would have returned to the Gilton Forest but for this task I placed upon him." The adept paused for a second and blinked. "How did I know that? Perhaps part of Brook is here with me."

How strange for Lillia, Aria thought. Her son was dead, but not quite. Lillia glanced at her and Aria saw that all the grief was now tempered to a low glow.

Aria asked, "Are you hurt? Can you walk, Adage?"

"Yes, I am whole, a few bruises only. But this body is young and will heal. And Rufus?"

"Gone," she replied. "Dead, I think. I hope..."

"The jewel?"

"Sophy is back...but...she's full of power. Lots of it."

Adage stared at her. "Power? The *given*, you mean?"

Aria nodded. "I can tap into it. It is leaking out of her. Oakheart lives, just. He was hurt badly and isn't conscious yet."

A wave of dizziness hit her. Fern put his arm around her waist to steady her. It was strange for him to touch her, yet not unwelcome. "We must get Oakheart out of here. Sophy, too."

Aria looked behind her and saw Sophy was still sitting where she had been placed, mouth slack and eyes unseeing.

"I will help you," Adage said. "Oakheart is a big man. It will not be easy, but with the *given* I am sure we can manage it. Can I leave you two to assist Sophy?"

Lillia nodded once.

"Yes, of course. Lord Fern, I feel better now." Aria eased Fern's arm from around her waist. The look he gave her sent a chill up her spine. It was full of desire and, worse, love, she thought. That just couldn't be. "Oakheart needs your help."

SUNLIGHT THREW SHAFTS INTO THE MOUTH OF THE TUNNELS, allowing them to see their way out. Aria held Sophy's hand and led her out of the warrens, but her friend was still in a daze. Oakheart, with his feet trailing in the dirt, was propped between Fern and Brook. Occasionally, Oakheart would bring his feet under himself and take a few steps to help only to falter, nearly dragging his companions to the ground.

Lillia kept looking at Brook surreptitiously. Aria thought that the forest maiden was living her worst nightmare and then she thought of

Mellow. What would he say or do?

Once outside they made it back to the camp where they had agreed to meet. Aria cast about, looking for Nasheen and the rest. But it was deserted. The guards had erected a large tent. Lillia suggested that Oakheart and Sophy both be placed in it. "Perhaps," she said, "being together will bring some healing."

Aria smiled at the thought. "Yes, that is best."

Getting Oakheart into the tent proved to be a little awkward. Lillia assisted by dragging him over a layer of blankets. She then loosened some of Oakheart's clothes and placed his sword next to him. She had tied it to her back to bring it out of the warrens.

"Bring Sophy in, princess. I will lay them together. She will bring him back. She just needs to find him."

Aria tugged Sophy inside and knelt, bringing her friend to the ground beside her. Sophy bent her knees easily. Lillia shuffled around behind her and stripped the gown from Sophy's shoulders. Sophy's skin was unmarked—it glowed alabaster white, flawless and pure. Aria thought of her own skin, still marked with bruises and scars that would perhaps never fade. Lillia undressed Sophy completely and pushed her down to recline next to Oakheart. Covering them with a large blanket, she reached under to tug Oakheart's clothes off too.

"What are you doing?" Aria asked.

Lillia didn't bother to spare her a look. "Assisting them to find each other. Skin on skin, breath on breath, they'll manage."

Aria stood and waited until Lillia had efficiently arranged the couple. Oakheart and Sophy seemed asleep. Aria hoped that having them close would be enough to rouse them. Surely the situation couldn't get any worse.

Aria stepped out of the tent with Lillia close behind. She blinked and then cast her gaze about. The Puri men's equipment was gone. She frowned.

"I don't believe it. He promised to watch our backs." Aria walked around the camp and double checked.

"I'll scout around for them and the others," Fern said. "The guards should be here, unless some of them fell during the diversion."

"Do you suspect treachery?" Lillia asked, her gaze directed to where Fern had disappeared behind boulders.

"I'm not sure," Aria said. "It's just strange. Can you fetch our gear?"

Lillia nodded curtly and jogged to where their things were stacked.

In a few minutes, there was a hail from Fern. When Aria angled her body in the direction of his shout, she saw him come into view. His face was ashen.

"What is it?" Aria asked, standing up.

Fern shook his head. "Dead, all of them. I can't find Nasheen's body though. But the other Puri man, Jeloh, and my guards are dead. Screavers or worse, I fear." Fern's face was screwed up in distaste. "The diversion worked all right but at a high cost."

"There was nothing we could do," Aria said, her heart heavy and palpitating with unease. But she couldn't pinpoint the source of her disquiet.

Adage spoke. "The princess speaks true. There was nothing we could have done. We had to take the risk even though the price was high. We have further challenges awaiting us."

Aria expelled a breath noisily. "More? What, exactly?"

"Argenterra suffers. We all will suffer. Your friend has sucked the *given* from the land. We must find a way to put it back..."

Adage's possession of Brook's body was giving her the creeps and the effect on Lillia was troubling. The forest woman cringed and looked on the verge of tears every time her gaze fell on him or heard him speak. "Great," Aria said with a sigh. "I suppose that means taking her to Glassy Mountain Retreat."

"Yes, that is surely so." Adage's voice had a strange quality in Brook's mouth. Not quite Brook but not Adage either. "I will need to return there as well."

"This isn't going to work. We can't keep calling you Adage or Brook."

His blue eyes passed over her. Aria resisted the chill his gaze invoked. "You wish me to take another name? You do not wish me to call this body Adage or Brook? But I have been Adage for five hundred or more years."

Aria shook her head. "You are neither and both."

Brook/Adage turned away, robes stirring slightly as he stared at the sky. "Then you must call me Meld. I cannot think of a better alternative."

"Fine. Meld will do. Lillia?"

The forest maiden's face paled. She swallowed and then nodded.

🌿 10 🌿

BITTERSWEET

Sophy dreamed of Oakheart. Cold, blue light cut through the images, separating her from those emerald eyes she clung to, and brought her to wakefulness. Blinking away the haze, she fumbled with the blanket and pushed her hair out of her face. She was uncertain, light-headed and weak. But it was her own hands and hair that she felt. Touch was a welcome sensation, a relief from the cold, hard existence that remained so fresh in her mind.

A warm body lay next to her. Her skin tingled when it made contact and she smelt a familiar scent. At once on her elbows, she peered at the person next to her and blinked because she couldn't believe her eyes. It was him, the real him. The enchantment that hid him from her was gone. Sitting up, she drank the sight of him in. The fine white brows, she caressed with her index finger. The full generous lips she traced with her thumb. Her heartbeat thumped as realisations flashed through her consciousness. She was free, Rufus was gone and the enchantment broken.

Oakheart stirred, shifted a shoulder, winced with discomfort. Sophy pressed her lips to his and leant back, watching him for signs of recognition.

His eyes snapped open, sparkling green. "Sophy?" His voice was quiet, thin, as if it had been overused. He didn't move to touch her, just held her with a surprised gaze.

Sophy nodded slowly and touched his ear, rubbing the lobe between her fingers. His hand reached up and grasped hers; his eyebrows drew together. "You are back? I am not dead and dreaming?"

Sophy couldn't quite smile. "Not unless I am dead or dreaming too."

His eyes tracked from her face down to her bare shoulder. With his other hand, he touched her. "'Tis really you. The real you I see..."

She nodded, smiling. "Yes, I think so. I see you too."

"Then we did it, defeated Rufus."

Sophy bit her lip. Her thoughts were smashed, but there was a thread of reason there. "The enchantment is broken so I guess you did defeat him. It's weird seeing the real you. You are dear to me, handsome or not."

Oakheart looked up to the roof of the tent and frowned.

"What is it?" she asked.

Half of his mouth quirked in a regretful grin. "I cannot move. I have no strength. My body is a dead weight." He clenched his jaw. "I cannot move my legs."

"Oh? But will you be all right?" Sophy creased her brow and ran her hands over his limbs to assure herself that nothing was broken. He seemed whole, but his arms moved limply, and the hand touching her face felt weak.

"I live, therefore, there is hope." He studied her face. "Sophy..."

Sophy stroked his face, her face set in a smile. Inside, she was concerned. Strength was so much of Oakheart. Having him weak was a new challenge and it disconcerted her. Her perception was clearer. She glanced around the tent and took in the familiar surroundings. She was back, she said to herself.

Oakheart's fingers brushed against her face, bringing her attention back to him, and then his hand flopped back onto the blanket "I want to..." he said, as his grin turned into a grimace. "This is not how I hoped our reunion would be. I have missed you, missed having you next to me..."

She smiled lopsidedly. "We have time for that. Perhaps if I..." She lay atop him, nuzzling close into his neck, revelling in the warmth and closeness. He groaned luxuriously and the sound of it thrilled her. "Is that better? I'm not hurting you, am I?"

His chest shook with laughter. "Hurting me? Only by tempting me." While he ran his hand over her back and down over her buttocks, he growled low in his throat. "You feel so good..." His eyes closed.

Sophy watched his face as it relaxed into sleep. Contented, she closed her eyes, sighing into Oakheart's arms with a smile on her face. He was right; it did feel good. She snuggled closer.

⚜

THE PRESSURE OF HER BLADDER WOKE SOPHY. ON AUTOMATIC SHE groped for her clothes and then touched the body next to her. Soft snores told her Oakheart was still asleep. Memories shifted and realigned. Aria was here. That nightmare of being caught in that cold, hard place was over. She was free of Rufus.

Her hand lucked upon her dress. She slithered into it. Put on her shoes. Then before she went outside to pee, she kissed Oakheart lightly on the lips. Pale moonlight cast an eerie glow over the camp. After creeping over to the bushes, she relieved herself with a heavy sigh. Everyone was asleep. It warmed her heart to know she was back with her friends. She righted her clothes and took a step towards her tent.

A dark hand encircled her wrist and tugged. Then before she could draw breath she was up against a man with a knife pressed close to her throat. The man was her height but stocky and looked middle-aged. She smelt his spice and sweat and tried to pull back. "Do not make a sound, Lady Sophy," the accented voice hissed in her ear.

Sophy nodded, repressing a shudder. He dragged her further into the bushes, away from the tent, away from Oakheart. A rustle of robes and she thought she knew what he was. He was a Puri. What was a Puri doing in their camp, and what did he want with her? She swallowed the lump of fear in her throat and tried screaming. It came out muffled. She kicked and fought but he had her in a hold that she couldn't break.

Oakheart! One part of her wanted him to wake so he could save her, the other part dreaded what would happen if he did.

Once they were some distance away from the camp, her abductor forced a scarf into and around her mouth. She lashed out at him, slashing the soft flesh of his neck with her nails.

Her captor thumped her on the side of the head. She fought for consciousness; the inside of her head felt fuzzy. Her feet moved, though, as she was dragged by her assailant. He kept going, moving quickly around rocks, dragging her upright when she sagged.

Suddenly he stopped. "Forgive me, my lady. I do not usually treat women so." There was a sound like a thump in her ears and everything blacked out. She sank down and down into the dark.

SOPHY WOKE, TRYING HARD TO BREATHE. SHE STRUGGLED AGAINST the wrapping around her. A blanket that smelled of horse and dirt cut out the light and most of the air. She was being jostled and bounced around. Sophy didn't know which way was up and wanted to throw up. Bile rose and burned the back of her throat. Calming herself, she guessed she was across the back of a horse that was moving at a fairly fast pace. She screamed around her gag and kicked the air ineffectually but could not dislodge herself.

A hand pressed on her lower back and then her rear received a stinging slap. She growled in response and kicked again. The second slap was harder. If not for the blanket, she was sure it would have bruised her. That made her quieten, but it didn't stop her feeling smothered or scared or cure her thirst. She tried to wriggle free of her bonds. Her feet were tied at the ankles and her hands were gathered together at the wrist and hung over her head. After a futile struggle, which made her sweaty and hot, she gave up and let her eyelids droop. She dreamed of being with Oakheart. Sadness welled up in her dream; she had been with him for so short a time before being ripped away.

LANDING ON THE GROUND PUSHED WHAT WAS LEFT OF HER BREATH out in a *whoop!* and snapped her painfully awake. Cool night air caressed her cheek. She was free of her confining rug. Her tongue was thick and numb and the chafing remained around her lips. And lord she was thirsty. She could drown in a lake and still feel unquenched. That thought made her throat feel all the dryer.

Lying flat on her back, Sophy blinked and looked around. The moon was up and the air was still and cool. The Puri man was moving about, settling his horse. He hadn't lit a fire. Of course, he didn't want anyone following them. She sniffed, the scent of food having caught her attention. Next to her head was some dried meat and a cup of water. Her hands were still bound, which made angling around and sitting up a struggle. When she was in position, she carefully opened her palms and placed her fingers around the cup. She didn't hesitate and drank the water, draining the last drop from it. The cup dropped from her hands and she lunged for the dried meat, stuffing it in her mouth. She was so hungry; she couldn't remember her last meal. The jerky was hard and difficult to chew. Hunger and need made her persevere. She needed her strength to get away. She needed it to survive. Eating her captor's food was the only way to do that: that and being clever.

Footsteps sounded close. "So you are awake finally. Praise the *given*," he said in his Puri accent. She noted the slight slurring of the 'r', slight lisp of the 's' and a softening of the 'p' sound. His accent was so like Hanal's, perhaps he was from the same clan. She wondered what he wanted with her. Anger swirled within her. She had seen Oakheart once again and touched him, if only for a fleeting moment. No chance to talk, no real time to be together. Blast this man. Her eyes stung with unshed tears. She had had enough of this place, this Argenterra. First Rufus, and now this.

"What do you want with me? Take me back right now and I'll make sure no one punishes you." She hated that she sounded so desperate.

He shook his head. "No, I will not take you back to the Argenterrans. Another wants you."

"Another? Who?"

The Puri man laughed, a merciless dry scrape against his throat.

"My kinsman and leader. His desires take precedence over Vorn's spawn."

Sophy blinked at his words. Her mind wasn't working properly as she had no idea what anyone would want with her. "You must take me back. I belong with them."

"No." The Puri man sat down and casually picked up some dried meat that had spilled from her serve. "Delivering you will right my wrongs, will bring favour to me and mine. What do I care for your Argenterran friends? They are weak and soft. Life has been too easy for them. We are stronger."

Sophy's mind worked frantically. She didn't know the situation or why the Puri man was there. Then the memory of the eyes came to her and the remembrance of those cold, blue eyes. "It's Hanal. You're taking me to him."

Coal-black eyes met hers briefly and then he continued to chew. So she was right. "You are mistaken though. He doesn't want me. I'm nothing to him. Ask him yourself."

He swallowed. "Oh, but he does want you, wants you desperately. You are the key to power in this place. Do you think me ignorant of what happened down in Rufus's den? Do you think I cannot feel what power lies within you?"

Sophy frowned. "Power? What power?"

She looked down at herself. "I can't use the *given*. I don't know anything about power."

His laughter mocked her.

"Listen! I don't know what you're talking about. I don't remember what happened in Rufus's den." Her words began to tumble forth. "I remember Gilly...and Oakheart—I remember blue and hardness—red and danger—wanting Oakheart...feeling sad. But it's all so confusing." She begged her captor with her eyes. "Please take me back. Oakheart needs me...I need him."

"Phah! What you want is not important. And Oakheart looked near death. He will need you no more."

Alarm seized her. Oakheart near death! "Please, don't do this."

He brushed his hands together. "Sleep now. I will wake you soon, and we will continue. We have to keep moving to stay ahead of them.

Your friends will follow if they are able." He stood and turned swiftly, sending his dirty robes to sweep against her face.

"Won't you listen to me?" she said to his back. "I need to go back to him, and to Aria."

He paused and said, without looking back, "I said go to sleep. If you talk again in that whining way, I will knock you out. I care not how you sleep, only that you do."

"But I need to pee!"

Her captor turned again and grimaced. Her feet were bound as well as her hands. She needed help or to be untied if she was not to soil herself. His forehead furrowed as he considered.

He pulled her to her feet. "Come." He untied her feet.

Sophy closed her eyes, heart thumping. He dragged her by the elbow to a place sheltered by rocks. Then he seized her hair. "Keep moving," he ordered. "Now pee."

Although her hands were tied, she was able to lift the skirt of her dress out of the way. She'd not put on any underwear. Her head was pulled back, the muscles in her neck taut. If only she was a gymnast or something, she could...what? Possibilities flitted through her mind.

"Finished?" he asked.

Sophy gritted her teeth. "Yes." She hadn't thought of a move.

In some sort of parody of dance, they moved away from the stones, him with her hair in a tight grasp. He swung her around to face him and grinned. His grip relaxed.

Using the momentum of the swing, Sophy surged forwards, her forehead smacking against the bridge of his nose. Her tied hands followed up with a side swipe and his head flung to the side. Her feet untied, she kicked him in the gut—and turned and ran.

OAKHEART STIRRED. HIS ENERGY LEVELS WERE BETTER THAN BEFORE but he sensed something was missing, altered. His bed was cold. A breeze played upon his skin. He brought an elbow beneath him, levered up on one side and looked around. Sunlight filtered through the tent flap. He was alone. "Sophy? Sophy."

Heart thudding, he threw off the blankets, noticed his nakedness and puzzled over it. Sophy had been there. He remembered that much. Footsteps drew closer. Dizziness and overwhelming weakness swamped him. His elbow shook and he eased himself flat against the bed. Darkness gathered at the edge of his vision. By the *given*, he was faint. What had happened?

Fern stuck his head through the tent flap. "What is it? Are you well? Where is Sophy?" Fern squinted into the tent. "Her clothes are gone."

Casting a concerned look in Oakheart's direction, Fern stepped back to the tent flap and bellowed for Lillia. "Ho. Ware." Fern darted off.

"Wait. What is going on? Fern?" But his friend was gone. He had been right to worry. Sophy had been there; it had not been a dream. They had succeeded in freeing her. By the feel of his body, at great personal cost. How had he made it there? His memory was patchy from when Rufus had attacked him.

Oakheart tried to sit up and failed. He sent his gaze in search of his clothes and found his breeches were half obscured by blankets. Carefully, he pulled the blanket, dragging the breeches closer and trying not to dislodge them. After he snagged them he tried to get them on. His legs were like floppy eels and his fingers could not quite grasp. With concentrated effort he managed to get a foot in, and then another. He had just pulled the breeches on when Aria and Lillia burst into his tent. He lay sprawled on the bed, exhausted and panting.

"No!" Aria shouted, her troubled gaze raking the corners of the tent, only to fall on Oakheart. "Where is she?"

He blanched at her tone. "Is she not with you two?" Dread rose up inside him as their looks confirmed his worst fears. Sophy was not just missing from his bed, she was gone.

Lillia frowned. "We left her with you. Both of you undressed. In that bed." She knelt, throwing blankets and clothing around. "Her dress is gone. Her shoes are missing too—" Lillia's voice choked off. She looked as if she had killed her best friend.

Aria held her hand to her head. "Do you think she's walked off...in a daze or something? She wasn't quite herself."

Oakheart saw their worried frowns and was afraid. Sophy had seemed herself. He recalled her voice, her body pressed close to his and the joy of being together. She would not have left him...willingly.

The sound of running feet heralded the arrival of Fern, who poked his head through the torn edges of canvas. "At least one horse," he began, panting. "One person possibly dragging another...Not sure when."

Lillia stared at him, desperation writ in her eyes. Her hands covered her swelling body protectively. It was not the time for more pursuit and danger, not with her child growing within her. Then as if making a decision, Lillia's gaze hardened and her mouth grew firm.

"Oakheart, can you travel? We must help her, of that, I am sure. Rufus must have taken her."

From behind them a voice said, "We cannot be sure it was he." It was Brook, using Adage's voice. Yet something was different. Oakheart could sense it but could not quite place it. He noted Lillia's pained expression but had to make room for the women so that Brook could come in. "Rufus was weakened and has probably fled. I fear he is headed for the Crystal Gate. It is his only means of escape."

A shiver of fear slid into Oakheart's gut. He remembered the last time he had seen the Crystal Gate. He would not lose Sophy that way. "Did Rufus take Sophy, Adage?" Oakheart asked.

A look passed between Lillia and Adage. "I am no longer Brookfell Treesinger or Adage. You must call me Meld from now on."

Oakheart realised that more had occurred in the Lower Warrens that he had ever imagined. Now was not the time for explanations. Sophy was his main concern. He needed to ready himself. He pulled on his shirt, but the effort to do even that taxed him. When he reached for his boots it hurt to breathe, so he paused, waiting for the feeling to pass. Aria's green eyes watched him. Her pity, her concern were anathema to him. His duty was to lead, to be strong. He could weep, he was so tired. Oakheart wished he understood what was going on. What had happened to him? If Rufus did not have her...then who? Then it came to him. "Nasheen."

Fern shook his head. "I am sure he is dead. The guards and the other Puri man were killed. There was not much left of the bodies."

"Did you find Nasheen?" Oakheart asked.

Lillia ran her hands through her short hair. "You said Nasheen's body was missing."

"At first I thought it was missing because I did not like him. Then when I thought about it and the state of the bodies, I thought perhaps he had been true to his oath after all and had perished in the holding of it. If he did betray us, it could be him. He could have watched us, waiting for time to ripen." Fern pushed his dark hair out of his eyes. "But how did he escape the massacre?"

Meld added, "More important is the reason why Nasheen has taken Sophy."

Aria's face had paled, and she played with her hair, trying to tame it into a braid. She shrugged. "I can't think why."

Lillia coughed. "Hanal of Puri has met Sophy. I think he had more than a passing interest in her. As Oakheart's oathbound wife, she would be valuable as a political hostage."

Meld knelt down, hands on his knees. "Sophy must be found. She is full of the land's power. When she was transformed into the crystal, she leached the *given* and pulled it into herself. Rufus's purpose was to use that power, to destroy us, perhaps to take it elsewhere. For whatever reason, Sophy has taken what belongs to the very land itself. It must be put back. If it is not, oaths will weaken, fray perhaps, and become naught. The *given* will pass from ordinary men to slide into legend. The people will forget their oaths and the land will become less than it was."

"And if Nasheen has Sophy then he is delivering her and all that power to Hanal," Oakheart said weakly, his eyes staring at the roof of the tent. By the *given* he was tired. "Hanal will not hesitate to take it for himself."

"You make it sound like Sophy's fault," Aria protested hotly to Meld. "She didn't do it on purpose, you know."

Meld regarded the princess. "It matters not the intent, only the outcome."

"No," Oakheart replied. "Intent is everything. Sophy will do what she can to make it right. That much I know about her."

"I hope so. Yet she is not here to make it right." Meld closed his eyes, and Oakheart sensed that the adept was reaching out to him because he detected an elusive thread of the *given* and then it slipped away. Meld opened his glowing blue eyes and shook his head. "I am sorry. I cannot aid you, Oakheart. You are alive, but not hale. The others must tend you for I have not recovered from Rufus's attack either. I fear Brook's weaknesses are now my own."

The look Lillia gave the adept would have frozen a lesser man. Oakheart was pained by Adage's words but did not have the strength to retaliate. He closed his eyes. Brook and Adage were now one? That was why he was calling himself Meld. That would explain Lillia's antipathy. He understood the forest maiden's pain. Her son was dead but she could not mourn him for his body walked and talked in front of her. He had never heard of such an instance before. Adage was the oldest and greatest of the adepts. It was fortunate that Argenterra had not lost him, but Brook was a good man, too. A young man with a life ahead of him, a joy to his family and to his clan. What a dilemma. Meld stood, his face showing no emotion, and left, dropping the flap noisily and leaving them alone.

Fern backed out of the tent to assist Aria gallantly. "Come, my lady. Let me help you get ready. We must go after them."

Oakheart ground his teeth together, worrying that his friend was infatuated and what disappointment that would lead to. Aria was married, bound to an unbreakable oath. Then to his surprise, Aria put out her hand and placed it in Fern's. "Thank you, Lord Fern. I will accept your help."

He watched them go with a heavy heart. Surely, Aria understood that her prior oath to Dellbright would prevent her forming a liaison with Fern. He shook his head, not liking what he was thinking or feeling. There was only heartbreak in store for Fern. For them both, perhaps. What a tragedy was Dellbright's life. He had made his marriage even more of a disaster than his parents'.

Oakheart suddenly noticed that Lillia had stayed in the tent. When his gaze rested on her, the grief spilled out of her. Oakheart opened his arms, and Lillia fell into them, weeping.

"I am sorry for your loss. Brook was a good son."

"He was our brightest beacon. Beloved by all...Mellow...how will he bear this loss?"

"I do not know."

She wept for a while, unable to talk. And then, calming, she edged out of his arms but lay by his side. "I have no medicines left to help you gain your strength. My son is...gone...replaced by Meld, and now all that we have fought for has been stolen away in the night. I cannot bear it. Poor Sophy! What must she think...feel?"

Oakheart stroked Lillia's head, soothing her sorrow the only way he knew how. "You did what you could, as we all did. If Nasheen took Sophy he would not harm her, I am sure. Hanal, though, I do not know. He would use her if he could, but she is oathbound to me. I see no point to this abduction."

Lillia pulled away, sniffed loudly and half smiled. "You seem so confident. But what about what he...Meld said? Oaths are weakening. Perhaps he will find a way around yours."

"That may be so. My oath to Sophy is strong. It lasted while she was changed into that jewel. It will last through this." *I hope it will last through this!*

Lillia managed a smile through her tears. "You always put great store in oaths, Oakheart. But Sophy has a strong will, stronger than any Argenterran oath, I think."

Oakheart smiled lopsidedly. "She is rather a handful. Perhaps Nasheen will return her before long, just to get some peace."

Lillia wiped her eyes and let out a chuckle. "Oh how I wish that were so."

☙ 11 ❧

A TASTE OF CRYSTAL FIRE

S ophy ducked and weaved through the brush, puffing and wheezing as she sped away from Nasheen. After her first mindless rush, she became aware of her surroundings. There was no path, no sure way to go. She kept running on blindly, but she had no idea of her destination.

Nasheen had taken her through some back way. There were no paths, no Argenterran roads, no people or landmarks. Winded, she bent over, gasping in lungfuls of air. It was hopeless.

Mountains loomed in the distance. The perspective on the Glassy Mountain Range gave her no indication of where she was. *Bugger! It all looks the same!* She had no food or water, couldn't use the *given* to help with that. No shelter, nothing to keep her warm.

Her heart lurched uncomfortably. There was no sign of rescue. No trails of dust or line of horses following. No sign of anyone.

The rustling of undergrowth grew louder as she paused. Nasheen was gaining on her. Wearily, she looked around, found a tree trunk to lean on and sighed. Her choices? There weren't any.

Sophy sat on the ground and stretched out her feet as she waited for Nasheen to come. She could do this the hard way, or she could negotiate terms. While she had no wish to go with Nasheen, she didn't fancy dying of starvation or wandering aimlessly where no one could find her. Not being tied over the back of a horse and bounced around like a milkshake was her preference. Could she bring the Puri around?

Nasheen approached warily. Sophy pretended to be resting, eyes closed and breathing steady. "My lady?" he asked hesitantly.

Sophy snorted and opened her eyes. "My lady?" She looked askance at him. "That's sweet. You trussed me up like a bunch of twigs and you call me, my lady?" Climbing to her feet, she stood opposite him. Her gaze dropped to the rope in his hand. Her eyebrows lifted.

"I regret the inconvenience." The Puri shrugged.

"You knocked me out. Is that how you treat a lady?"

"I required silence and stealth. I meant no disrespect."

"Disrespect? Are you serious?" When he lifted the rope and stepped towards her she stepped back and raised her hands. "You're not going to tie me up again."

Nasheen tilted his head, considering. "Then you will accompany me willingly?" He blinked at his own words.

Sophy clenched her hands into fists and tried to keep calm. "I want to go back to my people. Unfortunately, they aren't following us." She chewed her bottom lip. "What does Hanal want with me?"

Nasheen studied her silently. "You have power. If he could use it to help his people, it would be a good thing."

"I can't use the power."

"Hanal is gifted. He may be able to help you there. If not, I am sure he will let you go as you are no longer useful as a bride."

Sophy contemplated this. Nasheen was tricky, and she shouldn't trust him. If she could be free of restraint though, the passage would be easier. If by some faint chance she was to be rescued, she'd be in a much better position. She was putting a lot of faith in Hanal to be reasonable, though. "If I give you my word that I will not run away again, will you put your rope away and let me ride properly?"

"You would do that?" He chewed his lip as his dark eyes considered her. "What if your friends come close?"

Sophy grinned. "I won't lie. I prefer them to Hanal."

"Very well, I will do my best to stay ahead of them." He put out a hand. Sophy looked at it but didn't take it. Dark eyes glinting, he stepped back and gestured for her to walk in front of him.

A brief glance behind her and she sighed. Why weren't her friends following her? Hadn't she been missed? *Oh Oakheart! What will you think of me? I didn't run away.*

IT WAS EVENING AND THEY WERE HEADING NORTH AND WEST, INTO the sun as it was eaten by the mountain peaks. Sophy's mind was clearer. The mountains were part of the Glassy Mountain Range that cradled the valley and then broke up into ragged pieces before it split into the Upper Plateau and a smaller range behind Silverdale. The Fortitude Ranges, she thought they were called. Silverdale came to mind like a faded picture. Sophy sat behind Nasheen. She didn't like being this close to him but it was better than being trussed up and bounced around like a sack of potatoes. He had rounded up another horse but their stores were tied to that.

"It is strange to me," Nasheen said out of the blue, "that no one has spoken of your beauty."

"Really?" Sophy lifted her eyebrows in surprise. "Do you normally bash beautiful women around the head and drag them away in the middle of the night? If I had been ugly would I have escaped being bludgeoned and abducted?"

"No! No, of course I do not need to attract females in that way. Your invitation to the Puri required certain stealth. I am not trying to seduce you with my compliment. My wives are enough for me."

"Wives? But I thought..."

"Puri have ways to word their oaths that leaves them free to cleave to more than one wife."

Sophy stilled. "But I have an oath to Oakheart."

"Yes?" He changed the position of his reins before continuing. "You worry that I or Hanal would take you for a wife?" He shook his head. "Your existing oath prevents such. Argenterrans have no imagination, particularly when they swear oaths."

"That's good to know. So do all Puri men have multiple wives or, better still, the women more than one husband?"

He chuckled. "Most men cannot stomach more than one woman at a time. So not usual. As for a woman with more than one husband? Is that your fantasy?"

Sophy grinned. "I already have an excess of men in my life right now."

"True."

"So you beat them, then?"

He grunted. "Who? My wives. You are determined to make me angry. Mina, my first wife, does that when she wants me to bed her. Come to think of it, Amberlyn does the same."

Sophy swallowed loudly, and re-thought her tactics. She was not interested in going down that route. The topic just made her miss Oakheart all the more. Why hadn't he come after her? What was keeping them? "So, how many wives do you have?"

"Just the two. I have ten sons and two daughters."

"So your wives must be very sarcastic then."

"How so?"

"The number of children..."

He chuckled, and she felt the rumble of laughter where their bodies connected. "No. I am a good lover and my seed is strong."

Vomit rose to the back of her throat and she swallowed. *Eww!* Nasheen was oldish, fat and short, and she didn't want to even imagine him getting it on with his wives. Sophy rolled up her eyes and twisted her mouth at the back of his head.

"Have you no explanation?" Nasheen pressed for an answer. "Was it a secret?"

"Oh, you mean my looks? If you must know, Rufus put an enchantment on me, one that disguised my features, blurred them. That way no one took any notice of me. I looked very plain."

"Well, you are a beauty now. If you keep behaving in that annoying way I'll have to take you to wife."

"I'll watch my tongue. Really, I will." They both laughed because of the futile nature of his threat.

Some early stars were hovering in the dark purple, twilight sky.

Sophy could only guess where they were going. Both moons were out, the smaller chasing the larger. Nasheen had refused to answer her questions about their destination when she had sense enough to ask them. Unfortunately, she wasn't confident that Oakheart was hot on her heels. She worried that things were not well with him. If only she could remember what happened. Her memory was fuzzy.

She had vague recollections of Oakheart lying on the ground, mostly dead. But later she had spoken with him, but then he'd been weak, unable to hold her. Not that she'd been in the mood for sex, but he hadn't even tried to get her in the mood. They'd just cuddled. She bit her lip as she tried to work it out. The ethereal tie she had with him was thin, but not severed. He was alive at least.

Would they know that it was Nasheen who had taken her? Why was the Puri man anywhere near Rufus's caves, anyway?

As she grew tired, Nasheen's back was the only place she could lay her head, so she did. The smell of sweat was strong and so was the spice. She sniffed, trying to figure out what it was and then she knew. The dried meat he'd fed her was laced with it. If she ate much more of it she would smell just as pungent. She shuddered and closed her eyes. The horse's gait lulled her to sleep.

It was dark when she woke. Whispers filled the night all around her. She had been placed on the ground, the blanket tucked under her head as a pillow. Over the top of her was a colourful Puri robe. Surprisingly, it smelt clean.

A horse snorted, then another. They had company. She sat up warily, hoping that rescue was close, but Nasheen strolled leisurely from out of the shadows, a firestick in his hand. He shoved a handful of bread at her.

"Eat," he said like a grunt.

The flat bread was warm, freshly made. Sophy gestured with a bread-filled hand to where the sound of voices emanated. "Who are they?"

Nasheen's eyes narrowed, then he took a mouthful of bread, chewed and swallowed. "My clansmen. That tall one is my son Halif. Good looking like me, yes?" Sophy bit into her bread. He waited for her to answer and she didn't so he continued to spell out his plans. "We have fresh horses so we will make good time. Hanal will reward me greatly when I gift you to him."

Sophy watched the shadows play over his face. Dark stubble lined his chin and shadows ringed his eyes. He was worn out. "Are you sure? I'm worthless to him. He cannot use me or bed me. I am oathbound to Oakheart. Besides, I said I was coming willingly, so technically you can't give me to him. I thought you said he would be interested in this power." She struck her chest lightly.

Nasheen's eyes glistened in the reflected light. "You have a twisted tongue. Whether you think you come willingly or not, I have secured you and will deliver you. I know what Hanal values. As I said, even I can sense the power leaking out of you. Hanal is very talented. They say he can see into a man's heart. I do not give him credit for that ability, but he has ways, wait and see." He paused for a moment, waved to one of the other Puri and then stared down at her.

"You think me a savage, ignorant and untutored. I listened to the adept. He said you have the land's *given* in you. A lot of it. Right now, Lady Sophy, Gift of Crystal Tree Woods, you are more precious than even water to my people. Through you we will rule all of Argenterra. Veld will kneel before Hanal, and I will be a prince living off soft Argenterran soil. My sons will bed Silverdale's milksop women, and if those insipid females produce strong brown sons, I may allow those women to make an oath and become part of my clan, otherwise they will be whores like Tu Raenal, fit for nothing but bed warming and growing children."

Sophy's eyes widened, horrified by Nasheen's vision and his words about Rae. "I heard Hanal of Puri was an honourable man. It is of Rae that you speak, isn't it? The daughter of Kushlan, who went amongst the Puri to marry him?"

"Yes, Rae of the Valley. She opens her legs for Hanal, lives in his household without shame. So much for the morals of the valley folk."

"Wait a minute. The Rae I know wouldn't have done that. Not without a reason. Hanal is forceful, strong...he could have persuaded her."

"Hah. You women always make out that you are innocent and deny that you have ways and means to seduce a man. Rae had means at her disposal and she chose to use them. Hanal would not have bedded her otherwise. I know him and he does not seduce the pure of heart. In that way he is honourable. She is outcast and shamed."

"Honourable that Hanal is, he bears no shame in an act performed by two people. I see no fairness or honour in that. Why is the woman to blame?"

Nasheen grunted. "Enough. Sleep."

Worrying her lower lip with her teeth, Sophy thought back to the time Hanal had come into her suite at Silverdale. She had known then, or suspected at least, how close a call that had been. Hanal would have seduced her if he had wanted to. He came that close, and she had almost succumbed to his lure. It was only because she convinced him she was worthless, a nobody, that he didn't take her away. It made her angry that Rae was suffering because of Hanal. *Bastard!*

While Nasheen took a quick nap, Sophy stared into space. Two Puri men stood guard. Nasheen's son had already ridden off on Nasheen's horse to blur the trail. The remaining horses had their hooves wrapped in leather to disguise their tracks. Nasheen knew many ways into and out of Argenterra. Sophy despaired of rescue. That despair only made the pain of separating from Oakheart more acute.

Oakheart reined in his horse and waited for Fern to return from scouting ahead. Exhaustion filled his bones and his mind. Despite Lillia's best efforts, he had not returned to his previous strength. Because Sophy had been abducted, perhaps by the traitorous Nasheen, there had been little time to analyse what had happened to him. He knew he had been close to death as he had experienced his life unravelling. But what had Aria accomplished by healing him?

By her own admission, Aria knew nothing about healing. By instinct alone, she had brought him back from the edge of death. Her attempt had been sufficient to revive him, but not as yet to restore him. He was living a strange half-life and wondered whether there was hope of regaining his strength at all.

Meld had been too introverted, too concerned with his own

problems, to offer any possible theories or even use the *given* to heal him completely. The loss of the connection to Adage's body had caused the adept some measure of chagrin, as well as inconvenience. From what Oakheart could tell, Adage had not warmed to Brook in life and now ironically he was melded into the younger adept's body. His vow to Vorn held him against the force Rufus had thrown at him. By rights he should have perished, too. Now they had Meld, half man, half spirit.

It was indeed a strange and dangerous time. The *given* was fading, though his own tie to Sophy was still there, ethereal and light. Not as strong as it had been in the Gilton Forest, before this nightmare had played out. But what use was he now that he had nary the strength to pursue her? Nasheen would be able to knock him down with his body odour before Oakheart could heft his sword. By the *given,* he needed to heal so he could fight for her.

Fern headed his way, face grey and troubled. Oakheart braced himself for more bad news. Although the trail out of the Lower Warrens followed Nasheen's trail quite closely, once out of the immediate surrounds, the plains opened up. The Puri could have taken any number of ways out of Argenterra. The Puri leader had not used the usual, well-trod paths. If they did not find his trail, Nasheen would gain an advantage. Oakheart only knew one way into Puri, the trade route. But it was a long route that brought them close to Glassy Mountain Retreat. Oakheart sighed when he thought about the retreat. Could his learned brethren come to his aid? Could they stop the *given* from receding? He cast a glance at Meld and thought that they could offer little. Adage had been the greatest of them and now he was less than he was. That boded ill.

"Oakheart?" Fern hailed him as he rode up. "We may as well camp here. The trail is confused. I will need time to think on it. Nasheen's horse had one shoe that had an inlaid pattern, like a brand mark. Its trail leads vaguely north, along the trade route to Panal's Pass. But as I scouted around I noticed some muffled prints over there behind the boulders in between those scraggly bushes. But there are no tracks. I fear some subterfuge on the Puri's part. Imagine those savages being so smart."

Oakheart frowned; he liked neither the news nor Fern's views. "You may be surprised to learn they are not savages, Fern. The Puri are as cultured as we. 'Tis just that their ways are different. I have not lived amongst the Puri for a long period, but I have made a study of them. They are secretive and hide their knowledge from us, but they know the ways of the *given*, possibly more intimately than we do. They have to fight hard to use it. We may have to learn from them in the future if we cannot repair the land, cannot restore the *given*."

Fern's expression soured. "Now is not the time to lecture me about your admiration for the Puri. They have taken Sophy, for Vorn's sake." Fern inhaled through his nose and then let the air out. "We need to make camp." He slid from his mount and went to help set up the tents. Fern's mood was definitely bitter if he could not raise even a small jest.

Oakheart rubbed his pulsating head. He had never suffered from headaches before and found that he did not like it.

Meld walked up and stood near his horse's head, taking the horse's muzzle into his hand and stroking it with the other. "Will you not dismount, Oakheart?"

"I suppose I must." Oakheart took a breath. He barely had the strength to lift his leg up to slide to the ground.

"We will talk while I help you tend the horses. I fear you have not the stamina to listen to me afterwards. Already I can see the lines of tiredness etched into your face."

Oakheart suppressed a sigh. He was finding his condition galling; being found less than worthy by Meld did not help the situation.

Oakheart heaved himself out of the saddle and could barely stop his plunge to the ground. He landed on his knees, arms still clutching the leather straps of his stirrup. Luckily Meld held the horse's head, for it moved sideways. On his hands and knees, he fought the dizziness and waited for the world to stop turning. Closing his eyes helped. At least he did not throw up.

"Oakheart?" Meld enquired.

"I will be all right in a moment." Oakheart pushed back to a kneeling position. "Can you put the horse with the others?"

Meld nodded and led his horse away. A moment later, as he tried to stand up, he saw Meld dragging a sack of feed to where the horses were to be penned. It was not to be borne—the most revered adept doing menial chores! His chores. He staggered over to where the horses were penned.

"Please, Meld. Let me do that."

Meld looked up, blinked and tilted his head. "The bringing of the feedbag is already done."

Oakheart leant against the trunk of a tree. Hearing footsteps, he turned to see Lillia placing water for the horses, a small ration. It made his heart ache. All the horses were growing thinner; each day their strength waned.

"Come, Oakheart, tell me what to do with this feed now?" Meld asked. "The tending of livestock has not been a task of mine since my childhood. The last horse I tended was Vorn's own mount over five hundred years ago."

Oakheart nodded wearily. "Indeed, 'Tis is a long time. Place a small portion into their nose bags and hook it over their necks. Here, like this."

Oakheart placed a couple of handfuls of feed into a bag to demonstrate, then tipped some water in and mixed it with his hands. Lifting the bag carefully, he placed it over his mount's head. Meld copied Oakheart's placement of the feed with the rest of the horses. While Meld fed the horses, Oakheart went to unsaddled his. The saddle slid easily to the ground when he unstrapped it, although Oakheart could barely lift it. He slumped against his horse while trying to groom it, sweat pouring off him as he tried to brush the horse's coat and his breathing ragged. He was truly disgusted with his weakness.

Meld picked up the saddle and placed it with the others and then took the brush from him. "You must sit. There is little point in taxing yourself."

"Can you not do something for me, Meld? At least tell me what is wrong. Why do I feel like this at a time when I need my strength more than ever?"

Meld paused in the brushing, his back to Oakheart. "I understand your frustration. I am certain that I will be able help you soon. I have my own situation to deal with. Being a meld like I am…takes time to sort things through. You are not the only one to undergo something new. It seems to me that certain abilities I had were linked to my body rather that my spirit. I have to make...er...connections in this body. I never understood until now that the *given* and a person must have a certain understanding. Change the person and that alters the mix. I am not what I was, just as you are not what you were."

Oakheart's heart sank. "What do you mean? I have no wish to change. How am I altered? Will I stay weak like this forever?"

Meld handed the horse brush back to Oakheart and wiped his hands with distaste.

"Listen to me, Oakheart, and listen well. If you did not alter you would stagnate. It is in the nature of man to grow in either wisdom or experience. The very nature of living changes us, just as love changes us, or the death of a loved one does.

"The weakness is due to what Rufus did. He drained your life force. It may have seemed as if he struck you with power but that is not the way of it. He drew from you as he did me. Or should I say Brook." Meld shook his head ruefully. "I have had time to analyse what happened to Brook and me. I should have come on my own rather than risk another. But time was of the essence. Brook was closer to Valley Keep on his way to the Gilton Forest. Now it appears that it was a poor choice on my part."

"Then how did Aria save me, bring me back? You make it sound like I died."

Meld frowned into the growing darkness. "You did for a short time, I fear."

Oakheart exhaled loudly, remembering his oath that Sophy would not predecease him. But she lived. He knew Rufus had wanted him dead because that would null the oathbond, but he realised that if he died then Sophy would likely die as well, or at least lose the protection of his oath. He thought about the weakness he suffered when he had traded some of his life to save hers. He'd been weak, too. Was it the same?

"What is going on?"

Meld lowered his eyelids over the blue of his eyes. "That is a difficult question. From what I can tell, and half of this is guesswork on my part, Sophy, while in that crystal shape, created a vortex with her at the centre. She drew or bled the energy, or life force if you like, that is the *given* and stored it in herself. Just as Rufus drew force from you, so she did from the land. Aria used her talent with the *given* to bring you back. However, something happened in between. Your bond with Sophy, the *given* centred in the jewel, or just the passage of power that Rufus pulled from you. Something, you, the power, the *given,* has altered. Perhaps that is why it does not aid you. It is alien to your body and that part of you that can shape the *given.* You need to make new connections within yourself. I hope that in time both the power and you will adjust, thus giving you the strength you need to undertake your task."

"Task? You mean to save Sophy?"

"Yes...and other things yet to come. My vision of the future is lost to me. I thought I had glimpsed something once. The Crystal Gate had something to do with it, and Sophy, too. The visions I have of her are strange and distorted. More detail I cannot remember."

Oakheart rubbed his face with his hands. Meld's words sorrowed him. Not only for what they revealed about his own future but that the essence of Adage had been diminished. Argenterra had suffered a great loss and, at that moment, it weighed him down, adding to his lethargy. His failure to defeat Rufus also weighed heavily.

Meld stood. "Come, Oakheart. A meal is ready and you must gain your strength in conventional ways until that power nestled within you finds its path."

Oakheart stood and towered over the adept. "Meld...'Tis strange to call you that." He opened his arms wide, indicating the land around him as he walked. "Is this what Vorn dreamed? Has the binding oath been undone? Will the *given* fade completely?"

Meld's blue eyes focussed inwards. "Not knowing for certain tears at me. But I fear it is so. I cannot measure the extent of it as I am less than I once was. I curse myself for a fool. I would that my grandfather, Vorn, was in my place. He would know for certain and, perhaps, he could stop it."

Oakheart halted and Meld, sensing that he was not being followed, stopped and turned. "What is it?"

"I had a vision of Vorn, both Aria and I, at Valley Keep. Vorn spoke to us."

"Truly? His spirit lives on in the pool? Enough to communicate?" Meld shook his head. "What a wonder. I hoped that his essence would endure, but I never dreamed such a thing was possible." The adept stepped up closer, his hand touching Oakheart's chest. "Did he impart any wisdom to you?"

For the first time, Oakheart sensed nothing when the adept touched him. Before, there had been a solidness, an otherness and a vague tickling of power. Now there was nothing but a human touch. "He said the binding oath was undone...and he said another thing about the jewel—about freeing it and wielding it. I fear he meant Sophy."

Meld removed his hand and turned with a gentle swirl of blue robe. "Yes, he does mean her. Where best to hide a talisman than in a person themselves? How best to thwart the Ancient Evil because the vessel is not inert? No, this talisman can be altered, influenced and manipulated and loved..."

"You are speaking of my wife. Meld. Not some 'thing' to be used. She loves me. You underestimate her. She is free to choose."

"Yes, fortunate for us that she does. I pondered the issue of Sophy when I left Valley Keep. Rufus disguised her from us. It was his design to do so from the beginning. That his subterfuge included you, firms up my feeling that you were meant for each other and, despite those obstacles, you were still drawn to your destiny."

"'Twas not destiny, Meld, but choice. I chose her. I...I..." Oakheart flushed and he could not hold Meld's gaze. Lillia appeared further down the track, waving to them. "Come, we must eat," he said, quickly changing the subject. He was no longer certain about the veracity of his choice and the workings of fate.

Meld nodded and gestured for Oakheart to lead the way. "As you wish."

✣ 12 ✣

HANAL OF PURI

Five days later, stripped of strength, Sophy fell from the saddle when Nasheen stopped. A snatched nap against the Puri's back had not brought any cleansing rest. On top of that, he let her rest in the dark of night for only one or two hours. She was almost dead with fatigue.

That morning Nasheen had obtained new horses and fresh supplies from the Puri settlement they had passed through along the edge of Shabra's Plain. The settlement was made up of horse herders, the clansmen that stayed with the herds during winter, the unmarried men and the widowers.

Sophy shivered, remembering how they had looked at her with a kind of hunger in their eyes. She didn't know if it was from the power they sensed in her or the fact that she was a female and young and, she guessed, no longer ugly. Now more than ever she feared meeting Hanal and the other Puri. With no sign of pursuit and Nasheen's brisk pace, there was little chance that Oakheart or Lillia or any of them could reach her before she had to meet her fate. That realisation did little to boost her spirits. She hadn't worked out a strategy to deal with Hanal as yet and that worried her.

When she looked around at the wasteland of Shabra's Plain, the few trees and scrub blown by a cold wind, she was desolate. Hope had leaked out of her, leaving her as barren as the surrounding landscape. Shivering, she huddled in the Puri cloak and tried to block out thoughts of what lay ahead.

"It was said that Aria was fair upon fair, almost as beautiful as Prince Daken's whore, Veld's wife. Hah. The cuckold. Who would have thought that Veld's wife would have left Argenterra to be with the prince of Valley Keep!"

"What did you say? Veld's wife ran off?"

"Yes, left her husband and her son. But you must have heard the tale. You are Oakheart's oathbound, or so you say."

"Yes, I am Oakheart's oathbound wife. But what has that got to do with Veld and his wife?" A lump formed in her throat.

Nasheen grinned at her, patches of white teeth against dark skin. He finished lighting the fire, obviously no longer concerned about pursuit. The wind rippled the flames, sounding like soft drum beats, but Sophy could only note them. "I know that Oakheart was abandoned by love and for love...but he is the high king's ambassador, not his..." she said, and paused.

Nasheen chuckled, an evil sneering sound. "His son?" He finished for her before he fell backwards into the dirt, contorted by laughter after he'd looked at her expression.

With a strangled cry, Sophy looked around for a rock, but could only find rough, sandy dirt. She pitched a handful at Nasheen, sending him into a splutter, and bolted for the horse.

Within three steps, she was face down in the dirt, Nasheen's wiry hands clutching her. "Now, my lady, or should I say, princess..." He laughed some more. "I would not be in a hurry to leave. Surely a state visit to Puri is in order, your highness."

He dragged her upright. Sophy glared at him. "No!"

He grinned and dragged her back towards the fire.

Tears threatened to spill. How dare Oakheart do this to her? How could he marry her, make love to her and talk to her without mentioning that one important fact? He was a goddamn prince, the high king's heir. She thought back to see if Lillia had lied to her, but she could only remember the hints about Oakheart's importance.

Then the reason for Fern's dislike came to mind. Of course, who wants some gauche, ugly, outlander woman marrying the high king's heir? And the women at that ball, all of them falling all over themselves to get Oakheart's attention. Why didn't it occur to her before? It wasn't just that he was handsome. No, he was royalty.

Her legs buckled. *Aria! Aria knew. That cow!* Sophy clenched her hands. She ought to strangle Aria. How dare she manipulate her like that? Why would she?

Then Sophy recalculated her relationship to Oakheart—if she had known he was a prince, no, *the* prince, she would have stayed far away from him. They would never have been friends because she wouldn't have known how to act, would never have dared to speak her mind.

And bloody hell, she didn't want to be a princess! She hated the idea of it from start to finish. No privacy. Everyone fawning around you. No freedom to do what you want. No real friends.

"Oh shit," she said as Nasheen tugged her back to camp and she fell to her knees. "Stupid, stupid, stupid," she muttered under her breath. It clicked together. Hanal wanting Oakheart to marry Lyant, all of it. The resemblance. The high king and Oakheart had similar builds and they both talked loudly, sometimes bellowing. And the mannerisms...why he hadn't chosen a wife...political machinations, alliances...all of that...and her. No, she couldn't believe he'd bound himself to her for political reasons, for power. It just wasn't possible. Oakheart loved her, she was sure. Please god, she prayed, let love be the reason he married me. Yet, there was a newly inserted doubt there.

When she looked up, Nasheen flashed a smile at her. *Damn!*

SOPHY HAD ONLY JUST NODDED OFF AFTER AGONISING OVER HER plight for ages when Nasheen shook her roughly awake. It was still dark and her head was dull and heavy as she sat up. Still angry, she had the impulse to kick him in the face but couldn't think of what to do after that. It would only bring satisfaction, not anything else. Nasheen passed her a bladder filled with non-*given* wine, which she drank, and then tossed her some left-over bread, which she ate hungrily.

"We should make the Caves of Suval before nightfall. I will stop by the spring at Dereth so you may bathe and make yourself look more alluring." He patted a saddle bag. "I have appropriate clothes, which I picked up from the settlement, fit for a queen."

At her sneer, he chuckled. He climbed on and gave her a hand up. Once settled behind him and on their way, Sophy tried to keep her face away from his back. He kept laughing and it was annoying as hell. She hated his laugh, but she was tired, and she couldn't help herself. With the shortage of restful sleep, Sophy succumbed and slept against Nasheen's back, oblivious to their surroundings.

The sun was midway to the horizon when Nasheen slowed the horse. He sniffed the air and altered direction to ride the perimeter of a small dam. It looked like a dam to her, leastways. The water was muddy, a dull grey with a few clumps of spiky grass growing to one side. "There," Nasheen said. "It is clear. You may bathe." He slid off his mount and began untying the saddlebags.

Sophy glared at him. "I'm not the only one who needs a bath."

Nasheen chuckled to himself as he tugged the bag free. "I will bathe, too. I cannot present myself to Hanal looking like this. But I will wash in the lesser pool." Standing on the tips of her toes, she could see a smaller pool.

He lifted her down. Sharp stones dug into the soles of her feet. When she gasped and hopped from one foot to the other, Nasheen said, "I will give you some shoes after we leave. They will get muddy if you wear them now. Also, the sharp stones will stop you from running off." He untied her hands.

Sophy glowered at him, not afraid to show her anger. "I said I wouldn't run away."

He shrugged and unrolled a blanket. Within it were fine Puri clothes. "Dress in these." A sheer fabric made into trousers, lightly embroidered along the ankle, and a long tunic dress in pale pink with matching embroidery around the sleeves and neckline. Sophy tried to look unimpressed. It was feminine and pretty, something she didn't want to be for Hanal.

She swallowed. "I'm not sure I can wear those." She wanted layers of heavy fabric between her and the Puri leader, maybe some armour and a weapon, too.

Nasheen shrugged. "Very well. I can take you naked with nothing but a horse rug if you choose. It will save time at least."

Her expression dropped. She wished she had a stick so she could beat the smile off Nasheen's face. She turned round and gingerly picked her path to the water's edge. Her feet sank into the soft mud. It felt soothing after the sharp edges of the rocks and shards of stone.

"Do not go too far in," he called after her. "It is a deep pool. I will be back shortly. Be ready. I will give you a signal before I return so you can protect your modesty."

She watched him go, muttering under her breath. Her body odour was intense; sniffing one's underarms after more than a week in the saddle could be hazardous to your health. Stumbling to the water's edge, Sophy dropped the Puri robe and her dress, leaving them in the water, and stepped into the pool. It was cold, but she didn't mind. She squatted and washed herself vigorously. She'd never smelt so bad before and wanted to feel clean again, even if it was for the benefit of Hanal of Puri.

Once clean, she climbed out and used larger rocks to step on to keep her feet clean and then dried off with the Puri blanket before dressing in the new clothes. Nasheen was nowhere to be seen. As she looked around her, all was bare to the horizon. Then the screech of a large bird made her start. It dove to the ground some distance away, vanquishing some poor creature.

The pink tunic floated around her knees in a light breeze. Nasheen hollered and then came into view striding majestically towards her, vibrantly coloured cape trailing behind him, face clean-shaven and hair newly braided. As he neared, he wrapped his braids within his headdress. He looked to be in his mid-forties and was proud and imposing. A smile was on her face before she could hide it. Nasheen smiled back.

"Now you look fit enough to be brought before Hanal of Puri. If I did not have enough wives of my own, I would be tempted to take you into my household instead of Hanal's."

Sophy's face heated. There was something earthy in his comment that she couldn't quite ignore. After so long being slighted and overlooked because she wasn't beautiful, it felt so good to be complimented, to be noticed. However, she realised that she had to be careful. Vanity could be her undoing.

"So, do you love your wives?" she said as she mounted the horse. Nasheen brushed her feet clean and then tied pretty, embroidered slippers on her feet before he too climbed onto the horse's back.

"Yes, of course. Why, do you think me a beast such as Dellbright who beats and rapes his wife?"

Sophy gasped. "What did you say? What do you know of Aria?" Sophy had only a fleeting memory of Aria being there in Rufus's cave. It broke her heart to hear what Nasheen said.

Nasheen grunted and kicked the horse, and it jerked into motion. Sophy grabbed hold of him. Nasheen relented and told the tale of Dellbright's rape and assault on Aria. She listened hard to his words as there didn't seem to be any reason why Nasheen would lie about this. Had she not worried about her friend and her relationship with Dellbright? She thought back to the signs, her friend's reticence, those occasional unguarded looks. *No. Oh Aria. No,* thought Sophy as she wiped quietly at a tear. "I didn't know," she said when she could finally speak. "But I should have. Now that I think about it. There was something she never said, something hidden in her expression. Please take me back to her. I need to be with her."

Nasheen turned and said severely, "I cannot. So do not start nagging me again. Aria has the forest maiden to care for her. Fern, too, I imagine will sniff after her more now that I am not there to shoo him away. What good it will do him to hanker after her, I know not. Aria is bound to Dellbright. There is nothing but heartache for Fern if he continues to moon over Aria."

More surprises. Surely he hadn't been in her friends' company that long. Maybe he had, and his betrayal truly took them by surprise. She had better be careful.

"How do you know all this? Fern fancies Aria? Oh lord. He's so... well, nasty...I'm confused."

Nasheen lifted his hand for silence. "Enough, we must ride fast now." He urged his horse into a canter and all Sophy could do was hold on tight.

❁

HIDDEN BY THE DUSK, THE CAVES LOOMED LIKE DARK, HUNGRY mouths as they rode up. Nasheen made signals to unseen sentries as they neared. Boulders obscured the entrance, a low cave mouth that swallowed the light as they crossed the threshold. Sophy's stomach clenched and she fought the desire to scream and fight. As the horse slowed, she managed to find some self-control. She needed to face this calmly. Perhaps she could find a way out of this situation.

With another glance at the cave, she shook her head. It didn't look hopeful. Nasheen helped her to dismount. With the darkness deepening around her, her captor fussed with her clothes. She fought the urge to laugh hysterically at the oddness of his behaviour. "Bring light," he called to those who came to help with the horse.

A young boy ran up, holding a torch. Nasheen peered at her under the flickering light and then nodded to himself. As an afterthought he then peered into her face. "Are you ready?"

"No," she said in all seriousness.

"You will do." He bowed and urged her to precede him and she took that first step. "Come then."

The cave swallowed her up and, at first, she saw only an inky blackness. Testing the ground ahead of her with her foot, she took a few more steps. It was lighter farther in. Torches lit their way. She was in the Caves of Suval and soon to be delivered into Hanal's hands. She had to have a strategy. *Think, think, damn it!*

It was cool in the caves. The scent of fire and damp alcoves intermixed. They headed through a main passageway. Off to the side were smaller caves and hollowed-out dwellings. Shadows moved around fires and hushed whispers flowed around her as she walked deeper into the labyrinth of caves to Hanal's chamber.

Amid distant firesides and flickering torchlight Sophy hoped for a glimpse of Rae, or any friendly face. The faces were all in shadow, backs turned against her as if the Puri had no need to know of her existence. She guessed that, living in close quarters, they learned to ignore what did not immediately concern them. A false privacy. A prickling sensation began at the back of her neck and she knew that they watched her, hidden by veils and shadows.

Nasheen's hand separated a heavily embroidered curtain and he grabbed her and pulled her through it after him. Next, he tugged her down to the rug, making her kneel and bow low while he did the same. Out of the corner of her eye, she saw that his forehead rested almost flat to the ground. She refused to follow suit. When he let go the pressure on her back, she sat up on her heels, chin jutting, and stared boldly at the figure shrouded in robes and dimness

Hanal sat on a large, high pillow on a dais. He didn't move and she couldn't tell if he had even noted her entrance. Distracted, she looked up at the cave roof. The surface was smooth, probably ground down by water over time. It was a large chamber partitioned off with curtains only. She wondered who was on the other side of these, listening in.

"You are late, Nasheen." Hanal's voice had a hardened edge. Sophy's heart skipped a beat. Her gaze was again riveted to Hanal.

Nasheen lifted his head and shoulders but didn't look towards Hanal. "Yes, I was delayed, but I have brought you a gift."

"Why were you late? What were you doing? I have heard rumours of raids."

Nasheen bowed low again, twice. "Yes, Hanal. There were raids."

"You went against my orders?" The Puri leader spoke quietly but his voice had a deadly edge. Nasheen's hands twitched. *Good*, she thought, *he's not getting off easily, then*.

"Yes, I went against your orders with reason. I was provoked. Strange creatures walk the land..."

"Enough." Hanal's voice rang through the caves. "You have ruined my plans. I do not wish the Argenterrans to know my strategy or my strength. I do not wish them forewarned. Now they will make ready."

"I am sure I revealed neither..."

Hanal slammed his hand down, hitting the dais with a thwack. "Only half your men have come to the caves. Where are the rest?"

Nasheen had not sat up. Sophy thought he bowed even lower to the ground. She thought it politic to lower herself too. "I have ten to injury, and the other five are still in Argenterra," Nasheen answered, though his voice was quiet and muffled.

Hanal's posture was rigid and his voice without warmth. "I see...by this gift, this Argenterran maid, you hope to assuage my anger..."

The tension eased from Nasheen. He raised himself up, still keeping his head bowed.

"Yes. She is Lady Sophy, Gift of Crystal Tree Woods and oath—"

"What?" Hanal erupted off the cushion, sending his robes into a flutter. In two steps, he was dragging Sophy to her feet, examining her face minutely. "It cannot be..." His eyes studied her, hands roving over her face, fingers trailing down her long dark hair. Then his eyes widened. "Yes, it is her, but changed...more beautiful than I could imagine." Hanal glared at her with those cold, blue eyes, grabbing her face with his hands and bringing her near to him, so close she could see his pulse throb in his neck.

"What trickery is this? How were you able to disguise yourself? Or was it some conjuring trick of the retreat?" He almost hissed the last. Sophy was overwhelmed by his anger and suspicion. This was not the Hanal she'd anticipated. She began to tremble. "More likely Veld, though I did not know he could work the *given* so well. Speak."

She tried to shake her head, but he held her so tightly that she couldn't move. Then, through squashed lips, she managed to say, "Not Veld...Rufus..." Her words were muffled but the anger in Hanal's eyes lessened.

Nasheen then tumbled out the tale. Of Oakheart, Lillia and Fern travelling with Princess Aria and of Dellbright's treatment of the other Gift of Crystal Tree Woods. He detailed the rescue and the power he witnessed unleashed in the Lower Warrens. Nasheen also waxed lyrical about his own prowess and tactical thinking. He described minutely how he had thwarted pursuit. As he relayed his tale, Hanal's grip on her eased as he exhaled noisily.

"So you have brought her to me. You have provided me the key to undo Veld's hold on Argenterra."

Hanal seemed mesmerised by her. "No," Sophy said, unable to contain her anger. "You can't use me. I am Oakheart's. He will come for me."

Hanal pulled her to him until there was nothing but the sheer fabric of their clothes between them. Her flimsy Puri outfit didn't provide a sufficient barrier. The muscles in his chest, the bones of his pelvis and his firm thighs all pressed against her. "You have an oath? Did you lie to me when we met at Silverdale? That would earn you punishment."

What she saw in his face awed her. She shook her head. "No...I didn't lie. It happened after...not planned...on the way to the Gilton Forest." Sophy was breathing unevenly. His hand grasped her lower back, pressing her thighs to him. Suddenly her strength fled. Her arms fell flaccidly to her side. She should strike him for holding her that way but she couldn't. She was locked into that gaze, bewildered by those crystal-blue eyes that could see into her soul.

"Good," he said, his breath caressing her neck. "It pleases me that you did not deceive me. It angers me, though, that you tricked me into believing you were nothing." His other hand reached up and stroked her hair. "How was such beauty hidden from me? Truly your eyes are like the sky when the sun leaves its parting kiss, like the deepest twilight, and your hair as the night, cool and dark..."

Sophy thought it strange that he would speak such sweet words in front of Nasheen, but when Hanal released her she noticed that her Puri captor was gone. She was alone with Hanal, leader of the Puri clans. So far, she hadn't done a good job of resisting him. How could she fight this power he had over her? She began to fret that Oakheart's certainty that she couldn't break her oath to him was a figment of his imagination. Perhaps her promise to him was like a promise in her own world, a flimsy mockery that was easily discarded. Her father had discarded his vow to her mother, left her for another, younger and prettier woman. Her mother had abandoned her for her younger boyfriend. How could she stand against a genetic disposition to break promises?

The carpet was a relief after Hanal released her to let her sink to her knees.

"Tell me how it was done. How did Rufus hide you from me?"

Sophy found her voice. "Enchantment. Rufus put an enchantment on me from the time I entered Argenterra. It was not discovered until

I crossed the Lake of Reflections for the second time. I saw my face. And Oakheart's true one. I have only looked like this since I was freed from the jewel."

Hanal frowned. "Another unfathomable outlander. Who would have thought you both hide such power?"

Sophy tried to calm herself. *Both of us have power? Does he mean Aria?*

Hanal turned away and repositioned himself on his cushion, shoulders back, body poised regally. "Rae," he said in a normal voice.

Sophy had a hard time slowing her heartbeat and quelling the sensations in her stomach and lower down. The anticipation of seeing a friendly face was a balm that helped her steady herself.

The curtain parted and Sophy's gaze leapt to catch sight of the former maid. Rae bowed to Hanal without looking at Sophy. Kushlan's daughter looked at home in her Puri garments, her red and green headdress flowing down her back. Sophy was certain that Rae knew she was there, but as yet hadn't looked her way, hadn't acknowledged her at all. Sophy closed her eyes, praying that Rae was still her friend and that she would help her in some way, however small. Yet each second that Rae refused to acknowledge her, the more distant that hope became.

"Bring food for us," Hanal ordered the girl, barely noticing her.

Rae slid back on her knees, dropping the curtain, shutting herself off from Sophy's hopeful expression. The feeling of helplessness nearly overwhelmed her. She glanced nervously at Hanal, feeling her heart rate increase all over again.

"So..." Hanal said, lifting one dark eyebrow. "You are a maid no longer. Pity; that was not how I figured my prediction would come about. I thought it would be me to claim you."

Sophy looked him in the face and notched her chin a little higher. She'd had enough of Puri ways. So much for the prohibition on looking into another's eyes. Hanal had done nothing but gaze into her face and yet her soul seemed intact. "You will release me, now." She tried to sound as a princess would. From the look on Hanal's face, it hadn't worked.

Hanal almost smiled at her. "You think these Argenterrans are superior to us, do you not?"

Caught off guard, Sophy shook her head. "Not at all. It's just that I belong with Oakheart. That is all that matters to me."

"There we have a difference of opinion. It matters not to me, Sophy, that you have bound yourself to Oakheart. I may call you Sophy? Yes?"

She nodded, feeling a growing unease.

"Oakheart compromised my sister, Lyant, and in denying her an oath he has cut me off from an alliance with Silverdale. Now you tell me he is oathbound to you." He shrugged. "So be it. But he has a lot to answer for. He must provide me with a well-placed man to marry Lyant. He must compensate me through treaty and trade and position. For too long have we Puri been denied our rightful place. I have as equal a claim as Veld to the throne off Argenterra."

Sophy mused over Hanal's words and tried not to blanch at the professed equal claim. She had not heard that one before. "I'm sure it will be arranged as you desire. You don't need me to ensure that. Oakheart is honourable and if, as you say, he has made advances to Lyant, he will make it right. If you have a true claim…"

Hanal cut off with a bitter laugh. "You are naïve and stupid. Do you think Veld recognises my rights?"

Her fingernails bit into her palm. "I have no idea of the politics of this place. I haven't read any history or even heard a great number of stories. All I know is Veld is *high king!*"

"But you are his daughter now…"

Sophy chewed her lips. Why did she feel so trapped? Why did it all seem like some senseless game? "I didn't know who Oakheart really was when I made my oath. I never knew anything about his position so I don't have a daughter relationship to the high king, nor am I aware of his likes and dislikes…"

Hanal barked out another laugh, filled with derision. "Now you speak an untruth. How could you not know you bedded the heir to the throne? Such a prize is sought after. Even if he didn't tell you, the evidence was before your eyes."

Heated cheeks spoke louder than words. "I didn't know. No one mentioned it. I have a strong feeling that the facts were deliberately kept from me. And Oakheart was enchanted, too, from my eyes. The first I heard of it was from Nasheen. I still don't quite believe it."

Hanal climbed to his feet and paced. "*Phah!* Excuses. You are an intelligent person. Why did you not figure it out yourself? You knew he had direct access to Veld. And the women at court? Do you think I am ignorant of their behaviour? Of course, they would only abase themselves so for the high king's heir. Lillia the forest maiden knew of it for they have been fast friends these many years. I cannot believe she did not apprise you of the fact."

Sophy swallowed a hard lump. That was so unfair. Why did the forest maiden not tell her? Then she recalled a few hints, a few questions from Lillia. Had she been so easily fooled? It seemed so obvious now. "I'm telling you the truth. I didn't know. I didn't seek to seduce him, and I don't believe he bedded your sister, either."

Hanal's eyes widened. "I did not say that he did. I said he compromised her. Our standards are different."

She was glad her comment disconcerted him, but still floundered out of her depth. Knowing that Oakheart hadn't slept with Lyant was a relief. Her situation was complicated enough and she didn't need disillusionment on top of it. "I'm glad to hear it. No damage done, then."

He faced her square on, his robe parting slightly over his dark-skinned chest. "What do you know of Puri ways?"

"As much as I want to know. So far there has been trickery and betrayal. Let me give you an example. You tried to manipulate Oakheart but he was too careful. He would not have led Lyant to believe he wanted to marry her if he wasn't free, so you are wrong there. I'm sure of it. I recall he was always paranoid about the subject of marriage."

Hanal let out a sigh as if he had given up on the argument. Then he let his gaze travel over her. Sophy's skin prickled and her breath hitched. His sudden change of tack disconcerted her. "You are bold to speak so to me. You think you have protection."

Sophy froze. He knew she couldn't beat him or resist him. In an instant he was squatting beside her and running his fingers through her hair. "You think your oath to him can stop me?" he whispered in her ear.

She edged sideways, out of his reach, and gaped at him. Hanal was threatening her subtly and trying to confuse her. "I don't know what you mean." Yet the tell-tale pulse bounced in her neck.

He held her gaze, his face a hand's breadth away. "But I think you do," he said, dropping his voice a tone lower so that it vibrated down her spine. "You see, there are oaths and there are ways around oaths. I can make you want me so much that your oath to Oakheart will be tainted...and he will know it. But more importantly, you will know it...always."

Her skin chilled. "You may try to taint my oath, Hanal. But my love for Oakheart is stronger than any oath."

"We will see."

He stood before her and closed his eyes. Sophy bit her lip. She had thought that the fact that she had power had escaped his notice, but she was wrong.

His eyes flashed open, cold light in their clear depths. "So, my lady, what will we do with you?"

"Me?"

He lifted an eyebrow and a faint smile flitted over his face. "You are full of power. How do you suggest we take it from you?"

"I don't want it. You are welcome to it. I can do nothing with it. I can't even tell it is there. I have to take your word for it."

He lifted a hand and brushed a forefinger down her mid line, between her breasts to her navel. Stepping back, he studied her; only his breathing reminded her that he was still there.

"It is well shielded within you. I would have to break down your barriers to get at it."

"Barriers? You mean like my oath to Oakheart?" she replied.

"Your oath is one. There are others that protect you, ones you erect yourself. We all have them. I would only try to break your oathbond last of all as it is the hardest."

"So you break down my natural barriers and then you can get this power out of me. Free me from it?" Sophy knew her options were limited. If she didn't cooperate and didn't escape, then she'd have no choice at all. This way she negotiated.

"I can start with your natural barriers. Hopefully, we can release that power trapped within. Believe me, we have use for the *given* here."

"Once you have it, you can put it back into the land?"

He frowned at her. "It worries you that you caused Argenterra harm. Interesting. I would put the *given* back in the land, but in the Puri lands."

She nodded. It was all the same to her. Better out than in, as they said. "Then you will let me go?"

He tilted his head as he studied her with his clear blue eyes. "Yes. I believe I will. Perhaps I will exact a ransom for you as well. If you cooperate with me, it will go easier."

"What do you intend to do to me?"

"First, I will have to starve you; then, if that doesn't work, I will have to try to break down other barriers."

Hunger sounded doable. "Others?"

"Let you go thirsty. With hunger and thirst, your physical body will weaken. That should allow those internal barriers to drop."

"And then if those two things don't work?"

He inclined his head. "Here we come to the hard part. I would have to restrain you. Remove your clothes."

"My clothes? Why?"

"Because humiliation does tend to break down barriers. It will be like peeling layers of protection from you. With each layer I will try to take the power and then move on to the next. The last will be your oath. I may not break that, I may bend it."

Her heart beat fast and hard, her breath quickened. She was appalled. "You think this will allow you to take this power out of me? You're sure?"

"I am as sure as I can be. I can see it there, restrained. I just have to unchain it from its bonds."

Sophy let out a pent-up breath. She didn't want the power. She didn't want to be there with Hanal. The sooner she got the power out of her, the sooner she could leave. None of what he suggested was comfortable, but it was survivable. "We will try it your way."

"You agree?"

"If I can stop the process if I don't want to continue, yes, I do.

He pursed his mouth as he considered. "You can ask and I will consider it."

That seemed like the best bargain she could make. "Hanal, I don't want this power inside of me. I want it back where it belongs. I want my life back. I hope your plan works."

"So do I. We begin tomorrow. Sleep well."

❧ 13 ❧

FUTILE PURSUIT

Aria wanted to scream her frustration to the wind. She stood staring at the others, who were grouped around the fire, with her fists clenched. The firelight flicked shadows around the camp, casting a golden glow on their faces. Even the warmth from the flame did nothing to lift the mood. Everybody seemed so listless, so directionless. It made Aria want to spit. She had been through so much, suffered so much, and the stain of that suffering couldn't be removed. It had changed her, moulded her, and she wasn't sure that was a good thing. She wasn't comfortable with these new feelings of rage and anger and frustration.

Sophy was gone, for heaven's sake. Just disappeared without warning and leaving no sign. Aria wanted to pull her hair out. Maybe the pain would dislodge an idea or would make her feel better. Who was she kidding? All that work, all that risk, achieved nothing. Oakheart slept though the damn whole thing and even now had so little strength he could barely move. All he remembered was that he had spoken to Sophy, and touched her.

Oakheart's recovery was only one part of his problem. The attack had drained him, but Aria was sure that Sophy's absence affected him, too, perhaps mentally and spiritually. So much of his ego, his sense of self, was bound up in his physical ability and his desire to protect his oathbound wife.

Time. Time. Time. Sophy was further and further away with each minute they delayed. Meld was next to useless, meditating to recover his lost powers. It was a setback, for sure, but she wasn't going to give in to the feelings of weaknesses. She would not let Dellbright's words to her be true.

"We need a plan," she said boldly as she strode up to the campfire. Oakheart lifted his head wearily and nodded. *No more quick action from him!* She clenched her teeth to hold back a scold. Fern watched her keenly, nodded, too, brisk like a salute. His gaze lingered on her, his expression filled with warmth and admiration. Aria's heart fluttered uncomfortably and, like a twist of the knife in her stomach, she knew she had to discourage him. There was no future in him falling for her, only heartache and pain. Her oath stood solid and firm.

"What do you propose, my lady?" Lillia asked. The forest maiden passed Aria a bowl of soup when she reached the fireside. In it swirled green leaves and some dug-up vegetables boiled together. It was Forage Chowder, the name they had affectionately called it.

Aria sipped the hot brew tentatively. "If, as Fern says, Nasheen took Sophy, we will never catch up with him. His trail has disappeared and it appears he is too cunning to take the well-known route to the upper wastelands. We're travelling too slowly so we have to be smarter about our approach."

Oakheart pushed himself forwards wearily. "I..." He shrugged and gave her a helpless expression.

"Never mind, Oakheart. You can't help it, and besides, even if you were your old self, Nasheen has disappeared without a trace. He knows his way around these lands. The Puri have been raiding Argenterra for hundreds of years and they use paths unknown to us."

"Wait till I get my hands on him," Fern growled. His hands grasped thin air and squeezed, imitating a grotesque strangulation of someone's neck.

"Fern," Aria chided. "That doesn't help. What we need to do is think about why he wants Sophy. Do any of you have a clue? There must be something we're not seeing."

Lillia looked down, avoiding Aria's gaze. Aria turned towards Oakheart, and he cleared his throat before speaking. "Nasheen would not want Sophy for himself or to harm her. He takes her for his kinsman, Hanal. Hanal is the leader of the Puri..."

"I know of Hanal of Puri. What does he want her for? I don't get it."

"He seeks to gain some advantage." Oakheart sighed. "It is because of me that Sophy was taken. Hanal was insulted when Veld refused to agree to the marriage..."

Aria groaned. "More marriage politics? There's more, isn't there?"

"Yes. Sophy told me that Hanal came to her room at Silverdale when Lillia was absent. He acted strangely, said things about taking her away...but at the time the enchantment was upon her, he saw what we saw and thought her unimportant. I imagine that he has changed his mind..."

"Would he hurt her when he finds out that you and Sophy are oathbound?" Lillia asked, crouching down.

Oakheart's eyes glazed over then refocussed. "I think not, but he will use her any way he can. He may ransom her, or barter her for an alliance or marriage for himself or his sister."

Aria threw a stick into the fire. "But Rae went amongst the Puri to marry him. But then Nasheen said they did not marry. Curse it."

"Rae?" Oakheart asked, brows furrowed.

"Rae, my lady-in-waiting from Valley Keep. You know, the dark girl. She is cousin to Dellbright and to Hanal."

"Oh yes, I remember her slightly." Oakheart's eyes widened. "Hanal would not wed her, Aria. He would be saving himself for an alliance of power. I fear for your friend."

Aria sat for a few minutes absorbing all that she'd heard. She wasn't pleased about Oakheart's views about Rae. She loved her little friend and knew her heart would be broken if Hanal didn't marry her. As hard as it was, Aria had to weigh up what to do. "At least if Rae is there, Sophy will have a friendly face. Are you sure he won't harm Sophy?" she asked again, looking at each of her fellows in turn.

"How can he? Her oath protects her," Oakheart said, spreading his arms in an expansive shrug.

Aria sighed and pushed her hair out of her face. "I think we have different perspectives on harm. Her oath may prevent him from um... er...forcing himself on her sexually, but not much else. He could torture her or starve her, mistreat her in a number of ways."

"I am sure he would not do that," Lillia said. "I have met Hanal of Puri. I am not an adept, but I trust my instincts. He will try to bed her, I think. Her vow to Oakheart will counter that. But he will not harm her. It is not his way. Unless he is made desperate."

Meld looked up, his piercing blue eyes visible in the firelight. "You forget the binding oath is undone. Now all oaths may wither and fade; it is but a question of time. I would not put my trust in that oath to protect her. I can give you a more dire foretelling. He will sense her power and will stop at nothing, if what I fear is true, to gain access to it. If he finds a way, he could tap into her power. Then he would need no alliances nor a marriage for he would have access to the store of the land's *given* and we would be powerless against him."

Oakheart rubbed his hands over his face. "Yet I detect her oath. She is alive. How do you account for that?"

Meld turned towards Aria. "You have an oath to Sophy. Can you feel it as Oakheart does?"

Aria shook her head, sending her ringlets cascading around her shoulders. "No. I can't feel it...but my oath is different, Meld. I fulfilled it, didn't I? Oakheart has a different oath, more binding—a life bond."

Meld frowned. "You could be right."

Oakheart drew his hair behind his ears and wiped a stray hair off his forehead. "Meld has said that he fears what happened in the Lower Warrens changed me and I have to forge new connections to the *given*. I can still feel my oath to Sophy, but it is weak. I do not know if that is me or our oathbond."

Meld nodded. "It may be either or both. However, we must head for the retreat so I can study the matter further. I need assistance, and I need it soon, before the *given* fades for all time."

"I understand," Aria replied. Her heart was beating hard in her throat. She wasn't used to taking the lead, didn't really want to take the lead, but what choice was there? "Then we must trust that Hanal will not harm Sophy yet. We must hope that he will ransom her. The way to the retreat shares part of the path to the Puri lands. If we head there we can help Meld and send an envoy to Hanal to barter for Sophy."

Aria caught Oakheart's expression and tried to ignore the pain and fear she saw there. It was a dangerous gamble. Meld could be right. She hoped that Hanal would take his time before trying to wrench the power from her friend. Hopefully, Oakheart's link would give them warning. If he detected his bond to Sophy now, then surely he would feel it being tampered with or weakened.

Fern stood and dusted off his breeches. "To Panal's Pass then." He smiled at Aria, catching her eye with a wink.

"Fern," Aria said, returning his smile shyly, "Oakheart needs meat." She shrugged. "Something with more substance than soup. Can you go hunting?"

Fern nodded and went to fetch his bow. "Then we should move out in the morning," Aria said. Lillia went to check on the horses. "We still need to make up time. I hate that Hanal has spirited her away. I want to save her, but even more than that I have a feeling we need her. I know I need her."

"We do need her," Meld said, his voice solemn. "The adepts need to study her and find a way to release the *given* back into the land. We need to do that before Hanal finds a way to unleash it."

"Yes..." Aria whispered. "I need her more than you do, though. She's my friend and a person. Not a thing to be studied."

FERN'S HUNT WAS A SUCCESS AND AFTER A HEARTY MEAL OF FRESH roasted velder, Oakheart watched Aria head to her tent, followed closely by Lillia. Fern's eyes followed her too, his gaze devouring her every step of the way.

"You must forget this attraction, my friend. It will only give you pain," Oakheart said solemnly.

Fern smiled and examined his bow. "Too late. I am already in pain. I cannot forget her. She is magnificent! Beauty, courage and pain all mingled together. If she was a wine I would keep her close to me, and imagine how sweet she would taste."

Oakheart smiled. "You are a romantic. I never knew. I predict nothing but pain for you. She is wed to Dellbright. Perhaps if she had met you first, things would have been different."

Fern was shaking his head. "No. You would have stolen her then. I see how you look at her."

Oakheart looked at his friend askance, a blush stealing up his cheeks. "Truly? You think so? How do I look at her? She is dear to me, Fern, but I belong to Sophy. More than that, I want to belong to Sophy. Not having her near to me weakens me. I feel it, like a blanket is smothering me."

Fern took another piece of roast meat and dropped it onto his plate. "I would hate to be lovesick like you."

Embarrassment fell away. "Lovesick?" Oakheart chuckled. "At least Sophy is my wife and not someone else's. 'Tis you who is lovesick, but with no hope of ever consummating it or overcoming it."

Fern smiled but the joy did not reach his eyes. "I hate it when you are right, Oakheart." Oakheart lay back and pulled a blanket over himself.

Fern chuckled. "Are you sleeping there?" He looked up at the wind-swept sky. "There is no rain about so you should be fine."

"Yes. I will stay here. I like the way the air feels and I like the sound of the night." He did not want to admit that to move himself to his tent would tax him more than he would like.

Meld spoke from behind him. "I will keep you company. I, too, like the night, but strangely it is the rustling of the trees that thrills me. Some residue of Brook within me, I imagine." His tone was derogatory.

Oakheart closed his eyes. "Brook was a good man, Adage. Take care you respect his memory, for Lillia's sake, if not your own."

"Well admonished, Oakheart. You speak true. Long have I kept myself from everyday cares, from everyday people. Now I am thrust into them."

Meld fell silent and Oakheart let himself drift off to sleep, hoping that the rest would aid his healing. He reached out with his mind to stroke the tether that bound him to his oathbound wife. He could not feel her thoughts though, only the anchor of her life that bound her to Argenterra. He prayed that she was well and then prayed harder that he would see her again soon. He feared what was ahead for her, for all of them.

❦ 14 ❦

A COLDCLOTH TALE

Rae strode through the caves, lugging her laundry with a heavy heart. Now that Umri despised her, she had no female friends. While Hanal allowed her to remain in his quarters, he was cool towards her. She understood that he was punishing her and she was deserving of such treatment. When she had opened her legs and let Umri place Hanal's seed inside her, she knew he would not like it, knew it would make him angry. That she was desperate to marry him was no excuse. She had taken away control from him and she expected more bad treatment before he considered himself in control of their relationship again.

Then the outlander had come amongst them. Though she pretended not to, she had listened to their conversation and had not liked it. Not only was the plain outlander now beautiful, Hanal had spoken poetic words to her, revealing his admiration of her.

Gut-clenching jealousy seized her. She did not want Sophy anywhere near Hanal, even though she claimed to be oathbound to the high king's ambassador. Rae thought this was entirely likely, seeing how Sophy had gone off with Oakheart from Valley Keep. Despite the fact that Sophy and Oakheart had quarrelled a lot and Sophy's manner was at times awkward and offending, she suspected that they had had some kind of attraction. She had witnessed Oakheart with Sophy, particularly when he had stormed into Sophy's bedchamber and near ripped the covers from her naked body. Anger or love had inspired that reaction in the otherwise calm ambassador.

Whatever the relationship, Sophy had now complicated Rae's life, in much the same way that her friend Aria had done with Dellbright. Was she never to be free of these outlanders?

As she neared the place where the women washed clothes, she saw that she was not alone. Even though it was early, there were already five or so women beating their clothes against the rocks or rinsing them at the water's edge. Rae paused, her heart sinking. They turned towards her and then leant together in a huddle. Within the minute their laugher reached her. So much for a quiet space where ridicule could not reach her.

Ignoring them and dampening down her hurt, she knelt at the water's edge and stared at the dark rippling surface. She liked the smell of the water. The thought of immersing herself sent a ripple of anticipation through her. Of course, this was their main water source and swimming for pleasure was frowned upon. Only in Argenterra was swimming something one could do freely, as water was not so scarce and the rain fell often.

While she was engaged with reminiscences, with the dirty laundry lying forgotten, Umri snuck up behind her. Alerted to the presence by her distinctive perfume, Rae could not stop her start of surprise and fear. Would Umri make a scene? Would all the women know of her shame and Umri's machinations?

Rae looked carefully over her shoulder. Umri knelt, head bowed, waiting patiently to be acknowledged. "Yes?" Rae asked softly. "You want something from me?"

Umri lifted her dark gaze, made even more mysterious by the dim light reflecting off the water's surface. "I do not ask your forgiveness. I do not forgive you for your betrayal."

Rae looked down at the hands in her lap. "Why do you speak to me then, if nothing has changed between us?"

"We have unfinished business." Umri adjusted her headdress absently.

Rae shuffled around so that she was facing the other woman. She was confused. Last time they spoke, Umri was fit to rip Rae's hair out for confessing they had conspired to ensnare Hanal. Now she sensed no ire from the other woman and she did not understand. Puzzled, she knelt there waiting, and then it dawned on her. Sophy, the outlander, had been presented to Hanal the previous night. Word must have spread quickly. Rae said nothing of her guess and waited patiently for the other woman to speak her desire. Let her rain down insults on her head; Rae was ready for it.

"You do not ask what our business is? I will tell you then, for you are too affronted to ask me. Aurore's tale is still mostly untold. I will tell it to you."

Rae's head shot up. She shut her mouth and drew in a breath before speaking, using the time to calm her thoughts. "You will? Why?"

"Because the tale was woven into the cloth for you. It is right that you hear it."

Rae was suspicious. Umri was being nice, much nicer than when they were friends. "And what do you want from me?"

"Nothing in particular. I will tell you the tale, but it will be in a place of my choosing."

Rae's suspicion heightened but she could not anticipate where Umri's request would lead. "Your choosing?"

"Yes, and you must agree and then swear an oath on the life of your child that you will do as I ask."

"Swear on the life of my child?" She straightened her shoulders. "I will not do as you ask."

"Very well. A bargain, then. I will tell you the tale, in a certain place at a certain time. You will make it happen. Agreed?"

"Why do you not just tell me what you want? Then I can make a fair deal instead of binding myself without knowing the consequences."

"Ah, I forget you are a milksop Argenterran with no sense of adventure."

Rae waited but Umri said nothing more. She turned to regard her dirty laundry and lost all desire to wash it. "How do I know you are not out to take revenge on me? Hanal was very angry with you."

Umri laughed. "I was not angry with you for being honest with Hanal...well, not so angry that I could not recover from it. It was the exact thing I would have done in the circumstances. Hanal will get over his anger. He needs me and he trusts me."

Rae was surprised by Umri's certainty. If it was anyone else she would have considered that the person had lost their mind, but with Umri it was hard to tell.

"So do you agree? Do we have a bargain?"

Rae pushed her clothes into the water. "Yes, I will hear the Coldcloth tale."

"Good. You will take me to where Sophy, the outlander, is being held. I will tell both of you."

Surprised, Rae nearly overbalanced and fell into the water. As it was she splashed water down her trousers. "What did you say?"

"You heard me."

"But I cannot do that. Hanal has her isolated and tied up."

"Nevertheless, you will arrange it. I care not if Hanal knows of my visit or not. He will not prevent me, as he will be interested in my opinion. But he will not invite me...not after..."

"But—"

Umri climbed to her feet. "We have a bargain. I will be there this afternoon."

SOPHY STRUGGLED AGAINST THE SOFT BITS OF CLOTH WRAPPED around her wrists. Her mouth was parched, her lips covered in dry flakes of skin. Hanal had tied her up in a room, just off his main chamber. The floor was covered with woven mats and the weave left imprints on her bare feet. She could lie down and sit up but she couldn't move far because her bound wrists were tethered to a ring in the floor. Her agreement to this treatment was better in theory than in practice. It was still torture; she had to call a spade a spade.

Hunger punched hard in her gut. Yet she welcomed it. If being hungry meant Hanal could get at the *given* inside her, then the sooner she got really hungry the better. He could take the damn power and she could leave.

It was an affront to be tied up. Hanal knew this but had said it would help lower her barriers. It would humiliate her and prevent her from sneaking food. She could see his point. It would also make changing her mind moot. She was committed now. On a practical level, though, she needed to pee badly.

"Hello," she called out, not too loudly. She hoped Rae was listening. The rooms were divided only by cloth curtains, so if her friend was near she wouldn't have a problem hearing her. "Please, Rae. I need to go to the bathroom. I know you can hear me. Don't let me wet myself."

Sophy waited and listened. It seemed so quiet. At first, she couldn't hear anything, but then she relaxed, letting her eyes drift closed so that she could listen to the sounds of the caves. There was a hushed whisper that seemed to ebb and flow like waves on a beach. Occasional rustlings as many curtains parted, the faint sound of tinkling where pots banged, giggles of small children and a whimper here and there. These were the sounds of a community caught up with their usual activities. Her captivity, as yet, hadn't impinged on them. Over and above those humdrum noises, there was the cave, a mass of rock suspended over this gathering of clans. It dealt out a drip of moisture in various spots, spreading the scent of dampness and wood smoke and mingling it with the smell of humans.

Opening her eyes, she jumped. Rae sat there before her, the parted curtain falling back into place. Rae's dark brown eyes stared at her, though concern seemed to crease the skin around her eyes.

"Oh, Rae, thank god. Can you help me? I need to..."

Rae didn't speak but nodded. Sophy drew her knees under her while Rae draped a blanket around her and brought a chamber pot. Sophy was too grateful to worry about being embarrassed as Rae helped her loosen her clothes. She examined Rae's face while she worked. She looked like the same sweet girl, but she had an air about her, a maturity that hadn't been there before.

Rae's silence wasn't comforting. Sophy hoped to encourage her to speak. "Aria said you came to marry Hanal."

Rae's dark eyebrow shot up. She nodded barely perceptibly. When Rae stepped back and moved back towards the curtain, Sophy saw the telling bulge and gasped. "Oh! You're going to have Hanal's baby."

Rae ignored her as she stepped through the curtain, taking the chamber pot with her. The curtain opened again a few minutes later, and Rae passed hot towels to her. Sophy rubbed her face in one, sighing with delight.

Then she smelt food. Her stomach grumbled and her mouth watered. For a moment she forgot she wasn't to eat. Rae pushed a tray of food across the floor towards her. Sophy sighed with anticipation.

Rae knelt silently, watching with her dark eyes. Sophy gave up the idea of speaking, as Rae was so quiet and withdrawn it seemed to be a wasted effort. She wanted to know what the girl was thinking and whether there was any shred of friendship left, but it seemed so hopeless.

"Is that food for me? I am not meant to eat."

Rae looked to the tray, picked up a bowl and placed it in Sophy's bound hands. As she lifted the bowl, she caught a whiff of the seasoning. It was broth, meat broth with strong Puri spices. Was she able to have broth? She was confused.

It was too tempting. Lifting the bowl, she sipped. Flavour burst onto her tongue. It tasted good, so with another hesitant glance at Rae, she downed it all. Rae then handed her some bread. Sophy ate that too. She wanted to lick her fingers but refrained from doing so.

As the hunger eased, Sophy realised that she shouldn't have eaten. She had ruined Hanal's plan to break down her barriers. She had not kept her word. She hadn't even gone a day without food.

Now, she realised, it would get worse. Rae's presence offered her an alternative. Escape. Someone else could drain the power from her. Hanal was going to be pissed at her for eating. Hadn't she agreed to his strategy?

With her bound hands, she touched Rae's arm lightly as the girl picked up the bowl. "Help me, Rae. Help me get away from here," she hissed urgently.

Rae's dark eyes lifted and met Sophy's. "No." Her refusal was barely above a whisper.

Sophy wasn't sure she'd actually spoken. "Did you say, no?"

Bowing her head, Rae placed the bowl back on the tray and stood.

"Please, Rae. If you can't help me, I understand, but please talk to me. I'm all alone here. And I'm afraid of what is going to happen."

Rae half-turned away and said, "No. You are not afraid. You are never afraid. You are reckless. Now you have spilled yourself into my life, I can do nothing to help you leave it. My place in this household is precarious. I can do nothing to anger Hanal. My life and the life of my child rest upon how I behave. I have sworn my loyalty to Hanal, my clan chief."

Rae turned away and took soft steps through the curtain. Sophy was left to ponder her words. "But she brought me food," she said to herself. *I think I'm going crazy.* After staring at the curtain for a while longer, she huddled down to sleep, stretching herself out on the matting and cushioning her head on her arm. The sounds of the Puri in their cave washed over her and she slept.

۞

WHISPERING VOICES CLOSE BY STIRRED SOPHY FROM HER SLEEP. HER eyelids were heavy and her tongue was thick and dry. She opened her left eyelid and saw Rae and another beautiful woman sitting next to her. She pushed herself up into a sitting position, keeping her gaze riveted to that stunning woman's face. The grogginess was quickly shrugged off. The Puri woman had dark liquid eyes, lips of burgundy and a strange feel to her, like she had a mystic aura.

Sophy didn't bother to greet her. "Thirsty," she said thickly. She tried wetting her lips but she had no saliva. Rae went out and brought a jug, pouring water into a small round earthenware cup. Sophy gulped it down noisily and held out the mug for more. Being thirsty was going to be difficult to endure. Although, she wasn't hungry now that Rae had fed her. She prayed that Hanal wouldn't find out.

The other woman's gaze never left her face. She sensed her presence there, hammering away at her as if looking hard enough would reveal some secret of her soul. Across the woman's legs was a striped beige and white robe; Sophy wondered about it as she rolled

165

her tongue over her teeth, testing whether she could speak easily now her thirst had been quenched.

"Who are you and what are you looking at?" Sophy blinked at the sound of her own voice.

"She is Umri," Rae said with a tremor to her voice. Sophy tried to read the situation. Was that fear or dislike or something else?

Umri laughed. "So you are the outlander, the one that slipped through Hanal's fingers. How interesting that fate has brought you here."

Sophy smiled and laced her voice with sarcasm. "Hah. Fate. I thought his name was Nasheen."

Umri and Rae shared a look, then they chuckled together. Their laughter wiped the smile off Sophy's face. Just as quickly they returned to their previous blank demeanours. Sophy preferred this—better no emotion than ridicule. Umri made her feel uncomfortable, and she wouldn't be surprised if the change in Rae was due to this woman, too.

Sophy wrinkled her forehead. She hoped that Hanal had not tied her up in the general meeting area where the women came to gossip. Ridicule was further down the list of things to try to break down her barriers. A bit more mental preparation was required before she was up for that. She was still hoping that starvation, or better still, hunger, would do the trick and that she'd be out of there by the end of the week.

"Thank you, Rae, for showing the outlander to me. I will tell you more of the secrets in his Coldcloth if you like, in exchange for this favour," Umri said.

Rae's eyes widened, and the former maid nodded without sparing Sophy a glance. So, Sophy thought, Umri had surprised her, too. This should be interesting, she thought, drawn by the strange woman's gift and Rae's interest.

Umri lifted the cloth and caressed it with her face and hands. Then lowering it, she began, "Within this cloth is woven Aurore's secrets, the story of her life and loves. Care you to listen?" Umri was talking to Sophy now. Her voice fell like a cascade of slow-falling water that washed over her, liquid and warm.

Afraid that speaking would break the spell, Sophy inclined her head in a small nod.

Umri stroked the robe in her lap. Sophy noticed that Rae was transfixed, her expression halfway between awe and horror. Had Rae heard Umri speak of Aurore's past through the robe before? Was the woman some kind of charlatan, pretending to be more than she was?

Umri's eyes, those dark, limpid pools, focussed elsewhere. A sliver of quicksilver sped up Sophy's spine. She shuddered. Rae shivered noticeably and gripped her hands together.

Umri began. "I was born in Tobin's Foot, at the far end of the Valley. Kushlan was always there from my earliest days."

Umri spoke in her own voice but the nuances were Aurore's. The hairs on the back of Sophy's neck rose. *Dear god, it's like a séance.*

"From those earliest days I loved Kushlan. I loved the way he looked, how his smooth, dark skin moved over his layers of muscle. I loved the quickness of his mind and the nimbleness of his humour." Umri sighed as Aurore would have sighed.

"We shared our deepest secrets, the whispering of our souls and the longings of our hearts. I wanted to wed Kushlan as soon as I could, but Kushlan bade me to wait. I was not old enough and his farm was not prosperous enough to support us.

"In those days, we visited Valley Keep regularly for Daken was young and carefree and liked company. Daken, the then Prince of Valley Keep, was charming, handsome and engaging. I liked him, but he did not move me deeply or fill me with desire as did Kushlan. Daken liked our company, liked Kushlan's tales. He barely noticed me. I was too quiet, too dark in colouring for him to take seriously. But I did not mind at all. For when Kushlan looked at me the world seemed to stop and there was only us."

Sophy watched Rae's face and the other girl's eyes were watering.

"One day, when spring was on the land and birdsong in the air, we walked in the woods around Valley Keep. Daken was bored. The valley was small, and he wanted to explore. 'Let us go to Silverdale, Kushlan,' he said. But when Kushlan hesitated, he added, 'You may bring Aurore. I will bring one of the keep's maids as chaperone for her.' I wondered what lay at the heart of this desire. Daken was reckless, that much I knew already, but it was more than that. Valley Keep would never contain him. Now as I think about it, he was always thinking about other things: the land's mysteries, Crystal Tree Woods, the Adepts' Retreat. He studied them all. He did not just accept the *given*, he wanted to understand it."

Again Umri sighed in the way of Aurore, but her eyes were still transfixed—focussed inwards or outwards, Sophy didn't know for sure. Aurore spoke to them through the cloth she had woven and through Umri, who could tap into the threads. "I did not quite believe it then but I was young and naïve. What did I know of the world? Daken said, 'I am bid by Veld to pay my respects. So why not share the journey? You will see Argenterra in all its glory and meet the high king for yourself.'

"I must admit the idea did appeal to me. I had only heard Kushlan's tales and he had only read them or overheard them himself. Kushlan agreed, saying, ''Tis a bold plan, Daken. I hear tell that the High Queen Mara is the most beauteous woman in the land. Already, she carries Veld's child and the Silverlands rejoice at the hearing of it. I would also like to see the fabled tapestry of the First Comers. I would like to see the depiction of Vorn in his prime. That sight alone is worth my while.' So it was agreed. We travelled during early summer to Silverdale and there we made merry at balls and tourneys and competitions. With word and sword and song, we passed our time. There it all began.

"Veld was new to his throne and in his youth he was not always wise. He liked power, and thought he was clever. But he was blind. He was a fool." Here Umri's voice grew hoarse. Aurore's bitterness seemed to overwhelm her. The Puri woman's chest heaved and then calmed. Aurore once again spoke from Umri's mouth.

"At a great ball, Queen Mara did present herself for the first time since the birth of her son, Oakheart, who was a bonny child and as fair as she was. Veld was so puffed up with pride he did not see when Daken's eyes met Mara's. No, for in that moment all our fates were intertwined. Whether Veld knew of that instant or not, I do not know. Daken was smitten and, from what I could tell, so was Mara. She had green eyes and they glowed with warmth when they fell upon Daken, but when she looked upon Veld they cooled. Mara's marriage was arranged, brought about by the adepts of Glassy Mountain Retreat. Mara was actually more royal than Veld, had more of Vorn's blood in her, many times folded over and concentrated. The adepts advised the match and Mara wed him while still young. Everyone spoke of how great their offspring would be. Perhaps their son would be Vorn reborn.

"Daken managed to get close to Mara. I remember watching him, fascinated at how possessed by her he seemed. He walked towards her disregarding the smiles of other women, the words of men, the music so lively, the dancers so deft. Through them he walked to the corner where Mara sat in seclusion. She was not well enough to dance and Veld never took to the dance floor anyway. I saw her face as he approached, transfixed by him, so much so that she did not appear to breathe. He whispered in her ear and she seemed to swell with his words. Perhaps he told her of his love so immediate and strong.

"Veld then stood and shouted for all to listen. Daken was deep in conversation, his fingers touching Mara's arm, lingering on her hand. I was disconcerted. I worried that Veld would turn and see. But then the oath would prevent a breach of trust, but still I fretted. For even the thought could harm as much as a deed could.

"Veld called out. 'I would make a match. I know of one lady who is ready for marriage.' I remember looking around me, wondering who this person was, but he called my name. I blushed deep red and I was shy. I did not want to make a spectacle of myself in front of the courtiers and the fine ladies in rich gowns. But I glanced at Kushlan and he winked at me. So then I was willing. I stepped up and knelt at Veld's feet. Kushlan stood just behind me. I wanted him so badly. We had shared a kiss earlier, in an alcove hidden from view. I had felt it then, the powerful surge of desire. I begged him not to stop but Kushlan was stronger than me. I looked at Veld and wished he would order me to marry Kushlan right then. But Veld did not call Kushlan's name. No!"

Umri choked on Aurore's emotion. After a minute, she said, "I despaired at that moment. Veld named Daken as my husband. He called in a loud voice for Daken to come to him. Daken, hearing his name, let go of Mara's hand and, fearing he had been caught in a dastardly act, did hasten to the throne. Bowing like a practised courtier, he did speak these fateful words: 'I do as you command, *high king*.'

"My own heart near stopped in my chest. Daken looked around, catching my look, and paused. His brows drew together in puzzlement. I think he began to see his error, but I saw his mouth harden and perhaps his heart, too.

"Veld stood shakily. He was slightly in his cups. 'I proclaim that Daken, Prince of Valley Keep, is to wed Aurore of Tobin's Foot. Let the wedding commence now.'

"It pained me. I urged Daken to deny the high king. But he was too full of pride himself. He had said he would do as the king commanded. He would not speak to the high king to urge him to change his mind. I remember looking over my shoulder at Kushlan. I met Kushlan's eyes and all the pain in my heart was written there. They had been friends and Daken knew of Kushlan's love for me, but still he persisted.

"As everyone was already feasting and dressed in their finery, the resident adept was called forth so the ceremony could proceed. I heard Kushlan curse in a voice that scraped across my skin, flaying me with his bitterness and lost hope. He had only expressed what was in my heart.

"Daken took my hand. It was cold and clammy. His fingers trembled. I whispered to him urgently, 'Please, Daken, deny this. Do not do it.' But Daken replied solemnly, tears in his eyes, 'I cannot, Aurore. We will wed at the high king's command. I have pledged my word.' Again I tried to sway him but Daken only gazed at Mara and led me to the bonding chamber. I looked back for one last glimpse of Kushlan but he had been swallowed by the crowd."

Sophy couldn't resist a comment. "How horrid. Poor Aurore. I always thought there was a sadness about her. But why did she make the oath? Couldn't she stop it herself?"

"Quiet!" Rae almost spat at her. "This is my father she speaks of. It breaks my heart to hear it."

"Sorry," Sophy said, and then shifted because her foot had gone to sleep.

Umri's gaze never wavered from that elsewhere place where Aurore's story seemed to be woven. Her voice was strained now, whisper thin. Sophy had to listen closely to hear each word. Aurore's story was compelling.

"When Daken came to me in our wedding bed, I cried. For in my heart there existed only Kushlan. Though friendly towards me, Daken did not love me. I had seen him with the queen and I knew what it was to love and saw the same in the two of them.

"Daken was not patient with me. But he would see the bed sheets stained red, he would seal the oath right then. I tried to fight him off, tried hard. In the end, Daken hit me across the face, sending me tumbling to the bed. While I lay there thus suspended between wakefulness and dream, he did take me and filled me with his seed. The terror of that night has never left me. He did tear at me and filled me with all of his hate. For in that joining there was a desperation and an anger that had nothing to do with me. Only Daken knew the cause of it. I would only learn about anger later."

Umri spoke now, her eyes blinking away that otherness. "The sad thing is that it was the only time Aurore shared Daken's bed. From then on, he spurned her as she did him. Dellbright was born of that union from that night in Silverdale, when all their fates were woven together like the *given* into this cloth.

"For that time after, Aurore's life was filled with bitterness. Kushlan was angry, not so much with her, but with life. He had left Silverdale on the night of the wedding. Weeping and lost, he went amongst the Puri and stayed eight years with us. Left alone with a husband who did not love her, Aurore devoted herself to her son."

Umri sighed and withdrew her hands from the Coldcloth. "There," she said as she passed it back to Rae. "The tale is almost done. I am tired now."

Sophy said nothing. The tale rang like a bell through her head. Oakheart's mother ran off with Dellbright's father. Oakheart was some kind of inbreed, full of Vorn's genes. She blinked. How many years ago was it that Vorn lived? Why did Umri choose to tell the tale while Sophy was listening? "Why did you tell me that?"

Umri's wine-dark lips quirked at one corner. "Because I could. I can read you like I can read that cloth. You are the one, Lady Sophy. You are the one to change everything. Like a curse, you may inflict this land and dry up the *given* lore. Or you can save it and give us back what is ours. You are too unwieldy for even Hanal to hold."

Sophy narrowed her eyes. "I don't understand what you said. You got all that from reading the Coldcloth. I'm not 'the one'. Aria is."

"Oh no, outlander. Aria is not the one. She is of Argenterra. You are not."

"How can Aria be of Argenterra? That makes no sense."

"It is true. I do not know the how or the why."

Sophy shook her head, doubt mingling with fear.

"I read you while you listened to Aurore's story. While you sat drinking up her bitter fate, you opened yourself to me. I saw what you carry within you. I read the lines of your destiny. Split, it is. I like it not. You are an insipid creature. What skill do you have to choose our fate? None. Oakheart bedding you has not made you a woman. I have the measure of you. Beware of me."

With that, Umri walked out, setting the curtain aflutter as her robes flared around her legs. Sophy turned to Rae, who sat holding the Coldcloth with tears streaking her face.

"Do you believe her, Rae? Is it true? All of it? That I'm the gift?"

Rae turned, her face etched with a tragic expression. "I believe her...she sees true."

Sophy remembered what Lillia said. She had known of one who was wed when presented to Veld. They all knew about Oakheart. About him being Veld's son, about Mara and Daken. She'd always thought they were open and forthright with her, but the truth was always layered, hiding bits of fact in between.

Umri's words about her not being a woman bothered her. It spoke of things to come. Hanal's face loomed in her mind. Dear god, she thought, don't let him be the one to teach me.

Rae stood slowly and turned away, clutching the Coldcloth in her hand.

"Rae," Sophy said softly. "Did you know about it all, you know, about Aurore and your father?"

Rae didn't look at her. "Umri told me a snippet. But that is the full tale. I have never heard it from my father's lips. It is the one tale most fit to be told, yet he never uttered it. I am afraid, my lady, afraid for you and for me. I think out fates are intertwined and I would that it were not so."

"Amen to that," Sophy said, closing her eyes for a few moments. When she opened them again, Rae was gone.

❧ 15 ❧

WHAT TESTS AN OATH

T he curtain parted not long after Rae and Umri had left and Hanal entered. He looked different. Besides the determined look in his eyes, Sophy noticed that he had just washed. His hair, which was usually beneath his headdress, fell down his back. It was crinkled from being braided and hung heavy and thick to his waist. Instead of his usual robes, he wore loose-fitting white trousers and an open sleeveless vest that contrasted with his dark skin. Sophy was distinctly uneasy.

"Are you comfortable, Sophy? Are you hungry yet?" Hanal asked in a silky voice. His manner of speaking caused her to panic further. He was being too nice and somewhere deep inside she responded. Could Hanal have sway over her? In despair she tried thinking about Oakheart and her love for him. Yet, logic told her Oakheart wasn't coming to her rescue at that particular moment and she would have to deal with the situation herself. Chewing her lip, she took heart in the existence of her oathbond.

With his mesmerising crystal-blue eyes, he studied her. "You are not hungry enough." A fold of skin formed between his eyebrows and his lips tightened. "Disappointing."

Sophy lowered her gaze. She dared not admit to eating for it would void their agreement and he might resort to more drastic measures. "Can you sense the *given* more now?" she asked hopefully.

He undid her bonds. "Sit quietly while I study you."

Once free of her bounds, the blood rushed back into her hands and they burned. She rubbed at them and tried to keep quiet.

After a moment he got up and left the room. Within a minute he was back with a tray of food. The aroma made her stomach churn.

A smile lifted Hanal's mouth. "That is better. Desire for food will help you, I think."

Hanal held a plate under her nose. It looked and smelt like honey-baked toffel bread—Oakheart's favourite. Was Hanal trying to mock her? Aiming her face away from the plate, she clamped her mouth shut.

Hanal edged around to the side where she was facing, tilted his chin and dropped a morsel into his mouth. "Delicious," he said after he swallowed the food. "Are you certain you are not hungry?"

Sophy said nothing. Her stomach spoke for her.

He ate and watched her. Sophy tried to put him out of her mind, but she couldn't. Hanal was eating food in front of her to increase her hunger. She wanted to slap him.

He shuffled over to her. His breath fanned over her face, tasting of spice and honey. With a groan, she shut her eyes. Damn him. He was really pushing this hunger thing. What will he do when...if it doesn't work? *Please work, damn you!*

He studied her longer. "Your barriers are strong, Sophy. I will give it another day."

She nodded.

"Look at me?"

Sophy met his gaze. "Kiss me," he said.

Sophy shook her head. "That wasn't part of the deal. Hunger first, you said."

His gaze slid down her face. "It might be easier and faster to test your oath, slip beneath it, take the power."

"You said we should try hunger, then thirst, then humiliation... testing my oath is a last resort."

Sophy noticed when he stood up that he was aroused. The loose-fitting trousers did not disguise it enough. She closed her eyes to shut out the sight. He wanted to go to the last resort right now. He was playing a dangerous game...

"I did. Make sure you keep your part of the bargain. I will see you tomorrow."

The curtain fluttered in his wake. A few moments passed. Then, against the general background noise, she heard a frantic rhythm of bodies joined in mating. He was sating himself with Rae, she supposed. Thank god for that.

HANAL DID NOT VISIT HER FOR TWO MORE DAYS. RAE HAD obviously received correct orders as Sophy was allowed water but no food. Sophy was weakening. She lay flopped on the floor, not willing to move. Surely she was weakened enough and her barriers down.

Hanal burst in. He stood silently studying her. "It is not working."

Sophy braced herself in a sitting position on the floor with her hands. "I'm sorry. I can't help it. I don't even feel these barriers you speak of."

Clutching his hands together, he breathed, his nostrils flaring. "You do not know what it is like. When I go to Argenterra, I can feel the *given* around me. It is everywhere, in the ground, in the air that I breathe and in the food. Then I return here to the wastelands and my senses seek out the *given* with hunger, with need. I taste its absence. Little pockets exist. Small, thin layers like mist that imbue the water, the creeks, the places where it can seep through the earth. It is a loss. Something my people know only to a certain extent. Some are blissfully unaware of the *given* or its absence. They are the lucky ones. They accept their lot, the barrenness of the wastes and the eking out of an existence."

He dropped to his knees before her, catching her eye, holding it with his. "I know, Sophy. I know what it is they do not have. I feel the wrongness of that."

He pointed to the left. "Not far from here is the Crystal Tree. A chasm divides the land there and the *given* does not reach us. The adepts tell us that is why we have so little *given*. I tell you this. They lie. They keep the *given* from us. Deliberately."

Sophy didn't know how to respond. It was obvious that he believed that. She didn't know enough about the politics of the place or the intricacies of the retreat. Hanal believed it. Tension rippled from him. She was drawn to his argument and wanted to help him.

"Then deny me water. If you think that will help."

His gaze roamed over her face. "Are you sure?"

"Yes. How long do you think it will take?"

"I do not know." He stood up and went to walk away. "If it does not work I must seek advice." He clenched his fist. "I would that it did work—for our sakes."

◈

ARIA EASED HERSELF OUT OF THE SADDLE AND LOOKED OVER THE terrain. Trees and shrubs grew thickly around. The distant mountains had darkened to deep red as twilight glanced off their peaks. They were near to the valley, but were giving it a wide berth. None wished to encounter Dellbright, especially her.

Oakheart and Meld were making an enclosure for their horses. Lillia was directing their tent to be set up. Aria was thinking about food. The touch of strong hands around her waist startled her. She glanced over her shoulder to see that it was Fern. He was so persistent! She hated to hurt his feelings and she was lonely and miserable and he was nice to her. After so long feeling downtrodden, beholding to Dellbright for any small favour and bowing down to him, Fern's offer of friendship was as irresistible as it was doomed. Aria knew she walked a fine line. Could she act for the right and save Fern pain?

"Please, Fern. You mustn't get close to me. We've discussed this before. There is no hope..." His fingers pressed against her lips. Her eyes widened, but she said no more, startled by the shiver of pleasure his light touch caused. *Was it delight or fear?*

Then the pleasure intensified as he brushed his fingertips across her lips. It was painfully sweet, drawing her out of her well of unhappiness. It was so good to be touched like this, to feel treasured

178

and cared for. Sighing, she looked shyly into his face and witnessed the intensity of his expression. Dark grey eyes studied her. His mouth gentled, revealing full, sensitive lips. "Fern..." she began. He moved closer, his thigh brushing hers.

"Shhh..." he said. "I know." Leaning his head down, he touched his mouth to hers. Aria's thoughts surged. Guilt and betrayal screamed in her mind but Fern held her closer, without deepening the kiss. When he released her, she saw tears caught in his lashes. She was mesmerised by them. He felt deeply and it touched her heart in a way she'd thought it could no longer be touched.

Oakheart called out, and Fern stepped away, stepped back to his duty, leaving Aria standing still and barely breathing. Why had she made the decisions she had? Had Sophy been right all along? Had she failed to question? *Oh yes. I have chosen wrongly and what have I reaped because of it? Unhappiness and dissatisfaction for the rest of my days.*

Clasping her hands together, she struggled to order her thoughts. Fern's attention soothed Dellbright's neglect. Fern's gentleness soothed Dellbright's violence. Yet, there was nothing but pain if she didn't stop Fern from falling in love with her. Or worse still, her with him.

RAE SAT IN THE DARK, HUDDLED WITH HER KNEES PRESSED AGAINST her chest. Hanal had come to her after being with Sophy, but even in his sleep he whispered Sophy's name. Rae was concerned: Sophy was trouble, an object of desire. Nothing good was going to come of her being here. The outlander was not the saviour of the Puri, no matter what Hanal thought, no matter how much she cooperated. Rae could taste trouble on the air.

Was it jealously that plagued her? Had she not seen with her own mind that Sophy would replace her in Hanal's bed? Oath or not, Hanal admired Sophy's newly revealed beauty. Rae loved Hanal, more than her own life. Now she had doubts about his feelings for her.

Could Hanal even know what it was to love? Rae wished that she could teach him, wished she could show him what was in her heart. She lay back with a sigh, letting the cave sounds flow over her. She would be glad when they went back to their tents, to where the breeze blew and the sun beat down.

Sophy was mighty thirsty and beyond hunger. Hanal stood before her, bristling with anger and vitality. "It is not working."

Sophy pushed her hair back over her shoulder. "I'm sorry. I'm doing my best." She tried to recall what his next step was. Humiliation? She closed her eyes to fight the vision of what that might entail. She had thought the starvation and thirst would work before it came to that. Hanal had been patient, but she could see that he was no more.

"We must move to the next step. It is not pleasant. I will summon Umri to give me guidance. Perhaps she will see a way to lower your barriers." He sighed and his eyes travelled over her. "You need to take your clothes off." He lifted his hand, which held some rope.

"You're going to tie me up?"

"Yes." His bright eyes glittered.

Sophy wondered if he was as averse to this as he made out.

"Can't you go away and let Rae tie me up?"

Hanal pressed his lips together. "I could, but it would not make you feel uncomfortable. Well," he shrugged, "not as uncomfortable as stripping before me will."

Sophy hesitated, looking down at the clothes she wore, which weren't much. A loose tunic top and some pants. She licked her lips, stalling.

"You do not wish to help the Puri anymore?" Hanal asked.

Sophy's head shot up. She hadn't forgotten his impassioned speech about how the *given* felt and how the Puri were denied. She did agree that was unfair. The Argenterrans had a life of ease in comparison. Sharing the *given* wouldn't lessen what they had, would it?

Sophy stood up and loosened the trousers and let them fall to the ground. Her cheeks burned with shame as she lifted the tunic over her head. Hanal studied her naked frame. She wanted to slap him for daring to look at her like that. With what exactly? Desire? *No. He has Rae. He isn't interested in me. Besides, I have an oath to Oakheart.*

"Put out your hands."

Sophy let him bind her hands and then he led her to the wall where he secured her hands just above her head. To her shock, he took an ankle and tied it to a ring in the floor.

"Not my legs."

"Yes." He took her other ankle, held it as she fought.

Then he stood and regarded her. Her sex was exposed by her spreadeagled position, her breasts thrust out due to the position of her arms. She thought she saw contemplation in his gaze. Tying her up to humiliate her was just the beginning. What had she set herself up for? Hungry, thirsty and naked. It couldn't get much worse. Or could it?

❧ 16 ❧

THROUGH TO PANAL'S PASS

Oakheart woke up with Sophy's name on his lips, and blinked away sleep. He had been dreaming of her, dreaming of bedding her. What passion there was in that imagined mating. He lay back and wiped sweat from his brow. With a groan, he rolled over and buried his face in his pillow. Hanal would be hurting Sophy by now. He ached to be with her; wanted to save her, but that wasn't within his means. Hanal would not kill her, he reasoned, although that was cold comfort.

Lillia told him he was growing stronger daily, but he hardly noticed. His body was heavy and unwieldy. It was like he was wearing a suit of clothes instead of being in his own body. To be less than he was lowered his spirits. Improvement gave him cause for hope.

Hanal's probable actions churned him up—Hanal was making a terrible mistake. He would not be able to wield Sophy, even if he could tap into her power. There was too much of it, too potent.

Oakheart dressed and lurched from his tent to help with the horses. He was able to lift a saddle and strap it on. An improvement in health he had to acknowledge. Aria smiled at him when he led her mount towards her.

"You're looking better," she said.

"Thank you, but Sophy needs me. I feel her need through our oath. She is suffering at Hanal's hand."

Aria's green eyes clouded over, focussing her mind far away. "Really? I had hoped she would be all right with the Puri. It is impossible to break her out of there as we are. We must continue to the retreat as we planned. They should be able to help us." She patted Oakheart on the forearm. "I'm sure it will work out." Aria's browed furrowed. "The Puri lands are near the retreat. Do you think she'll feel that you are near? She could even escape. Sophy is very resourceful."

Oakheart thought carefully. "I hope in my heart that it will be so. I hope I have the strength to save her when the time comes. I hope the retreat can heal me, give me back my vitality."

"So do I." Aria's gaze travelled to Fern. Oakheart noticed and bit his lip. Fern deserved to give his heart to a woman who could return his love freely. Aria could never do that.

Daken, what were you thinking the day you conceived Dellbright? Oakheart thought of his mother and began to understand a little of what had driven her to leave her only child for Prince Daken. Love and desire were precarious things. They could loom large and obscure everything. Even logic.

It was logical to go to the retreat, but his emotions dictated a different action. He should ride to the Puri and offer himself up in exchange for Sophy. He ached to do so. But he could not travel on his own, not in his current state.

Meld walked up to him, his expression haggard. The adept had hardly slept since Rufus's cave and spent most nights and days meditating, trying to retrieve what Rufus had ripped from him. It was difficult.

Lillia's belly was filling with her unborn child. He caught her rubbing and stroking the bulge beneath her tunic, staring at Meld as if with longing. Poor Lillia, her good intentions had led her to this. But then again she could not have prevented it, or altered it. Brook chose his own path, had done since he came of age.

There was a shout. It was Fern. Oakheart swung round. His sword was in his tent, but without the strength to use it, it was useless to him. He gestured to Meld and Aria to stay. Aria dragged the adept by the sleeve and hid amongst the horses. There was a thrum of bow strings. Oakheart spotted Lillia crouched in bushes on the edge of the camp.

"What is it?" he hissed as he crawled near to her.

"Puri raiders," she replied, her keen gaze ranging out.

"Fern?" he asked.

Lillia shrugged. Then her eyes narrowed. She had someone in her sights. Her arrow shot from the bow. There was a muffled curse. "He is on the far side of the camp. I know not what has happened to him."

Oakheart slid a finger along the top of his boot, checking for his dagger. He tapped it and then scuttled in the direction Lillia indicated. It was quiet. That did not bode well. The Puri may have surprised his friend. He hoped not. For the first time in his life, he felt unequal to the task at hand. Stealthily, he edged between some bushes, listening to the sounds around him, those that he could hear over the sound of his heart beating. He heard the sound of shuffling, or of someone being dragged. He angled carefully under and through the bushes. He had to be quiet. He saw a dark, bare foot and had to close his eyes to prevent kicked up dirt from temporarily blinding him. Another pair of feet came into view. He waited.

There were only two Puri. Silently, he rolled over to change his viewpoint. He saw the edge of Fern's boot cocked at an angle; his friend was propped up against a rock. His chest rose and fell. The Puri raiders had bound him, somewhat hastily by the look of the twisted ropes. So, thought Oakheart, the Puri were not out searching for them. This was an opportunistic raid.

Then he thought of Aria. At first he thought her oath to Dellbright would protect her from possible Puri degradation, but oaths were weakening. Oakheart had to assume that Aria and Meld were well for the moment since Lillia guarded them. It was his job to save Fern without getting caught. The Puri would certainly recognise him. In his role as ambassador, he had visited them often enough and dwelt amongst their tents. His looks and size were distinctive too, so he knew they would recognise him whether they had seen him in person or not.

One of the Puri strode out of the small clearing in a swirl of robes, heading away. The other one, who was bearded and wiry, stood over Fern, dealing a swift kick to his friend's ribs that made Fern grunt. Oakheart thought that Fern may still be conscious, but faking stupor to his captives. Such a tactic would not last long against torture.

Oakheart measured up the distance. Using his bulk and taking a gamble on how alert Fern was, he crouched low and half lunged, half sprinted at the unsuspecting man. The Puri gaped at him while at the same time drawing his weapon. Oakheart focussed his will and landed on him, bringing him down with a thud. A *whoop!* exploded out of the fallen man as the breath was knocked out of him. His weapon spun out of his hand to scud in the dirt a body length away. Oakheart glanced down. The man's eyes were wide, the whites showing around his dark pupils. Oakheart had his dagger pressed to the man's throat. The man could barely swallow because the blade would cut the skin of his neck.

Oakheart put his lips next to the man's ear. "Stay quiet. Unwrap your belt, slowly, or you will not need it anymore."

With a nod, the Puri man undid his cloth sash with a shaky hand and dragged it from underneath himself. Oakheart took it from the raider and tossed it near Fern.

Sliding off his captive but keeping the blade at his throat, Oakheart whispered in his ear. "Now roll on your face slowly. I am not afraid to use this knife," he warned when he saw the calculating look that came into the man's eyes. That look was replaced with resignation. Oakheart would not kill the Puri but he would disable him if needs be.

The Puri man flopped onto his belly. Oakheart pressed his knee between the man's shoulder blades. The raider responded with a soft grunt but otherwise kept quiet. Gripping the dagger in his teeth, Oakheart deftly tied the man's hands and then his ankles. Next he ripped the edge of the Puri man's robe, rolled him on his back, shoved the cloth in his mouth and thumped him across the head. His captive lolled and then lay still.

Oakheart panted, close to fainting. Not a good sign for they were not in the clear yet. He staggered over to Fern and dropped to his knees next to his friend.

"Fern? Fern." His friend's face was ashen, his cheeks cool to the touch. Oakheart undid Fern's ties and chafed his wrist. "Fern, wake up.

We must move. For the life of me, I cannot carry you." Oakheart experienced anew the absence of his health and strength. He had taken it for granted and now, when he needed it most, it was gone.

Oakheart grew alert to the presence behind him before he heard any hint of movement. He surreptitiously slid his dagger back into his boot and turned slowly, still on his knees. A spear point was thrust nary an inch from his nose. He tried not to look at it.

"So...this is the *high king*'s ambassador. You will fetch a nice price," lisped the middle-aged Puri raider with an accent so thick Oakheart barely understood him. The older man regarded Oakheart from beneath his headdress. His ornate dagger hilt showed above his sash. He was stocky for a Puri, his eyes light brown, almost yellow. His teeth were brown stumps in his smiling mouth. Oakheart was not heartened by his pleased expression.

"Stand up and move away from my captive...excellency." He inclined his head in a mock bow.

Oakheart hesitated lest he fall on his face and reveal his weakness. He kept his eyes down; he did not want to reveal that Lillia and the others were still in the camp. He hoped to convince the Puri that he and Fern travelled alone. That thought was immediately quenched when Lillia was negligently tossed to the ground in front of him. She was unconscious. When he saw the blood leaking from her forehead, his stomach sank.

Four more Puri stepped out of the bushes and surrounded him. "Stand up or I will skewer you where you kneel."

Closing his eyes, Oakheart focussed on putting all his strength into his legs. He pushed up off the ground and climbed to his feet as elegantly and as neatly as he could. The dark eyes of the Puri watched him. He set his feet apart and locked his knees together, giving the appearance of bravery and vigour.

The old Puri bowed in the Puri fashion. "I am called Kraynen, after the silver-scaled lizard that lives in the wastelands. Nasheen said you might come this way."

Oakheart's eyes widened. Kraynen would gain enough from that mere acknowledgement alone.

Kraynen pressed his spear into Oakheart. Not with sufficient strength to injure him, only to bruise his flesh through his clothes. "Nasheen did not say what I was to do with you. Do you have any suggestions? I know that Hanal would like your liver delivered to him, or perhaps it was another piece of you that he was after." He dipped the point of the spear momentarily. Kraynen lifted an eyebrow with a menacing, brown, toothless smile. The other Puri men laughed at his joke.

"Let us go, then," Oakheart replied, hoping to lead them away from Aria and Meld. "I am keen to speak with Hanal myself, preferably while I have all my bits."

"Hah. I knew you would say something like that. Perhaps I should be the high king's ambassador." Kraynen pirouetted, an approximation of a courtly dance. "What do you think?"

Oakheart stood blank-faced. Underneath, he seethed at his physical impotence. If he had been whole the Puri would not be mocking him.

"No?" Kraynen smiled at Oakheart's expression.

Oakheart unclenched his jaw and curled his fists. "The Puri will pay for this outrage...I have travelled the Puri lands freely for years...yet you...threaten us..."

The spear came up under his chin. "But who will be left to tell of it? With the binding oath undone, we are free to rid this place of you." He gestured with his other hand, throwing it out expansively. "No one will ever know what happened to the high king's heir. And when we Puri rule, none will care."

"Kill them," someone shouted from the bushes behind them.

Kraynen's head jerked around in search of the voice. His men eyed the bushes around them, their faces puzzled. Oakheart grabbed the shaft of the spear and pulled. Kraynen overbalanced and fell to his knees. Mellow came flying out of a bush, landing on his two feet, and kicked another Puri to the ground. Next Illart and Raven tackled another and knocked him out. Kraynen knelt in front of Oakheart with surprise etched on his face. Fern chose that moment to wake with a loud grunt that made Kraynen flinch.

The Puri were subdued and huddled in a circle on their knees. Oakheart did his best to hide his weakness so he pulled his shoulders back and willed his fatigue into the background.

"When we leave," Oakheart said to the Puri raider, "go home and tell them of your offence. Nasheen breached every accord with Argenterra when he took my wife. Now you add to this insult. Tell your people we will send our demands for reparations soon, or every Puri man, woman and child will know the wrath of Argenterra. You know the binding oath is undone. Do you choose to visit death on all those you love? Be careful of who lets the first blood. The Ancient Evil will once again come to live amongst us and taint our world."

Kraynen's eyes widened. He trembled and bowed his head. "You speak true. I like not this place without the binding oath. There is much potential for violence in us. You will acknowledge that I have not killed."

"For that I am thankful." The old Puri put up his hands for Oakheart to bind. Oakheart knelt opposite him to undo his sash and wrap his wrists tight. "Thank you, old man," Oakheart said. "I appreciate you respecting the binding oath though it may no longer hold you." Oakheart looked up. "Wait!"

It was too late. Mellow clubbed the old man senseless with one thwack. Oakheart shook his head. With a sigh, he arranged Kraynen so he could still breathe and made him comfortable.

Mellow knelt next to Lillia and drew her into his lap. Anger and sadness mingled in his face. "Lillia. My heart. Please wake up. Speak to your Mel."

Lillia lay still, breathing quietly in her husband's arms.

Fern swayed on his feet. "Aria...oh by the *given*....Aria!" He staggered towards the camp, pushing bushes and branches out of his way.

Illart offered Oakheart a hand and a smile. Oakheart took it, but didn't climb to his feet. "I thank you," he said and gave a nod to Raven. "We must leave this place at once."

"But Lillia," Mellow said, grinding out the words.

"Bring her with you, Mellow. More Puri may be near. Illart, Raven, can you aid me?"

The forest folk exchanged glances and then came to help Oakheart stand up. He leant on them. "Thank you."

Mellow gathered Lillia in his arms and stood. A wiry fellow, Mellow did not look as if he had the strength to carry his wife. Yet he did and carried her back to camp.

"Brook!" Mellow shouted when he spied his son. He did a double-take when he saw the eyes and faltered. He dropped to his knees gently and placed Lillia on the ground, then looked back up at Meld. "Do I get no greeting from my son? What has happened to you all? Oakheart is as weak as a newborn babe and you...you are different. I fear to ask you...but you will tell me nevertheless."

"Mellow...now is not the time..." Oakheart began.

Mellow quieted him with a fierce flash of his gaze, his mouth an angry cut across his face. The forest man climbed to his feet and approached Meld, staring at the adept as if his eyes alone would reveal the truth. "No, Oakheart," Mellow said, his voice grounding out his dread. "'Tis the time...the only time. What has happened to my son?"

Meld returned Mellow's stare. "I am not Brook anymore," Meld replied, his voice thin and tired. The adept turned away, ignoring Brook's father and all the emotional ties to the forest folk. His blue robes fluttered and flared as he stepped away.

Mellow lunged, grabbing Meld by the shoulder, and spun him around. "What are you then if not the flesh of my flesh?"

Meld's blue eyes shone like gems out of Brook's face. "The Brook that you know is gone. I am called Meld. I was once Adage and Brook together, sharing a space, but now we are one."

Oakheart saw the rage, the hate, the despair come by turns across Mellow's face. If there was a man who looked ready to kill with his bare hands, then Mellow was it.

"Mel," Lillia called weakly from behind him. Mellow rocked back on his heels, halting the imminent attack on Meld's person. "Mellow, please help me."

Mellow spun round, his jaw grinding. Oakheart saw tears in the forest man's eyes. "My heart?"

Lillia's eyes fluttered open. "Mellow. Oh Mellow. Our son."

He knelt down next to her, taking her hands and rubbing his face against them.

"How can you bear it?" Mellow's shoulders shook with repressed sobs. He traced his hand across his wife's brow.

Lillia shook her head slowly. "I do not, knowing what you would feel, what you would do. It is difficult to mourn a lost one when his body is still living. But that...Meld," she swallowed "is not our son...anymore."

Oakheart looked away while Lillia and her mate comforted each other. He could only be an observer to their grief. Adage had been close to him. He was glad that Adage had not passed away completely. Yet this situation was perplexing to say the least.

Fern brought Aria back with him. She was hale, her hair only slightly more unwieldy than usual with a few twigs from where she had been hiding in the bushes. She supported Fern and bade him to sit so she could tend his head wound. Oakheart's friend was even more colourless than previously.

When Oakheart realised that he was still standing and that his strength had not failed him completely, he managed to smile. The addition of the forest folk had expanded their number, which was a good thing, but did make them more visible.

"Come, we must move on from here. We have not the means to take the Puri prisoner so we will have to leave them. They will free themselves eventually and we best not be close by when they do. I do not think they will follow us, but we may meet more raiders. The weather is warmer so they will be on the move. Soon their tent pennons will beat time with the wind at their summer camp. When they are gathered there, they may decide to attack Argenterra with a bigger force."

Lillia sat forwards. "Do you mean war? Then we must warn people."

"I fear it is so. We can warn Silverdale from the retreat for they have a talkstone there. Not too distant from there is the Puri's camp. I know where their tents will be. Aria...princess...I must go to Sophy's aid. Hanal harms her, wounds her spirit. Even now I feel it."

Aria looked up from tending Fern. Her eyes were haunted. "Yes, Oakheart. I understand, but you are still too weak to travel on your own."

Meld halted, turned back and strode into their midst. Ignoring all the others, he said to Oakheart, "You must seek the aid of the retreat. That is where you best serve Argenterra."

Oakheart swallowed his denial. "I hear you, Meld. But you cannot guarantee that the retreat will be able to retrieve Sophy. I feel her pain. I cannot bear her suffering. For now our path to the retreat and Puri lands is the same. I will wait till the parting of ways to decide which way I will go."

Mellow stood, ignoring Lillia's hands that tried to tug him back down, and said to Meld, "We do not move until you tell us what happened to my son, and why it cannot be undone." Mellow's eyes met Oakheart's. "I do not wish to withdraw aid from you, Oakheart, but the adept must explain himself."

"Mellow..." Oakheart tried to put some command in his voice.

"No...Oakheart, dear friend," Lillia said from the ground. Her chin was held proudly, and she did not bother to wipe at the blood that trickled down to her chin. "In this I support my husband. The taking of a life is a terrible thing. Although Adage did not intend it, his actions contributed to it. We must have an accounting so that Brook's tale will be told at the Heart Tree in Queens' Town."

Meld turned away, his shoulders rigid. "I do not have time for this. Go if go you must. I am not accountable to you."

"Adage," Oakheart said. "Adage...Brook was their son...they have a right, whether you acknowledge that right or not. I myself wish to hear how one as skilled and experienced in *given* lore as you was undone by Rufus. If his power was so great then why did he not use it before? Did he gain in power once he had Sophy?"

"You waste precious time, Oakheart." Adage turned his strange eyes on Oakheart.

"Please, Adage," Aria said, stepping away from tending Fern. "There is much I don't know about all of this. You hint, but that's all. Lillia served Sophy and me with selfless love and sacrifice. Brook served the Adepts' Retreat in the same way. Isn't an explanation a kind of payment for that?"

"I have explained already what happened. Rufus's power reached through Brook to me. I am sundered from my body—perhaps it is even now dead."

Lillia stook an unsteady step towards the adept. "Where is the spirit of my son, Brookfell Treesinger?"

The adept did not acknowledge them, but stared blankly at some invisible point. "Gone from here," he answered softly.

Lillia pressed on. "Gone how? How was it separated from his body?"

"It was not—separated." Adage glanced at Oakheart and in that look Oakheart saw fear.

Oakheart licked his dry lips. "Then Brook still lives?" he whispered in awe.

Adage sighed. "I think he must. That is why I call myself Meld. What was once Brook is part of me, and I am part of him. I am less than I was and so is he. Only time will tell me what that means. I cannot range out over the land using the *given* to reveal its mysteries. I cannot speak with the retreat. I feel so cut off. Not for five hundred years have I been so inept and unskilled.

"This body is strange to me. I experience things that I have not done for a long time: a stirring, discomfort, hunger and thirst."

"And Rufus? How did he get so strong?" Aria asked, walking up to stand behind Oakheart.

Meld's gaze passed over Lillia and Mellow, a faint smile of regret on his face. "In this I was a fool. Sophy...the jewel, is unnatural to this place. For many days, weeks even, it drew the *given* to it and stored it within itself. As the *given* lessened Rufus was able to draw more on his power, which is not native to this place. I surmise, I have no proof, that he could not use it freely while the *given* was so strong in Argenterra. It is sourced in the Ancient Evil. She, herself, cannot enter here as Vorn barred her way, but through her agent she can reach into the heart of Argenterra, feed him her power. As the *given* waned, his power grew."

Oakheart thought about the time since Sophy and Aria arrived in Argenterra. He remembered the arrow birds, the river, the forest...all subtle uses of power. "I see. He could not act openly at first. Else he would have taken Sophy straight away. No need for the attacks...no need for hesitation. Enchantments and subterfuge." Then Oakheart remembered the ball. "He was afraid of me so he must have been vulnerable then."

Adage seemed to sag. "I underestimated him. It saddens me for now the jeopardy is great. We must put aside our personal troubles. We must work together to prevent the *given* from being depleted. I must go to the retreat as soon as may be."

"And Sophy?" Aria and Oakheart spoke in unison and shared a glance.

"We need the *ungiven* girl at the retreat, too. But you are weak, Oakheart. Aria must not fall into the Puri's hands. She can wield Sophy's power. With the two outlanders together, Hanal will be invincible. For this reason we must take Princess Aria to the retreat and there work to deliver Sophy into your hands. I can see no other way."

"Let me go to the Puri." Fern stood a little shakily and glared at everyone. "I will barter myself for her release. He wants a husband for his sister. Why not me?"

Adage's laugh surprised them all. "You think you are worth the equal of Sophy to Hanal? I do not think so. Hanal knows by now what he holds. He is not without means. The Puri may not send gifted ones to the retreat but they are not without skill or learning. This much I know from gazing upon all the lands."

"I may not be Sophy's equal," Fern replied, eyes stony, "but I can offer him an alliance, a marriage for his sister. I am not so highly placed as Oakheart, but I am in line for the high king's throne if anything happens to him."

Oakheart watched Aria's face. She tried to hide her disappointment and did not voice a protest. She had no call on Fern. It made Oakheart proud to see her restraint, for he was sure one word from her would be all it took to turn Fern from this path.

Adage turned to him. "Does he speak true? I am afraid his lineage is unknown to me. He is not strong in the *given* and as such has been beneath my notice. I care not for these things normally."

"He speaks true. He is close kin. His offer may not satisfy Hanal enough to release Sophy, but it could make him more amenable to negotiation."

"Very well," Meld said, drawing his robes around him. "We will continue up Panal's Pass. Where the road divides between the retreat and the Puri summer camps we will consult again. Fern, your offer may be useful. But for now we must move."

Mellow sat caressing Lillia. The anger in his expression had dissipated now that she was awake and appeared unharmed. Oakheart hoped that the forest folk would accept Meld in time. Perhaps for Lillia and Mellow, the possibility that Brook still lived on as part of Meld would help to assuage their grief.

Oakheart shared a look with Fern, who nodded in return. It was ironic that Fern would give himself to save Sophy after all the taunts and ridicule he had aimed at her. Oakheart only hoped that Veld would agree to the match. His father was dead set against any alliance with the Puri. Yet Oakheart saw the political necessity, saw the pressures building between their people. And now the tensions between their nations had heightened. Oakheart could smell something dire on the wind. War. A terrible war. Without the binding oath, death would visit Argenterra and in its wake the Ancient Evil would come to feed and the *given* would flee. Such were the possibilities.

❦ 17 ❦

BITTER DRINK, POISONED CUP

Pain woke Sophy, a terrible ache in her arms that grew in her mind until she could no longer ignore it. She had fallen asleep with her wrists taking all her weight. Standing up, she eased the pressure, but the throbbing worsened, making her gasp. Then she noticed she wasn't alone.

The dark-eyed woman who had read Aurore's tale from the Coldcloth sat there looking at her. Sophy flushed as the woman studied her nakedness pointedly.

"This will not do." The woman shook her head and pursed her lips.

Sophy lifted her chin and narrowed her gaze. "What business is it of yours?"

"Hanal has asked for my help and you, outlander, are not suffering enough. There is not even a slight crack in your barrier."

The curtain behind billowed. "What do you suggest, Umri?" It was Hanal.

"Bring me a cane."

There was silence for a heartbeat or two. Sophy wasn't sure she'd heard correctly but her heart kicked up a beat.

"No. Hanal, we had a deal!" Sophy protested, trying to see Hanal behind the curtain. She couldn't believe it. Hanal was giving her over to this woman.

"Very well," Hanal said, voice low, hushed as if he didn't want anyone else to hear. Sophy thought it was shame. Damn straight he should be ashamed. Giving her over to this woman—a woman who wanted to beat her.

When Umri stood up, Sophy flinched.

Umri's mouth tilted in a small grin, her dark eyes bright as she drew near. "Strange that Oakheart found you attractive. Thin, pale creature that you are. Lyant would have pleased him in bed and bore him lusty sons." Umri pinched the skin of Sophy's upper arm, then cupped her right breast, shaking her head. "His loss."

Sophy bit back a response. Rae appeared at the curtain, bearing a thin stick as long as her arm. Sophy's eyes widened and she called out, "Rae? Don't let her do this. Please."

Rae kept her gaze lowered and shuffled back out of the room on her knees.

Umri laughed softly. "Do not look for comfort from Rae. She is Hanal's and is desperate to please him. You are nothing but an obstacle to her. Rae may have been an Argenterran milksop maid, but now she is a shrewd Puri woman, willing to do anything for her people...and Hanal."

Then without preamble, her arm flew up and flashed back down. The blow landed on Sophy's belly, followed by another across the top of her thighs. Sophy twisted away, but that just gave Umri access to her back. Umri dealt her many swift strikes, over and over. Paralysed by agony, Sophy was caught in a moment, unable to offer even fleeting protection to her body. Beyond crying, beyond pain, passing out gave her a short respite. Until Umri threw water over her. As Sophy regained consciousness, Umri sat on the ground and studied her.

"Well?" Hanal's voice came through the curtain.

Sophy opened an eye, looked down at her body and saw the welts and cuts. Blue bruises were spread across her thighs with raised ridges from the edge of the cane.

"No change. May I borrow your dagger?"

There was a hiss of breath. "Umri?"

Umri put out her hand. "Do you want my help or not?" Umri gathered her robes as if to leave.

A dagger was passed through the curtain. *Hanal, you betrayer!*

Sophy whimpered, thinking Umri was going to cut her throat, but she just grabbed Sophy by the hair and hacked at it.

Chunks of her dark hair fell at her feet. Umri was not gentle. Between cries of pain, Sophy said, "Hanal...please. Don't let her do this...We agreed."

"It was not working, fool!" Umri shook her head, still held by the hair. "He follows my advice now. Only I can help him access your power."

Umri's voice dripped confidence and...satisfaction. Blood trickled in Sophy's eyes as Umri cut her while denuding her scalp.

Sophy broke then, weeping as if she wouldn't stop. Umri grinned, leaving Sophy dangling exhausted and humiliated in her bonds. "More time," Umri said to Hanal as she left the room. "Bring people in to look at her in the meantime. Humiliation must be experienced. Privacy allows her dignity."

✦

THERE DIDN'T SEEM TO BE A PART OF HER BODY THAT DIDN'T HURT. Sophy stared miserably at the uneven roof of the cave and tried to move off her battered and bruised back. After a few tries and muffled whimpering, she found a spot on her hip that didn't hurt as much as the rest of her body and settled onto it. It took her a moment to realise that she had been covered up and her hands untied. She lifted the covers and found that she had been wrapped in a pale robe. From the way she smelled, she'd been bathed too. Blinking a few times, she rubbed her head, trying to piece together what had happened.

Her wrists itched, and she saw the welts from where she had strained against her ties. She didn't want to remember what had happened last night, or was it yesterday? Deep within the cave, she couldn't tell whether the sun shone or if it was raining.

Another visit from Umri would be her undoing, though. She didn't think she could bear it. She had thought Hanal was noble. Now she thought him a sadist because he had let Umri do horrible things to her. Umri enjoyed her struggle, and didn't care for her as a person. She was a thing, a means to an end, a toy to be played with. With a groan, she sat up. She had no memory of who had untied her. It was unlikely to have been Hanal. Rae, perhaps?

The curtain hissed open. Hanal stood there, once again in his loose-fitting trousers and a light robe over his shoulders. The look on his face made her blanch. He stepped out of the room and bellowed, "Who has done this? Who has untied her? Rae!"

Sophy cringed away from his anger. What had she become? After taking a few breaths, she steadied her nerve. She was cowed but not conquered.

Rae came, parting the curtain slowly, and stepped into the room and did not kneel as she usually did. Her ebony-coloured eyes passed over Sophy and then met Hanal's. His body sang with anger, muscles and jaw tensing, fist closing and opening. Sophy feared he would knock Rae out or throttle her.

"Who has interfered with the outlander?" he said in a low, dangerous voice.

"I did," Rae answered in a steady voice, never taking her gaze off him.

Hanal grew taut, his unfurled hair swinging around his waist. "You dared to interfere? You, who are nothing in my household?" His words cut through the air.

Rae held herself still, showing no signs of weakness. "If I am nothing," Rae lifted her chin higher and continued with a quiet dignity, "then I have nothing to lose by defying you and helping her. She was uncomfortable, unnecessarily so..."

Hanal raised his hand, but hesitated. Rae gazed at him, giving no ground. She was obviously with child. His hand closed and he lowered it.

"You think to strike me even though I carry your son?" Rae's expression was pained.

With clenched jaw, Hanal shook himself, puffed out his chest and pushed past Rae without sparing her a look. He spoke in whispers to someone outside.

On his return to the room, he squared his shoulders, shrugging his rage off like a wet cloak. "Did you feed her?" he asked in a business-like fashion.

Rae shook her head. "Not possible as she was unconscious." Something in her tone made Hanal mad. He swung round and yelled in her face. "Sit. You interfering fool."

Rae lifted her eyebrow at his tone, swept her headdress over her shoulder and lowered herself elegantly to the floor. She carefully avoided looking at Sophy and seemed to be staring at some fixed point on the wall.

Hanal sat. A pot of hot tea was brought in by a young male Puri, whom Sophy had never seen before. Rae made no move to serve him. With a wave of his hand, the youth left, but he eyed Rae though the girl refused to look at him. Hanal's face became impassive as he finally poured the tea into a cup and took a sip. "Do you know what you have done?" he said quietly, with an underlying tone of threat and anger. He seemed more in control of his rage, but Sophy shivered. He seemed colder, too, more removed from compassion than she'd ever perceived him to be.

Rae did not answer, nor did she look at him.

Hanal gestured towards Sophy with a sharp flick of his hand. "To break her down, she must be humiliated, feel abandoned, alone. Your act of kindness has taken the edge off our treatment. You have given her mental strength to resist me."

Rae deigned to speak. "You will not succeed. Sophy is too strong for you both."

Hanal scoffed. "What else do you know?"

Rae unfocussed her gaze from the spot on the wall and met his. "Umri serves her own ends."

Hanal stared at her, then sipped his tea. "You seek to recover your place in my household."

Rae shrugged. "You said I am nothing in this household. Therefore, there is nothing to recover."

He pursed his lips but before he could answer her, Umri was ushered in. The seer knelt and pressed her forehead to the carpet. "How may I serve you?"

Hanal did not smile. "Tell me, are you with child yet?"

Umri's inky gaze stilled while the smile on her dewy lips died. "I am not yet certain, venerable Hanal. I believe I may be..."

His look hardened. "You seek to trick me."

Umri pressed herself to the carpet. "I do not. Have I not served you well with this outlander maid?"

"Not really. Her barriers are intact."

Umri's eyes lifted to Sophy and she frowned. "Why is she dressed? Did you not do as I instructed?"

"We did but during the night there were..." his gaze flicked to Rae, "complications."

Umri clenched her mouth, taking in Rae and then Sophy. "Then my work was undone."

Hanal rolled a shoulder and shot a glance at Sophy. "No. There was not even a chink in her barrier. Looking at her now I can see it is as it was when she first arrived. You must think of some other way."

Sophy struggled to sit upright. Pain lanced through her, making her take in a hasty breath. Anger overflowed, washing away all thought of caution. "You did all that to me for nothing? You bastard. You *utter* bastard."

Tears leaked from her eyes. What were they doing to her? She thought she was helping but it was a joke. A joke on her.

Hanal's eyes flicked her way and then he glared at Umri. "What else is there to do? I can no longer be patient."

Something is his expression sent chills down Sophy's spine. A calculating man possessed by a need for power. Umri saw it too, she was sure. The older woman turned her dark gaze her way. Sophy had been wary of the seer, now she was terrified. Nothing would stop this woman. She felt it in her bones.

Standing up, Umri studied her. Something in the quality of the woman's gaze sent shafts of apprehension snaking through Sophy anew. Bile rose in her throat. She still didn't understand what was going on or what powers the woman had. If Umri could read thoughts and memories woven in cloth, perhaps she could delve into her mind.

Capturing Sophy with that elsewhere gaze, Umri loomed large. Fine droplets of sweat gathered between Umri's finely arched eyebrows.

Sophy detected no sensation, but her eyes widened when Umri began to pant and her mouth grimaced with effort. She hoped it was theatrics but there was a pinch and a sensation of burning inside her body. If not for the woman's closeness, Sophy would have waved it off as some flight of fancy.

Then the beautiful Puri woman collapsed to her knees and balanced on her palms, head lolling from side to side. With a trembling hand, Umri wiped her brow, pushed back to her kneeling position and pushed herself next to Hanal's right knee.

"Speak," Hanal demanded. "I would hear what you see in her, right now."

Umri poured herself some tea, hands shaking. After taking a sip, she lowered the cup gingerly and swallowed a mouthful. "There is something powerful there beneath the surface. I hesitate to describe it. I sense power—great power."

Hanal's eyes widened for a fraction of a second. He stared at Sophy, a touch warily. "Yes. Why does she not use it? Why can I not touch it?"

Umri looked her over. Sophy returned her gaze with a defiant stare. "She cannot, I think. Argenterra's *given* does not accept her alienness. She is solely a vessel, a container. She has not the will or the means to fight you for control of it. Fear not that power, as she cannot use it against you."

Rae gasped softly, covering her mouth with her hand. Was that pity in her gaze, Sophy wondered?

"Ahh...what you say makes sense. Nasheen told me of his sojourn with Oakheart. An adept was travelling with them, who constantly fretted because the crystal was drawing the *given* from the land. She is a talisman. Indeed, Nasheen said that Oakheart urged him to destroy the crystal if he and his fellows failed to return his oathbound back to human form. Do any of the ancient writings tell of this?"

Umri shrugged. "My knowledge comes from another place."

Hanal's arm snaked out and grabbed the seer's arm and shook her. "I must have access to that power. You must tell me how."

Umri's brow creased. Her succulent lips parted with an "Oh" of surprise. Hanal's eyes bored into her face, and he undid his grip slowly, never taking his gaze from her. Umri rubbed her arm when he released it. It took her a while to think up an answer or to calculate another plan. Sophy realised that Umri was desperate to appease Hanal, to win his favour. Rae, though, she was less sure about. Some struggle was going on inside the young woman, and she wondered if it was Hanal's obsession with his prisoner that was the cause of it. She hoped the girl would take pity on her and help her escape.

Umri bowed low then eased up off the floor, keeping her eyes lowered respectfully. "Drug her. Remove her conscious control and weaken her will. Only then can you touch her power."

"Yes!" Hanal radiated excitement.

"But not here—if you are successful you will hold a dangerous power in your hands. In our tents you must do this. 'Tis only a few days and we depart. Wait until then, I urge you."

Hanal smiled. "No. We leave for our tents today. Brew your drug, Umri. Tomorrow we will use it."

Sophy shivered in spite of herself and held her breath.

Hanal touched Umri's chin and smiled at her. "You will help me, Umri. You will guide my hand as my seer."

Umri shook, trembling with desire perhaps, as Hanal's fingers ran along her dewy lips. She swallowed once and glanced nervously towards Sophy. "As you wish, Hanal. I will serve you and aid you."

From within her sleeve, Umri drew out a small piece of folded cloth. She opened it and dropped a pinch of black powder into a cup, mixing in some left-over tea.

"Give her this. It will keep her docile for the move."

"Good," Hanal said, letting his breath sigh out of him. He stared at the cup, eyes glittering.

Hanal mixed the powder into the tea, and came to Sophy cup in hand. "Rae," Hanal said, in a voice laden with sugar. "Come, little sister, you will pour this into her mouth, while I hold her."

Rae was drawn to him, her expression once again one of love. Sophy saw her hand reach out. She couldn't believe the betrayal. Rae had helped her and now she would harm her.

"No. No, please," Sophy began. "I don't know anything about power. Please don't do this. I don't want power..." she babbled as Hanal closed in on her. He sat, dragged her to him and pulled her hard up against him. With his right hand, he lifted her chin, easing his thumbs into her jaw so that her mouth opened. Sophy got ready to spit the contents out. But Hanal held her nose. She tried to struggle free of his grip and suffocation but his powerful thighs held her. Her face hurt, her lungs burned, she had to breathe, and when she did, Rae poured the contents of the cup down her throat. Hanal covered her mouth with a hand, holding her jaw tight. The liquid burned the back of her throat and nose. A few drops dribbled from her nostrils. She stared up at Rae's face, pleading in her eyes as she bucked, fighting to the last.

Rae looked at her with a sad expression, rocked back on her heels and stood. When the last of the liquid had slid down Sophy's throat, Hanal's hold relaxed. When the curtain closed behind Rae, who followed Umri out, Sophy felt her world bottom out.

It was quiet in the room. Just her breathing and that of Hanal while he waited. Her heart began beating double time. Her senses were on high alert, searching for the drug's effect. It seemed that Hanal stared at her for about ten minutes without speaking—and then she was swallowed by fatigue.

⚜

STILL GROGGY FROM THE AFTER-EFFECTS OF THE DRUG, SOPHY CAME to. Her tongue was parched. She still hurt everywhere. Again, she was naked and bound and she vividly remembered Umri beating her.

Her thirst was great. A bowl of water was nearby. She edged over to it, despite the matting burning her knees. When she managed to angle her face over the bowl, she stuck her head in to drink deeply, spilling half the contents to the floor. It had a sweet taste, like the tea. Too late, she realised it was drugged and moaned in despair. Already the edges of the room were becoming fuzzy, so she closed her eyes and let the drug send her to oblivion.

Later, a light slap on her cheek brought her to wakefulness. Her vision clarified once or twice only to blur again in a drugged haze. "Wake up, whore," the woman's voice said.

Sophy blinked and a face she recognised took shape. Lyant? The graceful, contained girl she'd met at Silverdale stood before her. Hanal's sister and the woman seeking Oakheart's hand in marriage.

"What do you want, Lyant?" she said thickly with a dry mouth and tongue.

Lyant smiled and arched her finely plucked eyebrow. "You took my husband from me, did you not?"

Sophy shook her head. "I'm sorry if you thought he was yours. I didn't realise."

"Liar. I was there. Hanal spoke of it. You knew when you let Oakheart's manhood puncture you, that he was mine."

Sophy flinched at the coarseness of her expression "Yes, I knew Hanal desired the match. I didn't know that you did. If I hurt you I'm sorry for it."

Lyant laughed in her face. "Oh how precious you are. How was he? Hanal is more of a man, I think. What say you?"

Sophy had trouble keeping hold of reality. "What?"

"Do not act all innocent with me. You desire my brother."

Lyant's soft hand traced the curve of Sophy's breast. Then softly she ran her fingers along the welts on Sophy's back and buttocks and legs, as if mesmerised by the destruction Umri had wrought. "What did it feel like to be beaten?" she asked, breathing in short pants as if the sight of the harm was exciting to her.

Sophy wailed and choked off with a sob that left her gagging for breath.

"Interesting answer. I cannot afford to have my skin marked in such a way. But I do wonder what it feels like. The pain and the pleasure combined. To lose control and surrender to it, to another's hand, to really grovel, to beg for mercy and mean it with all your heart. I have never had the pleasure myself, but I often think about it." Lyant's eyes stared into space, no doubt imagining such subjugation. Sophy was sure the reality of it would change the other woman's mind. Lyant reached out to touch her again but Sophy pulled back. "Go away. Leave me alone."

"I disgust you? Me? Virginal me?" The Puri woman laughed. "You chose wrong, child, when you bedded Oakheart. Hanal was the right choice for you...but he is not now. There is danger for you now unless you give him what he wants."

Tears dampened her lashes; she was frightened by Lyant, so beautiful and so strange. "I know. Help me. Please."

Sophy was having trouble keeping awake. Lyant's image blurred, and faded in and out.

The girl stood and twirled around, her Puri costume flaring around her. Her embroidered trousers, the full apron, the headdress combined into a riot of colour. The sound of her laughter was in Sophy's ears as she lost consciousness again.

⚜

THERE SEEMED TO BE A LONG PERIOD OF MOVEMENT, VAGUE recollections of consciousness that didn't equate to awareness. Sensations of heat, of smothering cloth and smells that converged and overwhelmed.

Sophy emerged into wakefulness, but the odour of the caves was gone. The air was dry, laced with a fine dust that lingered in her nose and the back of her throat. The clean smell of fresh water neared, a cup was pressed against her lips. She drank deeply, greedily, and slurped the water till it ran down her chin. When the cup was empty, she dared to open her eyes.

Her eyeballs were irritated and scratchy as if layered in fine grit. Rae's face took shape in front of her. There was a smile around the younger woman's eyes.

Rae leant in closer and whispered, "Is that better? You can have more water but sips only this time. It will help flush the drug from your system."

Sophy nodded; it was all she could manage. The whole world seemed to vibrate when she moved her head. "Rae?" she asked, shocked by the sound of her own voice, which sounded like that of a lost child.

"Yes, my lady, 'tis me." Rae undid her bindings. Sophy lost consciousness for a minute or two, because when she was next sensible Rae was bathing her with warm scented water. Rae's touch was filled with kindness. Sophy nearly cried because of the young girl's tenderness.

"Rae? Did Hanal ask you to do this?"

Rae shook her head. "He will be angry when he finds out. But he is busy now, settling disputes amongst the clans. We have moved to the summer tents. Every year families vie for space close to the clan leader. Those who have lost favour go to the outer perimeter and those new to favour, or who have done Hanal a service beyond the call of clan ties, are brought closer or presented *dulab,* payment. His attention is elsewhere for the moment."

"I see. Then it is not over yet..."

Rae used a cloth to wipe Sophy's face. "No, not over yet. But you have a respite..."

Sophy clasped her hand. "Rae, you must help me. I have to get away from him. He broke our agreement. I don't trust him and I definitely don't trust Umri. They are going to drug me. With a drug stronger than the ones they have used already. I'm so frightened. Please...Umri is powerful. Together they will..."

Rae's brow creased. "I know. But Hanal is my..." Rae shook herself. "I am Hanal's by choice. He is obsessed with you, or this power he says you have. I cannot see it myself. I do not know if it is real. He is so focussed on you that it pains me, cuts my heart until it bleeds. Umri encourages it. For her own ends, I am sure." Rae sighed. "I cannot see where it will end. Hanal has lost his honour. He is diminished in my eyes."

Rae helped Sophy to more water and then assisted her to dress in a light robe. At least it was something to hide her nakedness. She shivered at the thought of what new humiliation Hanal would force on her in his quest for power. If she had power, she didn't know how to use it and couldn't even sense it.

This time, Sophy slept like the dead. Eventually, the pall of the drug faded, leaving her heavy and dull but with a glimmering of her old self. A yell of outrage woke her. Her eyes fluttered open and she let out a groan and then almost cried. Hanal was back with his seer in tow.

The Puri leader's hands flew into the air, sending his robe rippling with anger.

"Who has done this? By the water that flows with the *given*, it is Rae meddling again. Rae. Come here." His voice was as heavy as a club, his accent, usually controlled, thickened. Sophy's stomach clenched. What would he do to her helper?

Umri lowered herself to the woven rug spread across the tent floor, kneeling with forehead pressed to the ground. Perhaps Umri hoped Hanal's rage would wash over her and she would escape it entirely. Sophy wished the strange woman would bear the brunt of it.

Rae entered but didn't kneel. "Yes, Hanal. You called for me?" Rae asked in a composed voice.

"You dare interfere again after the warning I gave you last time? I left specific instructions that no one was to touch her. Again you defy me."

Rae seemed to be ignoring him. She stood up, walked past Umri and headed towards Sophy. Disbelief was etched over Hanal's face as he watched her. Rae knelt down and held a cup of water under Sophy's nose. "Here, drink this."

Before Sophy could take a sip, Hanal had swiped the cup from Rae's hands and sent the pregnant woman sprawling. "You dare to thwart me to my face! I will have you thrown out."

Rae ground her teeth together and stood to her full height, which must have been all of five foot. "You have no honour, Hanal of Puri." He growled, and clenched his fist. She lifted her chin higher. "No, Hanal," she said unwaveringly, like the words had been in her mouth for a week waiting to be spoken. "You will not throw me out. For if you do, I will return to the valley with your child in my belly. I will marry a farmer, an Argenterran one," she added for emphasis, "and there your child will live in mediocrity, unknown and untold in any tale. He will grow up ignorant of his heritage; he will marry a farmer's daughter and live all his days as the lowliest peasant."

Sophy was fascinated by Rae's threat. Hanal's face changed from outrage to horror with each of her words. "You carry a son?" he said weakly.

Rae spared Umri a glance. The seer was smiling, then covered up her enjoyment when Hanal turned to her. "I see that she carries your son. If you throw her out before she births the child you will have no claim to it according to our laws." Umri climbed to her feet gracefully. "If you strike her, you will have to face a gathering of the clans for judgement for you would endanger the child's life."

Hanal reacted to Umri's words. "I did not endanger the child. I wanted to slap her but withheld my hand." His face clouded over. "Manipulated by you both, I see it clearly. If I did not need you, Umri, I would throw you out of my clan, regardless that you are my brother's wife."

In two steps, he had Umri by the wrist, had her grimacing against the pain he inflicted. "Where is my nephew, eh? Time grows short. You will give my brother a child. I care not what sex."

Umri stared at Hanal, an expression of disbelief overshadowing her face. "I carry his child," she said through clenched teeth. "It is early days, but I..." Her expression let slip some of her deeper feeling. She was both devoted to, and despised, her clan leader. Sophy knew it and Umri's gaze slid to hers as if she too knew what she had let slip.

The Puri leader smiled and let her slide from his grip. "Then we are even. When you birth this child, this healthy child, you and Tarkel will start your own clan."

Umri gasped and said, "No."

Hanal nodded. "I will not have you near me after this. You think I am ignorant but I see your machinations quite clearly. I will not have you weaving your web of intrigue around me any further. If you do the same to Tarkel, try to manipulate him to your own ends, then I will ensure that he takes another wife. Your humiliation alone will be enough revenge for me."

Umri's eyes widened. "No, my husband would not do this. He is devoted to me."

"How long will he be devoted to you when I tell him of our relationship and how deep it went? You forget I worded his oath to you, woman," Hanal said, showing his cunning. "He was to cling to you, but not only to you. You are bound to him without reprieve, but he is not. You think you are smarter...but I have studied oaths." His face turned to Sophy and he nodded slightly, confirming to her that it was not over yet.

Umri bowed her head and acknowledged him silently. She would be a headman's wife; perhaps that was enough for her. Sophy didn't know. But she didn't like what she saw in the woman's eyes.

"Rae, you will leave us." He didn't look at the girl. Rae lowered her head, and then left the tent.

Sophy watched her leave with an inner wail. *Please don't leave me with them!*

RAE FLED FROM HANAL'S TENT, KEEPING HER HEAD LOW TO HIDE her tears. She was angry and she was heartbroken. Never did she think her love for Hanal would be tested in this way. She could see the wrong of what he was doing. Part of her thwarted him to save him from himself. She paused outside the immediate circle of tents. Hanal's shouts had probably been heard by everyone. It hurt her pride to have him yell at her, shame her. She'd given so much up for him, to be with him, for the love of him.

Sunlight beat down upon her head. Already it was hot. Dampness built under her arms and trickled down her back. She had nowhere to go. Her eyes fell upon a collection of urns. Water? She could collect water. It was late in the day for such a chore but at least she would be spared the stinging tongues of the Puri women as they gathered elsewhere; at least, she hoped so.

The path to the spring was winding, hidden by tall boulders and the occasional Neal Nut tree. Balancing the urn on her shoulder, she walked lost in her thoughts. There did not appear to be others on the path. With a sigh, she let her thoughts flow. There was much to consider.

At the water's edge, she knelt, watching the dark pool as the liquid slid into the neck of the urn. It was heavy. She tried to tug it loose from the mud. The small round bulge of her belly shifted slightly, making her start. The child had moved within her. A small rejoicing was called for, but a tear slid down her cheek instead. Ordinarily she would have gone to Hanal and told him of the new quickening of life within her. What point was there now, when he was obsessed with Sophy and her hidden power? Rae had thought she had won the battle with Umri, and now she realised with bitterness that Umri had snared her once again, entwining her in her intrigues to be the first in Hanal's eyes.

A dark hand landed on hers. A first she panicked and then realised someone was trying to help her lift the urn and put it on the bank. Blinking away the setting sun, she looked up and saw a dark shape, a man in silhouette. Before she could draw breath to speak, she was tugged to her feet and hugged.

"Father?" she asked as she took in the feel of him, more certain than ever that it was Kushlan.

"Oh Rae," Kushlan said, with a voice full of emotion. He relaxed his grip and held her from him, looking her up and down. "Please tell me 'tis not true."

The happiness inside of her froze to become a knife of dread slicing through her gut. She lowered her gaze, blinking back what once were tears of happiness. "Oh father, of what do you speak?"

She peeked at him through lowered lashes, saw his eyes widen when they dwelt upon the babe growing within her. "By the *given* I see that the tales I hear of you are true." His voice was almost a wail. "Come," he said grabbing her hand. "We must talk but here is not good. I have a tent over there, away from the settlement."

Urged along by Kushlan's hand, Rae scuttled after him. Although she dreaded what he had to say to her, she ached to empty her heart to him. Kushlan was a balm to her soul. And since she had heard the tale from Aurore's Coldcloth robe, she knew that her father would understand her love. His love had been forbidden too.

In the shade of a boulder was a small tent, the type a traveller used. She followed Kushlan to it wordlessly, noting how thin and haggard he looked. He crouched, opening the tent flap for her. There was not much room so she sat down straightaway with her legs crossed. Her father sat opposite her, his knees brushing hers. When she looked into his face, she saw pain and suffering etched there. He was unshaven and dirty, as if he cared naught what people thought about him, as if all that he cared for was gone.

"Father, please tell me what has happened. Why are you here? You look so ill. Can I do something for you?"

He shook his head, his eyes dead to everything. "Aurore is dead, murdered."

Emotion coupled with disbelief cut off his words. There had been rumours but nothing specific had reached her ears. Did Hanal know? She squeezed his hand. When he had himself under control, he continued. "I could not bear to stay in the valley once I had heard the news. Terrible things happened in the keep and the evilness has spread throughout the valley. The farm is gone, burnt by raiders, either Puri or Argenterran I know not who. Not that it matters." He touched her hand. "I fled under cover of darkness. My skin colour made me stand out. It was no longer safe. Once I saw Dellbright leading a search for me. My heart near broke at the sight of what he had become."

"Oh no, father," Rae said, sniffing back her runny nose. "How could you bear it?"

Kushlan sniffed loudly. "On my way here, I heard talk. Talk of you and Hanal. What they said made my blood run cold, made the cloak of shame fall upon my back. But I see 'tis true. You are Hanal's whore and carry his child in your belly. How could you have done this? Betrayed all that you were taught?"

He may as well have slapped her hard in the face for his words cut her deeply. Just as Hanal's had done. In the past she might have walked out and not talked to her father. Now she was desperate for him to understand her, desperate for someone to accept what she had done and why.

"Father, please....I cannot ask for forgiveness. What I did, I did knowingly. I have a passion for Hanal that you must understand—"

"Understand? How can I understand what you have done?"

"Father. I love him, more than my life I love him. I know you can understand that. I know how dear you held Aurore. I know it all, the whole story...you must understand me."

Her father paled and swallowed. Pain etched even more deeply across his face. "How did you know about that? Never mind me and what was in my heart as I can speak from a clear conscience. We never lay together, Aurore and me. You cannot compare our actions to yours."

Rae bowed her head low. "Father, I do not compare your actions to mine, I only point out that you understand my heart and what love can do. I am not as strong as you. I would not let Hanal marry me to some old widower. Not when I wanted him." Lifting her head, she wiped at the tears in her eyes. "I would not let someone I did not love paw me, make a child on me while I did my duty and smiled and made everyone believe I was content. No, that was not for me!" Her voice was harsh, full with determination. "I will not be forgotten and discarded. I am a woman, and I choose the man I want. I decide my own life." Her voice broke and she covered her mouth and then dropped her hand, looking directly into her father's eyes. "He does not choose to share an oath with me...but I will suffer the hurt and the shame as long as I can be near him. I bear the scorn from the rest of the Puri and live a friendless life and I do it willingly. This child gives me a place in his home, and for that I am content."

Kushlan's expression softened. "Do you really love Hanal that much? He wrongs you in so many ways. How can you love someone who hurts you so much?"

"I believe...I have faith...that his heart will soften. I must believe there is a positive end to this situation."

He nodded, watching her face. "This determination I can understand. You are not weaker than me, my sweet child. No, you are stronger than I ever was because you dared all for your love. Perhaps Aurore would have been happier if I had been stronger. If I had spoken out, demanded." He shrugged. "There is no use in repining about the past." He closed his eyes. "I cannot believe she is gone." He wiped his eyes, dashing the swell of teardrop before it fell. He smiled and sniffed. "I see clearly now. I have no right to judge you. If you can bear the shame and the hurt, I can bear it also. You must make the best of it and plan for a better day."

Rae threw herself into her father's embrace and some of her fear subsided. "Oh father! Thank you for understanding." When she disengaged and looked him full in the face, he smiled tremulously. Reaching out, she gently wiped the tears tracking down his cheeks.

He spoke, his voice coarse with emotion. "I now fear for your happiness, as there is much unrest in the world. This is why I stay here apart. I am not permitted to enter the camp, even though I am kin. There is no place for a storyteller here."

"But surely you said who you were?"

He nodded. "I did, but I fear that was not enough for the guards to allow me entry. They would not bring word to you. Warriors are gathering."

She shook her head and bit her lip. Her place in Hanal's life was precarious. Dare she even complain to him of her father's treatment? Not now. Not while he was obsessed with Sophy.

"Riders come from all directions. It is in my mind that Hanal calls a great council, which can only spell danger for everyone. I fear there may be war with Argenterra."

"If you only knew how much danger there really is and what Hanal's plans are." She dared not mention the outlander. "I can only guess at them, but I know he has ambitions. I can offer him nothing that fits in with his plans and that is why he withholds his oath."

Kushlan pushed dark hair from his eyes. "So you rely on the clan laws to protect you and the child?"

"Yes."

"Then you tread a dangerous path. With our home in the valley gone, we have nowhere to go."

Rae listened and tried to let the knowledge sink in. Her father had lost his home, all the years of hard work and pride he had put into that place. She would not walk the familiar paths around the homestead or sit at his hearth and watch a pot of stew boil. "What will you do, father?"

"Continue on. There are other camps; perhaps I will find a fireside to tell a story at."

For a heartbeat, Rae wanted to go with him, but knew she could not. Her path lay with Hanal for good or ill. "Where?"

"I travel further north. Perhaps in my aging sorrow I will collect more tales. I will return after my grandchild is born. Will you keep well till then?"

Silent tears dripped down her cheek and fell from her chin. She wiped at them and nodded. "Yes, father. I will."

"Go then and be well."

Rae parted the tent flap to crawl out. Kushlan touched her shoulder. "Is it true that he has the outlander, the one you brought to my house once?"

She froze. If Kushlan knew then it must be widely talked about. Rae bit her bottom lip and replied, "Yes, I am afraid it is true."

"This is very bad," Kushlan said, his eyes darkening with concern. "If you dare it, aid her. For the love of me, aid her. Do not stand by and let her suffer. We will all be the worse for it."

Outside, Rae cast her gaze to the sand below her feet. Her father's words echoed her own plans, except that the motivation behind them was different. She nodded and walked away, leaving her father staring after her. By the morrow, he would be gone. Although it had been a comfort to talk to him, and have him understand her situation, the leave-taking made her feel even more alone than before. There could be no going back. If Kushlan was not welcome in Argenterra, then she was not welcome also.

❧ 18 ❧

A HELPING HAND

On the path back to Hanal's tent, one of Lyant's maids ran up to her. The woman usually ignored Rae and was neither friendly nor unkind. "Tu Raenal, my mistress asks you attend her in her tent."

"Really?" Rae could not hide her surprise. Lyant had spoken to her occasionally but had never summoned her. Her gaze took in Lyant's tent abutted against Hanal's. The poor woman never left the tent, unless Hanal took her somewhere. She was a virtual prisoner, kept from harm and kept from life. There she played music, read poetry and conversed with her maids. That was all Rae knew of her. And now— right now, when Rae needed to be elsewhere, she summoned her. "Very well, I will come now."

The maid nodded and led the way back, the rich cloth of her skirts dragging in the dirt behind her. The maid's headdress was ornate, more than the norm, and the tail of it hung overlong down her back, a symbol of her wealth and virgin status. Rae found it, and her, quite off-putting.

When she entered Lyant's tent, she halted just inside the tent flap. Lyant lay naked on her stomach atop a backless lounge, its richly embroidered cover protected by a layer of plain white cloth. Two of her maids rubbed oil into her creamy skin. Her complexion was similar to Aurore's, one that tended to darkness in the sun but paled to ivory if kept shaded.

Lyant did not look up when she entered. She was moaning softly, almost sensually as the maids ran their hands over her oiled buttocks and thighs. The maid that had shown her in went to sit at the head of the couch and poured wine for her mistress. Lyant turned slightly to face Rae by the door, her cheeks slightly pink and her lips full and red. She looked like she had just finished making love. Thinking such, Rae cast her gaze around the tent to see if they were alone. Lyant smiled and nodded slightly. "I see that I shock you, little sister." She yawned widely and pushed herself up so that she straddled the couch. Her unbound hair fell to her shoulders. Dark and thick, it coiled around her waist. Unlike Hanal, she had dark eyes that arched slightly above her fine cheek bones. She was truly beautiful.

Rae gasped slightly and quickly hid it when Lyant stood and faced her, stretching her arms out so that her maids could drape a sheer, pale pink robe over her nakedness. Rae found her gaze riveted to Lyant's womanhood. For in place of hair, there were tiny jewels embedded in the skin, making a bejewelled vee and no other hair to be seen. Her legs glowed in the subdued light, smooth and hairless. Lyant was a fine, cultured lady and Rae felt more and more like a child the longer she stayed in her presence. She wondered what Hanal's sister wanted with her and shifted from foot to foot, eager to run away.

With her robe draped over her, Lyant arranged herself on her lounge. Her maids bowed low and then left. "We are alone now. We can talk in private though at least two of my maids will listen in secretly. They always do. Hanal pays them to spy on me. I do not know why as there is nothing to do here."

"You wanted to see me, honourable Lyant?"

"Yes, of course I do. I know what goes on around here. Oakheart's whore is there amusing my brother at your expense."

Rae's face fell at Lyant's unexpected bluntness. "You know about Lady Sophy?"

"Oh, yes. I visited her secretly. Said my piece." Lyant smiled, almost in the way that Umri did. Rae's eyes widened. Hanal's sister brushed a hand suggestively against her jewelled labia. "Hanal paid for this adornment. Do you like it?"

Rae shook her head and tried to ignore the blood that pounded in her ears. "Er...'Tis...a...unusual."

"Not really. Umri did it for me. You know, I like you." Lyant sat down again, parting her legs and sending the robe falling over her shoulders. She licked her lips and stared at Rae. "I have watched you."

Rae swallowed, heart thudding "Watched me? When?" Though in her heart she knew, though dreaded hearing it.

"Oh," she sighed and lay back on the couch, cushioning her head with her arm. "When you seduced him. You were good. Nowhere near Umri's calibre, but she only had a few days to teach you."

Rae hung her head. "Please do not continue."

"Why stop me from speaking? You were not ashamed to seduce my brother, not ashamed to open your legs to him whenever he asked, so why be coy with me now? I have watched him with other women before, you know..."

Rae could not resist. With a sickly sense of awe, she lifted her chin to speak, all the while thinking: *This was the virginal bride of the Puri, the pride and treasure to be nurtured and protected?* "Why?"

"Why what? Why did I watch you or why have I watched my brother in the past? He is rather well endowed and energetic. Oakheart is nothing to him, though Veld's ambassador is by far a bigger man.

"Strange is it not? Oh—I see by your face that you wonder how I know that. As I said, tent walls are thin and I am skilled at walking quietly in the dark of night. Umri instructed me in her arts, the loving arts that is....part of that was to watch her in action. She is very skilled. I watched her with Hanal often."

Lyant fanned her face with her hand. "I feared for Hanal, you know, in case he was held in thrall by her. He enjoyed her, revelled in her skill, exulted in her suffering when he chose to wring every whimper from her. I worried for nothing. He was playing as he usually does. He saw through her empty love. She wanted him, yes, but for what and who he was. There you have the advantage, for though your skill in the loving arts is paltry, you have something more."

Rae was tempted to run from the room. If this is what it was to be a lady then she did not want to emulate it. Yet she found Lyant's revelations fascinating, particularly her observations of Rae's relationship with Hanal.

"What is that? Why do you share these secrets with me? I do not wish to hear them. I know Umri was his lover, he told me so himself."

"Mmmm." Lyant stroked her chin idly. "You are so fresh and innocent, Rae my sweet, you see, that is the quality that has my brother in thrall. Although he knows it not. You see, I saw it when you gave yourself to him. Devotion...infatuation....loyalty and love. Yes, you love him, worship him, and that is like the sweetest honey. That is why you will succeed where others have failed."

Rae's mouth dropped open. She wanted to believe that Hanal would give her an oath and make her his wife. She had been manipulated by Umri and used by Hanal. Could she trust what this woman was saying or was she being manipulated again? Rae bit down on her doubt. "You still have not told me why you are telling me this."

Lyant rolled over on her side so that she was facing Rae. Her robe enveloped her bare skin like a layer of leaves, framing the naked torso and thighs. Rae wondered at her and then began to think that maybe Lyant liked having sex with women. The maids, the flush and ripe look and yet the virginal status. Rae lifted an eyebrow in speculation. She hoped that Lyant was not trying to seduce her because she had too many things to deal with at the present time.

"You must help my brother. He is obsessed with that thin, scrawny girl. You must get her away from here. I do not have Umri's sight but I know trouble and she is it. He talked of nothing but her on the way back from Silverdale."

"You want me to betray him? To go against his wishes. Why? Why should I do this?"

"Because if you want him you must get rid of her. I fear for him, truly I do. I see you look at me warily. I know Umri used you for her own ends but I tell you this. I love my brother. He is my life. Do you think I would agree to live like this otherwise? 'Tis only my devotion to him that keeps me here. I will do his bidding and marry where he chooses. If not for my love of him, my loyalty, I would have left this tent long ago. I would have lain with as many men as Umri has. I would have lived a life of my choosing."

"'Tis that all?" Rae suspected more, dared not utter it. "The way you live is not right. The way you think is not right to my mind. You are meant to be an untouched virgin yet you know things about..."

Lyant threw back her head, making her mane of dark hair ripple. "I am a virgin! My blood will stain my wedding sheets. That is my agreement with my brother. For that he allows me some simple pleasures. Besides, I am Puri, not some simpering Argenterran maid. If that is where he wishes me to wed, then I can hide that I am knowledgeable in the loving arts. I can act, if his plans necessitate it. And if necessary my knowledge of seduction could help seal an important deal."

"And how long will you keep up this agreement? Eventually you will age, lose your youth, your bloom and your ability to bear children. What happens to his plans then? What happens to you?"

Lyant's sultry smile dissipated. Her eyes narrowed. "I have time, little sister," she hissed. "Do you? Can you afford to let that power within that girl fall into his hands? Where will you be then? You will be nothing, your child nothing."

Rae was ready to leave. "No. I refuse to be nothing."

Lyant's smile returned. "Good. That is what I like to hear. You can leave now."

Lyant watched her from under lashes, a smile lingering on her beautiful face. As Rae exited the tent, she was sure that Lyant feared the fate that Rae described. Oakheart was lost to her. Who else was there? Glasshiver males? Perhaps. But they were wild and strange and their houses were full of women, all of them possible competition to Lyant if she were to wed there. Lyant would never survive amongst them. No, Rae thought, Lyant's eye was set on an Argenterran.

In turn, Lyant's revelations and observations had caused her heartache. Those words were not easily forgotten and they stirred up things in Rae. Things she did not want to face and a hope she did not trust. Just when she had been trying to find some quiet to think things through, she gets disturbed by others—first Kushlan and now Lyant. What would happen next?

HANAL TURNED TOWARDS SOPHY, A HUNGER IN HIS EYES. SOPHY WAS unbound but too weak to make a run for it. She tried to crawl away but Hanal grabbed for her. He held her by the throat, her head against his shoulder. "Umri, take off her robe. I know I will reach the power this time. I know. Now, feed her your potion. Make it double strength. It will lower her defences, weaken her oath today. I have run out of time. If I cannot reach this power, then I must make my move without it."

Umri stepped up to Sophy and tugged off the clean robe that Rae had dressed Sophy with. "Double? I dare not risk it. You could kill her."

"It would be a shame to waste such a lovely body, would it not? Yet I would have her power and wield it. Make it as strong as you dare. Do it now."

Sophy fought against his hold. Hanal tightened his grip. "Hurry."

She struggled as Hanal held her, forcing her to swallow. The liquid was thick and heady. The taste of it made her limbs tremble.

"That was effective, Umri. Now, you will work with me and guide me as I work around her oath and her resistance. This time I will take what I want. No more wearing her down slowly. I am done."

"Yes, Hanal." Sophy saw the woman's dark eyes glowing with triumph. "I am yours to command. Remember my service, venerable Hanal."

The pair of them forced Sophy to her knees. The drug was like an unexploded bomb. It crouched within her. Then like the first flash of an explosion, thirst hit her. "Water," she demanded hoarsely, hating herself for sounding so desperate, so feral.

Hanal knelt down in front of her and tilted her chin so that he could look into her face. "For water, what will you do? Will you give yourself to me? Will you show me what is hidden within you?"

Sophy shook her head but the tent began to spin around her. Hanal's image spun, too. Umri was chanting; her words wove through the air. Like knives they slid just under Sophy's skin. It was her own voice she heard yelling, tinged with despair and yearning, running in counter time with the strange woman's chant.

This was bad. Sophy tried to escape the horror, to make her mind go blank. But the drug held her. The fuzziness of her vision faded. Her mind snapped into clarity and the whole scene came sharply into focus. Then like a slice of blade across her back, Umri struck with a whip. Her smile dripped with glee. "Now, Hanal. Reach into her when I strike with the whip. The pain will distract her. Use your mind, search it out, delve it out." Thwack, another strike. "You see, the pain momentarily suspends her control." To demonstrate, she slashed the whip across Sophy's back. The tip of the flail nicked Sophy's breast and blood tickled down the white flesh of her stomach. Sophy was suspended in that moment of pain.

Hanal peered at her closely, then closed his eyes. The whip struck again. The pain was so intense she couldn't call out. It was like it possessed her will. Then she felt something alien inside her. Eager and hungry, it reached for her.

The whip fell again. Hanal's eyes opened, the pupils dilated. She could smell his scent; he was that close to her. His spicy breath mingled with hers. Sophy's consciousness slipped, even as the next lash fell. Her senses were wide open. She was wide open. There was clarity in pain and stillness.

Umri lowered the lash again, making Sophy's back arch. He was everywhere, surrounding her, penetrating her with his mind as the whip fell yet again. Her wordless scream died in her throat. His mind was inside her, peeling off the layers as he rummaged about. She was being ransacked, pieces of her smashed as he delved inside her.

The woman continued chanting, sending the knives into her skin, pricking her senses so that Hanal could ferret out her power freely. Hanal grew stronger inside of her. Thrusting away her defences and thumping inside her head in frustration when he couldn't touch her power. Umri's voice changed, lowered an octave, and Hanal speared ahead. Sophy grew taut, her mind invaded.

And then there was a blinding light. She blinked, dazzled by it. A bright blue glow reflected off Hanal's skin, burnishing his dusky skin to indigo, building in intensity. He seemed to be suspended, powerless. His breath heaved, in then out. But his eyes were transfixed and unseeing. There was a blinding flash, a surge of something, like a wave.

Sophy exulted in the sensation, revelling in the release from pain. The whip no longer fell.

WHEN SOPHY REGAINED CONSCIOUSNESS, SHE SAW HANAL LYING prone on the floor. His eyes were open and staring and his legs and arms twitched. Sophy lay on her side. She turned her head, the bones in her neck grinding. Her forehead furrowed, as to move a muscle sent her cringing with pain. Her back sung its misery all over her skin. Keeping her head still, she angled her gaze in the direction of Umri, who sat whimpering in the corner with her legs apart and her expression vacant. Her hair was burnt, and singed sections of scalp glowed red. Blood leaked out from between the woman's legs. Her unborn child had been forced from her body. So she had not lied about that then; she had been pregnant. Sophy was surprised that she experienced no pity for the pair. Not after what they had done to her.

Besides, what could she do? Sophy didn't feel inspired to help them even if she could. Her senses were raw: the pain on her skin, the burning, searing blaze across her mind. Slumped, she tasted the dusty air as she dragged in another breath. It was the drug, she was sure. It throbbed in her veins, still unpurged from her system. She wanted to move, but the merest twist of a muscle brought her awareness into focus and strummed her pain sensors.

Her robe lay in a puddle on the floor, inches from her face. Grimacing against the agony in her body, she inched forwards on her relatively undamaged stomach. Her breast was cut and twinged when she moved, but compared to the agony of her back it was nothing. Another caterpillar hump and she was a little closer to the robe. A dark hand reached down for it. Sophy let out a breath and sent her gaze angling upwards. Rae was there.

She dropped a pile of clothes onto the floor in front of Sophy's face. Her expression was unreadable. "Here, get dressed in these. We must leave now before they recover and raise the alarm."

"You're helping me?"

Rae gazed longingly at Hanal, crawled over to him and kissed his unfeeling lips hungrily. She ran her hands over his body, checked his breathing and kissed him again, whispering in his ear.

Sophy stopped breathing, certain that Rae would rouse him and start the torment all over again. But Hanal didn't react.

Rae turned to her again. "Hurry up! We have little time." She handed Sophy a flask. "Drink this. It will help clear your head."

Sophy eyed her, unable to let go of her distrust.

"Drink it. 'Tis water and will help you. I must prepare stores for the journey." When Sophy grasped the proffered drink, Rae snuck back out, dodging the prone Hanal. Sophy could hear the girl rummaging in the next chamber as she sipped the water carefully. Her throat hurt. She climbed onto her hands and knees and tried to put the robe over herself. The barest touch of fabric nearly made her cry out.

Rae came back in, realised her predicament and went back out. She returned with a bowl of ointment in her hand. "Quick," she hissed. "I will put this on your wounds. It will numb the pain and perhaps provide some cure. I have not time for more. We do not have healing bark here."

Sophy stuck her fist in her mouth as Rae quietly and quickly smeared the ointment across her flayed back. Not one whisper of sympathy passed the other girl's lips as she worked. On some level, Sophy was grateful for that because she didn't think she could have coped with a kind word. All she wanted was to escape.

The pain lessened quickly and she was able to turn her attention to the clothes Rae had brought. As she sorted through the clothing, she saw that it was a mixture. A thin shift of soft white material, like cotton. The next one she picked up was a thin Argenterran gown of pale ivory silk. The other bits were Puri trousers, an over tunic and a decorated apron. There was even a headdress. Sophy struggled into the silk dress. The fabric of the shift felt nice against her damaged skin. There were no other underclothes to speak of but she shrugged the thought away. The silk dress was so light that it barely added to her discomfort. It was better than being tied up and naked for days on end. Then she dressed in the rest of the clothes. She was staring at the headdress when Rae returned. The clothes weighed heavy and painfully. She moved carefully while she readied herself.

"Let me help you with that." Rae deftly tied the headdress. "You must keep your gaze down. I will cover you in this." Sophy shied away and eyed the dark stuff in a small container that Rae held out.

Rae whispered, "'Tis only soot mixed with oil and water. The sun is setting, so it will help disguise you. When we leave this tent, say nothing to no one. No matter what. Or we will both be caught, and you know what will happen to both of us. Understand?"

Sophy nodded and let Rae smear her face with grime. She was regaining her senses little by little. Her head was less foggy, though her tongue still felt thick and clumsy. Hope that finally Rae was going to help her escape threatened to overwhelm her. She bit back a sob; she couldn't lose it now.

Sophy's gaze slid to the corner. Umri sat in the same position, unmoving but still breathing. The pool of blood between her legs had grown dark. Hanal, too, was barely conscious. His mouth worked but no words issued. Despite everything he had done to her, he looked proud and beautiful. The Puri leader could have been a great man. Sophy shuddered to think about the path Hanal trod. She hoped he would be able to free himself from the darkness that held sway over him. He could have been a good man. What would he do when he recovered? Would he even recover?

Rae shoved a bundle into her lap, startling her out of her study of the Puri leader. Sophy gaped at the girl stupidly until Rae helped tie it across her back. Sophy cried out for even though the ointment soothed her marred flesh, the whip strokes still smarted terribly. Stifling her whimpers with her hand jammed in her mouth, she gave Rae a reproachful look.

"Forgive me." Rae's voice was soft but she said it in a business-like manner. "But you must carry that if our pretence is to succeed." Rae picked up another bundle. It seemed to be heavier than the one Sophy held. Once she had secured it to her back, Rae grabbed Sophy's hand and led her to the front of the large tent.

The former maid peered out of the tent flap and pulled back in. Someone went past the tent opening, so she huddled further back into the shadows. Rae's palm was sweaty and perspiration beaded on her forehead. After sparing Sophy a look tinged with fear, she edged forwards and peeped out. Sophy squeezed her hand companionably and detected the pressure of Rae's response. Rae tugged on her hand and drew her out into the clearing in front of Hanal's tent.

The twilight was enough to blur the tents, making dark patches against a lighter, grey sky. The stars were not yet out and there was no moon. The last traces of sunlight were receding. Pennons snapped occasionally, enlivened by a brisk, intermittent breeze. The air on Sophy's face was a balm; she revelled in the taste of freedom.

Some Puri still walked around. Men mostly, from what Sophy could see. Rae wove a path through the tents, darting from spot to spot. She held her bundle so that it wouldn't rattle, and checked that Sophy was well hidden with her in the lee of a tent's shadow. Her direction was directly out and away from Hanal's central tent. It was a while before Sophy heard the horses. The ring of tents thinned, leading to piles of feed and a small herd of horses corralled with rope fences.

When she looked around ready to bound forwards with Rae to the horses, a Puri male stepped out in front of them, barring the way. Rae halted and lowered her eyes. Sophy followed suit.

"What are you doing?" He sounded like an adolescent. His shadowed form looked tall, thin and rangy. He smelled of spice, too.

Rae looked up, sniffed as if she had been weeping. "Hanal has thrown me out of his household. He sends me home." She managed to sound convincing. Indeed, that is what the Puri leader would do to her, Sophy was sure. Hanal would not take betrayal well.

The man chuckled and spat on the ground. "Whore. What else could he do with you? I heard he beat you and threatened to cast you out. Next thing I know you are here snivelling as if you did not deserve such treatment."

Rae stiffened, affronted by the man's gall, Sophy suspected. A good swift kick where it hurt was what he needed. But he was probably speaking the truth. The tents as well as the caves left little to the imagination. Everyone must know his neighbour's business. Hanal's outrage would have been overheard by many. And that gossip would have floated on the breeze like smoke from the wood fires.

"What about her?" He pointed at Sophy.

Sophy kept her head low, trying to appear more servile. It wasn't

227

hard; she was near bent over double with the bundle Rae had strapped to her back. It was all she could do not to moan in pain.

Rae lifted her face. There were real tears streaking her cheeks. Sophy had to admire the girl. At that moment Sophy didn't care what her reasons were, only that she was aiding her to escape. "Nasheen sent this idiot servant to Hanal's household. She does not talk and is generally stupid, but she is sent to help me carry my things, just to the border. Hanal will spare no one useful."

Again the young man chuckled. "I see. Hanal is wise in his use of resources. Nasheen has grown cocky since he brought the outlander as a gift to him. Hanal's punishment of his gift will put Nasheen in his place. I like that. Nice revenge. My clan's tent had to go to the perimeter because of him. Go then."

"May your waters flow with the *given,* always." Rae's voice was full of regret. If the Puri man detected it, he didn't show it.

He pointed to the far end of the coral. "You can use that horse. The saddle and other gear are in the lean-to on the left hand side. Take it and be gone."

Rae lost no time. She almost dragged Sophy behind her as she arrowed directly to the allotted horse. A saddle was stacked in a lean-to as the guard said, along with other gear. Rae groped around in the dark and found one, muttering under her breath. Sophy kept quiet and jerked her head around in answer to every snort or nicker of the horses. From the tent encampment, there were noises, a few songs, laughter and the soft strumming of music. Sophy prayed that Rae would hurry for she dreaded that fateful cry, which would alert everyone to Hanal's condition and her escape.

Sophy stood by, panting, while Rae threw the saddle on the mount. After fumbling with the girth strap, Rae deftly bound Sophy's bundle to the saddle. The rope bridle was still on the horse. Rae untethered the horse and led them away from the tent settlement.

Sophy stifled her moans. Her feet were bare and every stone dug into the soft soles of her feet. She strode on, realising that the former maid from Valley Keep was going to succeed in setting her free. Yet, it was a long way from there to anywhere.

✤ 19 ✤

AN OATH'S RESONANCE

Thrusts of pain filleted Oakheart. He tossed and turned in his blankets, trying to rip free of his torment. He knew he was awake but could not open his eyes. Drawn he was, caught in a web of Sophy's making. Through the oath's tether, she reached out to him, called his name, and her thoughts were heavy and cloudy. He felt the sting and slice of a whip across his back and cried out, experienced the drill of pressure against his skull as someone tried to edge inside, hammering, applying pressure until his head would burst.

He had no strength to send her. Her dream sucked what strength he had and he ceased his struggles to lay half-senseless in his bedroll. Breath rasped along his throat. His heart lurched as Sophy's hold on him weakened and she slipped away into the grey background of his mind. He lifted a trembling hand to his brow.

Lillia's face hovered over his, brows drawn together. "What ails you? You called out."

Oakheart tried to wet his lips with his tongue. It took a few times before he could speak. "Sophy...he harms her."

The forest maiden put her hand to her mouth. "Hanal would do this? I can scarce believe it."

A tear slid down his cheek. It did not shame him, for he was overwhelmed by the hopelessness of it all—Argenterra's glory slipping away, the loss of life and oaths. "He has found a way to eat into her mind. Drugs, I think, and torture. He knows she has power and seeks to wield it. I thought my oath alone was enough to protect her. I have erred greatly and she suffers for it."

Lillia squeezed his shoulder. "Oakheart, you could not have predicted any of this. You are talented with the *given* and that is why you feel her pain through your oath. Others have not this gift."

"Gift?"

A smile lifted the corners of Lillia's mouth. "It is a gift to know that she lives. Yes, she suffers, but there is still hope, is there not? And if you can detect her presence, then perhaps she can sense you."

"Knowing that she suffers because of me is a terrible knowledge. I have failed her. I should have remained an adept at Glassy Mountain Retreat and learnt more so that I could have foreseen these events. If I had more skill I would have seen what she really was right at the beginning and would not have let Rufus or Hanal get their hands on her."

Lillia shook her head and clung to his vest to shake him. "No, no. You cannot wish that. Even Adage has been undone by events. If he could not discern Sophy's nature or the threats to her, how could you?"

"But I should have prevented all of this. Hanal wants her because I did not marry Lyant. All I have achieved is to make matters worse."

"Do you think Hanal would have ignored Sophy if you were married to Lyant and she fell into his hands? With her potential for power? I think not."

Oakheart chewed his bottom lip. "Perhaps...it is hard to..."

Lillia shook her head. "You love Sophy, Oakheart. You give her joy. I saw it. She has that to treasure, whether you meet again or not. Often I have parted from Mellow for duty, but we are bound with love and we find it again when we reunite. Believe in your heart that she loves you and then you will find a way through this."

"Love?" Oakheart tried to believe her. The forest woman was always pragmatic but she had a romantic heart beneath her tough exterior. He was caught between duty and the call of his heart. It had been easy to ignore love, to bury the hurt. Now, even though he had tried to cushion himself against it, he felt something akin to pain. Love was pain. "I do not—"

Seized by a sudden thread from Sophy, Oakheart's eyes rolled up as the breath was knocked out of him. A flash of blue-white burned across his brain. In the distance, he heard Meld cry out and heard feet running. Slowly, the sting of the blinding flash eased. Heartbeats fluttered, then became stronger as he slowly came back to himself. .

Lillia's shocked face loomed over him, but before the forest maiden could say a word, Meld was there, shaking, dark rings under his eyes. "By the *given*, he has touched the power. Did you feel it?"

Oakheart could not speak. Was all hope gone now?

Meld noticed Oakheart's distress. As the adept's trembling subsided, he lowered himself to examine Oakheart. With a sigh he touched Oakheart's shoulder. "He was able to touch her power, connect with Sophy, and the out-flowing has harmed him. I was watching, listening for them. Easier to see now they are in the summer tents."

Oakheart closed his eyes, reached out and detected nothing of Sophy. His strength was so depleted that he could not even sit up.

Lillia squatted next to Meld, the first time she had come close to him. "I've never seen Oakheart so weak. Not since...What can I do?" she asked.

"Not much in a practical sense. I will see what is to be done." Meld squatted silently, gazing at Oakheart or through him. "The Puri leader must have touched the power within Sophy, enough to overwhelm him, but not to take it. Yes, I feel that it is ebbing away. Not a full release but a touching." Meld shook his head. "This is bad news. My only hope is that Hanal has harmed himself, thus allowing Sophy some respite."

Oakheart groaned, not able to form words. Anger swirled within him, mingled with fear for Sophy.

Lillia gaped at the adept. "Respite? She is still a prisoner, surrounded by Puri. What rest is there for her in this? She is a woman, a courageous woman, and we have failed her."

Meld turned his cold gaze on her. "Whilst she breathes and holds the power of the *given* within her, we have not failed." Meld stood up, wavered for a moment and then drew his robes around him. Without a backward glance, he went away. Oakheart saw him pass into the shadows and assume a meditating position.

Lillia stroked his forehead, gently sweeping his hair away from his face. "I cannot speak my mind, Oakheart. I do not wish to disrespect the adept, but I cannot be easy about him. There is a ruthlessness there that is not savoury. And I cannot forget my son...trapped with him."

Oakheart moaned. He had no energy for talking or moving. "Some of my remedy for you, I think." Lillia slapped his hands that were resting across his chest. "No arguing."

The rest of the group had been roused by Meld's speech. Aria, hair tousled, stood nearby. Oakheart could only lie there unable to move, hoping that this encounter with Sophy's power had not sent his recovery backwards. Now, more than ever, he needed his strength.

Looking at the camp activity, he saw that Fern, recently returned from scouting, loomed behind Aria. Illart was absent—perhaps out searching for dangers further afield. Raven fed twigs to a small fire. He saw their concern and struggled up on an elbow. After swallowing a few times, he whispered hoarsely, "Go back to sleep. We'll talk more in the morning."

Lillia arrived with a cup. Not a hot broth, some potion that she kept about her. She helped him sip it. He hesitated when he tasted it.

"Yes, a touch of Nevin's Brew in that. You should sleep well and feel better in the morning."

Sparing him a pat on the head, she shot a quick glance at the adept meditating and then went back to her blankets. Oakheart stared at the sky, at the stars arrayed so far above him. He fought the sense of melancholy that came over him. It did not serve a purpose. What was self-pity when others dear to you were in need? Finally, after staring at the star-sprinkled heavens for a while, the brew helped him drift off to sleep.

The next morning brought both good and bad news. Oakheart found that his strength was rapidly returning to its former reduced level. He was still not his old self but he had not received a permanent setback. Illart brought bad tidings: more raiders to the east of them and Dellbright and his men to the north. Dellbright was apparently chasing Puri raiders, but Oakheart suspected he was hunting for his wife.

Aria's expression held true fear. She obviously thought so too. It wounded Oakheart to see it. "Fear not, princess. I will let none of them near you."

Oakheart thought of an alternative route. They did not have the manpower to engage with Dellbright and his men, or more Puri. "We will detour through Crystal Tree Woods. 'Tis still in Dellbright's territory but I hope he will not expect us to take that route. I hope awe of the Crystal Tree will keep the Puri out."

"But to backtrack? At least they will not be expecting it. But we will be cutting it very fine," Fern commented as he checked his gear. "It is very close to Valley Keep."

"What choice do we have? I will not risk Aria near either party," Oakheart replied. Would Dellbright guess at their destination? He hoped not, for Dellbright at the retreat while Aria was there would complicate matters.

"And well you should not," Meld added from atop his mount. "The princess must not fall into Puri hands. It is clear to me that Aria can wield Sophy's power. They came to Argenterra together for a purpose. They will be on the lookout for her. If we can work this out, so will Hanal. And we know what lengths Hanal will go to to obtain the power locked within Sophy. We tread a most dangerous path." The adept turned to Oakheart. "We should inspect the Crystal Tree as we traverse the woods. I wish to see whether events have affected it."

Nodding to the rest of his group, Oakheart urged his horse ahead. Mellow and Lillia scouted east and north, sending word through Illart and Raven and guiding the travellers away from danger. By midmorning, the woods came into view. The stark ring of trees rose out of the grassy plain. Bathed in sunlight, the trees seemed to absorb the light. Only the gentle sway of grass seemed natural. They headed south to the midsection of the woods. They kept a wide berth around Dellbright's semi-permanent campsite, the place where he had brought the two Gifts of Crystal Tree Woods on their arrival into Argenterra.

Pale sunlight filtered through the gaps in the canopy. The air cooled and was crisp at the edges. It was quiet, too, as if birds dared not disturb this place. A horse snorted and Aria and Fern chatted quietly. Oakheart caught sight of Lillia and Mellow amongst the trees. A creak of branches and he saw Illart and Raven leaping from bough to bough. The forest folk were happy to be amongst the trees and they signalled that all was well as they travelled.

The woods vibrated with a presence, not quite sentient but alive. Was that disquiet that teased gooseflesh from his arms and that left a metallic taste on his tongue? Further in, the party angled away from a well-worn path, picking their way through clumps of wildflowers and ferns with variegated leaves. It was quietly beautiful, a monument to all that was special about Argenterra. Oakheart sensed the pull of it, and found it soothed his disquiet.

The glade opened up before them and they halted on the verge. Meld slid out of his saddle and gingerly trod to near the Crystal Tree. No one spoke—for the sight was shocking. Oakheart had seen the tree a few times and had always admired the pure crystal leaves and its limbs stretched out in a symmetrical shape. But now the leaves were fallen, crushed and ruined at the base of the tree. The limbs were bent, misshapen and brown. The once fine stems at the end of the branches now curled like gnarled fingers clutching the air.

The sound of the adept's sobbing reached him. Oakheart could not but realise what the state of the tree signified. Aria went up to the tree and stroked the trunk gently. A limb bent above her. The sound of tearing reached him, but Fern was quick to act. He leapt and rolled away with Aria in his arms, avoiding the spot where the limb crashed down, bringing two other sizable branches with it.

The princess struggled upright and nodded to Oakheart to signal she was unhurt. Her expression was forlorn. Oakheart looked to the adept still on his knees, silently sobbing. He had never seen Adage express such strong emotion and he wondered whether it was Brook that mourned the loss of the Crystal Tree. No, Oakheart surmised. The condition of the Crystal Tree boded ill. And being a direct link to Vorn and how he spread the *given* through Argenterra, there was a sense of personal loss for Adage as well for he was Vorn's grandson.

Reluctantly, he urged the group on. "Come, Meld. We must leave this place."

Meld climbed to his feet wordlessly and groped for his horse's reins. Tears streaked his face. "Do you know what this means, Oakheart?"

Oakheart returned the adept's gaze. "Not every nuance of it, but enough to see that there is indeed less *given* in the land."

Meld seemed to realise that he had been weeping and wiped his face with the edge of his robe. "For the Crystal Tree to die bodes ill for all. There is not enough *given* here to nurture the tree. That means there is not enough to bind oaths."

The adept rode out of the clearing with Aria and Fern close behind. The forest folk took pieces of the dead crystal leaves and placed them in pouches. Oakheart wondered at their actions and thought that perhaps they kept the mementos so they could tell this tale at the Heart Tree. When they had finished collecting the dead pieces, they fled into the woods to shadow the rest of the party. Lillia's mount drew along behind him. Oakheart closed his eyes, groping for his link to his oathbound wife. "Soon, Sophy. I will be there soon."

They left the dying remains of the Crystal Tree behind them, leaving it alone to mourn for itself.

❦ 20 ❦

A WASTELAND WITHIN

Sophy followed Rae away from the cluster of Puri tents, away from the smell of campfires, away from the clutches of Hanal of Puri. They didn't speak. Sophy walked beside the horse, clinging to the girth strap and leaning more and more upon it for support. She yelped and complained of another stone digging into the soles of her feet.

"Shhh!" Rae hissed. "You must keep quiet. There are sentries, even this far out."

"Sorry," Sophy whispered back. "I have no shoes."

Rae's shadowed figure loomed closer from the back of the horse. "Soon...when we clear the outer sentries."

Sophy put her foot down on the ground, gingerly testing her foot. Stabs of pain shot up her leg, making her legs buckle. She made no sound and took the next step. She didn't want to be caught. The whipping was worse than sore feet, she told herself.

Before long, Sophy was taking a turn atop Rae's horse, gently swaying to the rhythm of its gait. Her feet were bloodied, ripped, blistered and were like numb lumps at the ends of her legs. Freedom didn't inspire raptures. Sophy was deadened, inured to suffering and quite forlorn. Rae helped her, and she was grateful. But she guessed there was more than good will behind Rae's assistance; she just hadn't figured out what as yet.

The air was still and the sky dark and moonless. Rae led her behind a boulder that barely reached up to Sophy's chin. There they paused. Sick of pestering Rae with questions, Sophy waited patiently. As far as she could tell, they were headed for the mountain range, the one that she had looked at so longingly in the days she sojourned at Valley Keep. How pitiful her concerns were then. Those happenings, Aria's marriage and being ugly were just cracks in her life. Nothing like now. After all that suffering, she was a woman grown. Unfortunately, she didn't like what she had become. The trappings of this womanhood were unwanted. Her innocence was gone forever, leaving only a sour bitterness. Her looks had returned free from enchantment but they served for nothing. They made not one whit of difference to her fate. Hanal cared not for them—her beauty did not stay his hand. She was nothing but a vessel of power, a means to an end....a talisman. Too bad this talisman lived and breathed and experienced pain and emotion and love. How perverse was the universe.

Rae gave the reins a tug. Sophy realised they were not stopping to make camp. Rae urged her mount on, along a convoluted, rocky path, around boulders and sand drifts. "What are you doing? Shouldn't we just gallop away and go wherever we are going as fast as we can?"

"No," Rae said in a bored voice. Her eyes watched the dark of the night with the help of starlight. "If Hanal knows where we are gone he can follow us and bring us back. We must take a path that is disguised. I use rocky paths where hooves will not leave a mark or the ways where many horses have trod before us, thus obscuring our path. I did not reckon on all these warriors heading for the summer tents. I see so many trails, many riders...I wonder..."

"I'm more worried about what they will do when they find Hanal. That shouldn't be too long."

"Yes, not long. Most likely they have discovered him already, but whether he is capable of directing them is unknown. He was completely addled from what I could tell." She climbed off the horse and helped Sophy mount up. "Try to rest while you can. We will not stop at daybreak."

"But what about you? In your condition you must rest."

Rae replied, sadness evident in her voice. "I am fine. When I need to rest I will climb up with you and ride. The horse is hardy enough to manage two as our pace is so slow."

They kept up their modest pace into the dark of night. Mild wind brought up dust and chilled her. Sophy closed her eyes against the stinging grit. Rae's hand gripped her arm, startling Sophy. Blinking away sleep, she suspected she must have dozed and leant sideways in the saddle. While she rubbed the crick out of her neck, she caught a glimmer of the sunrise. Rae's step hadn't slowed at all. They shared a quick look and then Rae let go.

"Why are you helping me?" Sophy asked. The girl's behaviour was confusing, as she risked a lot to help an outlander, yet there didn't appear to be any real friendship. Rae's manner had been cool and aloof. Hanal of Puri was everything to her and her abandonment of him had Sophy stumped.

Rae said nothing and kept walking with a brisk, determined step. Sophy glared at her, willing her to speak. She sighed loudly and thought of another tack. "I know back in the valley you were a nice, caring girl, but things have changed since then."

Rae didn't look round, but her shoulders stiffened. Without halting her stride, her words floated back to reach Sophy on the horse's back. "Nice, caring girl? I do not know whether to be insulted or not." Rae paused, as if collecting her thoughts. "I became Princess Aria's lady-in-waiting," Rae said with some measure of pride. "We became close after you left with Oakheart. I could see that she missed you sorely. I think all her spare moments were filled with thoughts of you. Her pregnancy was not easy for her...Dellbright was not always understanding or kind to her."

Sophy did not want to dwell on the unhappiness Rae's recollection of Aria brought. She missed her friend sorely. And the rumours she had heard of Aria's fate wounded her deeply. "So she gave you a promotion. That's nice...still you don't say..."

"I have not finished telling you and if you keep interrupting me I never will," Rae snapped.

Sophy frowned, hurt by Rae's harshness.

Rae's head lifted so that she was staring at the sky. Her pace slowed, yet she didn't turn around and look at Sophy. It was as if Rae didn't want to acknowledge her, didn't care enough to look her in the face. That behaviour made Sophy's gut clench, and feelings of distrust curled through her spine.

Rae's words were clear and clipped. "What you did not know was that I was sent to Valley Keep as a prospective bride to Dellbright. But by the time I arrived Oakheart had brought word from the retreat that the Gift of Crystal Tree Woods was indeed coming. The signs and portents had correctly played out.

"Dellbright took one look at me and bade me to serve in his keep, made me a servant. There would be no marriage...nothing. Aurore was kind to me and took me under her wing, but it was hard to watch you both. For you, I had some sympathy. You were overlooked, as I was. But even though Aria gained Dellbright as her husband I could still care for her. Her ways are so kind, her manner so gentle. She is everything you are not."

"Thanks," Sophy muttered under her breath. If she heard, Rae didn't appear to take offence.

"I watched the two of them. Dellbright liked it not that his bride fretted for you. He manipulated Aria, watched her and made sure she had little time to call you."

Rae's retelling of Aria's time brought all the threads together and wove a terrible picture. "Yes, I remember. After having the talkstone on hand, she hardly ever called me. I wondered why."

"I think he was the reason. I suspect he kept the talkstone from her. Although I left before the end and only heard through gossip that she had a male child, Gillcress. Nasheen brought dire tidings..." Rae glanced back at her then, a look that hinted of admiration. "Your daring rescue, sacrifice and metamorphosis...All this Nasheen did tell Hanal, and what he did not witness himself he gleaned from Oakheart. What he did see, though, was what had been done to Aria by Dellbright's hand."

Sophy winced; she had been selfish to leave Aria. She should have stayed, should have prevented it, shouldn't have led Aria into the tunnels beneath Castle Crioch in the first place. All of it was her fault.

Rae seemed satisfied by Sophy's woeful expression. "I believe Dellbright capable of cruelty. You did not see what I found after her wedding night. I dared not tell another soul, but now that I think upon it and all the happenings put together, I think the abuse began then. That very first night."

Sophy's throat clogged with emotion and her eyes stung with tears. "Please, tell me what you perceived? Here I was thinking you were shy and innocent, but you saw and felt more than all of us."

Rae slowed her steps until she walked by Sophy's leg, gazing up into her tear-stained face. "Do you remember when we put her to bed and the sweet nightdress that Aurore sewed for her? I found it in the waste, wrapped in some other things. It was torn, ripped in half and soaked with blood. I changed the sheets, too, while Dellbright and Aria ate quietly in the small sitting room.

"There was a lot of blood on the sheets, more than as if he had just bedded her for the first time—blood on the pillows as if she had a blood nose. I watched every time I brought them food. Aria was quiet. She would not look me in the eye, and she limped. Once, her eyes met mine, and I saw dark circles and her pain."

Sophy wiped the back of her hand across her face, smearing tears and grime. "Dear god. I thought there was something. It nagged at me, but I was so self-absorbed I didn't pursue it. She never said anything, not a word. Why disguise it? I guess she didn't want to admit that marriage to Dellbright wasn't all that rosy, or perhaps she hoped it would improve." Then Sophy recollected. "Oh no, and I made it worse, causing trouble and discord. I hope, Rae, that he didn't take my behaviour out on Aria. I didn't mean...I was so selfish then."

Rae patted her leg. "You sensed it, then. That shiver of something between them. I could not help her and could only be her friend in your absence. Only now I can piece it together. Do not blame yourself for not having seen or done more. I was never completely certain myself. I speak clear now from hindsight."

"Thank you for trying to comfort me but I must take the blame. If I hadn't been so wrapped up in myself I would've seen it, I'm sure. Aria and I have been friends for a long time. We were ten when her family moved near me. I lived with her family almost ever since."

Rae stepped away from the horse and drew her robe about her. "Gilly was left in Valley Keep with Dellbright, according to Nasheen. Apparently he used the child to make Aria stay. In her heartbreak, she had to leave him behind. I do not know how she stood it. I would die if Hanal separated me from my child."

There, thought Sophy, through her misery. Rae was leading her to the point. "Mmmm. You risk it though in helping me, don't you?"

Rae was quiet for a moment. The sunrise sent shafts of pale light through the clouds and spread a silver sheen over the mountain peaks. They seemed so much closer now, rugged and towering.

Rae paused and reversed her path to stand and search for signs of pursuit, leaving the horse to slow to a stop. She stayed there awhile. Sophy watched the snow caps change from deep gold to cream in the morning light. Her heart ached for Aria. How much had she suffered since she'd been left on her own? This land of hers, with its handsome prince, had shattered to a horrible reality.

Without doubt, Sophy's experiences paled in comparison. Of course, Hanal had broken their agreement and let Umri torture her, but she didn't love Hanal. The betrayal was less. It would be worse to be treated that way by the one you loved. Perhaps Oakheart was right. Dellbright was too needy and Aria was too beautiful...bad combination.

Rae strode on, her colourful robe billowing in the light breeze. The dark eyes that met hers as she passed were suddenly old. After she checked the path behind them, she said, "No one follows us as far as I can tell. By the end of the day, we will know for certain. The Puri like not the road to Glassy Mountain Retreat, which is the way we will take. They will not follow us past a certain point, I think. I hope they will not.'

Sophy noticed Rae frown. "What is it?"

Rae's dark gaze washed over her. "Many warriors march. I fear something is about to happen. We must hurry. I must go back to Hanal's household. He will need me."

"But you can't. He will harm you."

"No," Rae said. "He was tempted when I interfered with you. I have never seen him so angry. I do not believe he will harm me. Until I birth this child, he will not throw me out. Umri taught me many things; taught me to deceive, too." Rae grimaced. "The Puri like not the mixing of seed without oaths. But they do have a complex set of rules for the times when it happens. If Hanal injured me, or threw me out of his household before the child was born, he would lose his claim to it, he would deny his parental rights. However, once the child is born he may take the child and throw me out. Because of his position as leader, he would be free to marry me to one of his clansmen."

"That doesn't sound good."

"It is not. He could marry me to some old man, or make me someone's second wife."

Sophy screwed up her nose. Just the thought made her want to vomit. "A second wife? Good lord. Nasheen boasted to me that he had two wives. Something about the wording of the oath."

"I have not heard these oaths so cannot say. But I have not heard of more than two wives."

"So why doesn't he make an oath to you if he can take another wife?"

Rae sniffed and wiped her nose with the sleeve of her robe. "He wishes to wed an Argenterran. He believes they would not accept such an oath so he keeps himself free. Or else it is just that he cares not to wed me."

"Mmm...I guess you may be right about the Argenterrans. They do seem a bit particular. But if he treated you so badly, why go back?"

Rae turned to face Sophy. The hand holding the leading rein turned white around the edges. "He did not treat me badly. He is an honourable man."

"Well, Rae, I think we have different ideas about honour...but then again perhaps not. You are helping me, by the way..."

"I help you to help myself. I did not like him coming to me when he was full of desire for you. More importantly, you are dangerous. I cannot sense this power you have but I fear it. And look what has happened. Hanal is injured."

Sophy was at once enlightened. Jealously and fear. She was assisted because she was competition. Laughter bubbled up inside her and spilled out. Rae's frown deepened and she kept walking, shoulders hunched. Sophy realised that Rae hadn't wanted to admit such a thing. When her laughter subsided, her spirits had lightened. The heavy ache of sorrow that had pressed down over her eyes had dissipated. She realised, too, that Rae made her own decisions. Sophy didn't have to feel guilty about the consequences. Rae understood what she was doing. Well, Sophy hoped she did.

Sophy once again spoke to Rae's stiff back. "You really truly love Hanal, don't you?"

Rae swung round, lips quivering. "What do you understand about love? How can you understand what motivates me?"

Sophy shrugged and lurched sideways when the horse changed gait. "I know something about it. I am bound to Oakheart by an oath. I didn't seek it out though. I would have... ahem." Sophy searched for the local term. "I would have slept with him anyway. I didn't need or want an oath...What is more important to me is that I love him. I miss him. He is my friend. I trust him. I would do anything to help him."

Rae nodded. "I hear in your voice that it is so. Your bonding to Oakheart has caused problems though." Rae's gaze turned towards their path. Her shoulder relaxed and the girl no longer radiated affront.

Sophy whispered on the breeze, thinking of Lyant and Hanal. "It seems to have caused a few, yes. Not my intention. He just got under my skin."

A soft laugh rose from Rae. Sophy relaxed. Not friends exactly, but they understood each other.

Sophy continued to ride the horse with Rae walking beside her through a grey day and intermittent squalls of rain. As she huddled in her Puri garb, Sophy dozed occasionally. The effect of the drug was still with her as were the days of no food and water and the vicious beatings. Rae searched out fodder for the horse, splitting from the path and jogging to clumps of dry, coarse grass that dotted the wasteland sporadically. She tugged them out and brought them back, knotting them in a bundle and tying it to the back of the saddle.

Towards sunset, Rae pulled on the horse's reins as they neared a ring of tumbled stones. "Come, get off and rest for a while. The horse needs a break, for the next part is hard riding."

Sophy slid off the saddle and sagged to her knees. Grunting with the effort to stand, she slunk a short distance away and stretched out in the dirt. Rae nudged her awake a few minutes later and handed her some stale, flat bread and a section of dried spiced meat. Sophy took it and sniffed. Her mouth was pasty. "Is there anything to drink?" she asked, eyebrow quirked hopefully.

Rae shook her head. Her headdress had been unwrapped. Her long dark hair was braided to fall over one shoulder. "No. I gave what we had to the horse. But there is a spring nearby. We will stop there to drink and wash and give the horse more water before continuing."

"Oh, all right then." Sophy swallowed the last of the food, which sat like a lump in her stomach. The drug's effects still bothered her, the metallic taste in her mouth, the lack of real hunger but an exaggerated feeling of thirst.

"I found these. I am sorry I did not give them to you before." Rae threw her some sandals, which she automatically thanked her for. Although, looking at her feet she didn't know if they were going to help or not. The damage was done. She closed her eyes, fatigue pulling at her. She fell asleep, too far gone to even worry about the stones that pressed into her flesh.

All too soon, Rae shook her awake. "Come, we will walk to the spring and then we ride."

Sophy blinked away sleep. In the full dusk she found it hard to see anything. "Is anyone following us?"

Rae's brows creased together. "Not a soul, as far as I can tell." The girl sighed loudly and went to ready their mount. "I thought perhaps he would come after us."

Sophy heard 'me' instead of 'us' in Rae's slightly regretful speech. Perhaps she was disappointed her lover didn't pursue her. Sophy could only be grateful that Hanal wasn't chasing them. She would be happy never to see the Puri leader again.

Sophy climbed to her feet, a touch groggy, and strapped the sandals on her sore feet. "You are disappointed."

Rae tugged on the horse's reins and said nothing.

Sophy lurched after her, wincing with each step. She walked carefully to minimise the rub of the straps that rubbed against the blisters and cuts on her feet. "Well, aren't you?"

Rae looked at her sideways as Sophy caught up. "I thought he would try to stop you leaving. Perhaps he has tired of you now."

Sophy winced, from her feet more than from Rae's barb. "Oh?" She lifted a foot to adjust the strap on the sandal. "Maybe he is seriously hurt and still unconscious or even dead."

Rae's eyes widened with alarm. Sophy smiled wickedly to herself. "Speak not such things." Rae's voice caught in her throat. "He was breathing when I left him."

Sophy bit her lip, worried that Rae would weep, drop everything and ride back to Hanal's tent, leaving her stranded. Such thinking made her feel guilty for her jibe. But to her relief, the panicked look faded and Rae said, "No...he is not dead. He cannot be dead. There must be some other reason. One that worries me even more. He was so full of plans. Now I realise that I knew only half of them. I fear what this means. I will find out soon enough because I will travel back to him as soon as you are safely away."

"You're kidding me. Go back to him? But he will be so angry. He's been such a bastard."

"Perhaps. But for the reasons I have already explained I am confident he will not harm me or throw me out. I carry a son. Umri said so."

Sophy pulled a face. "And that's important? More than if you carried a daughter?"

"Not to me, but the Puri are a patriarchal people. Warriors and pride. Hanal would value a son."

Sophy nodded. "And you want to go back to that?"

Rae just glared at her and walked ahead at a brisk pace that Sophy couldn't match.

At the spring, Rae fed the horse and rubbed him down. Weak light illuminated a murky pool of water. Sophy cringed at the thought of drinking from it. It smelt disgusting. From what she could see, it was a muddy bog in the middle of nowhere. The fact that the horse had drunk out of it first made her stomach turn. However, extreme thirst made her swallow her pride and drink. The water was good, a little gritty but, all things considered, Sophy didn't think it would kill her.

Rae scooped water with her hands and sipped it carefully. Sophy watched her movements, surprised by how different the girl seemed. Even a short time amongst the Puri had matured her and brought out her skill and beauty. How far away those early days in the valley seemed. Rae filled the water bladders, too, and secured them to the saddle.

After a short break, Rae mounted the horse and gave Sophy a hand up. "I do not ride well," Rae said. "So hold on. We must ride like the wind to reach the next stop."

The horse jerked into motion and Sophy hung on precariously. She had to cling to Rae and the girl could hardly keep a proper seat. Sophy had to use her strength to hold onto Rae and the horse. Her jaw began to ache from the stress. They galloped for an hour or so, then slowed to a trot and then a walk. They walked the horse for another hour and then Rae spurred it on again. The way was clear and sloped uphill slightly.

They were riding in the open, vulnerable to attack. Sophy imagined someone spying them as they streaked across the wide plain. The mountain seemed to thrust up out of the ground in front of them and grow larger as the horse ate up the distance. Sophy had to catch her breath at the sight. The breeze was now tinged with ice, not quite freezing, but with a bite to it. The horse's stride began to shorten as it tired. No matter how hard Rae tried to urge the horse on, it refused to go further.

"We will have to dismount and lead the horse from here. We cannot stop," Rae said.

Sophy nodded and eased herself down to the ground. "Why do we have to hurry? I thought there was no sign of pursuit." She angled her gaze behind her, chilled by the thought of the Puri finding her and taking her back to Hanal.

"I see no signs. We must make it to the next spring otherwise the horse will die from thirst. The water bladders are not enough." Rae passed water to Sophy, which cooled her throat and helped clear her head.

Rae then fed the rest of the water to the horse.

Sophy groaned when Rae urged her to walk. She was more tired than the horse. Her stamina was not good and her feet had not had a chance to heal. Each step prodded her with pain. Rae had trouble persuading the horse. She persisted, and after a few jerks of its head and a couple of attempts at rearing, the horse fell into step. After a while, a sort of euphoria came over Sophy, making her lightheaded. All the kinks from riding had worked themselves out. Her feet dragged along the ground and because they were numb, she stumbled quite a bit.

The openness of the plain began to fade away; large upthrusts of rock and huge boulders muscled their way through the rough, grainy soil. A few large birds circled ominously overhead. When Sophy asked about them, Rae told her to pay them no mind. After a while Sophy found she didn't flinch when they filled the air with their chilling cries.

They walked for what seemed like hours. Sophy had only sense enough to put one foot in front of the other. Her eyelids hung down over her eyes, obscuring her vision. She was breathing with heavy, open-mouthed pants. The absence of hooves beating against the ground rhythmically didn't register for a while. She looked back and saw Rae tugging on the reins. The horse refused to go any further. Rae's head swivelled about, searching out something. Sophy turned back and shuffled near to Rae.

"What will we do?"

Rae ignored her and continued to study the landscape. Sophy patted the horse's muzzle idly while she raked her coarse tongue over her dry lips. It didn't help much as there was no moisture. Then as fatigue enveloped her, her head rested against the horse's sweat-matted neck.

"There," Rae said. Her voice was thin and scratchy. Sophy was grateful that her rescuer suffered from their trek too. She didn't want to be the only who wasn't up to it. The horse responded with both of them urging it into a hollow. "Come," Rae said. "Drink from the spring and then we will leave the horse here."

"But," Sophy began to say as she knelt down. She didn't even bother to note the colour of the water or the smell of the mud. She just drank and drank until she could drink no more. Panting, she fell to the side and lay down in the pungent muck. Blinking, she watched Rae drink and then feed the horse.

Sophy might have dozed. Everything seemed so hazy. The next thing she knew she was walking again, this time carrying a pack. The pain in her back brought her mind into sharp focus. The unguent that Rae had applied had worn off. The raw agony made her vision turn red. She heaved in a breath and followed Rae, ahead of her, back stiff and unbending, striding ahead as if fatigue didn't touch her. When the hurt eased a touch, she looked around. How did she come to be walking? She had no memory of standing up, only the memory of pain. She chanced a look over her shoulder; the horse was nowhere to be seen. She began to panic, thinking that she was hallucinating, but snatches of memory appeared in her tired mind. It was like a dream, a bad dream.

Rae kept walking and didn't look back, didn't bother to check that Sophy followed. It made Sophy angry. She sped up, wanting to reach out and grab the girl and swing her round and yell abuse into her face. But every time she sped up, Rae would quicken her pace and leave Sophy's hand flailing in the air.

By nightfall, Sophy staggered. Her tongue was like a dried leather strap inside a chalky mouth. Mud coated her teeth and her clothes. Her legs and feet throbbed and weighed heavily. Rae stopped and dropped her bundle on the ground. Taking that as a signal, Sophy let her knees bend and collapsed into the dirt. If Rae tried to rouse her, she didn't remember.

The sound of large wings flapping close by woke her. She blinked against the hard light and brisk chill in the air. Rae lay quiet beside her. Sophy sat up quickly and the bird, dull grey and brown with a hooked beak, flapped its wings again. Sophy waved her arms and yelled and the large bird took flight. But it circled, angling its head at them. Something about the creature made her nervous. The bloody thing was sizing her up as its next meal, she was sure.

Rae stirred. The girl had also slept where she fell, removing neither robe nor preparing a bedroll. Her dark eyes were bloodshot and rimmed with darker circles. When she stood, it was with less energy than before.

Out of her bundle, she took some rations and handed them over wordlessly. Her gaze roamed about the surroundings and she sniffed. "Quick. We must drink and then go."

Sophy crawled to her feet and pushed herself up to stand. The horizon tilted and then steadied. The salt and spice meat in her hand was hard to chew. She didn't have enough spit to swallow. She tried sucking on it, while she numbly followed Rae to a spring.

The puddle between two markers was even more disgusting than the last one. The water was yellowish and smelt like sulphur. "Are you sure we can drink that? Isn't there something better?"

"We have no choice. 'Tis hard to call water here, unlike in Argenterra. There is less of it and there needs to be cracks in the rocks."

Sophy said nothing. Rae knelt and put her face in the water. She sipped it carefully and then used some to wash her face. When she stood and moved out the way, Sophy knelt too. But she found it hard to drink. Holding her nose, she put her lips to the water. It felt slimy and she nearly retched.

On the other hand, she knew she couldn't walk without fluids, no matter how disgusting they were. Like Rae, she splashed some of the fetid water on her face, noting absently that she wasn't sunburnt. It was spring and up there on the wasteland the winter wind still blew. She hated to think what the winter was like. No wonder the Puri took shelter in caves in the coldest months.

Rae had moved on, and Sophy had to lope after her with an ungainly stride. Her feet hurt and she was stiff in various joints. Rae's pace was relentless. What was worse was that she didn't talk. Perhaps she didn't have the energy.

Another day eked past. Just as the sun was setting and sending shadows and shades of red about, Rae paused. Sophy staggered on for a few more steps and noticed that the land dropped away steeply. Fear quaked inside her. It was a chasm. Sophy backed away, her stomach spinning like a whirlwind just at the thought of it. Walls of ice and rock rose on the other side.

She noticed Rae was staring at her with her dark eyes, her mouth grim. "Here is where I will leave you."

Sophy broke into a sweat. "Leave me? No...you can't leave me here. I have no idea where I am. And I can't survive. Not here."

Rae pointed to the chasm. "This is the edge of Puri lands. I have to go back now—I must go back." Her face looked haunted. Her young, pretty face was marred with dirt and dark thoughts.

Sophy took a step towards her. "But I'll die here. Do you want me to die?" Her voice was near hysterical. "Was that your plan all along? Just get rid of me and forget it ever happened? Is your jealousy so great?"

Rae shook her head. Her dark hair was loose from her braid. It hung in dirty clumps around her face, which now had sunken cheeks. "You will not die." Rae dropped to her knees and then rummaged through her bundle. She pulled out a familiar beige and white striped robe. It was the one Umri had held while she told the tale of Aurore and Daken.

"Here, take this. 'Tis Coldcloth and will keep you warm." Rae looked down, suddenly humble as Sophy weakly put out a hand to caress the material.

"It's precious to you. Are you sure you want to part with it?"

"I can travel no further with you. Every minute I waste here means I am further from Hanal. Take the robe. Keep it safe. You will return it to me one day. You see? I do not wish you dead but whole. Come on, take it quickly." Rae pushed the robe towards her.

Sophy took it, scrunching it in her hands. It was steeped in the *given* but Sophy was beyond complaining about that. Somehow the *given* in it didn't bother her, like it was less potent than before. "Thank you, Rae. But I don't want you to leave me. I am afraid and I hate feeling like this."

"Sleep here this night and cross N'Brell's Chasm tomorrow," Rae added as she sorted through her bundle. "On the other side is the way to Glassy Mountain Retreat. Help will be there for you."

Sophy chilled at the name Rae had given the chasm. From experience, she knew that places were named for significant events, reaching back to the times of the First Comers.

"Why do I not like the name of the chasm? Did someone die here?"

Rae's expression became solemn and she lifted her tired, dark eyes to hers. "The tales tell us of N'Brell, who was Vorn's cherished wife. On a visit to the mountain with her husband, they became separated during a blizzard and she fell to her death here." Rae pointed to the rent in the earth.

Sophy stood on tiptoe and looked to where Rae pointed. She swallowed the lump in her throat. "I was right. I don't like it." Sophy's brief spurt of levity had no effect on Rae. "Please don't leave me."

"In the morning, just after sunrise, gaze in that direction. Do not oversleep. The sunlight reveals a bridge built in crystal. You must go then for 'tis not visible at other times. If you are too late, you must wait for the next morning, understand? It is dangerous to cross at other times.

"I thank the *given* that I listened to Kushlan's tales as well as I did. He told tales of his treks through here in his youth. It was the memory of those tales that led me to the springs and to the forgotten paths." Rae paused and for a moment, Sophy thought she would cry. *Praise to Kushlan for our deliverance!* But Rae didn't. With a slight shrug, Rae continued her instructions. "You must cross the bridge quickly."

The sinking feeling was back and reached to Sophy's knees. "What happens if I'm slow in crossing?"

"When the sun reaches a certain height, the bridge fades from view. 'Tis still there, mind, but hard to see. And then there are the winds, strong enough to rip you from the bridge and fling you to the depths below."

Sophy's eyes widened. "Isn't there another way? You don't know for sure that I'll see this bridge. How will I find the retreat?"

"I am as sure as I can be without seeing it for myself. And no, there is no other way. Not here. I fear to direct you to Panal's Pass for it will be guarded and it is far. If Hanal sent pursuers, there is where they would look for us. He would not think that I knew this way, for 'tis an old trail, not often used and perhaps forgotten."

Sophy eyed the chasm and swallowed loudly. "Oh well, I guess that's something at least." She twisted the Coldcloth robe in her hands.

"As for the retreat," Rae added, "I cannot help you. It is there. I know not how to find it."

Sophy gazed at the mountain on the other side of the chasm. No hint of habitation could be seen from their vantage point. She really didn't want to be left alone. She had no strength and she was afraid, afraid as she had ever been. She wasn't reckless anymore; now she was thoughtful, and considered the consequences. She could die. Die and not see Oakheart ever again. She would hate that more than anything.

Rae ignored Sophy's pleading gaze, while she busied herself by assembling her things and retying her bundle. "I will leave now and by the time I find my horse he will be rested enough for me to ride home." She turned away and then paused to face Sophy and put out a hand to clasp her shoulder. "I hope you find peace in all this, Sophy. And may you reunite with Oakheart. He is a worthy man."

Sophy reached up to pat Rae's hand resting lightly on her shoulder. "Thanks." Her eyes burned and the back of her throat tightened. "I hope you don't suffer for helping me, Rae. I hope you can help Hanal find his honour."

Rae nodded, a ghost of a smile on her lips, before she strode away, disappearing into the shadows of early twilight while Sophy, motionless, watched her depart. She hugged herself. What would happen now? On the other side of the chasm was a sharp incline like a slab of rock and ice pushed up by forces unseen, and from there rose the mountain range, craggy, corrugated bedrock. Winter snow drifts clung to it. The way looked impassable.

The wind whistling through the crevice sounded as if it was singing her death song. Slowly, a sliver of Walker moon rose, soon to be followed by Chaser the smaller moon. By its dim light, Sophy lay down, sitting up quickly to pull on the Coldcloth robe. It itched, but with Sophy's other pains the irritation paled in comparison. Rae had left no food or water. Her stomach punched and pounded, making its emptiness known.

In the morning, she had to find help on the other side of that chasm or she would die. She wondered what help could be found. Would she be able to find the retreat? Would there be sign posts? Someone waiting to direct her path? Her life opened up in front of her, as dark and as daunting as the depths of the chasm beside her.

✵ 21 ✵

A PARTING OF THE WAYS

A ria eyed the split trail sadly. One rough, beaten roadway led up through Panal's Pass, the other wound through the foothills and up into the Glassy Mountain Range. The jagged mountains cut the sky and from where she sat she could taste the ice on the wind. The other horses were slowing behind her as the riders took in the view. Aria couldn't believe she'd come this far. She never thought she'd have the courage. She found it hard to identify with the young girl who'd come to this place just over a year before. Argenterra had seemed so welcoming then, and in many ways it still was, but she had changed.

There was a reality to living here that she found hard to accustom herself to. A wedding oath was binding till death. A good thing, perhaps, because it meant you couldn't be unfaithful if you tried. On the other hand, it could be a terrible burden if you chose unwisely...as she had.

How different it seemed in those early days, recalling the attention, the handsome prince, the feel of the *given* flowing through her. Who would have thought that there was a layer of malice here, a rotting thread of corruption. Rufus didn't make her say yes to Dellbright's proposal. That had been her own doing. And it shamed her more than anything. Sophy's advice had been sound, yet she had turned away from her friend, creating all the misery that followed.

Oakheart sat on his horse next to her, gazing longingly up to the mountains. He had been so good to her, had shown her how well she could use the *given*. But would it be well enough? She couldn't use it with finesse. Didn't she fail to heal him properly, fail to bring him fully back to himself? Every day she saw the lines of worry around his mouth and eyes cut deeper, the fatigue etching into his spirit. Someone as active and strong as Oakheart would, understandably, find it difficult to manage with a sudden and all-encompassing weakness. There was never any reproach in his words, or looks, about her failure.

"My lady," Fern said quietly from the other side of her.

Her heart did a quicksilver leap and she dared to look into those grey eyes of his. They reminded her of a storm. She was overwhelmed by his gaze, so full of love and sadness.

"Yes, Fern? What is it?" Aria tried to keep her voice neutral; difficult because she found herself responding to him in all kinds of ways. His allure was almost too much for her to fight, yet she had to.

"We must part ways here."

Aria's breath caught. Already they were at the crossroads, and Fern was insisting on offering himself to Hanal's sister in exchange for Sophy. They had discussed it over and over during their trek, but Fern was persistent. She couldn't help showing her innermost thoughts. She could not have him herself. What right did she have to stop him doing some good for Sophy? Was she that selfish?

Fern reached out and touched her hand lightly. "Do not be sad...my lady..."

"What if he refuses and takes you captive? Then everything will be for nothing. I can't help but think that it is a waste of time." Panic rose inside her. She wanted Sophy back, but wasn't convinced Fern's plan would achieve it.

Fern shrugged. "Why would he? He wants a connection to the Argenterran throne and I can supply it."

Fern's hand strayed up her arm. His touch thrilled along her skin. Her body trembled in response. It was so confusing. Everybody was looking to her for leadership, and all she wanted was to be folded into

Fern's embrace—the one thing she couldn't let happen. She couldn't trust herself. She needed to be wary of men, but Fern wasn't Dellbright. What harm was there in being receptive to Fern's advances? For wanting some tenderness, some love and adoration?

Oakheart dismounted and rested his head against his saddle, suddenly looking exhausted. "We should camp near here this night," he said wearily. "There is a travellers' hut ahead, nestled behind the trail. There should be supplies and a roof over our head. Unless, of course, the Puri have raided it."

Glad of the chance to put off Fern's departure, Aria said, "Yes. Let us stay together for one night more." She was going to say something else, but Fern's look stopped the words in her throat. Perhaps he wanted to be gone, for there was an expression of longing and pain that came over him momentarily.

"The path to the travellers' hut is that way," Oakheart said. He took a while to raise his head from the saddle but finally he grabbed the reins with a sigh, smiled at the horse and stroked its muzzle. Fern moved ahead, and Oakheart led his horse after his friend. Aria kicked her mount to follow after them at a walk.

There wasn't much vegetation and there were vertical thrusts of rock breaking through the ground, creating an unusual twisting forest of rock. Ahead of her Oakheart checked for signs, such as lines nicked into the sides of the rock face, and led them through a winding and convoluted path. All of a sudden, in the shadow of a huge spear of rock, imbued with multicoloured layers, was a hut. It blended in because it was made of the same rock. Round and quite large, it could easily contain a dozen men. At the rear was a stable for their horses.

Aria must have been gaping because Oakheart chuckled when he looked at her. "There is a spring as well. Plenty of fresh water for us and our mounts. We should be able to bake bread if we can light the oven."

Aria took her gaze from the hut and smiled at him. He seemed heartened by being near the retreat or the hut or food or maybe all. "Warm bread? That sounds great. Do you know how to make it?"

His smile faded. "Ah, no. I thought perhaps you might."

Aria repressed a groan. She loved warm, fresh bread whether it was white bread or coarsely ground grain bread, but she had no idea how to make it.

Lillia took Aria's horse's reins to lead the tired animal to the stables. Aria tried to catch her eye but Lillia seemed bent on avoiding it. "Um, Lillia," she called out, "you don't know how to...er..."

Mellow stood still, watching Lillia's hastened step. He turned to Aria, a slight smile on his face. "No. She does not," he said. "However, I do." Mellow was quite handsome when he smiled, Aria thought. It washed away his dour expression. Perhaps his bitterness would not be permanent.

She beamed a smile at him. "Oh. Would you be so kind as to make some bread, Mellow?"

Lillia's husband glanced sideways to the hut and grinned. "I will try. Let us hope that Oakheart's promised ingredients are still intact."

Oakheart patted Mellow on the back companionably and led him towards the hut. Meld's horse was between Oakheart and the hut. Oakheart looked up at the adept.

"Will you not dismount, Meld, and join us? Mellow is going to make fresh bread."

The adept avoided eye contact and looked at the surroundings. The strange adept had been meditating while in the saddle and was only coming to realise where they were. "We are close to the retreat, now. We should push on. Why do we stop here?"

Mellow's frown returned, causing a vee of creased flesh between his eyebrows. The forest man stepped back and then went into the hut.

After sparing Mellow a quick, concerned glance as he walked away, Oakheart sighed. Aria took a few steps closer so she could hear the exchange. "We stop because we have come to a parting of the ways—and we are tired." Unable to keep the weariness from his voice, Oakheart said, "Best to tackle the last part of the journey well rested and with our stomachs full."

Meld's eyes took on that otherness quality that was once Adage's trademark. He flicked his gaze to the mountains and then looked at the camp and at Oakheart and Aria. "I see I cannot persuade you otherwise. Very well." The adept tossed his reins to Oakheart and climbed off the horse. He moved stiffly, suffering from being so long in the saddle.

Later that evening, the fire filled the hut with comforting, golden warmth. Mellow had baked his special bread, which sat tantalisingly on a wooden board in front of them while they watched and waited for it to cool. To accompany it they had found a mature cheese that crumbled when cut. Aria's stomach grumbled and she smiled weakly in embarrassment. Oakheart laughed, then Fern joined in. Soon they were all laughing at Aria's stomach noises.

Except Meld. Aria saw that everyone bar the adept was looking at the bread. He shared their fire but not their companionship. Brook's body was thinner than it was. Adage, as Meld, didn't take good care of it.

Each of the faces gathered around the fire reflected a secret and sad thought. The laughter faded and the mood became sombre. Oakheart had been sleeping while Mellow baked the bread. Now his green eyes were alert. They didn't sparkle with joy but they had lost that haunted look. Aria thought he had hope now. Unfortunately, he had detected nothing from Sophy across their link since that spectacular time when Hanal had touched the *given* within her. Aria and Oakheart both were sure that Sophy was not dead, but that was all they were sure about. So many things seemed to be happening across the land. She couldn't put her finger on it but it was there, a nagging feeling that something bad was about to happen.

Lillia knelt beside her, disturbing her thoughts. She handed her a decoction of herbs. "Drink this, my lady. It will aid your strength."

Aria eyed the brown-tinged liquid. "Ah thanks. But doesn't Oakheart need it more than I do?"

"Yes, that is why he has a double dose. I have been able to replenish my supply of herbs and cures here. I have made a fortifying brew for everyone."

There was a faint groan from Oakheart's direction, but when Aria caught his eye, he winked at her and sipped a mug of Lillia's brew.

Fern took his portion meekly, as did Illart and Raven. Meld didn't acknowledge the forest maiden as she placed the mug by his leg.

"'Tis time," Mellow said, startling more than just Aria. He pulled a knife out of his belt dramatically and plunged it into a large round loaf. He had made more than one but the others were for their journey. Steam rose from the brown dough. Aria's mouth watered at the aroma. Such a simple thing and she was in raptures.

Lillia handed around large chunks with a portion of the cheese. Meld ignored her when she held out his serving. Aria thought she heard the woman's teeth grinding. "Hearken, adept," Lillia said in a voice half anger, half despair. "You must eat. Your body has weakened through your lack of care. You endanger us all by doing this. We have a hard road tomorrow."

Meld's blue eyes focussed on the forest woman. Slowly, he looked around and then down at the portion of food she held out to him. With a slight nod of acknowledgement, he took it.

It was strange watching Meld place the slice of warm bread, steaming lightly, into his mouth. A look of relish overshaded his features for a moment but was soon replaced with his usual austere look. Aria guessed it was the part of Brook that still lived within his body that had surfaced, for only bread baked by his father would have provoked such a reaction. She hazarded a glance at the forest folk. Lillia was wild-eyed and the rest of the forest folk shared a hopeful but hesitant look. The adept finished eating, then drank Lillia's fortifying brew. Resuming his previous pose, he sat staring into the fire, meditating on some obscure thing that probably none of them could understand.

After a time, Aria looked up from her own plate to see Meld staring at her. Could he read her thoughts? She hoped not. She cleared her throat and Meld returned to studying the flames.

Oakheart leant back and wrapped himself in his blanket. Aria could tell by his breathing that he had instantly fallen into an exhausted sleep. Not even the prospect of a second helping had kept him awake. She smiled. There was so much to like about Oakheart.

Fern was quiet. She thought his expression spoke volumes. His eyes were dark grey in the firelight, and when their eyes met he gave a lopsided smile. Stupidly, she sat and stared at him, unable to voice all the things she felt. When she needed something he was there, attentive, solicitous and loving. Fern turned on his side and rolled himself up into his blanket.

Aria wanted to stretch her legs. Her thoughts, her emotions, wanted to fly in every direction. She tried to focus on the rough-hewn stone wall of the hut to calm herself. She'd never sleep otherwise. No, she had to step outside. She needed the clean night air, she needed the stars, the mountains...

When Lillia finally quenched the firestick and only the soft, red light of the embers shed light over her sleeping companions, Aria eased herself to her feet. Between her and the door there were pallets, light wooden frames that kept sleepers just above the stone floor of the hut, that had to be negotiated.

Everyone's breathing appeared to fall into a rhythm, a rise and fall that almost mesmerised her. Her tangle of hair was in her face. She ran her hand through it. She waited another moment and, with her blanket draped over her shoulders, she tiptoed between the sleepers and finally tugged the door open. Hesitating in the blast of cool night air, she shored up her courage and slipped outside into the night.

Despite the barrenness of the area, it was alive with sounds. The horses nickered intermittently but that was overshadowed by the sound of frogs, and other things that chirped and sang into the night. Aria let the sounds flow over her and wash away her dread. It was good to be alive.

The sky was bright with stars. How lovely. Why hadn't she taken the time to notice them before? She ran her hand over her lip, healed now. When she walked, she didn't ache. Her scars had mostly faded. She still felt them though. Every scratch or nick or cut was writ upon her body where only she could see. She could never forgive Dellbright for what he had done to her. He had fractured her love, turned it against her in a twisted way she could never understand.

She sighed loudly, letting her tension and bad thoughts ease out into the night. She didn't know how long she'd been there when she suddenly noticed Fern's outline as a dark shape against the stars. A shiver of trepidation snaked through her. She should go back inside, keep away from him and all the possibilities that could have been if she had met him first. It was best they not be alone together. Yet, some impulse, some deep-seated desire, held her where she stood. Surely she deserved some happiness.

Fern took a few more steps, his face still in shadow. "Aria," he said as if her name was everything to him. The texture of his voice thrilled her, made her skin prickle pleasantly.

Aria stood very still, waiting out the moment, enjoying the sensations aroused by being with him like this. "Fern," she answered finally when he was close by, not touching her, but near enough that his warmth flowed over her.

Then his hand touched her hair lightly. "Aria—how good it feels to touch you."

Aria went to brush his hand away.

"No, please...let me...touch you this once. Tomorrow, I will be gone...perhaps forever." His voice caught.

Aria dropped her hand. "Fern..." She turned to face him, closing the gap between them. "I don't want you to go." Seeing his eyes widen, she took a half-step back. "I'm sorry. I know it was wrong of me to say that. I have no right."

"Aria." His voice was a caress.

"I...I should encourage you for Sophy's sake, I know that. But I find that I'm selfish...even though there is no hope...of...for us."

Fern's fingers brushed softly against her lips. "Shhhhh," he whispered in her ear. "Speak not of it...I have to go...You know I treated your friend most unkindly...falling under your spell is punishment for it I am sure."

"You were unkind to Sophy? I don't understand." Aria frowned, tormented by the fact that Fern could do wrong, and to Sophy, who needed acceptance more than anything.

"I am sorry for it. Truly I am. My quest to save her, to sacrifice myself for her should earn me some forgiveness. Say you forgive me. Do not let it stand between us. Already there is so much that does."

"I don't understand. You who have been so kind to me was unkind to Sophy? I don't see how you could be cruel to anyone, particularly Sophy. She is a wonderful person, brave and strong and beautiful. I know her looks were affected when we first came here...but beauty isn't everything. It is only one part of a person."

"Yet in you everything is combined. Beauty within and beauty without. I am so smitten."

She touched his hand lightly, a tingle at the touch. "Fern...I wish...I wish things could be different."

"Hush now. Worry not about the future. Who knows what the future will bring...but now there is only this moment, you...me and the night." His lips brushed gently across her brow.

Aria lifted her head and Fern was there, mouth soft and smooth, kissing her. He stopped suddenly, breath short and excited. "Forgive me. I did not know if I could and then I did." His voice was full of wonder. "The oath does not prevent us sharing this touch."

"This will only lead to pain. But I do not want you to stop, even though you should." Her fingers laced through his and she brought her body closer so that she was wrapped in his warmth. When his mouth found hers again, the kiss was no longer sweet but demanding and filled with passion. Aria wanted his touch, wanted his kiss so badly. Her hands found his ears and she stroked them and then they went to his neck where she pulled him even closer. Her passion exceeded his. She wanted to drown in it. She needed it...wanted to die for it. Wanted to wipe the bad memories away.

Fern broke off and panted loudly in her ears. "Oh Aria...I...I...thank you for this moment. If 'tis my last I would be happy for it."

She touched his lips with her fingers. He nipped them with his teeth. "Do not speak of death or of parting..." She didn't realise she was crying until Fern wiped a tear from her cheek with his thumb.

"We could leave Argenterra, Aria. Like Daken and the high queen. We could love each other, unhindered by your oath. You would not leave any sadness behind you."

Aria gasped at the possibilities—and then responsibilities and other ties intruded. She loved this place and her child was here. Gilly needed her.

"Gilly...I cannot be near him just now, but to leave would separate us forever. I could not do it."

"I am selfish and needy. I thought only of my own desires. Forgive me."

Aria sighed and leant into him, fitting herself to the curve of his body and feeling the muscles of his chest against her cheek. "I thank you for talking of it. Such thoughts have been in my mind for a long time now. I have been in torment, thinking I was inflicted with Shabra's curse the moment Kushlan told me of it. But now with my feelings for you, it is more than a thought...it is true."

With both hands to the side of her face, he eased her head back gently to gaze into her face. "Hush now. We can consider again... after....I must go to your friend's aid. I must go through with the wedding if Hanal agrees to it. But it will not end there. My heart will be yours even if my body cannot."

Aria couldn't respond. To say that she didn't want him to make love to another was what was on her mind. Perhaps he would enjoy it, perhaps he would not love her afterwards. And what right did she have? None. She was bound to Dellbright. The memory of his striking her flashed into the forefront of her mind; the feel of him ripping into her with his flesh made her quake. The memory so easily bidden was quashed but not before Fern took note of it.

"What is it? You tremble but with fear not with desire."

Aria sucked in a breath. "It's nothing...just a memory..."

Fern's brows furrowed. "Of him? Of what he did to you? How I wish I could erase his touch. The man is a coward. Indeed, to call him a man is an insult to the rest of us. In time your hurt will heal." He stroked her hair. "I am sorry. I should not have reminded you. I am a beast myself."

Aria made to turn away. But Fern pulled her to him and wept on her shoulder. She found herself weeping too. Not just for Fern but for herself and all the sorrow that welled up inside her. In the end she admitted her fears. "I find I am jealous of the thought of you with another woman. What if you do not desire me afterwards? What if this feeling you have fades?"

"Hush, hush. Think not on it. I will always feel this way about you. From the moment I saw you I was smitten. Your gentleness and your bravery have only made your claim on my heart stronger. Why worry about a future none of us can control? We can only think and feel and be of this moment."

In the night, while the sounds of the wilderness washed over them, they embraced. Feelings of guilt arose. "We must go inside. We shouldn't be doing this," Aria insisted.

Fern stepped back from her. "You go. I will wait out here. I am not ready for sleep. There is much to dwell upon. I must head to the Puri tents soon."

His eyes spoke of his feelings. Aria couldn't resist the passion that swelled in them. She stepped up to him and pressed her lips to his. A wave of warmth swept over her, stirring her. But she thought of how this would end and tears leaked from her eyes. Abruptly, she pulled away, hastened back to the door and swept inside.

Meld was sitting up when she entered. His strange eyes glittered with the reflected light from the embers. Aria swallowed her guilt, nodded to him and sought her blankets. As her thoughts settled, they turned to Fern still outside in the cool of the night. She was warm from his embrace, tempted to test her oath's boundaries. With a sigh, she decided not to venture out again. It would only lead to disappointment and heartache. Her dreams, when they came, were pleasant this night.

When she woke to the smell of toffelporridge, Aria was conscious that Oakheart's gaze held pity. Did he know that she had left the hut in the night and that Fern had followed her? Surely Meld would not have said anything. She tried to shrug off the unease. She had not slept with Fern but her kisses and her words and her thoughts were all a betrayal of Dellbright and her oath. She might trifle with the details but, in essence, it was the same.

Outside the hut, they waited in readiness to farewell their comrade. His gear packed, Fern was serious and determined as he led his horse towards them to say farewell. The sensation of cool iciness flowed over Aria and she swung round. Meld was watching her, calculation in his gaze. She tried to ignore it. Nothing but Fern's departure was in her mind. When he was gone, she could think about Sophy.

"Take care, Fern," Oakheart said. "Remember the route I showed you. The main Puri camp is there, just over two days' swift ride. Hanal will be holding court. They harvest the wild grass during the summer. They depend upon it for food, cloth, rope, fodder...everything. Add what you can to your inducement to Hanal in cash and in-kind tribute.

I will try to meet it. Beg for safe passage to the retreat. The Puri like not the retreat but if they can get what they want from the alliance, they will do it."

"I hear you. I will do my best. By my life, I will." Fern climbed onto his horse. His eyes met Aria's. "Farewell, princess. We will meet again." He sounded certain.

"G...goodbye, Fern..." Aria looked away and casually wiped a tear from her cheek. She would not cry, she told herself, but Fern's departure was like an ending. She could see no other outcome.

Lillia and the rest of the forest folk farewelled Fern in their way. Meld said nothing. Aria stood and watched the dust kicked up by his horse's hooves until he was in sight no more.

Oakheart walked over to assist her to mount up. She studied his face while he checked the horse's hooves, the girth strap, the bridle. He must have sensed her scrutiny because he looked up and blushed. His eyes were haunted. Sophy's suffering was nearly his undoing.

"She'll be all right, Oakheart. I'm sure of that."

He nodded, helped her mount and then moved off to check his own horse. Comfortable in the saddle, it surprised her how well she rode. She'd learned so much since leaving Valley Keep. She knew if she looked behind her she'd be able to see the valley wreathed in mist, but she couldn't bring herself to do it. Her son was there and he was lost to her.

CHAPTER 22

N'BRELL'S CHASM

S unlight played over Sophy's face. She licked her dry, cracked lips but her tongue had the texture of a coarse stick running across her savaged mouth. She could barely swallow saliva. Easing up onto her elbow, she looked around, a touch disorientated from lack of food and water compounded by fatigue. A brittle landscape greeted her: roughly hewn rock faces gouged by wind, a smattering of ice and dusting of snow. It seemed so grey and lifeless.

A troublesome bird swooped her. She waved her hands about and screamed. The vulture-like bird banked to the left and landed noisily on a rocky outcrop. It was still early. With a sudden thrust of alarm, she scrambled to her feet. The bridge was only visible at a certain time. If she missed it, she'd have to wait for another day. She didn't think her strength would last that long.

Even her eyeballs were dry and her vision was blurry. She blinked a few times and rubbed her eyes so that she could see the crystal bridge. Picking her way carefully along the edge of the chasm, she stared hard, looking for the way across. The sun was angling higher, sending shafts of light through a dip in the mountain range and making the ice-laden air glisten.

Around the bend of a cliff face, a shaft of light lanced the gloom and settled upon a smattering of silver, a play of brilliant pale blue light. She had to shade her eyes with her hand to keep looking. Like a spray of hoary dust floating down, a thin bridge spread out before her to span the chasm. It had no handrails from what she could see. She ground her teeth in frustration. To cross that thing was to risk her life. To stay was equally hazardous. Sophy didn't like not having choices. *Bugger this place!*

"Best get close to it." She lurched over. If she looked down she lost sight of the bridge and had to stop and locate it all over again. The higher the sun rose the more concrete the construction became. As she drew near she decided it looked like transparent plastic. A few steps more and she would be at the edge. As well as not having railings, it wasn't very wide. A death trap to the unwary. A horse could, perhaps, be led across it, but Sophy didn't think a horse would ever want to be. She knelt down, tied the Coldcloth around her waist and tentatively put her hand on the bridge, just in case she imagined it was there. Its texture was like glass, cool and smooth. When she looked up the world seemed to tilt around it. Just what she needed, a dose of vertigo. She supposed closing her eyes would help but then she'd fall off the bridge. There was nothing to hold on to, just the bridge itself. It wasn't a short bridge, being at least ten times her body length. It was going to take an age.

Because of the chasm gaping below and the lack of guardrails, Sophy thought crawling across would be the best way. She would have to keep three points of contact with the bridge at all times. She gulped down a few breaths and put her hand on the crystal fabric of the bridge. It bore her weight. She edged out a little further and began to tremble. She didn't know where to focus her gaze: straight ahead or on the bridge in front of her. Gazing down into the chasm itself was not an option.

Taking it slowly, Sophy inched along. The tug of a breeze from out of nowhere surprised her. She gripped tighter with her hands. Unfortunately that didn't firm up her hold. Her hands were sweaty and the bridge was smooth, like glass rolled and blown in one piece. Lying flat, she hugged the bridge until the wind settled, letting loose some tears. Cries flew out of her mouth and disappeared down the chasm.

The wind left her shaking with fear. She pushed back onto her knees and continued crawling. Then she remembered what Rae said about not taking too long to cross because of the winds and the bridge fading from view. She panicked and tried to crawl faster. Her hand slid beneath her and she lost her balance. A scream sped out of her mouth and was gone. Sweat gathered at the back of her neck and at the base of her spine, and she was more than slightly queasy. Again she steadied herself, then crawled onwards. All too soon, she paused and began to shake, paralysed by nerves. No amount of telling herself to be calm seemed to help.

After a few deep breaths the trembling eased. "This is not helping anything, Sophy," she said to herself.

She continued on, trying to ignore the pain in her knees caused by the hard surface. The bridge was longer than she thought. Once out in the middle, instead of the occasional tug of a strong breeze, the wind became more persistent. Her hair flew across her face. She spat out the strands blown in her mouth. Shaking her head, she tried to keep her vision clear. Presently, she couldn't lift her hands to tie her hair back for the wind would tug her clear of the bridge if she let go her hold. If the wind grew any stronger she'd be done for.

Tired of crawling, Sophy tried another way. Grasping the sides of the bridge, she pulled herself forwards, sliding along on her knees. This seemed to work better than crawling for it allowed for a better purchase. The wind shifted again, blowing her hair out of her face. She took the opportunity to measure how far she had to go.

"Oh no!" The far end of the bridge was disappearing. It sparkled and shimmered as if it was dematerialising. Gaping stupidly was not going to help, but gape she did, long enough to confirm that the bridge was indeed disappearing. "Damn it."

Sophy picked up her pace. A sound, more like a vibration, began to build around her. Distracted, Sophy slowed and dared to look around her. The dark chasm beneath her loomed large. She swivelled her head, trying to see the source of the sound. Buffeting wind danced around her, but there was more coming. Wind. Strong wind.

With the next push along the bridge, she lay flat against the surface using her arms and her feet to anchor herself, hoping that the wind would slide over her.

At the onslaught of the gale, she thought she would survive, but then, impossibly, the wind grew stronger and her grip began to fail. Prayers leaked out of Sophy's mouth, snatched away by the wind. For a mindless moment, she lost touch with the real world as she fought for breath.

The wind abated ever so slightly. Taking that for a sign, she began to move, snake-like, undulating her body towards the other side. Whimpering, Sophy edged along on her stomach, gliding along by the pull of her hands and the push of her thighs. Another strong burst of wind made her legs slide sideways.

A scream tore from her throat at the nothingness beneath her left foot. She pressed herself flat and managed to get her leg up to join the other. Hand pull by hand pull, she inched across the bridge. She cared not to look if it was there or not.

Her time on the bridge went on forever. She kept crawling, not taking note of the change in the feel of the ground beneath her until she sensed that the ground beneath had become rougher and firmer. Perhaps she'd made it. The sound of the wind funnelling through the chasm was like a wild beast roaring. That was the last thing she heard before she lost consciousness.

Shadows were lengthening by the time her eyes fluttered open. There was some snow, a light dusting, dry and cold. Coming to herself, Sophy looked around. Her feet still dangled over the edge of the chasm, but the rest of her was on terra firma. She pulled her feet towards her and hugged her knees. The wind was less powerful—and the bridge was nowhere to be seen. Whoever had made it must be insane. Surely, no one normal would think up such a construction and expect others to endure the crossing of it. She bet it kept the Puri away.

Her arms and legs pained her; her feet and hands were numb with cold. She groped at the Coldcloth around her waist and struggled to put it on. Immediately, she was warmer and the wind penetrated less.

Behind her was a wall of rock. She studied it, then realised it was riddled with pathways. On unsteady legs, she stumbled down one. Her hand trailed along the wall of rock as the path angled and turned like a corkscrew shape bored into the mountain.

It was so cold Sophy could no longer feel the blisters in her feet as she shuffled along. It grew darker the further she followed along the path that became a tunnel. A few more steps revealed it was a dead end. She almost wept. She turned, resolutely tugged her Coldcloth robe around her, shutting out the biting wind, and reversed her path. She didn't realise that she was moaning and crying as she lurched along. She was losing her mind, it was so surreal. She could not have imagined a place like this, an ending like this.

Returning to her starting point, she chose the next path along. It had corners and sharp twists. Time was running out. She was cold and hungry and near the end of her stamina. Panting as she loped along, hoping this path would lead her somewhere, she ran smack into a wall that marked the end of the way. Dazed, she stumbled backwards, face smarting from the impact. "What the hell!" she croaked and rubbed her stinging nose.

"Is it a maze? God no! That's not fair," she cried out, followed by a wail of despair. She had the inclination to sink to her knees and forget about finding a path. The pain would be over then. But she resisted the urge. Picturing Oakheart helped. Picturing eating food, being warm and his smile was even better.

Wiping a frozen tear from her cheek, she swung round and stepped determinedly back towards the main path. A least six other paths ended in dead ends. One split off and left her confused and unable to trace her way back to the beginning for hours. The light was fading; she no longer thought of food and water. Her insides felt empty, as if she didn't really exist and at any moment she'd float away on the breeze.

At the main path for the umpteenth time, she looked up and around, searching for a clue. Tall, smooth rock lined the path. She trailed her hands along the stone, using it for support and guidance. So many paths crisscrossed it, leading down and around or to the side. It was impossible. Anger welled up inside her. Such a futile attempt to end in death, for that is what she faced without a doubt. She sagged to her knees and reclined against the rock face. She tried to weep but there were no tears, just an empty feeling that stretched out and out so that her essence was thin and ready to be tugged away by death.

Sleep, she needed it, wanted it and couldn't fight the downwards pull of her eyelids. She'd done enough. She'd crossed the chasm. There must be help nearby, she thought to herself as she huddled against the stone walls, clinging to the warmth in her Coldcloth robe.

SOPHY WOKE WITH A START, A JERK OF THE EYELIDS. SHE HAD trouble remembering where she was. What had woken her? Her sleep had been long, almost a death sleep devoid of dreams. It was eerily quiet in the still of the night, lit only by a quarter moon.

Silver tendrils of light bathed the pathway. Gaping for a while, she didn't understand what she was seeing. It was a pretty, bejewelled glow. Narrowing her gaze, she looked again, finally comprehending that the light was coming from within the stone path. She crawled along, and saw there was a glowing stone set in the ground. Looking along the path, she saw that the stones continued along the ground, like runway lights. It was a map.

Sophy hugged herself against the cold creeping through the folds of her robe, holding it closed with her hands. There was a hint of snow and ice in the breeze. She struggled to her feet. Was she really seeing what she thought? Taking a few more steps, she rounded a corner. When the gentle moonlight hit the path, sections of it seemed to glow. At first only faintly, then as Walker moon rose the stones shone more brightly. Sophy stumbled along, shaking her head because she thought she was hallucinating. Maybe she was dead and this was the pathway to the other world. Didn't they always say follow the light? Was this the path to heaven?

Sophy giggled. Surprised, she stopped and touched her cold, numb hand to her face. Another giggle escaped. Goodness, she was losing it. She followed along a bit further, not daring to believe and knowing that if she hit another dead end it would be her dead end.

When she came to an intersection, the reflected moonglow only lit sections of one path. Was that the road she had to take? How weird!

Was the same person who made the bridge responsible for these guiding lights? *A nutter, for sure. Should be hung.*

Sophy traipsed along the glowing pathway. Many other paths intersected with the one she was on but she held true to the lights. So far she hadn't hit any dead ends. That had to be a good sign, because in all her other tries she'd reached the dead end by now. She frowned and chewed her lip. How could she tell? She was losing her sense of time and surroundings. It had to be a dream.

As she continued on she saw paths cut out to the side and disappear. It was definitely a maze or labyrinth but something made her think it wasn't man-made. Rather, someone had altered and enhanced what was already there.

Walker moon climbed higher as Sophy came upon a niche in the wall. She paused, drawn to the spot. Intricately carved from the stone was a lacework pattern of curved scroll work. Sophy angled her head so she could make out the picture. The moon rose a fraction higher, and then she could see. Carved from the rock was the image of a beautiful woman, eyes closed and lips smiling. Her breasts were large and well enclosed in a gown and her hands were folded across her partially pregnant body. The depiction of the woman was well crafted. It reminded Sophy of a picture of the Virgin Mary, so tranquil and still. Sophy thought about the chasm. "N'Brell," she whispered.

Whoever crafted that woman from the stone loved her. Every wee detail exuded adoration. Sophy sighed. It was time to move on. She needed to pass through the labyrinth before sunup.

It seemed that she walked forever, beyond fatigue and into a sort of death shuffle. All she could see was the glowing path and all she could feel was the wall of rock around her. All her thoughts focussed on moving on, pushing one foot in front and then shifting her weight to take the next step. All her will was concentrated on survival. Even under Umri's torture, she'd never felt such desperation. She had known that Hanal wouldn't allow her to be killed. Now, though, she knew what mortality was.

Life was a fragile thing, easily lost in recklessness, in unthinking acts. What a child she had been! How infantile her attempts at love. Would she find comfort in Oakheart's arms again? She wondered whether the horror of what had happened to her would fade. Would she ever feel carefree and laugh again? The thought of Oakheart's warm and strong embrace taunted her.

The path abruptly ended; the rock wall guiding her was no longer there. Disconcerted and weak, Sophy dropped to her knees. There was something up ahead, a blur of white and blue, moving and shifting in and out of focus. Was this the help she sought? In one breath, her strength failed her. Her face pressed against the ground and darkness swallowed any further thought.

✺ 22 ✺

GLASSY MOUNTAIN RETREAT

It took three more days along the winding path up into the mountains. Surprisingly, the road was well kept. There was a natural tunnel that led under a glassy-looking overhang. The forest folk exchanged a few wary glances, but Meld's face was serene. As the group's horses entered the mouth of the tunnel, the echo of their hooves reverberated. The sound layered itself until it was like a chant.

Inside the tunnel the light was muted and ethereal. Aria looked back, but all she could see were rainbows of colour. Excitement made her giddy. This was truly the most wondrous thing she had seen. How skilled were its makers? Those First Comers who had arrived from other worlds, perhaps even her own world. She pulled her cape closer around her shoulders to fend off the chill air. Although, it was not as cold as it should have been this high up in the mountains. Some strange enchantment seemed to emanate from the ground itself.

The music of the horses' hooves continued to serenade them, beautiful, but making conversation difficult. Aria spied Oakheart's expression: resignation and despair had given way to hope. She realised that Oakheart put a lot of faith in the retreat and the ability of the adepts to help him save Sophy. She hoped his faith was not misplaced. Meld hove into view, taking the lead. A chill washed over her. If he was the best of them, perhaps she didn't have much faith at all.

As they neared the far end of the tunnel, the music started to thin and the rainbow shafts of light gave way to the gloaming on the other side. Aria edged her horse behind Oakheart as he led them up a sharp incline. The horses walked slowly, picking their way up the path. Aria leant sideways in her saddle, watching the path pass under the horse. Then she noticed that the ground levelled out. The group pressed on around a wall of ice and crystal, the last traces of light ebbing away.

"Lord. Is that what I think it is?" Aria saw a building made from the same material as the tunnel, a crystalline structure, faceted and reflecting pink, mauve and ochre light left over from the sunset. It shone out the light, brightening the little valley it lay in.

Behind, the mountain speared straight up like a knife thrust into the air. It swallowed the light emanating from the retreat, letting starlight fall unimpeded. Aria sat on her horse, bedazzled, with her breath misting around her. The retreat was triangular with a tall spire that reached upwards at a steep incline. She supposed the snow would slide right off it. At the base struts wove together and seemed to plunge into the earth like the roots of a tree.

"It's magical," she breathed.

"'Tis," Oakheart said, stopping beside her. "Your face mirrors what I experienced when I first beheld it. It overshadowed all my pain at the time. I was abandoned, alone and miserable. But the wonder of it was so that I found it hard to leave."

Aria frowned and glanced at Oakheart. "How did they build it? It looks like it would be impossible to build and to maintain."

Oakheart frowned. "I know not how it was built. Like the keep in the valley, some of that knowledge has passed from us. The First Comers hailed from many lands, some with a vast store of knowledge. Some of the secrets were kept, others were let to fade and become part of the mysteries. The retreat, perhaps, is a monument to those early achievements, a celebration by the refugees that fled here from their lost worlds. They made an oath to the land, and with it brought freedom from the Ancient Evil that they fled."

The last of Oakheart's words chilled her. But she had to know because there was no use in hiding any longer. "What is the Ancient Evil? It sounds so ominous. But what is it exactly?"

Oakheart gazed at the retreat, his voice barely above a whisper. "'Tis not an it, but a she. The Ancient Evil is a she."

"What? But what of Rufus? I thought he must be this Ancient Evil."

"No. He was but an agent methinks. The greater power and malice lies in his mistress."

Aria's heart chilled. Rufus was an agent only—worse was yet to come. "Oh god, help us." Aria urged her mount ahead. The heaviness of her thoughts dimmed the wonder of the structure before her. She almost smiled, though, when Meld's horse sprinted ahead, kicking up a light dusting of snow. He was keen to be inside its walls, to once again find succour. Aria had no idea what lay in store for her but she hoped her future didn't include the Ancient Evil. She'd had her fair share of strife.

The rest of the group increased their speed. At the base of the structure no one stirred. There was no welcome, no movement or sound. Aria cast a worried frown in Oakheart's direction.

"'Tis normal, my lady. The adepts stay within."

As they drew nearer, Aria saw that there was a covered pathway that led to the centre of the base. Buttressed with the same crystalline material, it reflected the light, casting a blue haze around them. Up ahead was a set of doors. In contrast to the ornate beauty of the retreat, the doors looked like those at the front of Valley Keep: heavy wood, studded in metal. They looked like the dark mouth of some elegant creature. That analogy gave Aria pause.

The doors swung open as Meld neared. Ducking his head, he rode through. After a moment's hesitation, Oakheart followed. The place was so delicate and clean that riding an animal through the front door seemed like sacrilege.

Aria nudged her mount with her heel and, once through the door, found she was surrounded by people and horses. The forest folk were there, Mellow and Lillia sharing the same mount, and Illart and Raven clinging to one of the pack horses. Her horse followed Oakheart's to the side, where the stables were. Oakheart lifted her down and then tied her mount to a post.

There was no one around except the new arrivals. It seemed odd. Oakheart's gaze travelled around and he bit his bottom lip as time stretched out. They shared a look and his eyebrows lifted.

Before Aria could remark on the absence of a greeting, people came out in a flurry of robes. Lots of adepts lined up in front of another set of doors, which were made of crystal and carved with intricate patterns.

Meld, free of his horse, walked straight towards the growing line of adepts. Swirls of robes in white and blue and brown shifted and swayed. Curious, Aria fell in behind Meld. She didn't want to miss a word of what was said. Oakheart took her hand, squeezed it once and walked with her. The forest folk brought up the rear.

Meld's robe fluttered as he strode purposefully between the two lines of adepts and headed for the doorway. Before him, standing on the threshold, was another adept in darker coloured outer robes. When Meld reached the end of the line, he fell to his knees dramatically and bowed his head to the adept standing there. Not a face amongst those gathered showed any emotion or reaction. She noted as she, too, walked down the line of adepts, that some were as young as twelve and others as old as seventy. A prickling of fear sped up her spine when she took in their faces devoid of welcome. Again Oakheart squeezed her hand and, when she glanced at him, he smiled. "Fear not," he whispered.

The adept in front of the door stepped down and stood in front of Meld. His robe was a darker blue than the others and contrasted with the hem of his white under tunic.

"Welcome Brookfell Treesinger—tell us, what has happened? A great wrong has occurred to Adage."

Meld climbed to his feet slowly and squared his shoulders. "I am no longer Brookfell Treesinger," he said in a loud voice that echoed and amplified around them. "I call myself Meld, for I am Adage within Brookfell's body."

His words caused a ripple of whispers amongst the adepts. Their murmuring was cut off by the lead adept, who raised his hand. The lead adept's face was calm, yet Aria thought she saw the look of fear hastily covered up in his eyes. "Then truly we have a cause for sorrow. We will speak together soon. Be welcome amongst us, Meld."

The lead adept then directed his gaze to Aria, Oakheart and the forest folk, examining their faces by turn and taking in their dishevelled appearance. "I am Lianal, Lead Adept at Glassy Mountain Retreat. Be welcome."

The line of adepts turned and the doors groaned as they were pushed open. The adepts filed through the door, leaving the party waiting. Lianal stood with them, smiling beatifically and not speaking until the last adept was through the doors. "If you will come with me." Lianal turned slowly away from them. Meld walked a step behind Lianal with his head bowed like a penitent.

Apprehension tickled Aria's skin as she followed with Oakheart at her side. Occasional groupings of adepts lingered and stared at them silently. It was like there were a hundred eyes staring at her from the turrets and doorways or hidden niches and a thousand whispers flying through the air. But no one was speaking.

Oakheart looked at peace. She was anything but comfortable. She happened to catch a glimpse of Lillia. Instead of the expected awe, Aria saw anger etched in Lillia's face; a deep seething anger. Perhaps it was the lack of emotion they showed for the loss of her son. Perhaps it was the retreat itself. She wondered if Lillia would ever explain it. But since Brook's essence had been quenched, Lillia had hardly spoken of her feelings.

Aria discovered that the inner courtyard had many doors leading off it and seven levels above. Adepts slid away into them, disappearing through doors and up staircases. A staircase dominated each corner. Aria looked up to see that they wound around in a spiral with the flutter of blue adepts' robes evident. The adepts disappeared entirely, leaving Lianal alone with them.

When the lead adept had their attention he said, "You must rest from your journey now, take as much time as you want. Oakheart knows the way to the guest quarters. I must consult with Meld. I hope you understand our need for urgency. Someone will call for you tomorrow, towards the evening. Perhaps, Oakheart, you can show our guests the Great Library tomorrow after you have rested."

Aria glanced from Oakheart to Lianal. "But...but..."

Lianal smiled gently. "Forgive me, princess. Your sorrows have been great. Yet, what I have to consult with Meld about is very important and cannot be delayed. Even now Adage's body is near to death."

Oakheart spoke, his voice displaying shock. "I thought Adage's body was already dead."

Lianal's expression was dour. "Close to; I fear it cannot be long," he replied. "Our hope is small. To restore some semblance of order Meld must see Adage straight away."

"But I must save Sophy..." Oakheart burst out. "My oathbound wife is stolen." Lianal's eyes widened. "This is more urgent than you think, Oakheart. We will deal with your missing Sophy in due course." With that he turned and sped off.

Meld was close behind Lianal without even giving them a backward glance.

"What does he mean?" Mellow asked. "Adage alive...then our son..." His mouth shrunk to a tight frown. "By the spirit of the trees, I trust them not."

Aria agreed with his sentiment. There was something underhand in the way they were behaving, she couldn't quite put her finger on it though.

"Yes, excellency," Lillia began. "I want to see what happens. Can you not intervene for us? What of Sophy? What of our aid?"

Oakheart sighed. "I understand your feelings. I am not privy to all the retreat's secrets. I can only guess what Lianal means. There is naught to do now but take Lianal's advice and rest. You will find that nothing happens quickly at the retreat. The daily urges that drive us do not have sway here. Indeed, it can be quite peaceful."

"Peaceful? How can you rest? What about Sophy?" Lillia's expression soured as she spoke.

Mellow grunted, a sharp sound of anger. Oakheart turned away and they fell in behind him without another word. After another quick check that Illart and Raven followed, Oakheart led them up the left hand corner staircase, stopping at the first level and exiting to walk down a corridor.

It was like walking on glass, Aria thought. The floor, ceiling and walls were transparent yet she could see only reflections or refractions of light and colour. The temperature was steady, neither filled with chills nor overly warm.

The passageway had an arched ceiling, with buttresses joining the edges of the ceiling to the wall. Then she noticed how clean it was, and the light scent of wildflowers permeated the air. It was truly amazing.

At the first doorway, Oakheart paused and opened the door. "These rooms are big enough for four people. It is a suite. Two bedrooms joined by a common area. Perhaps, Lillia?"

Lillia stepped into the room. She sniffed once. Facing Oakheart, she nodded like a salute. "Where will you be, Oakheart?"

Oakheart took a sideways step and pointed to a door opposite. "Here."

"What about Princess Aria?" Lillia asked.

Mellow spoke then. "She will stay with us. We will share with the others to allow the princess the privacy of her own room."

Oakheart raised an eyebrow. "There is no need to be so crowded. There is a room next door for Aria."

Aria nodded. "Thank you, Oakheart, but I would rather share with the others." With the loss of Fern's company, she needed the distraction of others to keep her from dwelling on it. It was difficult to tell Oakheart of her unease at being at the retreat. He had such regard for the place.

Oakheart sighed. "Very well." His face showed all of his fatigue. It had been a hard road, and how his heart must ache for Sophy. Aria thought of Fern's quest and tried not to. She was tired, too. Hopefully there was a bath in the room, because she needed to soak away her saddle soreness and sleep for a week.

Aria reached up and patted Oakheart on the shoulder. "You go rest, Oakheart. Tomorrow we will find some answers. Meld will ask the right questions. It is too important for him to overlook us."

Oakheart put his hand over hers and patted it. "Thank you, Aria. I will sleep now but I will eat first. You will find food already in the room." He bowed to them all, a sweep of his left arm embellishing the movement. Then he turned and opened the door to his room.

Aria smiled and let Lillia guide her within their suite.

✣ 23 ✣

WHERE THE SPIRIT DWELLS

Oakheart stood in the middle of the familiar suite of rooms. To the side was the bed, and next to it a study table, topped with a nest of firesticks glowing softly. Fresh food was laid out for him to eat. For many years these quarters has been his. When he was a child, he had shared them with another adept. At the age of ten, Aran, an adept many years his senior, had taught him and befriended him when he had lost his mother to the Crystal Gate. This suite was filled with fond memories of those times, except perhaps that first time when his heart was laid bare from loss and abandonment.

He remembered the great chase clearly, memories of strong emotion, desperation and feelings of abandonment as he chased Daken and his mother, Queen Mara, through the land and up here to the mountain ranges. That time was forever etched across his mind. He wondered why the recollection came so strongly.

He had been at Valley Keep, visiting his kin with the high queen. He had never liked the way Prince Daken had looked at his beautiful mother and was too young at the time to understand the depth of feeling between them. At the keep, the prince never bothered to mask his desire, not in front of his wife, Aurore, or anyone else. He had wondered during that visit why his mother had not taken Daken to task about it, why she had not told him to cease his bold looks and overly gallant gestures.

One night a few days into the visit, he had heard whispering outside his door, words that floated in the air and hovered in the shadows. Daken spoke of the Glassy Mountain Range and of the Crystal Gate. His words were urgent, demanding. His mother's response was restrained, saddened. Oakheart had wondered what made her sound so forlorn. There had always been joy and love in her face and voice. He remembered feeling anger towards Daken. He liked it not that the prince made his mother sad or frightened.

Then through a crack in the door he saw them kiss and clench hands desperately. Daken seemed to possess his mother, his hands in her hair, holding her to him. Surely she did not allow him to do that to her. But after, when Daken released her from his embrace, she had laid her head upon his breast and wept softly. Oakheart recalled his confusion. His young mind did not understand. The sight had sent his heart a-beating and his mind reeling for what his father, Veld, would feel if he knew of it. He vowed that he would not tell, that he would keep the secret—and that he would never trust Daken.

Before sunrise, he had woken to find his mother gone from her bed, and her belongings too. He stood in that empty room, finding it hard to breathe. In his heart, he knew she had left him behind, and a great loss cut into him at her abandonment. The keep was full of his kin, but they could not replace his most treasured mother. For his beloved father, he empathised. What would he say to Veld? How would the high king react? He could not bear to even think of it. Perhaps it was his fault, some deed of his that had made his mother leave him behind.

Yelling with fright and disturbing all those within the keep, he had dashed through the bailey and to the stables where he mounted his horse, Bravefoot, and bounded down the road and out of the valley. Of what happened within the keep when Daken was discovered missing as well, he did not know. He had never asked. Both Aurore and Dellbright never spoke of that day. It was as if Daken had never existed in their lives. But Oakheart knew his father's desertion had left an indelible mark on Dellbright. Aurore's face had always held an expression of sadness, but after that day the lines were cut deeper. Dellbright clung to his mother, monopolised her life and bent her to his whims. Yes, this was the notorious prince of Valley Keep's doing. Daken, sufferer of Shabra's curse, and much harm he inflicted on all those involved, willing or not.

Oakheart had clung feebly to his mount, through storm and cold, but he could not catch them. He could not distinguish the days of pursuit in his memory; they blurred together, threaded with heartbreak and exhaustion. That he fell from his mount many times he did acknowledge, because he remembered climbing back into the saddle and digging deep inside himself for the strength to keep going. He had even slept on his horse.

Teardrops had mixed with rain as he doggedly followed their trail. He did not say goodbye. Even if he had had the opportunity, he did not think the words would have come. How does one say goodbye to the most precious thing in one's life? His mother was kind, good and so regal. She had grace, manners and flawless beauty in her creamy skin and red, sunlit hair.

Veld had always been in awe of her. Oakheart had never guessed that she loved another. She had always treated Veld well in his presence. He arrived too late to prevent the fleeing couple from departing Argenterra through the passageway that Vorn had used to bring the First Comers so long ago. He had glimpsed the blazing light of the Crystal Gate as it diminished to become nothing. In that empty space, heartbroken did he kneel, letting his head fall to his chest to weep. His mother never came back for him. No amount of tears would undo what had been done. His pleas were whipped up by the wind and blown up to the mountain peaks to be heard by birds alone.

That is where the adepts had found him, huddled in the cold, hungry and near death. They requested permission to keep him at the retreat, citing ill health, and Veld gave it. For ten years Oakheart stayed at the retreat, learning their ways, and he only saw his father through the large talkstone in the heart of the retreat. Veld held the other stone in Silverdale. The main communication link between the two citadels, one talkstone was at the heart of learning, the other at the heart of government.

So here he was again...but a student no longer. He had visited since he left the retreat and so much had happened since his last sojourn. He ran his hands over the walls of the retreat, revelling in their exquisite beauty. The walls were cool to the touch but the air was warm near them. They did not pulse as Valley Keep did because the crystal mined from the range was not imbued with Vorn's spirit. It was the design and the manufacture that was its greatest virtue. None could build such a construction again; the skill had died out long ago.

Oakheart picked at the food and drink: some cold meat, bread and dark brown ale. A weariness crept up on him. Tomorrow he would seek answers. He stripped off, washed and then slid between the sheets. His body remembered the bed and how easily it adjusted to him. With the translucent glow of the walls washing over him, Oakheart fell asleep.

A powerful dream was fresh on his mind when he woke. *Sophy!* Her beautiful face floated in his dream; her dark eyes pleaded with him. Oakheart was tormented—he did not like feeling so helpless, so unable to do what his heart wanted. He decided then that in the morning he would demand that the adepts aid him, and once his strength was restored he would wrest Sophy free from Hanal. That decision brought hope and a purpose to that day.

"Aran," he whispered to himself. "My old friend will aid me. I know it."

With that thought, Oakheart threw off the blankets and went to wash. In the chest were his retreat clothes, a pale blue robe with an over-cape of white. He donned them, feeling relaxed and whole. While he ate some fruit, cheese and bread, his unbound hair dripped water onto his face. He searched for a cloth to dry off for there was no need to bind it for it was not the fashion at the retreat.

The door opened behind him, he heard it creak. Towel in hand, he was still in the process of drying his hair vigorously when he spied Aran entering.

He dropped the cloth to the ground and in two steps grasped Aran to him in a bear hug. "Aran."

The older adept stepped back from Oakheart's embrace. "'Tis good to see you, my friend. So much has happened in the world since you were here last." Aran's eyes narrowed, his grey eyebrows rising. "Something is amiss with you." Aran stepped around him, staring at him and trying to fathom what was different.

Oakheart told him of his loss of strength after the fight with Rufus in the Lower Warrens. "Yes, many things have happened. Can you study me? Can you return me to strength? I must away as soon as it can be achieved."

Aran's frown grew more severe. "My friend, so much haste. I had thought you more considered. My sight is not what it was. I cannot aid you, even though my heart wishes it. I cannot discern what it is within you, only that you are different, altered from what you were."

"But Aran..."

The older adept held up his hand for quiet. "I will use my voice and my influence to see that the retreat offers you aid. Fear not. Now tell me what has happened and about the guests in the other room for I have heard naught but rumour. I was on duty at the time of your arrival, hence I was not able to greet you then."

Oakheart gestured for his friend to sit and put some water on the boil. "Come, drink some tea with me...the tale is a long one." He was well into his tale when there was a knock at the door. Oakheart stopped mid-sentence and rushed to open it. Aria stood there with the forest folk ranged out behind her. She was a vision in the white robe of the adepts. Her hair, clean and unbound, fell near to her waist in a wave of chestnut and golden curls. Oakheart grinned. The forest folk had not relinquished their own garb, stubborn to the last, he thought. He was not displeased; he had nothing but admiration and the deepest trust of his forest folk companions.

"May we join you?" Aria asked with a tentative smile. She looked well rested except for the worry in her eyes.

Oakheart stepped back and Aran stood. "This is Aran, a very old friend. This is Princess Aria, Lillia of the Quick Bow, her mate Mellowbark, and their fellow forest folk, Illart and Raven."

Aran bowed his head. "Welcome to Glassy Mountain Retreat, travellers. Let your hearts and minds be eased here. Oakheart has nearly told me all that has befallen you." Aran's expression grew grave.

"Indeed, my heart is heavier for the hearing of it. Now that you are gathered here, I will show you around. I believe the Great Library will be of interest to you."

Aria's eyes widened and her smile turned to a frown. "Forgive me...but..."

Lillia gaped at Oakheart, her throat working on a retort. "The library? But...we..." She snapped her mouth closed so fast her teeth clicked.

Oakheart smiled. "Yes, the library...then Lianal and Meld will meet us. Aran tells me they have been closeted together for most of the night."

Aran nodded, his expression grave. "Much to discuss, to analyse, and decisions to be made." Aran hesitated, glanced to Oakheart and back to the forest folk. In a soft voice he said, "Meld refuses to see Adage's body. He claims there are more urgent things to be done."

"Like what?" Mellow asked. "I confess I am confused and uncomfortable here. What will happen if Meld sees Adage's body?"

Aran spread his hands and shrugged. "Nothing like this has happened to us before. Adage knew more than any other adept. He is Vorn's grandson, kept alive by his oath to his grandfather. He was one of the first born in this land. Who knows what mysteries lay embedded in his mind? The library contains much of his work."

Aria shared a concerned look with Lillia. After a moment's hesitation, she said, "Very well. But we have come a long way just to see a library. We need answers and help. Oakheart needs his strength and he needs it now."

Oakheart patted Aria on the shoulder and gestured for them to precede him out of the door. Aran stepped in front of them and opened the door. "If you will follow me." Aran strode out into the corridor with slow, deliberate steps as the others stepped back to make way for him. Oakheart let Aria go ahead of him. The forest folk, led by Lillia, closed in behind Oakheart.

Aran strode down the corridor, his pale skin bluish from the reflected light in the corridor. He was composed and unhurried. Oakheart tried to relax as they entered the stairwell. The staircase spiralled down underneath his feet as he trod. He breathed slowly, trying to calm himself as he normally would while staying at the retreat. He could not quite manage it. His dream of Sophy lingered and still unnerved him.

Aria said, "The floor is like walking in water. Quite amazing."

Oakheart lifted an eyebrow; perhaps it was like that. He was accustomed to the magnificence of the building and, while he never took it for granted, his amazement had decreased over the years. The party reached ground level and passed under the large ornate archways to the main stairs that led to the library vaults below.

Aran's pace remained unhurried. As they descended into the basement level, the blue-tinged light faded. Soon the glow was yellowish and reflected from walls made from hewn stone, smoothed with the *given*. Only the ceiling was made with crystal and it glowed with a prism of colours and shards of the morning sun. Light from candelabras full of firesticks cast an ambient glow around them as they walked along another corridor. Large and smaller rooms were arrayed on one side: studies, storerooms and meeting rooms. On the right hand side was the library.

Aran pushed the heavy oak doors open. Oakheart caught a whiff of incense and smiled as the scent aroused pleasant memories. The walls were carved in intricate designs that matched the swirls and interlocking circles that were found throughout the retreat. Bookshelves stuffed with parchments and hand-written, weighty tomes crammed into the available the space. Here was the history of Argenterra, recorded diligently throughout the years, and also a collection of handed-down remembrances of other worlds and other lands from where the First Comers had originated. Here were even words of Vorn himself and Shabra's scribing of his kinsman's terrible dream—the dream of an *ungiven* land.

Oakheart had read the dream scroll but once, and was taken aback by how vividly the words sprang to his mind. It was as if the vision of Vorn that he had beheld in the depths of Valley Keep was on him again.

Vorn's words echoed in his mind:

I dreamed a terrible dream in the night, but at first the touch was light. For in my dream, the land was bountiful and our descendants were prosperous. The binding oath had brought peace and sustenance to all. The land had barred the way to the Ancient Evil and all who dwelled upon the land never knew her touch. But, then, just as I savoured this most hallowed vision, the hand of the Ancient Evil reached out and touched the land. Where once there was silver and brightness, there remained only the dull tarnish of the dark detritus of violence. Oh how this dream rends me, for my deeds are never far behind me, and I can never escape from what I had wrought in my younger days.

It pains me that my seed is to be thus tainted, for what connection do they have to those acts that brought the Ancient Evil to me? Surely a man's deeds are but his own. Oh that I had never seen her, or felt her bewitching touch. For she will never be free of me, or me of her. Oh no, that Ancient Evil will ever be a part of me. 'Tis as if I had made her with my own hand. Then, as my vision waned and the pain and the terror that had been visited upon me forced me to wakefulness, I did see a glimmer of hope. A jewel, so fair and bright, did glow within the land. And there in that moment did I perceive that hope was yet in sight.

These were the words of Vorn, the first High King, as written by Shabra within a week of entering Argenterra.

Heart beating painfully, Oakheart realised that his mind had wandered, so possessed he had been by his recollection. Aran stood nearby waiting patiently, and already Aria was running her hands along the shelves, casually sizing up the collection that no other place in Argenterra could rival. The forest folk stood together, watching and guarding Aria as if some adept might leap out and attack. Oakheart shook his head and smiled. Aran patted him on the shoulder. "Are you well, Oakheart?"

"Yes, Aran, only caught up in memories and recollections of my time here." Oakheart was hesitant to reveal what he had just been thinking. "I always like to be here in the library. I spent much of my youth here."

Aran chuckled. "I remember it well. I had the task of preventing you from climbing the bookcases to reach the highest shelves and of teaching you to turn the pages gently. I remember well your innumerable questions that had to be answered in all haste."

Oakheart smile broadened. "Yes. I remember it well. It was you who instructed me in patience. But you seemed to enjoy it, if I recall. I remember Adage offering another to take over the task and you refused."

Aran nodded. "Adage and I argued over it. I enjoyed your agile mind and innate ability. I won that round. To tell the truth, 'twas the only argument, or should I say debate, I ever won against Adage. Tell me, what were you thinking of when you entered? Your face seemed so stricken. If you were remembering something it must not have been pleasant."

Oakheart walked over to the large table and pulled out a chair and Aran joined him. Oakheart looked over his shoulder and saw that Aria was talking quietly to another adept, who had come up to explain the various collections. Perhaps he should reveal all to his old friend as he had no need to hide anything from the adept. "When I stepped through the door," Oakheart said with his voice lowered, "I recalled, word for word, Vorn's dream that I read here in my youth."

"I see. You knew it off by heart by the age of twelve, you know. You were quite taken with Vorn's vision." Aran's smile was full of fondness.

Oakheart lowered his voice further. "I know. I have never forgotten the words. But the way they sprang out of me was strange. The time of Vorn's dream is upon us, I fear."

Aran's eyes widened. "'Tis not certain, Oakheart. Even here in the retreat there is no agreement about what the current events mean. Adage thinks as you do, and his opinion will sway many. But there are those of us who have hope that the dreadful time is not upon us."

"Hope? When the binding oath is undone? Aurore was murdered in Valley Keep. Her blood stained its very fabric."

Aran's expression grew appalled at Oakheart's words. "Then Vorn's resting place is defiled?" Aran stood, shivered and began to pace.

Oakheart wondered why the news of the events at Valley Keep was not widely known. Aran was not high in the hierarchy, yet all should know of it, surely? Had Dellbright been hesitant to communicate to the retreat? But that made no sense, because Adage had been there.

"No, not defiled. Aria and I, we used the *given* to cleanse it. I went to the bonding chamber and drew some power to help me. Aran, I must tell you. I saw a vision of Vorn in the bonding chamber as well."

"Surely this cannot be. You did not mention it when we talked. I thought you had told me all."

"I talked a great deal, but those few hours that we had were insufficient to tell all that has transpired. So much has happened, and Sophy is upmost in my mind."

Aran folded his arms. "I understand. You said Aria assisted you?" Aran turned his head and studied Aria. "Then she is as strong as you? Untaught, she could assist you?"

Oakheart nodded. "Yes. If she had been born in Argenterra she would have been an adept..."

Aran's brown eyes glowered at him, reviving their age-old argument. "You would have been a great adept, Oakheart, if you had stayed here and applied yourself." He seemed to let that old regret go and asked, "What made you draw upon the *given* in that way?"

Oakheart closed his eyes, trying to discern what his motivations had been. He could not answer his old friend and mentor lightly. He respected Aran too much for that. "Desperation and instinct, I think. I drew upon Vorn's essence in the pool, drawing as much of the *given* into me as I could withstand."

Aran's expression was thoughtful. "I see...Meld spoke not of this."

Oakheart's head came up. "You have spoken with Meld?"

Aran dropped his gaze. "For a short time only. We passed each other in the corridor."

For the first time, suspicion haunted Oakheart. He would never have expected his good friend would lie to him. But it hung between them, a slight untruth. Oakheart let it pass. The adepts did not always reveal everything. Their code was complex, their ways mysterious, even to Oakheart, but still... "I see."

Lillia coughed. "Excellency, when do you think we will see Lianal and Meld once more? We wish to...see...our son before we return to the far forest."

Aran stood and faced Lillia, glanced quickly to Mellow and the others. "Please stay awhile with us. Your worn appearance suggests that you are in need of rest and nourishment."

Lillia glanced down to her abdomen and then lifted her chin higher.

"I am hale, Adept Aran. Once within the woods of home I will be safe."

"That may be. But your road has been long and hard. The child growing within you needs good food to make it strong."

Oakheart raised himself up and stood behind Aran. "Lillia, dear friend, Aran is skilled in the healing arts. Please hearken to his words. The retreat is a haven as well as a place of study. I know that it is strange to you, but no more so than Valley Keep or Silverdale. Rest while you can and take nourishment as Aran suggests. I would not have the life of your child on my hands."

Lillia's grim mouth softened. With a sideways glance at Mellow, she said, "We will stay for a week at most."

"'Tis all I ask," Aran answered. "Now, Oakheart, pray let me speak with the princess, the fascinating outlander that wields the *given* so deftly. Oh, and I recollect she wields another power, the blue flame from the gem."

"That is so." Oakheart gestured for Aran to precede him.

Aria looked up at their approach, smiled tentatively and whispered to the adept assisting her with a book. "Hello, Aran, isn't it? I'm pleased to meet you. This library is fascinating, the whole retreat is a marvel..."

"Yet your mind and heart are troubled," Aran said knowingly.

Aria faltered and sought Oakheart's gaze. "What can he see in me?"

Aran chuckled. "Worry not. I see not your thoughts, except those writ upon your face. But there is something within you, not quite the same as I see in Oakheart."

"It must be Sophy's power you see in me. I took some because I wanted to heal Oakheart, but all I did was hold him to this life with the *given*. Over time, he has regained some of his strength. I can see something in him, sense a knot of power, but I don't know how to help him. I can't see inside myself but I guess there's a residue of power yet within me. It is vague, like a stomach ache or a mild headache. Not enough to complain about."

"Interesting. I am sure Lianal would be interested in this. Meld too."

"Did Meld speak of it to you?" Oakheart asked Aran. "He never spoke in depth to us about it. He was a touch absorbed by other concerns at the time, so we did not press the issue."

"Not that I recall. As I said, I only had a brief meeting with Meld. 'Tis possible that he cared not to discuss it with me. Adage's ways have forever been a mystery. I heard that he was harmed by Rufus and 'twas a severe harm. Perhaps that was the reason he failed to mention such an important occurrence." Aran's eyes dwelled on the forest folk. "Indeed, a blow that affected more than Adage and Brook and may yet have far-reaching consequences."

Aria touched the adept's arm lightly. "Can you help us, Adept Aran? If you can see this power inside of us then perhaps you can aid me. I can draw the rest of the power and weave it through Oakheart. Then his strength may be restored."

Aran shrugged. "What you suggest is pure guesswork. I do not have the skill and I could not risk harm to either of you. With assistance, I might be able to look more deeply inside you and understand the nature of that nestled there. Others within the retreat will assist you. I cannot go against my authority." When Aria's expression soured, Aran patted her hand until she withdrew it. "Let me speak to my fellow adepts. Lianal is still locked in consultation with Meld. I must bide my time, as must you."

Aria glanced at Oakheart, begging assistance. "Pray forgive me, Aran. But there is no time to waste."

Oakheart wanted to argue, but Aran's look stilled his words.

Aran turned to Oakheart. "You know as well as I do the ways of the retreat. I cannot rush this. This power you speak of, which I discern inside you, could be dangerous. Think of what we have here in the retreat, the knowledge stored here and the talent gathered here to learn. What if that power unleashed could destroy us? I could not risk that no matter how urgent your request nor how dear you are to me in life."

Aran bowed slightly, inclining his head. "Forgive me for speaking passionately. I am not often with company these days." He turned and went out of the library doors, his robe flaring behind him. There was no more opportunity to argue or beg.

Aria touched Oakheart's hand as he stared at the door.

"Can we wait? What do they do in an emergency if they take so long to decide things?"

Oakheart held her hand. "This is an emergency, but the adepts... who can understand them? Vorn gave them a mission and even I do not know what that mission was."

Aria snatched her hand back. "So what do we do? Stay in the library and wait?" Her voice was tinged with anger, voicing the frustration that he could not.

He sighed loudly. "We will use our time wisely, and I will show you some of the treasures. After that, I will take you back to our rooms and we can rest and eat. I know the way. If by sunset we have not heard, I will seek an audience with Lianal. 'Tis my right as ambassador to claim one, although I have never enforced that right before."

Aria's chin rose and her pink cheeks exposed her anger. "All right. We will do it your way for now. But we have travelled a hard road, and I will not sit still and let them ignore us. Not when Sophy is in need and others risk their lives. There is much wrong in Argenterra. Don't they care about that, the raiders, the fear?"

Oakheart led Aria to show her his most treasured books. The thought came to him that he should search out other texts relating to these turbulent times. Surely there were more of Vorn's writings. He noticed that the librarian adept had departed, leaving them alone. "Come, let us look over here. This is the oldest section. Perhaps there is something useful here."

His fingers traced the spines of the old books. *A Treatise on the Ancient Evil*, by Adage, son of Farlow, son of Vorn stood out from the others. Oakheart's gaze travelled further. *The Nature of Argenterra— Early Discoveries of the First Comers*, by Vorn, First High King, was a book that he remembered from his youth. He hadn't remembered that Vorn had written it. He left the old books and began to rummage in the old scrolls. Some were inside cabinets. Aria, close behind him, took a moment to check the door. The librarian had not returned.

"Open it," she urged. "Before the librarian comes back. He stopped Lillia and me from going near this cabinet."

"Really? How odd." Oakheart was truly surprised. He did not recollect ever being prevented from perusing the contents of the Great

Library. Although in his childhood, he had many texts set for him to read, which had prevented any serious broad search. He did not know for what he searched for now, but perhaps something would jump out at him. There was nothing better to do, leastways.

Oakheart grabbed a handful of the fragile scrolls and unrolled them carefully on the table. The first few were maps of the valley and plans for Valley Keep. He shook his head. The next scroll he laid out gingerly. It smelt musty and some of the edges broke away. The old writing was faded and hard to understand. "*My world was once alive, a green world full of vegetation and plenty.*" The words seem to thrill within him. "I think this is the one," he said in hushed tones to Aria. She rolled up the remaining scrolls and put them back in the cabinet. Then she urged Oakheart to hide the scroll in another book. They both sat down to read it, just as the librarian returned.

Both of them leant over the scroll. It read:

Now my home is called the Deadlands. Yulandir, the dead world. Ravaged it was by war, fought over the years. With my mighty sword did I strike at my foes. With my heart did I long for her touch. Unesta, that most alluring of women, gave herself to me. Oh how tender was that day, when birds still sang in the trees and the oceans were filled with life, when I did woo her. I was young then and foolish.

I lied to her, tricked her, took what she offered, without even listening to her bargain. That she wanted my soul, I did not understand at the time. But when I entered her sweet realm and let her put her hold on me, it was my undoing. A stranger to my world, a star traveller, she said, but her body was the same as other women, so I did not believe her, did not understand the true nature of her.

I fled from her, afraid of her hold on me, but she pulled me inexorably back to her, drawn by a web and reeled in. I fought her and was successful. And then the burnings came. High above the world light beams descended, casting red death all around. I gathered my forces, my hand crusted with blood and calluses as I fought with men. It seemed that many years passed, when there was a lull in the fighting, a reprieve from destruction. My dreams were full of her, but now the vision she cast me was evil and twisted. Not so her body because it stayed the same, but the mind within. I shudder to think on it.

Aria gasped. "The Ancient Evil was his lover? But..."

"That is what his words imply but his meaning may be different from what we understand today. I remember what he said about the dream...something about the Ancient Evil being wrought by his own hands and the result of his own deeds. 'Tis more than a woman scorned, though."

Aria's eyebrows shot up. "You think so?"

They buried their heads in the scroll again. Oakheart felt close to Aria at that moment. As the librarian passed close to them, Oakheart hunkered his shoulders so that he could not see what they were reading. The librarian checked the cabinet and walked on. Such subterfuge was normally beyond him, but at that moment Oakheart did not care.

He read from the scroll some more.

I heard tell that Unesta possessed a great weapon, one that could destroy us all. I had to prevent her using this cruel device against us. Rumours sprang up, perhaps of her own making, of how she had destroyed many worlds, leaving them dead and hollow and devouring the souls of all those who dwelt there. Indeed, her power did seem to grow the more people died and the more we did fight against her.

I was desperate. I blamed myself and I had the responsibility of other lives. I made an arrangement with her. She desired me, wanted me body and soul, and so I agreed to it. But in my heart was another plan, a risky, almost doomed-to-failure plan.

Unesta did send unto me directions on where to meet her and I came early to the place in the hope to find a way through her power. It was then that I first beheld the Crystal Gate. She did summon it in the middle of the plains and I saw the wonder of it clearly. From within the gate she drew soldiers, brutal combatants that scoured my world from end to end. Here I thought she had tricked me. For did she not say that she came from the stars; did not her fire fall from the sky?

Perhaps both were true. I wanted her to take me to her 'ship' so that I could destroy her weapons. At the appointed time, I greeted her warmly. Her manner was strange. With power she did hold me and I did sleep. When next I woke I was in a room with no windows. I did not know if I was in her 'ship' or below the ground. I was bound. Instruments surrounded me: sharp knives, bludgeons and all manner of cruelty. I had sought to trap her but she had caught me. She entered the room, smiling in a way that put fear into my heart. From her hands,

I did feel a pain so great. She used me, almost butchered me until she was spent. 'I like you,' she had said. 'I'm going to keep you forever.'

She put potions into my veins. They burned my blood, expanded my mind until I could feel the place around me, sense the breathing of others and see the blackness of her. I knew her intent. She meant to finish the job she came to do. I caught the fringes of her mind, the thirst for violence that would never be quenched. These revelations gave me an insight. A world without violence would not sustain her. That was my goal: to take the survivors of this apocalypse and find a new place, a place where we would all abjure violence. A place where she could not touch us. I found the source of her power and brought it with me.

In that last battle for our freedom I lost my mighty sword 'ere I summoned the Crystal Gate and fled with the small number of survivors. Within the pathway between worlds were other people and they joined us. The gate brought us to Argenterra, the Silverlands as I had named them.

In the end, the Silverlands, the power of Argenterra, was proof against her.

Here the scroll ended. Oakheart ran his hand through his hair. Aria gazed into space, her expression thoughtful. He did not know what answers the scroll provided, but it confirmed his view that these were the times that Vorn spoke of. The beginning of them, at least. When all the power was gone from Argenterra there would be nothing to stop this Unesta from entering. Vorn lived longer than any other man —that must have been from the potions that creature had put in his veins.

Aria still stared at nothing, though thoughts seemed to play on her face. Perhaps her mind was occupied with Fern, or perhaps of the terrible wounds Dellbright had inflicted on her. He knew then he loved Aria. A brotherly love, but love nonetheless. He could see why Sophy loved her friend. It was not just her grace, or her smile or her beauty, there was a quality to Aria, a depth that repented for her misdeeds. He could not say that she was perfect, for perhaps in hindsight in her dealings with Sophy she had not been so, but there was the potential for greatness in her. He wanted to touch her hair, for its beauty always drew him, so like his mother's. Such sad times.

"'Tis enough," Lillia exclaimed, jerking Oakheart from his reverie and Aria from her daze. "'Tis there no aid to be had here in these books? No answer?" Lillia's gaze was like a spear as it sought the librarian. He raced to the door, bowed and left. With eyebrows raised in query, Lillia regarded Oakheart.

"Perhaps we should return to our rooms and eat. That will make us feel better..." Oakheart smiled. Unfortunately, Lillia seemed immune to his charm.

Hands on hips, she stood near the door, eyebrows like arrows in flight. "I like not this treatment. We have travelled long and hard, much have we seen that has never been witnessed by others in this land, yet these adepts leave us wallowing in a library as if we are on a pleasant visit. This is urgent, Oakheart. Do you not see what is happening? They are stalling."

"The adepts?" Oakheart laughed at the absurdity of it. But underneath that he grew uneasy and Lillia was only voicing the deep doubts and suspicions he held.

"Yes, the adepts."

Aria stepped closer, after the adept had shut the door. "I agree. Something isn't right. I feel it."

Oakheart looked from one to the other, smiled at them, watched them relax a little in response. "You do not understand the way things are here. Matters need to be mulled over, discussed. Trust me, they will aid us. Trust them, for my sake."

Mellow grasped Lillia's hand. "We will for a while longer. But I fear 'tis your loyalty to them that makes you not see clearly, Oakheart. I have no loyalty to them. My son is dead, and they show no pity or sorrow. They do not even acknowledge the great harm. That is enough for me to see they think not like ordinary folk. They do not feel in the right way and that makes me most uneasy."

"Come then, let us eat. I will press matters further, believe me. For now we should rest." Oakheart opened the door and held it as the others filed past. The librarian was nowhere to be seen, so he darted back in and quickly stuffed Vorn's scroll back into the cabinet. Caution dictated that he not reveal what he had learned.

After closing the door softly behind him, in a few quick strides he caught up with the rest of his party. With Aria by his side, he passed

Lianal's study. A shiver up his spine nearly made him falter. He paused. Aria gasped and held her hand to her chest.

They shared a look. "What was that I felt?" she asked with a look of horror.

Oakheart frowned, unable to answer. The sensation had scared him to his very bones. "Perhaps 'tis some use of the *given*. Let us continue."

Oakheart climbed the stairs slowly, his mind preoccupied. Coming so closely on top of reading Vorn's words, the echo of power that he and Aria had experienced was disconcerting. Could the adepts be stalling, as Lillia said? Could his own thoughts and feelings be blinding him to the true situation? His expectation was of immediate action, and it was Aran's caution about not rushing that held him in check— that and the lack of access to the most powerful adepts. 'Twas perhaps the kind of passive resistance to be expected from the retreat. They had not even tried to help him when it was obvious he needed succour. That sort of neglect was unusual.

They reached the visitors' level. Lillia opened the door to her room and invited Oakheart to join them. Food and rest was what he needed. It had been his intention to eat with them so he readily joined them. He tried as best he could to eat with appropriate vigour and to think positive thoughts, but doubt clouded his mind. Looking at the rest of his party, he could see that they struggled with the same doubts. None of them commented on his lack of appetite, seemingly caught up in their own thoughts.

Later, as Oakheart slept, he was plagued with unease, which soon coalesced into a vision accompanied by sensations of pain. Rising up through the layers of dream, he found that he could not dislodge it. Images and emotions kept rolling over him, drawing him further and further into a maelstrom of power. It lanced through him. He cried out as he fought free of it. The more he fought it the more the tendrils of power drew him in. Blue pulsating light, fingers of power, grasping through his flesh. *No! Let me be!* But a beautiful, pale face with dark, succulent lips appeared. Sophy. All the fight went out of him. Her eyes were glowing coals of dark blue power. Her face was neither sad nor happy, a serene mask drawn over her suffering.

Her dark hair swirled around her face, tousled by an unseen wind.

She seemed to be looking straight at him. Those lips opened. "Oakheart...Oakheart?"

"Sophy?" His own voice sounded so lost and forlorn. "Where are you?"

"Near...I am near...come...help." Her voice was rich and then it faded to a thread. Just before the image of her face dissipated, he saw lines of pain take shape around her eyes, her mouth stretched in a grimace and a wordless cry of anguish.

Panting, he sat up. He was covered in sweat though the surrounding air was cool. He used the sheet to wipe himself down. It was the black dead of night. The walls of the retreat no longer glowed. He reached for a firestick and summoned the flame. In that light, he found his own clothes, not the borrowed adept's robes.

He padded to the door and slipped it open a crack. He would never have thought to use stealth in the retreat but the sense of unease was high in his blood. The forest folks' door was shut. Oakheart peered left and right; no one was about. He was not being watched. Firesticks dealt out a small amount of light as he made his way to the basement. Something in Lianal's study drew him. He tried not to think of all the rules he would be breaking as he trod the empty corridors.

There were sounds of footfalls when he reached the ground level. Oakheart huddled in shadow and waited for them to pass. A group of young adepts, breaking from midnight meditation, he guessed, talked quietly amongst themselves as they made their way to their beds.

They disappeared into the doorway that led to the novice's wing. He waited until his heart slowed and checked carefully for more adepts. It was quiet and still—how unearthly it was. With his feet covered in soft boots, he dashed to the next pool of shadow and then the next. Near the main staircase leading to the basement, he had to hide again.

There seemed to be a lot of activity below, hushed voices, the snick of doors opening and shutting and the flurry of robes. As a phalanx of adepts entered the stairway, Oakheart searched for a better hiding place. A pool of shadow would not hide him from so many. Their voices flowed over one another and mixed with echoes, making it hard to distinguish more than a few words. He backtracked and hid behind a column that supported one of the archways. The group of adepts split up and headed to their various quarters. Oakheart lifted an eyebrow. Many of these adepts were high ranking, and he found it curious that they would be all drawn together in the place he wished to go. He shook off his doubt. He knew the ways of the retreat. Subterfuge was not one of its methods.

When the last adept had slunk out of sight, Oakheart set off for the basement. He trod the stair quickly, descending into the darkened corridor with only muted light. He knew which room he needed. Pressing himself against the walls of the corridor, Oakheart edged forwards. There were two adepts standing on either side of the door. Guarding it? Oakheart paused; in all his years of living at the retreat he had never seen a doorway guarded. If one accidentally went where one was not supposed to go, you apologised and left.

Secrets. Oakheart's mind screamed the realisation at him. What had happened here? Lillia's instincts were right, but if he allowed that idea then all he held dear was a lie. It was the unbinding of all he knew; like the oath being unravelled in the land, so were the bindings of loyalty in his life.

He tried to think of an approach but all he could think of was the rage inside of him fed by thoughts of betrayal. The only way seemed to be the direct way. He straightened up and strode confidently towards the door. The two adepts noticed him immediately.

"Greetings, excellency, what brings you here at this time of night?" said the first. Oakheart remembered him slightly. He was called Luume.

"Greetings, Adept Luume. I would enter this room here and speak with Lianal. Please stand aside."

"We cannot," the other adept replied. Oakheart did not know the other adept but he knew he did not like the man's scowl.

"Yet you must. I have business within," Oakheart replied, clenching his fist. "I never thought to use force with an adept. If you care for yourselves and your wellbeing, I suggest you stand aside."

"Please, Oakheart, do not do this. Go quietly back to your quarters and I will pass word that you wish an audience," Luume begged.

"I will not leave." Oakheart stood straighter.

The other adept sent a charge of *given* towards him. It resonated within him as he hit the wall across the corridor. Shaking his head, his eyes refocussed. Both of the adepts were unconscious, legs and arms sprawled with heads at angles. "What?" He stood and shook himself again, touching his hand lightly to his chest. The skin still tingled from the force the adept had thrown at him. Unusual, to say the least. He never even knew the adepts studied ways to use the *given* as a weapon. He had been taught that the *given* was only for good. How had the power been reflected? He suspected that it was not meant to react that way. Could it be Sophy's power that Aria put inside him? Shaking his head in bewilderment, he knelt to check the fallen adepts. Luume still breathed but the other he was not as confident about.

When he tried to open the door it would not budge. Slowly, he stood and braced himself by planting his feet wide before the door. He reached out with his sight to see if it was sealed by use of the *given*. He had not done this before, but his senses advised that *given* had indeed been used in sealing the room.

With a sliver of power drawn from within, he pushed against the door. Just that slight use made his head reel. So weak he was, but what had rebounded the adept's attack? Perhaps there was power there, and he knew naught about how to use it.

The door edged open slowly. The resistance to his use of power weakened. Whoever had sealed it had their minds focussed elsewhere. A final push, and the door flung open and crashed against the wall. The room was filled with blue light, reminiscent of the light Sophy in jewel form had cast in Rufus's chamber. He stepped into it, shading his eyes. He could make out Lianal and Meld—they were standing over someone.

They turned towards him, surprise etched across their faces. Oakheart's vision adjusted, and he took another step. "By the *given*," he yelled. The surprise ripped the words from him. He fell to his knees as shock and fatigue caught up with him. "What have you done?"

Aria took a bath in the middle of the night. Too restless

and troubled to sleep, she thought a hot soak would help her relax. The tub she used was small, nowhere near as elegant as the amenities of Valley Keep. The waist-high, small tub was full of warm water that smelt of minerals. Perhaps it came from a spring. She was towelling off when she felt a vibration of power. It was more than the tremble she'd felt outside that room downstairs. Something was happening.

She dressed quickly and slipped into the corridor. Just ahead, she made out Oakheart creeping through the corridor. If what she had sensed had also woken him and drawn him towards it, then she would follow. All the time she trailed him, the power throbbed around her. Her teeth ached with it. It couldn't be her imagination. There was Oakheart skulking through corridors that he had every right to stride down. No, something was up.

When adepts emerged out of a stairwell, Aria was hard pressed to find a place to hide. By the time she did and calmed down enough, Oakheart was out of sight. She guessed he'd gone below, to that room. Yes. It was the only place.

An explosion of power made her fly backwards and land on her rear. She tugged her wet hair out of her face and crawled along the floor cautiously. In the dim light, she saw two adepts with their limbs at strange angles sprawled on the ground. She climbed to her feet and quickened her pace. Blue light spilled out of the open door. As she entered the portal, she saw Oakheart kneeling.

"Oakheart? What happened?" Then she was next to him, staring into the faces of Lianal and Meld, and saw who lay beyond. "Oh my god."

✹ 24 ✹

THE JEWEL WITHIN

"A ria?" Oakheart whispered beside her, roused from his stupor.

Lianal stepped around the bench and moved closer. "Oakheart, what brings you here?"

Oakheart climbed to his feet, fist clenched. "Sophy brought me here. How dare you!"

Sophy was on a table, a few scraps of cloth barely providing decent covering. The adepts had rigged a large, faceted crystal and had the tapered end suspended over her. Her eyes were closed and surrounded by dark smudges. Oakheart could see how thin she was, her ribs sticking out, cuts and abrasions seeming untended. He walked around her and saw that her feet were cut and blistered. A complete mess. How could they neglect her hurts?

Myriad thoughts assailed him. Had they done this to her or was it Hanal's work? Even if they had not inflicted the wounds themselves, they had not given her aid or tended her wounds. Worse still, they had hidden her from him. He was certain that she had been here when he arrived. The rage inside surged and he wanted to smash things.

His voice was low and controlled as he spoke. "How could you hide my wife from me? How could anyone bound by the oath leave her in this condition and not offer healing?"

Both of the adepts showed the whites of their eyes. He guessed they had never been spoken to thus. Or did they fear him? Sophy's eyes fluttered open, her face creased with pain. "Oakheart?" she said faintly, voice filled with hope.

Aria was weeping behind him, murmuring Sophy's name over and over.

Oakheart pushed Lianal out of his way and went to his wife. Her hands and feet were bound to the table. He undid the ties and placed her flaccid arms around his neck. Carefully, he lifted her to him. He was shaking with rage. Never had he experienced such a powerful emotion. He had been betrayed by those he would have trusted with his life.

"Where will you take her?" Meld asked in that emotionless voice of his.

"Away from you. Away from this place. You have betrayed us...you have betrayed me. Betrayed all that is good."

"We were examining her, Oakheart," Lianal interjected. He moved to stand between Oakheart and the door. "We did not harm her. We were trying to drain off the power so we can give it back to the land. Surely a little suffering is worth that?"

Oakheart tossed his head, sending his unbound hair out of his face. "But she called to me in pain. Even now she suffers. Are you so blind that you do not see it? Are you so caught up in yourselves that you cannot feel as others do?"

"Yes," Aria agreed. "I felt it too. She suffers a lot."

Sophy's hand touched his mouth feebly. "Oakheart...Oakie. Is it really you? Don't be angry. They asked me if they could look at me...I said yes."

Oakheart ground his teeth as his anger had not lessened. "Did they tell you that I was here?"

"No," Sophy whispered. "But they were busy trying to take back the power and give it to the land. I just want it out of me. Everyone wants this." Sophy's hand reached up and stroked his hair. Her expression was one of wonder, as if she had never expected to see him again. He glanced at Aria's tear-soaked gaze. What to do? All his instinct said to leave, to walk away with Sophy and never look back. Too much betrayal, too much deceit.

"Aria?"

She came to the table and took Sophy's pale hand into her own. "We have her now. Let us take care of her and deal with them," she inclined her head in the direction of the adepts, "later. The morning will shed new light on things."

He nodded. "Come, then."

Sophy was light in his arms. Back in the corridor, they found that Oakheart's bellowing had brought other adepts at a run. With faces full of sleep and disbelief, they lined the hallway and the staircase. Oakheart kept a close eye out for Aran: he needed that adept's healing skill. He gazed into Sophy's face, asleep in the cradle of his arms. Dare he trust Aran though? Surely his friend had known all along.

"How long do you think they had her there?" Aria asked him in a quiet voice. Oakheart could tell that the adepts' subterfuge had disturbed her as well. He had asked his friends to trust the adepts and now he was doubly betrayed.

"I am not sure, princess, but I think since before we arrived. We would have noticed if she arrived after us." Oakheart had to stop talking because he wanted to yell and scream and hit something real bad, and that would serve no purpose other than rousing more adepts.

When he reached the level of his rooms, Aran was waiting by the door, his face full of concern. Oakheart harboured doubt. Had his friend suspected what Meld and Lianal were up to and kept it to himself? Well, in any case, Oakheart would use all the pressure he could bring to bear for he needed Aran's help to cure Sophy. Aran must have healing bark as well as the retreat's own specialist healing powers.

"I am here to serve you," Aran said with a bow. His face grew paler as they approached with Sophy. Surely her pain must speak to him.

"Aran, please, you must provide healing. Sophy suffers greatly."

Aran bowed and opened the door for Oakheart. The room became crowded as Lillia and the forest folk, roused from sleep, squeezed into the room behind Aria. Oakheart shared a look with Lillia who nodded and spoke quietly to her mate. Mellow and the others slipped out the door to stand guard. Lillia returned after fetching her own healing supplies from her room.

"Put her here," Aran said. Oakheart draped Sophy over his bed, placing her arms carefully by her side. She looked too pale and fragile against the sheets.

Aran leant over her, raised his hand and held it above her. When he moved his hand, Sophy began to glow. It was the crystal leaf that had burrowed into her chest when she first entered Argenterra. The leaf had grown so that it was everywhere inside her. Sophy *was* the crystal leaf. It was the jewel within. She squirmed and murmured while Aran evoked the power within her. Then Aran's brow creased and he began to sweat. Within the centre of Sophy's body glowed a dark blue spot. It faded from view when Aran sagged to his knees, panting.

Sophy's skin was a normal colour but none of her wounds were healed. Oakheart grabbed Aran and shoved him against the wall, facing him almost nose to nose. "What were you doing? I need you to heal her."

Aran's eyes were wide. "I know what you want." He shook his head from side to side and then returned Oakheart's stare. "Forgive me, I had to see for myself. 'Tis true: she is the jewel and her power is untouchable."

Oakheart grabbed the adept by the neck of his robe and shoved him higher up the wall, so now they were indeed nose to nose. "You satisfy your curiosity while she suffers? I did not think it of you. Is there no one here who has compassion? Get out!"

He released Aran, who dropped to his feet and fought to right his clothes. "Forgive me...I am a man no more than any other. I will try to aid her but the *given* wanes."

Lillia stepped up to the adept, her fist clenched as if she too wished to throttle the adept. "Healing bark? Have you none? Herbs? Bandages?"

Aran nodded, still trying to settle his breathing. He straightened his robe, but did not lose his look of dishevelment. Oakheart growled, "Bring it now."

"I will. But does the bark work on her? I heard she was resistant to the *given*." Aran dropped a hungry gaze on Sophy's sleeping form.

"Hear this," Oakheart spoke in a coldly controlled voice. "I will brook no further opposition from you or any other within this retreat. I am disillusioned with you and all that you taught me. 'Tis a myth that you seek to aid the people of this land. You are nothing more than men drunk on your own sense of power.

"Here is my wife, suffering at the hands of another through no fault of her own, and you have done *nothing* to aid her, to succour her. You gape at her and prod her as if she is some oddity to be studied. She is a woman, my oathbound wife." He thumped his chest for emphasis. "You have angered me. You will provide the aid I seek or forever will the retreat be cut off from my house and the Kingdom of Silverdale and all the lands that it governs. Do you hear me?"

Aran gaped at him as if Oakheart had lost his mind.

"No Argenterran will be permitted to come to the retreat. No adept will be welcome in Argenterra. We will teach our own."

Aran nodded solemnly and left without a sound. Lillia was already warming water. Oakheart looked to Aria, gave a helpless shrug and plopped down on the edge of the bed. He was close to weeping; the foundations of his life lay in ruin. He rubbed his face with his hands.

"I see what you are thinking and I feel the despair radiating off you. You did the right thing. They cannot get away with acting the way they have. I stand by what you said." Aria gazed down at Sophy's inert form. "Should I try to heal her, do you think? I am not sure I can but her injuries seem to be surface wounds...though I am sure Hanal's torture would have scarred her on the inside."

Oakheart swallowed the lump in his throat. "What choice do we have? I would see her pain lessened. I would take it from her myself."

Aria edged to his side. "Turn her for me. I will start on her back."

Reaching his hands under Sophy, he gently rolled her over. Aria peeled back the remains of clothing, hand shaking. She said nothing for a long time. Each slash, cut and abrasion, she examined. Then Oakheart sensed a feather-like touch at the edge of his mind. Sophy's skin glowed softly as Aria reached for her power. With her fingers, Aria traced the pattern of the wounds and they sealed up. Not even healing bark could accomplish such a miraculous healing. There were no scars.

Aria's ministrations on Sophy's back seemed to go on for hours. Silently, she concentrated as she worked on Sophy's feet and progressively worked her way up her body. Oakheart's gut clenched. Hanal was going to pay for what he had done to his oathbound wife. Aria moved on to heal Sophy's face, smoothing the hurt with a gentle touch to her brow. Sophy struggled against the touch, throwing her head from side to side.

Lillia stood mesmerised by what Aria was doing, for this was no ordinary use of the *given*.

Aria sat back on the bed and put her hands on her lap. She blinked and shook her head before lifting her face to gaze at Oakheart. "How's that? Aran said the power was dangerous and that I shouldn't use it."

Oakheart had tears in his eyes. Her simple words belied the great work she had just accomplished. "Aria....thank you...praise the *given*." He grabbed her hands and kissed them. Her heard Lillia weeping behind him.

Sophy gave an inarticulate groan and fluttered her eyelashes. Lillia edged around Aria and held a shallow bowl of foul-smelling brew under Sophy's nose.

Sophy screwed up her face, but then opened her eyes—clear and blue.

Lillia moved the bowl away as Sophy struggled to sit up, placed another pillow behind her head and eased her on to it. Sophy was healed, but still weak.

"Drink this now while it is hot." Silvery tears shone in the corners of the forest maiden's eyes, too, and her nose was a touch red.

Sophy took a hesitant sip and screwed up her nose. "Horse piss. Geez!"

Lillia laughed. Aria giggled and Oakheart could not help but smile at the familiar words.

Oakheart shifted his gaze back to Sophy. Their eyes met and then she said, a pink blush burnishing her cheeks, "Right then. I am the obedient invalid once again, stood over by the high king's ambassador, a princess and a forest maiden and forced to drink dubious-tasting concoctions." She took a big mouthful of the hot potion, swallowed, and her head fell back on the pillow. "I could really murder a pizza right now. Or maybe some fried chicken."

Aria's smile was wide. "Oh, Sophy. I'm glad you're back. I'll see what food we can get you." Eyes sparkling, she went to Oakheart's food tray to see what Sophy could eat.

Oakheart wished he and Sophy were alone that he could soothe away her fears and her guilt. He could tell by her blushes and by the way she avoided looking him in the eye that she was shamed by being sick again and blamed herself for her misfortune. His dear oathbound wife cared for him and his opinion. Hanal had harmed her in many ways, and she was but a victim. He wished to rid her of her anxieties.

At more urging, Sophy sipped the brew, lay back and closed her eyes. Aria gave her some slices of fruit and small morsels of cheese. Sophy took these without complaint. Lillia wanted to fuss some more and started tugging on the sheets and fluffing the pillows. Oakheart touched her elbow and nodded in the direction of the door. The forest maiden paused, and then nodded. While Lillia made for the door, Aria stroked Sophy's head and kissed her brow before she, too, stood to leave. "I'll leave you alone with Oakheart. I'm quiet tired now myself."

"Thank you, Aria," Oakheart said as their fingers touched and a shy smile lit Aria's eyes as she said farewell.

৩৩

SOPHY SAW ARIA LEAVE AND DREADED THIS MOMENT WITH Oakheart. After all her longing and all her suffering, she found she didn't have the courage to face him. The smattering of haphazard images of what Umri had done to her and what Hanal had almost achieved plagued her mind. They were like a smear on what she really was; they made her feel less of a person.

Yet there was a feeling of comfort in being with Oakheart again. How could he ever love her after all these things had happened to separate them? How could he love a woman that was part jewel, who had a power she couldn't wield? And he a prince and heir to the high king! He knew all about duty and honour and she only had the strength of her convictions. She was no princess. It was laughable that she had any claim to him or his love. Part of her wanted to crawl away, to hide, to die, and the other part never wanted him to leave her again and wanted only to be rolled up in those arms of his and feel his caresses.

A weight on the bed signalled that Oakheart was near. His firm fingers stroked her hair. "Sophy?"

There was so much love and longing in his voice she couldn't help but meet his gaze. Those emerald eyes were dark with worry, his face thinner than she remembered. And his hair was a halo of white-blond around that handsome face of his. He touched her lips lightly with a finger, his eyes travelling over her face as if he was drinking every detail in. On his chest hung the familiar medalion, the one she'd seen when waking while sick in those early days during her trip to Silverdale. She couldn't forget all the troubles she'd had back then. Still had trouble following her around. "I cannot believe I finally have you here. I have so much to say to you. But the first thing is this: you have nothing to be guilty or sorry for, my love. What Hanal did to you was underhand, criminal. He tried to break your oath and he did not succeed, even though all oaths are fading."

Sophy couldn't stop the sob rising in her throat or the tears burning in her eyes. "I'm sorry. It's not as bad as that. I bargained with him. He wanted some of the *given* for his people. He was so passionate about it that I thought I should let him. He detected a barrier protecting the power inside me. I agreed to being starved, being made thirsty. I even agreed to be humiliated, although I hoped it wouldn't come to that. I don't know what this barrier is and I had no control over it either.

"It was his seer, Umri, who took it beyond what was right. She had some hold on him, I think. When he asked for her help when my barriers didn't drop, everything changed for the worse. He became desperate, you see. It's my fault."

Overcome by emotion, she furiously wiped the tears away. Swallowing a few times helped her to keep from breaking down.

Sophy didn't want him to see her cry, but to her surprise he knelt on the floor and buried his face in the bed beside her. He cried with her, for all the pain that they had shared. All the straps on her emotions snapped. Gut-wrenching sobs shook her frame.

When the tears subsided, she reached out and stroked his hair, revelling in the feel of it. With the corner of the sheet, she wiped her face and sniffed. It didn't matter if her face was red or her eyes bloodshot. The wall of pain she'd been hiding behind was gone. That connection to Oakheart she thought was lost was there again. Honesty bound them. There was no hiding. How could there be?

"You felt what happened to me, didn't you?" she asked in a voice clogged with left-over tears.

He lifted his head and wiped his face. "Not the details, but your suffering. You called out to me. I am sorry for my part in it. If I had married Lyant he would not have taken you, would not have had any interest in you."

"Then you would have married her? I did wonder. But I think Hanal would have wanted the power anyway. There was no changing that."

Oakheart took her hand in his and kissed her knuckles. "I thought it was best to marry her. I did not love her. But the alliance would have kept the peace. I struggled with the decision from the time I was at Valley Keep, when you arrived. I thought about it long and hard as we journeyed to Silverdale. I was drawn to you then; perhaps that was why I seemed moody, so changeable. I was not free to choose from the heart. When I suggested the marriage to Veld, he said no and sent me from Silverdale."

Sophy's brow creased. "But if your marriage would keep the peace why did he say no?"

"Because old prejudices linger. Veld has his opinions, which he doesn't care to change. He would never consent to it." Oakheart shrugged. "He did not think the Puri were a danger. Silverdale is impregnable. The passage up the Upper Plateau is impassable with our troops holding a defensive position."

"Nasheen and Hanal told me you were Veld's heir, the high prince. I was shocked. Why didn't you tell me? Didn't you trust me?"

Oakheart took her hand in his and kissed it. "I did trust you...and I was going to tell you when I realised you did not know."

Her dark blue eyes were wide. "Of course I didn't know. I wouldn't have come near you if I knew. Me married to a prince? Heavens, that's insane."

"Not insane."

Sophy wanted to argue the point but she had other questions. "When were you going to tell me?"

"I was thinking when we officialised our oathbonding, if someone did not blurt it out beforehand."

"But why not tell me before? I was the only one who didn't know. Aria must have known, but she kept it from me."

"Aria thought it best. She said it would spook you."

"She's not wrong there. When was this?"

"When we were planning the trip to Silverdale. Aria thought you wouldn't come if you knew about my relationship to the high king."

Sophy shook her head and screwed up the sheet. "But...but that was wrong of her. I feel so angry about that."

"You would have come if you had known?"

"No, of course not. And, if I had been persuaded to, I would not have said a word to you."

Oakheart sighed, undid her grip on the sheet and lowered her hand to the bedcover. He reached out and drew her face in his direction with the tip of his forefinger. He gazed into her eyes, appearing as open and honest as he could be. "Then we would not have had this." He touched his lips to hers.

Sophy lifted her head away from the kiss. "I know. I don't know what could have been. I am messed up by this. By the subterfuge. But not by you."

Oakheart let out a sigh. "It pains me that you would have avoided me if you knew what I was. It is not the ordinary reaction. Usually, women want me because of what I am. You do not know how wonderful it is to be desired for just me.

"I wanted you to like me for who I am, not what I am. From the beginning you treated me as an equal. At first, it rankled when you treated me with such disrespect, and then I saw a deeper meaning in your treatment. You wanted nothing from me but trust and honesty, where everyone else wanted something. Even my good friend Fern."

His hand stroked her cheek, and Sophy smiled. "So what do we do now? I will make a terrible princess." She furrowed her forehead. "You do know that, don't you? Would you be interested in abdicating?"

Oakheart's brows drew together in a worried frown. "You would ask that of me?"

Sophy studied him for a few minutes. "Not really. Just a thought." He was born to duty and he loved Argenterra. She loved him and would not ask him to change anything. "I will ask for extra understanding for me. I won't like it and I won't be good at it. Better you had married Aria. She enjoys that stuff."

Oakheart laughed. "But I do not love Aria in that way."

Sophy lifted an eyebrow. Now that she was feeling better, she could be persuaded to be with Oakheart in that way. She initiated a kiss that Oakheart joined with heartily.

Brushing his fingers through her shorn-off hair, he smiled. "In the morning we make it all official. Everything else can wait. Right now we are just going to talk and hold each other."

Sophy nodded, but made no room in the bed for him. Oakheart stayed by the side of the bed, keeping his hands folded. Sophy lifted her chin, firming up her resolve. "There is so much I don't know. Nasheen spoke of Aria and Dellbright. Is it true?"

A frown marred Oakheart's forehead and his lips pursed. "Yes. He beat and raped her. Dellbright has Gilly."

Sophy's heart leapt. "And?"

Oakheart stroked Sophy's forehead repeatedly, soothing the worry that was creasing her brow. "He hurt her terribly. She does not talk about it."

A tear leaked out of Sophy's eyes. She swallowed and asked, "How could she bear such a thing? She loved him deeply. Rae told me some of what passed at Valley Keep after I left. I bear some of the blame. There was no evidence of abuse then, but there were signs that things were not well between them. I couldn't put my finger on it. I should have done more to support her."

Oakheart considered her with bright green eyes shining with admiration. "I can understand your regret for what has happened to Aria. What about your suffering?"

Sophy sighed and squeezed his hand. "I didn't love Hanal so there

315

was no betrayal of the heart. I was always wary of him so the threat to me was there from the very beginning. What Aria suffered was different. Dellbright had her love and he turned it all around and mangled it. Oh, what Aria must have suffered. I can only imagine if...sorry, I can't bear even to contemplate it."

Another tear slid down Sophy's cheek. What had happened to this place? Was Rufus to blame for all that had happened or had it always been there just below the surface? The violence within, waiting to break free. Her eyes met Oakheart's again. He was gentle in every way but strong as well. How glad she was that she had waited to know him and love him.

"Will you sleep now? You look very tired."

Sophy nodded slowly, drowsiness already sneaking up on her. Yet she managed a smile, one that would remind him of the old Sophy. "If you will sleep beside me and hold me, I will."

"Finally," he said with mock exhilaration. "If you can stomach me close to you, then maybe we have a way ahead, after all."

"Oh, I wouldn't worry about that. I've been thinking of this moment for a long time now."

Oakheart wasted no time and stripped off his clothes and with utmost care slid next to her in the bed, sighing at the sheer luxury of her warmth, and gathered her up into his arms.

⚛ 25 ⚛

A BOND SEALED

The light brightened in the room. Sophy had been awake for some time, listening to Oakheart's breathing while she thought about things. The walls of the retreat visitors' quarters were quite magical, unlike the walls in the basement rooms where she had been held. The strange adept Meld's words troubled her. He and Lianal had tried to drain the power from her. Or so they said. Sophy could neither feel nor use her power. It was just there inside her, like she was some vessel. And everyone seemed to want it, except Oakheart. Her oathbound husband knew what it was like. Didn't he suffer the same thing? Friendships and adoration not for who he was inside, but his looks and his position. How frustrating to be overlooked for mere trappings you had no control over.

The two adepts had not hurt her physically. They hadn't helped her either, and they had lied to her. She had asked for Oakheart constantly while she was on that table, but they'd said they didn't know where he was. And then there he was. Was that a betrayal? Was no one to be trusted, except her close companions?

Thinking about how Aria kept secrets from her made her grind her teeth. Bloody hell, was Oakheart the only one she could trust? But he had kept information from her too. Staring at the ceiling, she tried to reorder her thoughts. It wasn't black and white. So much grey in her head she was lost in a fog.

Oakheart's arm jerked in his sleep. She stroked it. This was a special man; he didn't rush her, didn't press her or ask her any questions. His patience pleased her. Now that he had slept beside her the whole night, without any sexual advance, she was even more at home with him. The disquiet and the awkwardness were evaporating while they stayed together. Now she wanted that bonding with him, wanted their reunion to be special.

When she turned and stroked the hair from his face, she found he was watching her, his expression thoughtful.

"Hello," she said.

He smiled. "Hello yourself." Propping himself up on his elbow, his gaze lingered on her face.

Feeling awkward with his appraisal, Sophy tried to divert him. "So what does a girl have to do to get breakfast around here?"

With his eyes twinkling, Oakheart twitched her chin. "I will feed you shortly, but first there is a small matter to settle between us."

Sophy's heart sank. "Oh? What would that be?"

Oakheart slid to the floor and reached across the blankets to grasp her hand.

"Lady Sophy, my precious jewel, I humbly ask if you will wed me this day. I know I have failed you, that I am unworthy of your love. But I ask you from the heart of me. I know I have denied it even to myself...I love you Sophy, and my life is yours."

Speechless, hot blushes flushed over Sophy's face in waves. Tears and happiness fought for control of her tongue. "Dear Oakheart, I will marry you. There's no way you can get out of it. We are oathbound already. Besides, don't think you have failed me. You have not. And I already knew you loved me. I knew it ages ago. I was waiting for you to realise it."

Oakheart kissed her smiling lips. "Did you now? You jest with me. How could you make jokes at a time like this? Does not every woman wait for the day when a man pledges all to them?"

"I'm not 'jesting'. You have loved me since the Gilton Forest."

"What?" He frowned at her.

She put her arms around him. "I'm glad you can admit it."

His eyes lit with mischief and his frown melted in a smile. "If you do not keep quiet...I...I will let Lillia feed you herbal concoctions for the rest of the day."

She smiled broadly, her heart free of misery. "Oh no, please no!" She put her hand to her forehead in mock dismay. Sobering, she added, "I'll be good. Just feed me because I'm starving. I want my strength for later on." She winked at him.

Oakheart paused and blinked. "Later on?" A smile quirked at the corner of his mouth. "I see."

With enthusiasm, he pulled on his clothes, and bustled about preparing breakfast. Pulling out bowls and then going out the door. A couple of minutes later he was back, carrying a tray. Sophy's strength was coming back in dribs and drabs, probably because her spirits had lifted. It was such a luxury to be pampered by Oakheart. He fed her, rubbed her back, talked to her of inconsequential things. A soft knock on the door and Aria poked her head in. "May I?" Aria asked, her wild hair tied into a plait. Her eyes looked bright.

"Of course, come in," Oakheart said before Sophy could say anything. "I must organise a few things so I will leave you two alone for a while." He squeezed Sophy's hand and left the room.

Sophy studied Aria. She was thinner, and her face showed some of the misery she'd experienced. Aria came over to the bed and picked up Sophy's hand. "I'm so glad to see you again. I wanted to tell you that you were right about everything...about me."

Tears gathered in Sophy's eyes and she rubbed at them with the back of a hand. She did not feel superior for being suspicious of Dellbright and Argenterra. It made her sad that Aria's dreams had not come true. "Aria, don't. You didn't know...I didn't either. I was bitter and scared. What happened really? And Gilly?"

A sob burst out of Aria. "I miss him, Sophy...truly I do. But I had to help find you and Dellbright wouldn't let me...he...even when I stayed behind he kept Gilly away from me." She shrugged and met Sophy's gaze. "I sent you into danger, to Rufus. I've come to appreciate how brave you are, just by having to be strong myself. It was a powerful lesson."

"And Dellbright...will you go back?"

Aria shook her head vigorously, her mouth a grim line. "Never!" Her voice shook and Sophy thought the very mention of her husband's name made her tense.

"Tell me what happened. What did Dellbright do to you?"

Her friend slowly shook her head, this time with lips trembling and the march of tears still evident on her cheeks. "I would rather not speak of it."

Sophy lay there saying nothing, letting Aria control herself. "But you had an inkling that he would treat you badly..."

Aria's eyes widened, the question evident.

"Oakheart mentioned something to me..."

Aria stilled and moved her gaze to the wall. After a minute of silence, she began to talk. "Yes. I think I did, but I tried not to believe it. I thought my love would make a difference. But I should have known...you see, it started on the wedding night. I thought it was me... that I was deficient. Oh god, Sophy, he hurt me when he...I can't say he made love to me because that is not what it was. He took me, delved everything out of me, pain and blood and tears.

"He was remorseful afterwards, and most of the time while you were there he behaved well, tried to at least. There were moments of anger, a pinch on the arm or the chin that wasn't gentle or affectionate. I felt so isolated...I withdrew into myself...I guess it was depression. I found out little things about him, his treatment of Rae for one, and then how he treated his mother. Her life was his. She did everything for him and did his bidding, too afraid to question him.

"I was confused, especially when he said he understood our friendship, but then he did his best to prevent me from contacting you. He took the talkstone. Demanded I not ask to talk to you. In the end, whenever I did we argued and he became violent. Sophy," she lowered her voice, "he...he raped me while I was pregnant."

Sophy caressed Aria's hand with her thumb, something Oakheart did when he wanted to listen and soothe at the same time. Her heart was heavy. She had a share of blame for what had happened to Aria, as she was responsible for leaving Aria alone and for not doing more to prevent the wedding. "I failed you, Aria. I could have done more."

Aria chuckled, a sad sound, full of self-loathing. "No, you didn't fail me. It was my decision to make, and I had to deal with the consequences. I treated you badly for my own selfish ends. I could have done more to make your life easier. I should never have done what I did. Even now, I still think of myself before you. You put me first but you shouldn't; I don't deserve it."

Sophy propped herself up on both her elbows, running her gaze over her friend. "But you have power. You can use the *given*. You healed me, and Oakheart before that. You saved me from Rufus."

Aria got off the bed, took a few steps away and then turned back to Sophy. "Oh yes. I can wield power, use the *given*, which is now fading from the land. I have done nothing to deserve it and nor do I know how to wield it properly.

"Coming to Argenterra and finally being more beautiful and important than you ended up being a curse. What good did it do me? I liked the attention and had little compassion for you. It went to my head. I acted like a bitch to you and all along people attributed kindness to me when I didn't deserve it. Yes, I can act with good manners and appear sympathetic. I pushed you away from me, for a man who was not worthy. I fell for his looks, a few kind words..."

Sophy slid her legs over the side of the bed, wrapping the sheet around her body. She was lightheaded, but Aria's remorse had to be addressed. "No, no. You are kind. Most of the time you do things I never would think of, and you're gentle, too, and sweet. These are good things. I'm not like that. Sometimes I think Oakheart wished I was. I remember what you told me, how you could see people were true. Remember. I recall you saying it was overwhelming. Surely that had to do your head in big time. I think I would have gone crazy if I had experienced that."

Aria's eyes narrowed and she pinched her fingers together as she held them in front of her waist. "I see, you're out to stop me beating myself up. Yes, it was like that. If I have an excuse then that is part of it. The overwhelming wonder of Argenterra and the *given*. As for the rest of your 'oh so nice' little speech, well, that's crap. I have owned my badness, you have to accept it."

"Fine. Evil Aria. What next?"

Aria lips lifted in a smile and her green eyes twinkled with light. "Oakheart loves you. He may have tricked you into an oathbonding but he does nothing hastily. He is considerate and smart and, more than that, he is a good and gentle man. I am envious of your good taste." With that said, Aria smiled. "I hope you don't mind that we've become close friends. Brother-like, if you know what I mean."

"Ah, but you failed to tell me who he really was. I'm not sure I'm going to forgive you for that. The princess gig is your thing, not mine." Sophy frowned and Aria drew in a breath.

"Oh, Oakheart told you that was my idea." She winced. "Sorry."

"Sorry? Is that the best you can do? You've condemned me to a lifetime of good manners, obeying the rules and setting a good example. How horrid!"

Aria gaped at her. Sophy could not maintain the semblance of outrage and her lips twitched. Then they both burst out laughing.

When she'd gained control, Sophy added, "I'm glad you are close."

Sophy was filled with sadness for Aria's suffering. At least she had some support in Oakheart. He'd be a life-long friend and supporter. There was another knock at the door. Aria swung around when Lillia poked her head into the room. From what Sophy could see of the corridor, the forest folk were guarding her door. She immediately thought of Oakheart and smiled. When he distrusted someone, he really went the whole hog in making up for past mistakes. The adepts had broken faith with him, and he was unforgiving.

Lillia had a tight expression on her face; something was worrying her.

"What's wrong," Sophy asked.

"Meld asks permission to enter. Will you see him?"

Sophy wondered what Lillia would do if she refused. "Let him through."

Meld stepped inside, brushing past the forest maiden, who carefully avoided touching him and could barely keep the revulsion from showing on her face.

"Forgive my intrusion. I see that you are healing nicely, my lady. Good morn to you, Princess Aria."

"Good morning to you," Aria said, not taking her eyes from the strange adept.

Sophy sat a little higher on the pillows. Meld was being polite, which seemed odd. "I'm fine, getting stronger by the minute. Did you want something or were you seeing if I survived the night?"

Meld bowed his head slightly. "Your straightforward manner is interesting. I detect bitterness in your words; perhaps they are deserved. I ask a boon of you."

"A what?" Sophy gaped at Aria who sat down beside her on the bed, eyeing the adept warily.

"He asks a favour," Aria translated.

Sophy grinned and then studied the adept. "What do you want?"

"I ask that you let me perform the bonding ceremony between you and Oakheart. He is dear to me, if one such as me can have feelings."

Aria's fist clenched. "Don't let him, Sophy. He's not normal. He doesn't think the way everyone else does. Meld's been so cold to Lillia, even though he's riding around inside her son's body."

"What are you talking about?" Sophy stared at Aria. "Adage is the closest adept to Oakheart." Turning back to Meld, she asked, "Why would he want you, Meld, instead of Adage?"

Meld's eyes glowed blue momentarily. Sophy stiffened, realising that she was missing something important. "I am Adage in Brookfell Treesinger's body. Brook was the son of Lillia and Mellow, hence their reaction when they are near me. I was struck by Rufus when we attempted to free you from your crystal prison." Meld bowed his head slightly, acknowledging Aria. "What the princess says is true. I am not normal. I do not think or feel like others do. Yet I ask this boon anyway."

Oakheart slipped quietly in through the door. The room was becoming crowded. Sophy caught his eye and Oakheart nodded slightly, the signal she'd been waiting for. "Yes, I would be honoured, Meld."

Meld bowed low, turned and acknowledged Oakheart before leaving.

"Why are you letting him do this after everything that has

happened?" Aria demanded, anger staining her cheeks red. Her outraged gaze swept both Oakheart and Sophy.

Sophy lay back on her pillow, not quite up to arguing after a rather taxing morning. She hoped Oakheart would answer for her and he did. "I have spoken with Meld and he has explained a few things to me. Becoming a meld with Brook damaged both of them. Adage's body is still alive. After the ceremony Adage wishes us to go with him to view his body. He fears that seeing his body will trigger his final death. He says it is his time."

Aria stood with her fists clenched at her sides. "And that's sufficient to forgive him...forgive what he did to Sophy and how badly he treated the forest folk?"

"Yes," Sophy said softly. "It's enough. Adage's passing is a big thing. There is no one his equal. When I became that crystal, I sucked the power from the land. Because of that Rufus was able to bring more of his own power to bear, as there was a gap, a weakness where none was before...I am the cause..."

Oakheart strode to the bed in two steps and knelt by her. "Do not blame yourself. 'Tis prophecy, enchantment and many other things beyond your control."

Aria considered Sophy's words. "Okay, if you say so. But you haven't seen how he has treated Lillia and Mellow. I am not going to forgive him until he makes amends to them."

Sophy closed her eyes; images and memories clicked together. Now she understood what Meld was, it made sense. "Meld suffered a lot, Aria," Sophy said. "I'm not as perceptive as you, but Meld has been close to me since he came here. In taking power from me, I saw much. He's hurting. He feels as if he let Argenterra down. His oath is shattered. It was meant to keep him alive to fight the Ancient Evil, but that's broken. He's going to die and he can't stop any of this from happening. Can't you see what that's doing to him?"

Aria lifted her chin. "I can't believe you can say that. You didn't see how it was. Anyway, I'm going to get ready for this ceremony. I wouldn't miss your wedding, Sophy, not if Rufus himself was saying the bonding prayer."

SOPHY HAD REQUESTED A LOW-KEY CEREMONY. THEY DIDN'T HAVE the time or the resources to do anything nearly as elaborate as Aria's wedding. Even though she was marrying a prince, there wasn't going to be any pomp and ceremony. It wasn't appropriate at the present time, nor was it to her liking. As much as possible she kept her relief hidden. She and Oakheart hadn't discussed the details of royal life. He had asked to marry her so he had to take her how she was. She suspected it was going to be difficult. She hadn't planned on being married at all, but she'd grow accustomed to it, she supposed. She had a strong friendship with Oakheart, and she thought he understood her. It was a good basis to build on. They should be able to tackle what normal life threw at them. Trouble was that normal seemed likely to be a long way away. With a sigh, she realised her life had never been normal.

Lillia helped her to bathe and dress in an adept's white robe. "There you are, my lady," she said as she dried Sophy's hair. "You need nothing else for your beauty is now apparent to all. This simple robe and your hair...um..." Lillia tried to arrange the hacked locks, covering the bare patches of scalp with dampened tufts of hair. "I do own that I would prefer a little more flesh on you. You look half-starved."

"You're not wrong there." She patted her stomach. "Oakheart has been feeding me so I won't be this thin for long, so don't worry."

Lillis sniffed and tried to smile.

"You are kind to me, Lillia. I know you have suffered a lot through your choices. I hope I bring you no more grief. But please remember, whatever happens, you will always be welcome where I am, and if you need it, I will help you."

Tears trailed down Lillia's cheeks. "There, there. No need for such fine speeches. Who has not suffered in this? We are all touched by misfortune, even the land itself. I fear for the future though. My unborn child will come into a world with little of the *given*, and perhaps the hand of the Ancient Evil will enter here."

Sophy patted Lillia on the shoulder. "I would stop it if I could."

Lillia turned Sophy around and put the final touches on her clothes, tugging here, smoothing there. "Oh, I know that without saying. I have always known you for a brave heart. I have doubted your motives at times, and for that I am sorry."

"Really?" replied Sophy. "To me you were always a good and true friend."

Lillia breathed out a sad sigh. "Your memory fails you. I recall how it was in the Gilton Forest." She stood back and looked Sophy up and down. "There, at last you are ready."

Sophy nodded, remembering how the forest folk treated her at first. But she understood how it was. They couldn't 'see' her and she was rather rowdy.

Sophy waited while Lillia checked her own clothing and hair, then out the door they went—into the crystal corridor bathed in midday sun. It sparkled and shimmered like a sheet of clear ice. Sophy was a little disconcerted by the sensation of walking on water. Aria was further up the corridor leading the way. Because of Sophy's aversion to the *given* they were to be bonded in the main courtyard.

Sophy ground her teeth when she saw how many adepts were gathered there. The threads of their soothing song reached her. Some things one couldn't change and had to live with. She wished more than anything she could see, touch and use the *given*. Then she wouldn't be the odd one out and Oakheart wouldn't have to make excuses for her. Oakheart could have had his ceremony in the bonding chamber here in the retreat with the *given* resonating around them. But in deference to her sensitivities, he had requested this venue.

She caught a glimpse of Oakheart clad once more in his blue and white robes. Her heart fluttered at the sight of him. He looked so different in those robes. They disguised the contours of his body, making him appear bigger. Yet they added a mysterious air to him, as if he was powerful and full of hidden knowledge. Like a wizard. He smiled when their eyes met across the distance and he walked up slowly to grasp her hand. "You look very well, little jewel."

All of Sophy's doubts fell away. "So do you," she responded, arching her eyebrow as she assessed him.

Meld stepped out from between Lianal and Aran. "I call all here to witness the solemnisation of the oathbonding of Oakheart, Silver Bow, Ambassador to the High King, acknowledged high prince and heir and

Vorn's direct descendant, to Sophy Sinclair, Gift of Crystal Tree Woods and Argenterra's talisman."

Meld's words made Sophy uneasy. Oakheart squeezed her hand. "As these two are oathbound and their oath has been sealed in blood and thus witnessed by the land, we need only offer witness to their vows and offer our support for their union."

Oakheart turned towards Sophy, using the pressure of his grip to draw her to him.

"My lady Sophy, in Gilton Forest I did obtain from you a vow and I did return it. But hear this: my life is yours until I die. With this body and heart of mine, I will serve you and no other. My love, my heart, my body and all that I have is yours."

Sophy's mind went numb. Suddenly she felt so unequal to the task. She gazed into Oakheart's green eyes, seeking support. They were bonded already, now she must repeat another vow in front of witnesses. Her hand trembled but Oakheart soothed her with his thumb.

She smiled in response to his touch. Why had they not discussed vows and rehearsed them? "Oakheart," she said and coughed. "My love for you is stronger than any oath. My life and love is yours until I die and, with this body and heart of mine I will serve you and love you and no other."

She closed her eyes, suddenly shy, and lowered her head to his breast. Her heart was beating loudly in her ears. No matter how much she loved him, promising him like that in public was hard. Meld was already midsentence when she noticed that he was speaking.

"....we do witness this bonding ceremony."

Lianal walked up to them and bowed low. When he stood again, he could not look Oakheart in the face. "We have prepared some refreshments. Will you partake of them with us?"

"Food?" Sophy said cheekily. "Oakheart never says no to a good meal. Lead on, Lianal, and thank you."

Oakheart's eyes widened and then he chuckled. "Sophy, I should be angry with you, but I am not. I think I understand this humour of yours."

"Angry with me? Why? Am I wrong? You're not hungry?"

Oakheart laughed out loud. "Of course I am."

THEY HAD BEEN EATING FOR AN HOUR OR SO WHEN MELD STOOD UP from the table. He inclined his head to Sophy and Oakheart, then to the forest folk and, lastly, Aria. Taking that for a signal to follow, Sophy swallowed what she was eating and took a gulp of water. Oakheart took her hand and led her to fall into step behind Meld. After some negotiation, Aria, Lillia and Mellow were to accompany them. Of the adepts only Lianal followed. It was a quiet procession. Adage's body, she was told, was kept below in his old study. As they headed lower, the comparatively darker walls comforted Sophy. Despite the beauty of the upper levels of the retreat, this basement seemed normal and much less ethereal.

Lianal hurried ahead and swung the door open, careful to shut it after Aria, Lillia and Mellow entered. Adage's slight form reclined on a bed, the cheeks sunken and his skin pale. His chest rose and fell slightly. An adept stood beside the bed, eyes closed as he breathed with Adage's body. His eyes opened slowly then widened when they beheld Meld standing at the forefront of the group.

Meld took a place at the end of the bed. He looked resigned to his fate. However, she didn't know what was going to happen next.

The eyelids of Adage's almost dead body fluttered. The cold blue of his gaze met Meld's, while both of them trembled. Meld spoke with great effort. "I know not," he said, his voice thin, "what to expect from this."

His shoulders slouched and then his head lolled back and then forwards to sit on his chest, and he dropped to his knees. Through gritted teeth, he said, "Brookfell is near. He grows stronger as I grow weaker. I bid you...I bid you farewell. May you preserve the land." His breath was sucked in a noisy death rattle. Meld's gaze met Sophy's, the otherness fading, letting brown eyes show through. "Beware the Crystal Gate..." Meld toppled to the floor.

At the same time that Meld dropped to the floor, Adage had sat up in the bed, but grew rigid and fell back to the bed, eyes wide and staring.

"So passes Adage, the greatest of us all," Lianal said with hands raised. "I believe Brook has returned to us."

With a cry Lillia rushed to her son's body, Mellow close behind, to draw Brook into her lap. The adept was deathly white, his breathing shallow. Yet while he lived there was hope. The suffering of Brook for her sake twisted Sophy's gut. Why did she feel so responsible? Brook took a few more shaky breaths then opened his eyes.

"Mother," he said. Turning his head and reaching out, he grasped Mellow's hand. "Father. I was never far from you. Forgive him; he acted for the best, or so he believed."

Mellow swallowed slowly. "My son, I never dreamed that you could be returned to us. He never admitted it to us."

"Perhaps because he did not know if he could save me. He was a man with a mission."

Lillia's joyful weeping swelled up while she stroked Brook's hair and rubbed his shoulders.

Mellow took a deep breath. "Will you return to Gilton Forest with us? Will you return home?"

Brook glanced about until his gaze rested on Lianal's. "Yes, father. I will come home."

Sophy sniffed away her tears. It would be hard to part from Lillia but it was time to let the forest woman live her own life. Suddenly she thought of the child she had conceived at the same time as the forest maiden. Her child was gone, taken, she was sure, by some art of Rufus's. Her eyes locked with Oakheart and she saw his grief. Adage had always been special to him. Yet it was time: *their* time. Sophy rubbed her abdomen thoughtfully.

Oakheart went to Adage's body and spoke quietly. After touching a hand to the man's forehead he turned away. Catching sight of Sophy he came over and hugged her. The forest folk gathered up Brook and led him from the room. Aria followed behind. Oakheart draped his arm over her shoulder and led her out. After all, they were now officially husband and wife.

❧ 26 ❧

SOULS ENTWINE

Sophy couldn't help noticing that things were not as they should
be with Oakheart. The day's activities had left him fatigued.
She hadn't had a chance to find out everything that happened
after she was rescued from the jewel and Rufus. Nor had she found out
what had transpired during and after her abduction by Nasheen.
Something important had happened. That much was obvious.

He noticed her worried frown and kissed her brow. "Do not fret,"
he said and held her gently around the waist as they walked along the
corridor.

"I'm not fretting. I know that you're mourning for Adage, but
there's more to it than that. I can feel it, see it. What has happened to
you? You're not normally so easily tired. Is this why you didn't wake up
when Nasheen broke into our tent? Why you didn't come after me?"

Oakheart avoided her gaze. "Please give me a moment, little jewel."

Aria was just ahead. Oakheart sped up, though his gait was heavy,
dragging Sophy along with him down the corridor. "Aria," he called. "A
moment, please."

Aria slowed and smiled hesitantly, her skin and face as beautiful as
ever, though her expression was forlorn. When Sophy drew near, she
noticed that her friend's eyes were red from weeping. She looked down

to avoid meeting Aria's gaze. Was Aria upset because Oakheart had wed her? Aria said they'd become close. Sophy hated herself for thinking it. She hadn't failed to notice the bond of friendship between Aria and Oakheart and until that moment had refused to be jealous.

With a shake of her head, Aria said over-brightly, "Shouldn't you two be elsewhere?"

Sophy's head snapped up and she faced her friend. "Yes," she answered a mite too forcefully. Aria's mouth spread into a wide grin. It didn't quite mask the bloodshot eyes but it did improve her looks. Sophy leant back against the wall and pointedly gazed up at Oakheart. He blushed, making her want to laugh. Oakheart embarrassed? Now I've seen everything, she thought.

Her husband's expression grew serious. "Aria, would you come to my...our quarters. I need to discuss an important matter with you."

Aria's puzzlement was evident as she chewed on her bottom lip. After giving Oakheart the once over, she agreed to join them and together they ascended the stairs. Once inside the room, Sophy sat on the bed and pouted. As much as she loved Aria, having her in their room on her wedding night was enough to make her angry, jealous... She couldn't help frowning. She wanted Oakheart to herself, wanted all of his attention. When Oakheart sagged into a seat, giving the impression of supreme weariness, Sophy sat up. "What is going on?" She glared at Aria and then at Oakheart.

Aria sighed loudly and began to pace, her unbound hair bouncing as she walked. "When we rescued you from the crystal, Oakheart was nearly killed. Rufus drained his life force. I used your power to save him, but all I did was keep him alive. He was weak, very weak for a long time."

Sophy's gut clenched. She remembered that Oakheart didn't stir when she was taken by Nasheen. "But, but..."

"I am well, Sophy," Oakheart tried to reassure her, even though he could barely sit up straight in his chair. He appeared to have aged. Lines were etched into his forehead and around his mouth and eyes. Sophy's eyes burned with the sharp sting of tears. Were none them unscathed? She had been defiled, battered and bruised practically since the day she set foot in Argenterra. Aria had been beaten and raped and now Oakheart nearly ripped from life.

It twisted her heart with anguish to think of Oakheart being less than he was. Strength in person and in character was Oakheart. How could he bear being anything less?

"Over time he has regained some strength, though he is not like he used to be." Aria turned and stared at Oakheart. "That's why you asked me here, isn't it? You want me to use Sophy's power to heal you as I did her."

A spark of enthusiasm lit his gaze. "Yes. I know it is selfish of me. But it is a special night for me. If Sophy agrees I would welcome your healing for it seems you have grown in skill. The finesse you used to heal Sophy could be used on me. If you look deep enough. I have waited so long to be whole...now is the most important time for me and for Sophy. You have it in your power to help me."

Aria wrung her hands. "I know I healed Sophy but I don't really know how I did it. It was instinctive. I think I'm getting better at it but I could hurt you. Remember what Aran said; I wouldn't want that." She shook her head and turned away from him, clearly distraught.

"Please, princess... Aria?"

Aria turned to Sophy and they shared a long, deep look. Sophy nodded. If Aria could help Oakheart, she wanted that more than anything. "It's his choice, Aria. I want this night to be special too, but more than that I don't want you to leave him like this, less than he should be, especially if you can help him. I'm assuming it doesn't hurt you to heal."

Aria chewed her bottom lip. "Oakheart, I followed you when you went in search of Sophy in the basement below. I saw the bolts of *given* power the adepts threw at you. Saw them rebound from you and back on them. What if you send that power back at me?"

Oakheart buried his head in his hands. He spoke though his voice was muffled. "I did not know the adepts could use the *given* so. I did not consciously send their power back at them." He rubbed his face and met Aria's gaze. "I do not know what it signifies or how it happened and 'tis too late to ask Adage. I fear we will never know. It could be some skill I unknowingly wielded, or it could be a result of the power already residing in me."

Aria worried her bottom lip with her teeth some more and shifted her gaze to Sophy. After a few minutes of contemplation, she said ever so quietly, "I could try a little power at first, a gentle healing probe. If that works then I'll try to heal you."

Oakheart smiled again, his eyes flaring with hope. "Yes, please. I will be ever in your debt."

Aria laughed and blushed. "I've lost count of who is indebted to whom. Let's just do it. But relax, okay? No sending power at me and frying my hair."

Oakheart nodded solemnly.

Face taking on a serious expression, Aria's green eyes locked with Sophy's. It was a strange sensation. Sophy knew Aria was drawing power from her, but all she could perceive was a bluish light all around her and a faint tingling in her hands and feet, like a weak electrical current. Out of the corner of her eye, she saw Oakheart stiffen.

Time seemed to stand still. Aria didn't recoil as she had expected, so obviously Oakheart was taking in her healing. Aria closed her eyes, finally releasing Sophy's gaze, yet she still drew power from her. Oakheart's hair flared out, spiking with power and residual traces of blue arcs of light. A bluish glow haloed him and seemed to pulse through him. The lines of strain eased away from his eyes and mouth and his skin returned to the tanned healthy glow of old. The whites of his eyes glowed, overshadowing his green irises.

Then it was over and the power ebbed away. Sophy drew in a loud, gulping breath, not realising that she'd been holding it in, then half lunged, half crawled over to the chair to eagerly drink in Oakheart's transformation. He was panting and had sagged back into the chair; his head lolled momentarily. Certain that he was healed, Sophy's attention was drawn to Aria, who looked ready to faint. "Aria?"

Aria smiled wanly when Sophy touched her shoulder. Her eyes were bright and feverish, and she looked pale. "I'm all right," she said. "That was interesting and difficult. There wasn't an injury to heal so much. More like every part of him, every cell lacked life. It took a while to work out how to get them to take the power in. Let me know how he is in the morning. It was the best I could do." Aria clasped her hand on Sophy's forearm and then lurched drunkenly to the door.

Aria was nearly out the door when Sophy said softly, "Thank you, Aria." Aria left without looking back.

Gazing over to Oakheart, Sophy realised she was shaking with fear. He hadn't spoken. With a trembling hand she reached out and stroked his hair. There was a faint zap when she touched him. He lifted his head and smiled.

"Well?" she asked, full of tension. He looked better, healed, yet she couldn't be sure. "How do you feel?"

Oakheart leisurely stretched out his limbs, stood and bent his legs. "I feel whole. I feel alive with energy, probably more than I ever felt before. It feels so good to be like this." He gave her a lop-sided grin. "I never want to feel so drained ever again. Thank you for letting Aria have use of your power."

"It's not really my power. My body is kind of a rental. I can't do anything with it."

He lunged at her and swung her round, lifting her off her feet. Sophy let out a squeal of surprised delight. Their eyes met and the attraction seemed to leap between them. She didn't know how long she gazed at him before he thoroughly kissed her. He didn't stop, but kept on and on with the kiss as if it was his last. She was breathless, but still uneasy. She found it hard to relax into his lovemaking. She wanted the horror of what had happened to her to disappear, yet it was there, rearing its ugly head and spoiling her wedding night.

As if sensing her hesitation, Oakheart ended the kiss and parted from her. "Sophy," he said softly. "We should talk about what happened. It will ease your mind."

Sophy rubbed her hands over her upper arms, suddenly chilled. Umri said that she wasn't a grown woman, but she felt that she was now. That young girl who had entered Argenterra had been replaced with a woman. The difference was hard to describe. Yet, she had to face up to her fears and tell Oakheart her thoughts and feelings. It was the only way their relationship could continue—or end, she thought miserably.

"I don't really want to talk about it, although I realise that I have to. We must deal with the things that stand between us. You vowed your love for me today. I feel I don't deserve it. I responded to Hanal... he made me want him sexually. We didn't...you know...but still..." She paused, trying to control her shameful tears, which were imminent.

Oakheart pushed her chin up, smiling ever so sweetly at her. "I wish I could wipe away what Hanal did to you, for I was the cause of it. But let it go now. Let me fill your mind with my touch, let yourself be pleasured by me, let my love enfold you. I have naught else to give you. There is no other comfort that I can give, except myself. Aria has given me back my strength. This night is the official start of our life together. Let us make it our own."

Sophy wept, a torrent of pain sweeping away her defences. Oakheart embraced her, soothed her with a balm of soft, meaningless words full of endearment. When she was ready, he helped her remove her gown, stripped his own clothes and gathered her up in his arms.

With wonder she watched him touch her gently, his face enraptured by her body and face. Their eyes met, and yes, she felt the passion in her, the falling away of her fear and self-loathing. Their lips met and a frisson of excitement ran through her body. His hot mouth devoured hers, and then her passion rose, reaching out so that desire snaked through her body. His touch exhilarated her skin, making it burn. Her body quivered with love as she dragged her hands through his hair, bringing him even closer. Their lips met once again. Then Oakheart placed her on the bed and lay full length on top of her. It was a heavenly sensation, encompassed within the frame of his body. His bigness, his strength drew a sigh of satisfaction.

"Sophy," he said sensuously, holding her face in his hands. "I am yours to hold. I would make a child with you this night and in this place."

She clasped him close, running her hands over his muscled back, revelling in the strength of him. He pleasured her. With his mouth and hands, he delved out pockets of ecstasy. Oakheart pushed her over the edge and a sweet sense of fulfilment enveloped her. Her body shook with the force of her enjoyment and then he was inside her, moving with all his strength deeper and deeper. She moved with him, licking the sweat from his chin, nipping his lips with her teeth.

All of her senses were crying out with wonder. She was with Oakheart, the one she loved. Afterwards, he rolled her into his arms and held her, talking to her softly as the light around them ebbed. Oakheart's lovemaking had cleansed her, rid her of guilt and filled her with something else.

Twice more during the night they made passionate and sensual love. Oakheart stretched out the time he touched her until she nearly screamed her frustration. She made love to him, making him tremble and groan as her lips travelled over his body, teasing his skin with her teeth. His shout startled her, but before she could understand what was happening he was tumbling her to the sheets once again fired by a passion so strong, ignited by her lovemaking, that he was mindless with it.

Near morning, they lay exhausted and entwined, speaking their innermost thoughts and dreams. Sophy learnt of his love for Aria, a tender bond. At first when he spoke of it, she was tempted to be wounded, but then she understood him. Aria was like a sister. He admired her, cared for her, but he didn't desire her. She found it hard to keep her face straight when he told her of Fern's infatuation with her friend and how he was doomed to heartbreak.

"But if oaths are fading, wouldn't they be able to be together one day?"

Oakheart's face showed his horror. "That will be a sad day...for then the *given* would have been swept away entirely."

"No, I don't believe that. The *given* will weaken but never disappear. It is the heart of this place. If you continue the way of life that you have, it may even come back. Rufus caused the oath to be broken, but if the people hold true, then I can't see why it would not come back, like strength after a long illness." Sophy spoke from her heart, from belief. She had no facts to offer him.

"Is this knowledge you have? Some truth you have? Or do you torment me with false hope?"

Sophy propped her head on her elbow and draped her leg over his. Drawing circles with her fingers on his wide chest, she said, "How can hope be false? If I believe it, then that is like faith and in this place there are many wonders. Your average person may not be able to work the *given* anymore, but it will always be there for those who can see it. Vorn made an oath that bound everybody. But what is there to stop an individual making an oath? Wouldn't the force that heard Vorn hear them?"

Oakheart smiled. "You have been thinking hard. You cannot sense the *given*, or use it, but you believe in it. You are a marvel. I will do all I can to stop the *given* from fading and prevent the hand of Unesta, the Ancient Evil, from touching this place."

"I remember you told me about her."

Oakheart told Sophy about the scroll he found in the library and Vorn's words inscribed therein. She found no comfort in them. It was all too plausible. She yawned and closed her eyes. She went to sleep feeling Oakheart's light caress along her back and the scent of him all around her. In her sleep she sighed and smiled. What a wedding night.

The sound of voices in the corridor jolted Sophy awake. She blinked. The walls glowed faintly but it was still night. Oakheart tensed as he too was roused from a deep sleep. The noise became louder and centred outside their door. Sophy groped for some clothing, while Oakheart placed the sheets strategically over them. A pounding on the door sent Sophy's blood pounding. Before Oakheart could say enter the door burst open. On the threshold stood Fern, with Aria close behind him. The forest folk were there, too, but they hung back.

"Fern?'" Oakheart shouted, bolting upright in bed. In a few strides Fern was there, kneeling on the ground with head bowed.

"Forgive me," Fern said, then raised his eyes. "'Tis true. Aria said you were within," he said to Sophy. "Perhaps these tidings are not as dire as I thought."

Aria was standing behind Fern. She touched his shoulder hesitantly, as if he had risen from the dead.

Oakheart clapped Fern on the shoulder. "Yes, my wife is hale as you see. But what tidings do you bring? How do you come to be here instead of amongst the Puri?"

Fern stood up, and twisted his hands together as if to encourage himself to speak. "I took the road you described to me and rode hard. There were many signs of horses and men traversing the wasteland. My instincts were on high alert and I rode on. A few patrols were around, but they were filled with the old and the very young. I slipped by them easily."

"Hanal?" Oakheart asked softly.

Fern shook his head. "The tents were near deserted. I snuck into the camp under the cover of darkness. Nothing but women and children remained, and even then not as many as should have been. I fear something has happened."

"What other signs were there? Anything else that struck you as odd?" Oakheart clasped Fern's shoulder and shared a look with Aria.

"No, nothing..." His eyes glazed over as he ran through his memories. "Except—I did see feathers...Glasshiver feathers."

For some reason they were all silent. Sophy could see Lillia whispering to the others. Oakheart and Fern had locked gazes. Then Oakheart nodded. "You did well, my friend. I cannot tell you how happy I am to see you." Oakheart squeezed her hand and smiled at her. "Rest now, and we will discuss these things further in the morning."

Fern hesitated, so Sophy asked him, "What is it?"

"On the way here I saw markings of horses. They looked like Argenterran horseshoe tracks. I think I overtook the party, but I fear they will arrive soon."

"Dellbright?"

Fern nodded once.

Aria's face paled. Then Aria took Fern's hand. "Come, Fern, I will show you to your room."

Sophy's heart stopped for a second when she saw the raw desire in Fern's expression when he took her friend's hand. "Oh dear," she whispered to Oakheart as the door shut behind the couple.

"Now you see my concern. 'Tis a terrible thing for Fern and for her."

"But if Dellbright is coming here then there's going to be a confrontation."

Oakheart sighed, his expression clouded with worry.

❧ 27 ❧

SIGNS AND PORTENTS

U rgent knocking on the door disturbed Sophy and Oakheart later in the morning. The walls of the retreat sparkled with reflected sunlight, making Sophy squint. Oakheart pulled on his breeches and opened the door.

A gaunt but excited Aran stood there. "You are looking well, my friend. May I come in?"

Gesturing for the adept to enter, Oakheart smiled. "Of course." He winked at Sophy, who due to the lack of speed in donning her clothes had to cringe under the bedcovers. She waved to Aran while trying to hide her blush.

The adept seemed suddenly conscious that he had disturbed the newly wed and reunited couple. He coughed gently after he took the seat Oakheart offered. "Forgive my disturbing you. I thought you would be anxious to know that signs have been reported."

"Signs?" Sophy asked.

"The gate?"

Aran nodded. "We are not sure of the exact timing but the early signs are there."

"You're talking about the Crystal Gate? Is that a bad thing that it's coming?"

Aran glanced her way. "Not bad in itself. The Crystal Gate comes rarely. We have not been able to predict with certainty until we detect signs."

"Early signs? What are the latter ones?" Sophy tugged the blanket higher and shared a smile with Oakheart.

"Well...." Aran's eyes widened. The floor began to shake. With a yelp, Sophy surged out of bed, dragging her blanket with her. The unearthly groan that accompanied the shaking made her teeth ache. The firesticks wavered, the whole structure tinkled like a large crystal bell, and then the tremor died away. During the whole thing, Aran had sat quietly and gripped the chair he sat on.

Oakheart's smile was gone. "That is a latter sign, I would say."

"But won't the Ancient Evil come through?" Sophy asked.

They both turned to her. "No. Vorn left a warding that would prevent her entering Argenterra," Aran explained.

Oakheart rubbed his chin. "This is why she worked through Rufus. She would need great power to break the warding and enter here."

Aran lifted a finger. "Or the land to be without the *given*. While it is less, it is not gone completely. I believe we have some time before Unesta can come enter here. We are not the *Ungiven Land* yet."

"Oh, so what are the signs of this gate approaching?" Sophy asked, glad that they weren't facing the imminent arrival of Vorn's nemesis.

The adept appeared to be calculating and then spoke. "There should be two more tremors and then the gate will appear. Not since..."

Aran saw Oakheart's pained expression. His gaze, filled with uncertainty, flicked to Sophy.

"Since my mother ran away so long ago," Oakheart finished for the adept.

"I am sorry to say this is so. But the signs over the years have been recorded. I have it on good authority that the Crystal Gate will open. It is such a rare occurrence. Do you not want to see it?"

Sophy's interest was piqued. "I do. Oakheart, let's go and see it."

"'Tis a rare marvel," agreed Aran.

Oakheart suddenly looked ill. "I am not certain. There could be danger. Did not Adage say something before he died? Beware the Crystal Gate. I do not want you..."

Sophy understood his feelings. She was an outlander, a stranger in a strange place. His mother had left him through the Crystal Gate and there was a fear in him that she would take the opportunity to leave. Part of her was angry that he thought like that. How easy it was to be insecure in love. "I don't want to leave you, Oakheart. I only want to see the gate because it is special and rare and unique to Argenterra. I know Aria would love to see it too. If it hasn't opened for so long then I may never get the chance to do so again."

Aran was nodding in agreement. Oakheart went to the door and opened it. The adept took the hint and stood up to leave. When Aran passed over the threshold, Oakheart said, "I will think on it. Thank you for letting us know."

Oakheart shut the door and stood facing it with his back to her. His back muscles were clenched, his shoulders tight. Hadn't she assured him that she wasn't going to leave him? She walked up to him and laid her face against his back. "Does it really bother you that much?"

He turned around to face her, expression half agony. "I know in my mind that you do not wish to leave Argenterra and me, but my heart fears that you will. I know this is a child's insecurity yet I ask you not to go to see it."

She touched his cheek gently. "We can discuss it after breakfast. We will have time to think things over."

Another knock at the door interrupted them. This was definitely not to be a wedding week. This time it was Lillia inviting them to eat breakfast before the forest folk departed with Brook. Lillia's eyes angled to the other room. Sophy guessed that was where Aria had spent the night....with Fern and not under Lillia's watchful eye.

Sophy smiled brightly. "We'll be there in a minute. We have to wash and dress."

Oakheart frowned while he pulled a clean shirt over his dripping hair.

"What?" Sophy said, knowing what was bothering him. "If the oath holds true, they have done nothing wrong other than give each other comfort. You can't deny Aria that, can you?"

Oakheart turned towards her, his frown still evident. "You do not understand. Fern will suffer torment and she will too. I wish they had the will to...to..."

Sophy gave up trying to arrange her tattered locks. She looked like a porcupine. "Not love each other? Resist the temptation. Hah."

Oakheart's stern expression softened. "I see what you mean. After Brook leaves with his family, we too must think of returning to Silverdale."

"I guess you're right. That's my home now, isn't it? But what about Fern's news? Is there trouble, do you think?"

Oakheart shoved Sophy gently out of the door. "More trouble than the breaking of the oath? The retreat's betrayal of me and those I love dearly? The abduction and torture of my wife by the Puri? Aria and Fern's predicament and possibility of Rufus on top of that? I fear no trouble in comparison to all that at all."

"Rufus?" Sophy's blood turned cold. "I thought he had been dealt with."

Oakheart realised that his attempt at levity had frightened her. He rubbed her back as they stood in the corridor. "I did not mean to give you cause for concern. Adage had doubts about Rufus's demise and so do I. I was not conscious at the time and know not what befell him. Aria seemed convinced that he was no more. And truly the evidence of his malice has not been clear since she freed you from the crystal. But still...I fear."

Sophy slapped his arm lightly, companionably. "You are real worry wart, aren't you?"

"A what?"

Sophy didn't have the heart to explain what a wart was, a little, annoying growth. "You worry too much."

He cast her a sideways look. "I am an ambassador to the high king, his adviser and his heir. 'Tis my role in life to worry, as you put it. One must remain open to possibilities."

That brought another thought to mind. "Hey, now that we're married, you aren't going to run off on your ambassador adventures and leave me behind, are you?" Sophy had now found something to worry about herself.

"Ah...so the Gift of Crystal Tree Woods seeks to tame me." He grinned, and before she could respond they were at the other door.

They entered the forest folks' room. "Good morning, all," Sophy said. Brook looked better than the last time she'd seen him. A bit fuller in the face and his complexion had improved. Lillia must have been plying him with her remedies and every morsel of food she could find. It occurred to Sophy just then that they were about to say goodbye.

Lillia had been so much a part of her life and now it would seem empty without her. How would she cope without her counsel? Heavens, she was going to be a princess. It would be a disaster without Lillia. A wash of sadness put Sophy off her breakfast. However, Lillia noticed and made sure Sophy ate more than her fill. Sometime after, when the conversation had hushed, Aria edged through the door followed by Fern. The atmosphere was strained. Aria didn't assist matters much. She blushed but pretended she wasn't and smiled way too much.

Sophy was dying to know what had happened between the couple. Fern's gaze never strayed from Aria; like he was bewitched. He answered the forest folks' banter absently and with monosyllabic answers.

Together, Lillia and Mellow stood in front of her. "'Tis time to bid you farewell, my lady," Lillia began, her eyes jewelled with tears.

"Don't say goodbye," Sophy said, hugging them both in turn. "We'll meet again. I'm married to Oakheart now so I can travel with him freely. No need for a chaperone. We'll see you soon and come and visit your newborn."

Oakheart's hand pressed against her shoulder. "Indeed. We will endeavour to see much of you in your home." Mellow's angry expression eased when Oakheart said the last, perhaps comforted that his mate was not going off on any errands again.

Mellow grabbed Sophy and hugged her all over again. "'Tis good to see you whole, my lady. I have not always been kind to you and I am sorry for that. Perhaps you will find it in your heart to forgive me." His dark eyes assessed her and she was too taken aback by his speech to respond. A slight smile lifted his lips. "Take good care of yourself and Oakheart. I will not have Lillia worry over you two needlessly. I want her mind on home."

"We will take very good care and thank you for everything." Oakheart braced arms with Mellow before pulling him into a bear hug. Fern and Aria waited until the forest folk had filed out.

"Sleep well, my friend?" Oakheart asked Fern, with an undercurrent of anger that surprised Sophy.

She elbowed him in the ribs. "You must be tired from your journey, Fern. I guess you and Aria had a lot to talk about.'"

Aria cast a worried glance at Oakheart. "Yes, we did," Aria said. "We've heard about the Crystal Gate." She lowered her voice. "We're going to see it..."

Oakheart groaned. "You dare not."

"What?" Sophy asked, looking at each of their faces in turn. Fern avoided looking at her.

Aria shrugged, looked around to see if anyone was near. "We've talked about it. We want to be together so we're leaving this place. We are pretty sure the gate will take us to our world. There I will contact my mother."

"But...You cannot—"

Aria leant in close, grasping Oakheart's forearm. "I cannot see Dellbright. Please understand. This is the only way, otherwise he will seek me out."

Fern added, "We will survive. I will take care of her. Once we are established we won't need help." Fern took Aria's trembling hand and stroked it soothingly.

Sophy thought she heard Oakheart's teeth grinding. She elbowed him again. "It's their decision. You can't make it for them."

Oakheart snapped, "I was not trying to."

Aria shushed them with her hand. "Please, keep your voices down. We don't want the adepts to know in case they try to interfere. More importantly, we don't want Dellbright to find out. We're relying on you to help us," Aria said earnestly and drew closer to them.

Fern touched her elbow lightly and said, "I know this is painful for you, but please, Oakheart. Help us."

Oakheart's complexion had a greyish cast. Shakily he drew his fingers through his hair. It took a few moments for him to form words.

Filling the gap, Sophy asked, "Why do you think the adepts will try to stop you?"

Aria's expression became neutral. "Well, no particular reason, but now that we've made up our minds we don't want anything to get in our way. And if the adepts find out they might tell Dellbright..."

Oakheart cleared his throat. "I will keep your intention from the adepts. More I cannot vouch for."

Aria wiped a tear from her face and stood on tiptoe to kiss Oakheart's cheek.

Conflicted feelings roared through Sophy. Foremost, she would miss Aria. She couldn't contemplate her not being there in Argenterra. Her ambiguous feelings about Fern were harder to deal with. Could such a jerk be good for Aria? Did Aria have really crap taste in men?

Then the thought that made her heart pound: did she want to go too? If Oakheart came with her, she would, but he'd never do that. He had responsibilities and duties. He would be high king one day. She'd already promised to be with him.

Her eyes rested on Aria's eager expression. Could Aria leave Gilly and have no misgivings? It was a big step to leave her child, with no sure means to get back. These were obviously questions that Aria must have had to deal with.

A loud roar sounded, thinning to a high-pitched groan. The floor beneath her feet shuddered. She reached for Oakheart and clung to him, hating the churning sensation in her stomach. The groaning died off and then came again, stronger, making her cringe. The crystalline structure seemed to chime louder this time, making her ears ache. Sophy gazed up at the ceiling, heard the voices of the adepts as they scurried down the corridor talking excitedly. The rumble grew stronger. Some plates toppled off the shelf. The tones emitted by the retreat structure grew louder until it became like the sound of a large church bell. The note played for long minutes after the tremor had ceased. It seemed that a trip to this gate was definitely going to happen.

Fern ducked out of the room and soon rushed back in. He

exchanged a nod with Aria—his gear was packed, a knapsack slung over one shoulder. Aria had still to go to the adjoining room to put her things together. "You will come with us and see us off then?" Fern asked, holding Aria's hand tenderly while he gazed at them earnestly.

Oakheart shook his head. "I will say goodbye here. I do not wish Sophy to go near the gate."

Sophy crossed her arms. "But..."

The look Oakheart sent her quelled any argument.

Fern staggered back. "But you must," he said, oblivious to Oakheart's mood. "You must see us safely through the gate. I ask you as your friend and kin."

Oakheart's mouth turned down in a frown. "I do not agree with what you are doing, but I venture no protest. It is your decision. But please do not ask this of me; do not ask me to see you depart through that gate."

Sophy swung around. "Oakheart, what is it?" This was more than just a moral objection. The hand holding hers trembled.

He wouldn't look her in the eye. "It's me, isn't it? You think I'm going to leave you through the Crystal Gate." She shook her head.

Aria slipped away to pack just when Sophy could have used the backup.

"You do not recall Adage's final words. He said 'Beware the Crystal Gate'. I did not think much of it at the time, but now I do. Something warns me that we should not go near it. Call it a premonition." He gazed at her. "I fear to go near it."

Sophy remembered the powerful adept's words. But Aria was leaving. "We can't let them go off alone."

Oakheart's gaze zeroed in on hers. "Sophy," he said softly, a thread of desperation evident.

Aria returned to the room, a bag swung over her shoulder. "So are we ready?"

Oakheart nodded as if Aria's assumption that he was coming had sealed his fate.

Sophy dropped her arms and smiled. "Give me five minutes. I have to get something warm on."

While she dressed she thought about how Aria would be

returning to her mother, Maralain, and her stepfather, Jeff, and they would work out their lives and leave all thoughts of Argenterra behind them. Aria would be able to tell her mother what had happened in the tunnels beneath Castle Crioch. It was ironic, though. Aria was the one who had been always at home here in Argenterra, yet it was Sophy who wished to stay, even though she was the odd one out.

Oakheart tugged her by the arm to stop her from exiting the room. "Listen, you talk to Aria and I will talk with Fern. Perhaps we can talk some sense into them before we reach the gate."

"Oh? You are really against it then." Sophy screwed up her face. She remembered the last time she tried to talk to Aria about her decisions regarding Dellbright. But Oakheart's earnest expression shut her up. He was serious and it meant a lot to him. "I'll try, but I don't think it will do any good. I'll ask her to walk with me, you do the same to Fern. But I think we're wasting our time."

Oakheart let her step ahead of him and then he called out to Fern.

Sophy had changed into breeches and a shirt and caught up with Aria in the corridor. "Hey, Aria, are you sure you know what you're doing? It's a really big decision."

The smile on Aria's face died. She tightened her lips. "Yes, I do." She turned away, but Sophy went with her. "Oakheart sent you to talk me out of it, didn't he?" She turned to Sophy, fixing her with a look.

"Well, yes, of course he did. He cares about you both. Cares about oaths and cares about this land."

"And what do *you* think?" Aria asked in a serious tone.

Sophy grew wary, narrowing her gaze. Aria would never ask her that and expect an honest answer. "I want you to be happy. Can Fern do that? You don't know him like I do. He can me mean and cruel..."

Aria let out an impatient sigh. "But he's sorry for that. He told me what he did and he wanted to make up for it. He went to offer himself to Hanal in exchange for you."

Sophy's shoulders sagged. "He did what?" Struggling with disbelief, she tried to digest what Aria said and respond. "That was nice of him to try...but better if he had not been cruel to me in the first place. Would you forgive Dellbright if he said he was sorry for what he had done to you? Would it make him a different man, would you trust him?"

Aria's lips twisted into a scowl. "Just how low are you prepared to go to do Oakheart's bidding? Trust you to bring Dellbright into this. Fern is not Dellbright. He's kind and caring."

"But would you? Could you? Wasn't Dellbright kind and caring in the beginning?"

Aria frowned and crossed her arms across her chest. "No, I couldn't forgive Dellbright for what he's done. Yes, he was kind and caring in the beginning like you said. You warned me. I didn't listen." Aria's tears fell silently, anger preventing her from dissolving into sobs. Her fingers clenched and unclenched, rucking the fabric of her breeches. "But this is different."

"I know you think it is."

"Sophy, just don't take Oakheart's side in this. Please."

Sophy had to agree to that. "Could you make love with Fern last night?" Sophy asked, more with a desire to satisfy her own curiosity than interest in the details. How weak was Aria's oath now?

Aria blushed, her creamy skin almost crimson. She coughed. "I don't think that's any of your business."

Sophy grinned. "It's not, but I asked anyway."

Aria took a few halting breaths and checked that they were alone. "I...we...lay together naked. It was beautiful to be looked at by him, to feel his soft caresses after...what happened. But giving pleasure only turned to torment." Her watery gaze met Sophy's. "It made the longing for each other worse."

"Did you try to, you know...um?"

Aria nodded and wiped a tear away. Sophy thought she understood. The sexual desire between them had peaked, teased by their petting, but with the inability to consummate their relationship on a sexual level, it had grown to frustration. Aria and Fern were probably still in possession of that strong, unsated sexual desire and that could be influencing their decision. But for the life of her, Sophy couldn't see what was wrong with that. She knew what physical torture it was. As for Dellbright, after what he'd done, he was a beast and deserved to be abandoned and shamed.

"So this desire drives you from here," Sophy commented without judgement. "That's why this sudden decision. But how will someone like Fern cope in our world? Would he still be loving and sweet to you in the rat race? When he has to work to support you, deal with the crime and the rush of the city and commercialism? What will our world make him? Will he still be the knight in shining armour he is here?"

Aria straightened and lifted her chin. "I think you've said enough. I don't want to hear anymore."

Sophy nodded. "Okay. Sure." Without another word she headed back to her room to confer with Oakheart. She wasn't angry with Aria. She paused and looked back at her friend.

Aria leant against the wall, studying her hands. "Aria, please be careful. I think you're angry at me because you know I'm telling the truth. You have doubts. You like it here, love this place. You and Argenterra are made for each other. It's been that way from the beginning. But for the love of Fern, your overwhelming need for a man, you will leave this place just so you can..."

"Sophy," Aria hissed at her. "Shut up. I won't listen to you and this poison you are pouring into my heart."

"Sure, I'll shut up. I love you, you know. I care about you, more than you care about yourself. One last thing: who will wield my power after you leave?"

Aria gasped and her eyes widened. Obviously she had not expected that question. Perhaps she thought Sophy would bring up her son, but Sophy wouldn't do that. That was too low a blow.

"I don't know." Aria brought her fisted hand to her mouth and bit on it. Sophy left her there to contemplate the magnitude of the ramifications of her leaving Argenterra.

❧ 28 ❦

THE CRYSTAL GATE

Sophy was wrapped in the Coldcloth robe Rae had lent her. Aran had returned it to her possession when he came to accompany them to see the Crystal Gate. It successfully kept out the icy wind, for which she was grateful. It irritated her skin but she was prepared to live with it. She shivered in spite of the robe. It reminded her of Rae...and that led to thoughts of Hanal. Not that these were ever distant. What was he up to? Where had he gone?

Her thoughts of Rae were ambivalent. The girl had left her for dead, not caring if she fell to her doom in the chasm or if she died in the mountain maze. Sophy put her survival down to pure chance. The adepts who had found her had only happened to stumble across her. Then again, perhaps they knew somehow that she was there. It was too late to ask Adage for the truth.

Under her robe, Sophy wore a comfortable pair of breeches, a shirt and leather vest; a parting gift from Lillia. The way the wind blew, one second curving then next arrow straight, the trousers served better than the adept's robes she'd been wearing. The latter fluttered and swirled, letting the cold wind bite. Her soft leather boots kept the chill of the stone path from her feet. After her ordeal, she never wanted to be cold again.

She supposed that as a princess she should be wearing a beautiful gown, but the plain travelling clothes made her feel relaxed and ready for anything. Besides, once they returned to Silverdale, her life would be governed by protocol and manners and the need to look the part. She caught herself frowning and uncreased her brows, with an effort. As long as she and Oakheart understood and cared for one another, then the marriage would work out. No point worrying about things yet to come.

Aria, too, was dressed for travelling, almost matched with Fern's plain shirt and grey breeches. They held hands as they walked ahead. Aran came with them, supposedly as a guide, but when they got out of the retreat the path to the gate was obvious. Looking at Aria and Fern she realised the poor adept had no inkling of the pair's plans. He chatted amiably to Oakheart as they walked, talking about old times.

A sudden gust of wind parted the Coldcloth, making her teeth chatter. She grabbed the ends of the garment and shut it tight. Oakheart's blue cloak flared out behind him as he stepped up an ice stair behind Aran. Above, Sophy saw a barren tree, gnarled limbs stretching emptily to the sky.

"That is the original Crystal Tree. The one where Vorn first worked the *given*," Oakheart said to her. "The limb he took to Crystal Tree Woods became the tree that yielded leaves to you and Aria when you found it."

"Wow. It looks nothing like the tree in Crystal Tree Woods."

The tree loomed larger as they climbed the stair. It looked dead and large, and the boughs creaked in the wind. Once she reached the top stair, she had to hold her robe shut again. A fresh gust of ice-damp wind tried to pry it from her fingers. Her face burned from the small ice particles blown up by the wind. Up ahead, near the mountain face, was a largish alcove. There seemed to be enough room for ten people to stand shoulder to shoulder.

Aran knelt in the sleet beneath his feet, either praying or meditating on the alcove. Sophy glanced over to Aria and Fern and saw him place a tendril of Aria's hair back over her ears. It was a tender moment between them. The look in Fern's eyes made Sophy soften towards him and maybe even forgive him for all his previous unkindness. Aria's expression was pinched and worried. Perhaps she was having second thoughts, after all.

Aran stood. "It will not be long. Soon the last tremor will herald the arrival of the gate. Do not fear it, though it is expected to be a strong one."

Sophy's gaze roamed, seeking out rocks that might tumble from above. There wasn't enough snow for an avalanche, but she didn't know for sure. She was trying to soothe her anxieties. Oakheart looked forlorn as he looked about, probably musing over some horrible memory of his mother leaving him behind. He barely glanced at the two lovers, who stood apart whispering and holding hands, apparently cloaked in a cocoon of togetherness.

The adept stood with them quietly, his gaze flicking here and there in expectation. Sophy was unwilling to intrude on Oakheart or the lovers and stood by herself. Kind of a sad way to end a friendship.

"Does the gate stay open long, Aran?"

He met her gaze. "'Tis recorded that the time it stays open varies. Sometimes it appears for a moment and then fades quickly. Other times witnesses say it stayed open for half the hour. 'Tis hard to say for certain. Its workings are a mystery."

Oakheart's eyebrows furrowed. He rested his hand on Sophy's shoulder and addressed the adept. "Its workings? Then 'tis a mechanism that can be controlled?"

The adept looked down at his feet and hesitated before answering. "There are some writings by Vorn that suggest it may be controlled. Indeed, he must have operated it to bring the First Comers here." He shrugged. "None alive know how it works or how to control it."

"Why aren't there more adepts here to witness the gate's appearance or to study it?" Sophy asked.

"Over the years, there has only been one adept to witness the gate's coming. This is to confirm the signs and portents. Alas, Adage has left us. As for others studying the gate, how can we? 'Tis a fleeting thing, a phenomenon. Some adepts fear it. You are here to allow us to make some recompense for our treatment. I asked of Lianal for permission for your presence as a boon."

Sophy shared a puzzled look with Oakheart.

"Has anybody else tried to study it?" Oakheart asked.

The adept looked uncomfortable and averted his gaze. He cleared his throat and cast Oakheart an uneasy glace. "Prince Daken came many times to study the gate. At the time he said it was to discover knowledge and add to ours. Any notes he made would have been archived after all these years. But we were ashamed of what transpired later and by how Daken misused his knowledge. Veld was sorely pained and...angered. We have been careful since...that is why we do not study it."

"Oh," Sophy managed to say. Talk about asking the wrong question at the wrong time. The last person in the world she wanted to hurt was Oakheart, yet she did it however unwittingly. "I'm sorry." She squeezed Oakheart's hand. "Aria and I came through Crystal Tree Woods, not through the gate."

"Yes, the wanderer is a strange phenomenon. It has deposited a woman in Argenterra every one hundred years. We think it is a natural phenomenon rather than a mechanism like the gate."

Sophy considered his explanation. How could something natural just happen to deposit women in a new world at regular intervals? Then again, there was magic here, so who knew? Even the Lake of Reflections defied explanation as it defied the *given*, or so Oakheart had said. Mysteries.

A slight vibration teased the bottom of Sophy's boots. A quick look to Oakheart and she knew he felt it too. The gate was coming. Reflexively, she stepped back, bringing Oakheart with her. Aria's eyes grew wild, her hair almost twitching with energy. Sophy frowned. Was that supposed to happen?

The lovers stepped back too, though she noticed that Fern clenched his belongings and Aria's hand tighter.

"Well, well, what have we here?" a familiar voice said from behind them.

Dellbright! Sophy's head came up. Somehow Dellbright had come upon them without them noticing. Aria let out a cry and spun around. Fern leapt in front of her.

Oakheart squeezed Sophy's hand and moved to place her behind him.

"The whore is..." he glanced at Fern and then at Aria, "...running away? You dare use the Crystal Gate?" Dellbright drew out his sword and lifted it. His dark eyes glittered as they studied Fern. "Get away from my wife."

Fern was not armed. Having been told that people in the other world didn't wear weapons, he'd left his behind. "Step back, Aria," Fern urged.

"Dellbright! You cannot do this." Oakheart's voice rang out with command. Aran was gaping, swinging his head between the two parties.

A tremor rumbled the ground beneath their feet. Fern struck, kicking Dellbright's blade out of his hand, only to land badly, stumbling to his knees. Dellbright fell back and Aria was hard pressed to keep her feet.

The vibration grew stronger. Sophy staggered. Rock groaned, filling her ears with its agony. Grit and fine particles of ice rained down from above. Only Oakheart's hold on her centred her. Aran's eyes were round with fear. His robe billowed as he ran from the alcove and increased the distance between himself and the gate. Sophy became concerned. Just how big was this thing? Instinctively she took five more steps back, not resisting when Oakheart pulled her back even further.

They struggled to stand, lurching from one side to the next as the tremor reached its peak. A sigh in the earth beneath their feet heralded the arrival of colours and lights in all the hues of a rainbow, spilling seemingly out of the air in front of the alcove. Dazzled at first, Sophy shut her eyes and then squinted behind her hands to see the gate arriving.

An archway began to materialise. It was made from a substance that Sophy couldn't name. Not crystal; it was too insubstantial for that, though she could see how the gate got its name. Something swirled within it, a radiance or energy. The last of the tremors faded, leaving them gasping with the final shake of the ground. Standing in front of them and towering above them was the Crystal Gate—its aura lit the alcove and be-silvered the light dustings of snow.

A scuffle behind them distracted her. Dellbright was up and

wrestling with Fern, who landed a punch. Dellbright fell down and didn't move. Aria dragged Fern away from him and towards the gate.

The Crystal Gate hummed and the rainbow light was so dazzling that Sophy nearly missed the two figures emerging from it.

They strode confidently out of the white light, haloed in colour. Their features were undiscernible, but teasingly they kept walking while Sophy held her breath. The adept was near collapse at the surprise of it all.

The gate stayed solid behind the pair and gave no indication that it would soon dissolve. Fern grabbed Aria's hand ready to dash through the gate, but she was caught by the sight of the new arrivals and pulled him back. Not wanting to wait, Fern talked urgently in Aria's ear, but she shook her head. With a dazed look, Aria stared at the two newcomers.

The newly arrived couple stepped closer. Aria dragged Fern with her as she headed for where they stood, partially obscured by the residual light of the gate and a mist from evaporating moisture. The mysterious couple's voices could be heard.

"We're back," said the man with a satisfied tone.

"Home again," said the woman's voice. "Alas, my oath is still in place." The woman sounded forlorn.

The man answered. "Mine is not. I am free."

As the mist blew off in fine fingers, Aria edged closer. The couple turned towards her. Sophy clung to Oakheart's hand, unwilling to let him venture to the light, lest he become caught in the gate. He was spellbound by the figures before him and the voices. His eyes widened as their words drifted towards them.

"Aria?" cried the woman, when she saw Aria approach her. The figure of the woman and Aria embraced.

"Mum!" Aria answered, her voice half excitement and half heartbreak. The wind blew shavings of mist and the figures grew more distinct.

"See, I told you they would be here," the woman said. "Is Sophy with you?"

Sophy's heart pounded. It couldn't be. "Maralain...Jeff?"

Oakheart glanced to Sophy and then at the figures, but his face was transformed as surprise, pain, hope and embarrassment all seemed to possess his features in turn. Sophy was puzzled: what could the visitors from Earth in the gate possibly mean to Oakheart?

The blurred figure of Aria headed back towards them, arms linked with the woman. Fern followed them like a shadow, his face a thundercloud. They stepped out of the light and, after a moment's bedazzlement, Sophy could see them properly.

Dark haired, with a goatee, the man stood smiling, and next to him was a woman with red hair braided and arrayed on her head. The couple held hands and blinked as if they had not seen who was near them. "We're back," the woman said and sighed.

"Maralain?" Sophy gasped. "It *is* you. But how...I don't understand. How did you know to find us?

Beside her, Oakheart made choking noises. Sophy turned to him. "What is it?"

Maralain froze, her eyes riveted to Oakheart. She looked ready to cry. "Oakheart?" she said at last, holding a shaking hand out to touch him. "My son?"

Jeff bowed eloquently. "I thought we'd find you two here in Argenterra. The signs seemed to fit. Didn't know the wanderer took people from that Scottish castle, but in the aftermath I thought that this is what must have happened. Particularly when they didn't find your bodies in the rubble." He smiled as he viewed the gathered party. He blinked when his eyes fell upon Oakheart and his smile dimmed a little.

Sophy shut her mouth. "Jeff? If Maralain is Oakheart's mother...you must be..."

Oakheart growled low in his throat. He had not moved towards Maralain, had not acknowledged her at all. Aria was spellbound from what Sophy could see.

Oakheart said for all to hear, his voice devoid of warmth, "His name is not Jeff. It is Daken, Prince of Valley Keep, who stands before you."

"Daken? But..." Sophy looked from one to the other, her mind working overtime. But would that mean Aria had married her own brother? Sophy was near to fainting and was dying to know what Aria was thinking.

"Daken?" Aria said, coming forwards a mite shakily. "I'm confused. How did you...why did you..." Tears fell unchecked down her cheeks. Maralain gave Oakheart another mournful look and went to embrace her daughter. She ogled Fern for a moment, then bent to her task.

"There, there. Jeff...Daken said he thought you might be here. He didn't know that the castle tunnels were a gateway. The authorities sealed them after your disappearance, so we couldn't come after you right away. We had to wait for an opportune time and find our way to the Crystal Gate. But you are all right! And Sophy too, though, she looks different." Maralain smiled at Sophy.

"Sophy is my wife," Oakheart said, taking Sophy's hand in his and placing his body in front of her. "Why have you returned? I do not understand. What is your relationship to Aria?"

Sophy squeezed Oakheart's hand, willing him to know that she understood what he was going through. Here he was suddenly faced with his mother, who had abandoned him all those years ago. The appearance of the Crystal Gate had rattled him and brought back all those old feelings of abandonment. Now his mother was right here, and things were seriously twisted.

Maralain squared her shoulders and lifted her chin. "Aria is my daughter—and hence your sister."

Oakheart's body twitched. The Crystal Gate was still open, bathing them in its unnatural light. Fern looked longingly at it, but began to look resigned to not going because he could sense the change in Aria. It was an unexpected reunion for them all.

Jeff stood taller and Sophy could see the resemblance to Dellbright. She shivered, remembering the words of Aurore told from the Coldcloth. He'd done some bad things in his time. But how could it be him? Surely they would be older. Maralain didn't look old enough to have a son of thirty.

"We came back because...for many reasons...we were concerned for the girls," Jeff began. "If they were not here we would have continued our search. But you see, look at her...Maralain could not be parted from her daughter. She fretted so much I couldn't bear it. And we want to come back home. It's been so long. We want to seek forgiveness for what we have done to others."

Jeff seemed close to tears. He breathed out. "I am free of my oath," he said. "You cannot imagine how fantastic that feels." He gazed wonderingly at Maralain. The former high queen closed her eyes and waited. She heaved in a breath.

"I am not free of mine. Veld lives yet."

Oakheart took another step in their direction, his body riddled with tension. "How callously you speak of my father. Like he is some burden you have to bear." Oakheart near yelled at her: "You left us! Abandoned us! Me!" He thumped his chest. "For him." Oakheart paused. Sophy had never seen him so distraught. He lowered his voice. "You dare to come back to flaunt your disgrace...and Aria...Aria?" Oakheart's anger dissipated as he beheld his sister.

Aria, it seemed, understood what he thought. Gilly was the result of incest. She looked near to fainting. Fern put his arm around her waist and she sagged against him. "Oh god," she said in a terrible voice. "Gilly!"

"What is it? What has happened?" Maralain demanded like the high queen she was.

"She married Dellbright and had a child," Sophy said.

Maralain's beautiful brow furrowed. "I do not understand? Married?" Her eyes dwelt on Fern meaningfully. "He is not Dellbright, surely."

All was silent. Oakheart shifted his feet. "Did Aria marry her half-brother?"

Maralain's brows furrowed. She glanced between Aria and Oakheart. "No. I carried Aria within me when I fled Argenterra." Silent tears were tracking down Maralain's cheeks. "Daken and I never had a child together." Her eyes grew sad. "Aria is your sister."

"Yes," Oakheart replied, keeping a tight rein on his feelings. "I love her like a sister. Now many things make sense to me. Why she was marked with the binding oath, for one."

Maralain took a step towards him. "My son, I ask forgiveness. If I could have taken you with me, I would have. But your life was here with Veld, with the land."

Oakheart held his breath as he struggled with his emotions. She wanted to smooth away his hurt, tell him it was all right, but she could do nothing but stand there and witness it all. "You left me, abandoned me. I followed you here to this place..."

Maralain's hand reached out, clasping air. "My son, I am so sorry. For years I've hidden away my grief at losing you. Now I've come back, perhaps I can make amends."

Oakheart blinked back the tears that stained his green eyes so like his mother's. "Will you honour your oath? Veld loves you still."

Maralain paled. She shared a look with Daken. "I...I..."

"Well, well, well. What have we here?" Dellbright said as he groggily climbed to his feet and wobbled the few steps he needed to be abreast of them. "So, Aria, you are the daughter of a whore as well as being a whore yourself." Dellbright chuckled, an evil sound. "So very touching, this scene of reunion."

Daken's eyes immediately went to his son. "Dellbright? So grown? So much like your mother."

Dellbright flinched and reared back, away from his father. "You? Do not speak to me. If it would not break the binding oath I would kill you where you stand. I have come to claim my whore of a wife."

The spell over the group dissolved: Fern darted protectively in front of Aria; Aria took two steps back and looked ready to flee in any direction; Jeff tried to grab Dellbright and missed.

"Whore!" Dellbright shouted as he surged forwards and backhanded Aria. Her legs crumbled, as she fell backwards.

In that moment Sophy thought the light from the gate developed a red tinge. Then it faded. She blinked, trying to focus, but the confused shouts and words distracted her. Could the light now be pinkish? Was that normal? Her mind was in turmoil. Oakheart grabbed her around the waist and tugged her away.

Dellbright stood preening himself as he lurched over Aria's prostrate form. "'Tis so fitting," he said and pointed at Maralain, "that you are *her* daughter."

The next instant Fern laid him out with a swift punch to the jaw. Jeff went to his son's aid, though he looked perplexed and saddened. "What is going on here?"

362

Fern hissed his words contemptuously at Daken. "He is possessed by something evil. That is what your deeds have wrought. You are responsible for what has become of him."

Fern looked at them all, desperation staining his cheeks red and darkening his eyes almost black. "I love Aria. I would die for her," he near shouted. He was trembling and kept clenching his fists. Sophy thought he would strike Dellbright harder, perhaps fatally, if he tried to interfere with Aria again. "We came here to use the gate. We wanted to flee so Aria could be free of her oath, just as you did. But I think our motives are better than yours." He pointed at Dellbright, who was trying again to climb to his feet. "He would kill her if he could. He is that twisted."

Dellbright jerked awake and spat blood as he righted himself. "You will die for what you have done." Dellbright raved like a man possessed. "Aria is mine, no one can take her from me." He writhed as his father held him back and would not be soothed.

Oakheart looked sickened to his stomach as he locked gazes with Sophy. She smiled tentatively at him. "It doesn't do to hate, does it?" she said. "This is what hate does, it twists and distorts. Forgiveness doesn't allow it to fester."

Swallowing, he shook his head and gazed longingly at his mother. "Sophy is right. 'Tis time to forgive." He held out his hand and Maralain took it, held it to her face and wept. With his other hand, Oakheart soothed his mother's hair and then drew her closer, letting her sob on his shoulder.

Sophy stepped backwards away from the various reunions and utterings of anger. Aria climbed to her feet and in a daze put her arms around Oakheart and her mother. Sophy realised then that Aria was a princess, had *always* been one.

When Aria's eyes fell upon Fern, her expression changed. There was longing and hurt and confusion. Sophy stepped back. She was out of place here, like she always was. Emotion clogged her throat. She was happy and sad at the same time. She wiped her nose with the back of her hand, and took another step back.

Suddenly, Aran called out, "My lady Sophy, do not step any closer to the gate. Please. Stop!"

Sophy turned to look behind her. The massive maw of the gate loomed above her with a swirling mass of colours in the centre. Mesmerised, she was unable to step away. Tendrils like red smoke appeared to be forming within it. She tracked them with her gaze, saw that they were leaking out of the rock face and working their way into the light-filled substance of the gate. That colour of red reminded her of Rufus—and that thought made her stomach drop to her feet. Taking a quick step back, she was disconcerted by the action taking place behind her.

Half-turning, she watched as Dellbright exploded out of his father's arms. Finger pointing, jabbing at her. "You!" he shouted at Sophy. "The Ancient Evil come again. Let me wring the life from you now." He was nowhere near her, but his anger and aggression scared her to the marrow of her bones. Wordlessly, she gaped at Oakheart. Denial. Distress. Dellbright came at her with a roar. Instinctively, Sophy stepped backwards.

"Sophy?" Oakheart called, his gaze taking in the gate. "Ware. 'Tis Rufus."

The hair on Sophy's neck pricked up and sweat tickled on her scalp. She dared to look behind her to see Rufus's form coming into being, woven together from red smoke. Why couldn't she run?

Sophy was in a web. Time seemed to stand still, and she became the observer. Aran was shouting at her: "Step back, by the *given*, step back! You are stepping into the gate!"

Dellbright was heading for her, broken free from his father's hold. Everyone's attention was divided amid the commotion, seemingly undecided on which was the worse threat.

"Sophy, come to me," Oakheart called in a desperate voice, stepping towards her. She willed herself to obey. Felt the power of him calling to her. She took a halting step, and then was wrenched, jarred by the warring power around her.

Behind her, she detected the vile presence, the festering glee of Rufus as he reached out to her with his mind. The filth of him stuck to her, oozed down her body to drip at her feet. Gripped by horror, she could move neither forwards nor backwards. Her body was held in a weird stasis.

Then there was a shift, a moment of satisfaction emanating from Rufus, and concurrently Dellbright lurched drunkenly towards her. She tasted it: a surge of malice. A shaft of red emerged from Rufus behind her, the power of it pushing her back. He was drawing from a well of power somewhere beyond the gate. The structure of the gate grew taut. It was going to close, to reflexively snap shut. Her heart beat frantically and her cry of warning could not break free of her constricted throat. With helpless eyes, she saw the beam of power heading towards Dellbright. There was a blur and Jeff stood in its path.

Dellbright was thrown by the impact and writhed on the ground, smoke wafting from burnt patches of his clothes. Jeff fell to his knees as the life was instantaneously sucked from him. His eyes were but smoking holes, his mouth a jagged and charred orifice, and then he toppled forwards.

Oakheart, distracted by Jeff's murder, took his eyes and attention from her. Sophy sensed his power ease off as Rufus's grew stronger. Blue smoke filled her gaze. It wove through the tendrils of the red. With a sickening sense of slowness, she was tugged back. The light within the gate surrounded her. The world of Argenterra lost substance as Sophy was drawn into the gateway between worlds.

EPILOGUE

The maelstrom seethed around Sophy, tugging her essence through light and darkness. Heat seared her like the inferno below. Her mind screamed in pain. Thought was torn away. She grasped at the thread, followed it out of mind and body. Her oath swelled as a fattened slug then split apart, severing her from Oakheart.

Following soon after was the memory of him, the sound of his voice fading, the feel of his hands on her, lost in the collection of sensations. His face melted like wax too close to a furnace. He was lost to her. She no longer knew his name, or shape, or face.

Agony ripped through her at the knowledge of her loss. Would she ever see and feel him again? All that she had was gone. Laughter was around her—and fear. The red spot on her mind reached for her but it too was caught in the storm and it too was hurled through the gate between worlds. But then the memory of red faded and there was only knowledge of existence, a blind knowing without understanding. Sophy was, and that was all she knew.

An eternity later she woke to the feel of stones digging into her back. The light was strange: pallid and brownish. What place was this? She tried to sit up but every muscle in her body protested. Her clothes were burnt and ragged. They fell off in scraps as she struggled into a sitting position. Barely three bits of cloth remained to cover her. She adjusted one so it covered her breasts and tied the end. The other two she pulled down over her hips so that she had a kind of short skirt. A little further away she saw a boot, twisted but still whole. She crawled over to it, wincing with pain. Then she noticed the landscape—the light, the two moons.

Above her was a twilight sky, pale grey and with high cirrus clouds etched against the heavens. Two moons hovered, pock-marked and close. The landscape was monochrome and barren. Nothing but rocks went for miles in every direction. Dark holes dotted the landscape like hungry mouths big enough to huddle in, deep enough to fall in. Sophy shivered. Something watched her, she could sense it. It was like the teeth of a comb travelling up and down her spine. Nothing came to greet her. This was a deadland.

A sense of danger prompted her to stand and try to lurch away. In any direction; it didn't matter. Her mind was fuzzy. She thought hard to recall where she had been and how she had come to be in this dead place, but nothing would come to her. She was alone: bereft and empty. She was certain she'd been somewhere else. The memory of green eyes flared for an instant in her mind, pale hair wafting around a face that she didn't recognise. A rich voice calling to her out of nowhere that made her heart trill.

Full of fear and confusion, she sobbed heartily as she picked her way across the stones. It was gone, the voice, the memory, the person. She had lost something, that much she knew. Not knowing who and what felt unbearable. With her tortured muscles, she laboured across the stony plain seeking out those that watched her. No thoughts in her mind and only the sound of her panting breath in her ears. In the distance, tree trunks glowed brightly as the light around her faded. They drew her like a beacon. Then her strength petered out and she collapsed into a dreamless sleep.

The End

PREVIEW OF UNGIVEN LAND

THE DEADLANDS

Wind rippled a strip of her torn and scorched clothing as she lay inert on the ground. Another gust dumped grit onto her head and spilt dirt onto her face. With a splutter, she woke, wiping at her nose and mouth and licking her dry lips. Sitting up, she coughed and then groaned as a sledgehammer of a headache slammed behind her eyes. She knew only pain. Toes, fingers, knees, elbows and even the tips of her ears radiated agony in slow waves.

Wincing, she cracked open her eyelids. Even blinking was like rubbing broken glass against her eyeballs. Rapid opening and closing of her eyes helped clear the accumulated irritants. Through a blurry gaze, she could see she was in that strange, barren place. Looking about, she realised it was empty and dead. Nothing moved, only the dust. She hadn't stumbled far from where she'd found herself at first...but she couldn't remember much about before, or before that. It was a blank wall of nothing, impenetrable. Even though she couldn't remember, she knew there was something before now. Before this.

Panicked, she scanned her surroundings for a place to hide. Although what she was hiding from she didn't quite understand. All around was a dirty, grey landscape, streaked with sulphurous yellow smears. Barren, dry and lifeless. Probably toxic too. The same muted colours smothered the sky, the worn, pallid rocks and the distant smoke-obscured hills. An inhalation of stale, tainted air added weight to the feeling that death and isolation surrounded her. This was a nothing place, a forgotten place. She could breathe the atmosphere, but there was no indication that anyone else lived here, no sign of life.

How long would air alone keep her alive? She exhaled, the taint of old smoke lingering on her tongue. She continued to scan the landscape, coughing a few times as her lungs drew in more of the left-over air. The pull of tender ribs, the cuts and scrapes all over her body, made her wish her cough would ease. What had happened to her? A quick inspection revealed scraps of clothing, looking burnt and torn. She tried to remember. But her head only ached more. It looked like she had fallen. But from where? Her head angled up to the sky. Nothing except the stringy strains of dirty-looking cloud. She was just here.

Alone.

Afraid.

Confused.

When her eyes adjusted to the light and the texture of the place, she discerned more geographic features. Behind, the land rose up to form a scarred ridge marked with clefts and tiny holes. Hidden behind the yellow-grey clouds was a sun that did little to lift the miasma of old smoke. Near the horizon she saw a pale, blurred patch. It looked like a wood, except there were no leaves to be seen, no suggestion of life or abundance. No green. White, spindly growths speared out of the ground, stretching up to the sky like the limbs of drought-stricken trees.

The wind picked up, nailing small pebbles into her arms and legs. She scrambled up, shielding her eyes, and yelped as each little missile pricked her skin. With three dust devils at her heels, she aimed for the shelter of the ghostly wood. Sharp rocks cut into the soles of her boots, hampering her progress. At times, she crawled with eyes scrunched shut against the wind-blown debris, picking her way carefully through the rocky obstacles and occasionally falling, only to leave a trail of blood on the stony edges.

Whimpering, she reached the edge of the wood and panted, relief coursing through her as the wind was less in the shadows of the trees. She shivered as the air cooled around her and took in her new surroundings. The shapes of the distorted trunks made her think of tortured, naked bodies. Edging further in, she stepped carefully around roots and holes, like puncture wounds in the ground. Close up, the growths looked like bleached trees, empty of colour and life. Even the crab-like roots, which clung to the ground as if someone had tried to pull them out, looked dead and stark white against the blighted ground. Dry twigs crunched under her feet and dead leaves rolled out of her way as she trod carefully. Dry brown vines and long fingers of dead leaves reached down from the sparse canopy, giving the impression that life was once vibrant. Now only the echo of life remained.

The bony looking roots were waist high and had dark hollows between them, appearing to lead to burrows beneath the trees. The dark gaps unnerved her, made her think she was being watched. She avoided looking into them. The faint memory of lightless, closed-in spaces made her shiver. In the wood, the rocks littering the ground thinned out and she could walk more freely and without adding to her injuries.

Choosing a large, thick root to park herself on, she decided to check the damage to her toes and the soles of her feet. Slipping off a worn boot, she began to clean her big toe with a bit of spit on her finger. It hurt but that particular spot did not appear too bad.

Fatigue weighed upon her. She needed to sleep. The light grew dim, a slow leaching of day. As dusk paled the sky, the tree trunks glowed brightly, illuminating everything. Leaf mulch was black against glowing roots grasping soil. Surprised by the phenomenon, she rose and continued further in, pressing through black drapes of leaves and vines. Scanning alternately overhead and along the ground, she searched for life. Nothing moved. Ahead was a large tree with thick roots that embraced a bed of leaves like loving arms. She headed to it and, kneeling, checked there was nothing living in it and then lay down to sleep.

WITH A START, SHE WOKE, STIFF AND SORE. IT WAS MORNING. THE tree trunks no longer glowed and the pallid sky indicated the sun was up. What had woken her? She drew in a breath. Sounds assaulted her ears: *click, click, clicking.* Her heart skipped a beat. What was that? Swinging her head around, she tried to detect which direction it was coming from. Behind her, beside her, in front of her, beneath her, it kept changing, moving.

Surging to her feet, she rubbed dirt out of her face and scampered over the roots, heading deeper into the wood. Soon she was surrounded by the pale dead trees. The sound of her panting was overly loud. Turning in a full circle, using her hand on a root to balance herself, she looked to the tops of the trees, seeing nothing except the empty grasping limbs. The *click, click, clicking* returned, more deafening than a forest full of chorusing cicadas in midsummer. Trying to calm her panic, she put her fingers to her ears. The sound would not be shut out.

What was it? Where was this place? Who was she? The memory of who she was hovered there, just out of reach, if only she could grab it and hold it for long enough. Something was missing. She knew that. She suspected that. And, then, the sounds overwhelmed her, stopped her thinking, and filled up her mind with fear. The noise grew even louder and she screamed for it to stop. Her voice was drowned out and she despaired, but then the crescendo of clicks lessened on its own, like the wind dying down after blowing a gale. Her breathing relaxed and her ears ached. She didn't trust that she could hear nothing.

In the distance she heard someone calling a name. Surprised, she began to make her way out of the wood. Her progress was slow, hindered by the roots that had to be walked around or climbed over. The source of the deep voice was coming closer. "Sophy. Sooooophhyy?"

A familiar voice—she didn't understand her reaction to it. Her stomach clenched and fluttered as if hundreds of butterflies were taking flight. *Sophy? That's me! That's my name.*

The voice was now in the wood. The trees deflected the sound, making it hard to pinpoint. The clicking sounds were rising again, over the sound of crunching twigs. Whatever was approaching was large, large enough to smash its way through the trees. She heard a ripping sound, then a crash followed by a mindless screech. A sound that made her shake uncontrollably. She no longer moved towards the voice. It was moving towards her and all she wanted to do was flee. Turning on her heel, she darted away, limping, stifling a yelp when she stubbed her toe and then hit her already bruised elbow.

The *click, click clicking* drowned out the encroaching voice. Her eyes darted around. She could hear movement around her, like cockroaches swarming. Then a tree collapsed near her, bringing down another one with it. She went to run and instead her foot was caught. Looking down, she expected it to be caught in a root, but there was a multitude of tiny hands around her ankles. Horror swept through her, as if she had seen a spider. A yell and then she tried to stamp her feet but as soon as she lifted one, the hands tugged and she dropped to her knees. A scream escaped her. She didn't want to be pulled down into the ground, down into the dark places.

Over her panicked screams, she heard the voice again, the one approaching, the one that ignited strange fear inside of her. The ground-hands tugged urgently. She was now thigh deep, her legs dangling into the empty space beneath the trees. The hands pulled at the strips of her clothing, pinching her thighs, her buttocks. She dropped into the hole, just managing to snag the root above her head with a desperate grasp. She gritted her teeth, fighting the pull of the many hands.

Another crash sounded as a tree fell. In the aftermath floated that voice, caressingly soft, yet loud enough to hear. "Sooophyyy! Come to me. Come to your angel."

As if they too were listening to the voice, the clicking creatures subsided, but the grip of the hands strengthened.

"Sooophy," said a sweet angelic voice. "Come to me, my sweet. I know you are there waiting for me."

Sophy let go of the root in preparation to cup her hand around her mouth to call out a reply. But before she could draw breath, the hands jointly yanked her down into the dark. Before she could let out a yell, hands covered her mouth, stifling her voice. Her eyes were wide in the dark. The creatures were there with her. Hundreds of them moving around her and on top of her, crowded in. As one they hushed as the creature with the seductive voice drew closer. Through the gap made by her passage, she could see the world, as on a television screen. She saw a rat-faced creature as he moved into view. Saw him sniff the air. "Know you are here, little one, little jewel. Come to me now."

There was no answer. He sniffed again. Did that mean he could smell her?

"You may hide for now, little jewel. But you will come to me eventually. There is no life here, no food, no shelter. I am your only hope of life. She wants to talk to you. Only talk. No harm will come to you if you come now and freely."

Even if she'd wanted to go with him, the hands held her firm and quiet. Yet the image of him was familiar. The memories came back, painfully and slowly; she had to fight to get them to the front of her brain. *Rufus*. His name was Rufus and he meant danger. There was more there, she could tell, but she couldn't remember. Just the sensation of danger and of past history where he had abused her, hurt her and those she loved.

Loved? There were people she cared about. Wide green eyes loomed large. She could not remember the details and could only recognise the gap in her life where these others she cared for had existed. Perhaps other memories would return, like the one of Rufus. Now at least she knew her name: Sophy.

A loud thump drew her from her reverie and then another. More trees crashing to the ground marked the passage of Rufus as he ploughed through the wood. After a while it grew quiet. The air smelt stale in the dark place and she could feel the little creatures moving against her, like a wave of rats. Panic made her thrash and then one by one the hands dropped away from her mouth. Then the creatures began to click again, soft, gentle clicking.

They had saved her, prevented her from giving herself up to Rufus. That meant there was intelligence there. Also, prior knowledge of this Rufus. So this was where he came from. There were more memories hovering, but they splintered and drifted out of reach. No point in forcing it or being angry with herself. If the memories were there then they would return. They had to.

Now that she had recovered from her original panic, the sound of the little creatures relaxed her. Her panting eased, her heart ceased thumping painfully and echoing against her rib cage. Without sunlight, she could not see the creatures, but she could sense them, hundreds of them. Yet they did not move to harm her, or bite her or make any other threatening gestures. So, what next? She couldn't stay down in this little hole forever.

Before she could assess her surroundings, the hands snatched at her again, dragging and pushing her flat and then tugging her along what appeared to be a tunnel. Her nose brushed the ceiling and then occasionally an elbow or knee caught the earthen sides. Fear took hold of her again, particularly when fine grains of dirt rained down on her face, so she closed her eyes and let the little creatures take her. It wasn't as if she had a choice. A scream perched in her throat, waiting to pounce.

Time passed slowly as she was carried through the tunnels. She scrunched her eyelids shut as she was passed along like a parcel moving along a conveyer belt, the smooth transfer from little hands to more little hands appearing seamless. Then there was a change. The air felt cooler, fresher, and the feel of the soil being so close subsided.

Opening her eyes, she found that she was in a small cavity dug into the ground. It was suffused with dim light. The hands lowered her to the ground and the creatures moved away. She sat up, her head gently brushing the roof of the small cavity, in time to see the tail ends of the creatures disappear into a multitude of holes. She shook her head, not sure what she had seen. Curling into a ball, she huddled, waiting for what came next. Yet there was nothing, except the occasional soft hissing click. She could, if she tried, stretch out here and lie flat. To stand up, she would have to fold over double and shuffle around. Better to crawl, she realised. As her eyes adjusted to the low light, she saw about twenty dark holes in the sides, roof and ground, which appeared to be tunnels leading away—a dark, tiny labyrinth. At the base of the opposite wall was a small pool of water.

On all fours she shuffled forwards. The creatures stared out at her from the tunnel openings, a series of small glowing lights that she reasoned must be their eyes. She could hear the soft clicking noises that they made. Were they afraid of her? Why? They had grabbed her and dragged her down here, so why would they be afraid of her?

"Hello?" she said quietly. "Is anybody there?"

A rising choruses of *click, click, clicking* responded. None of the creatures dared to put in an appearance. "Bugger," Sophy said to herself. "I guess I'll have to sit here while you guys work up the nerve to let me go or at least talk to me."

Her stomach grumbled loudly. "I'm hungry. Is there food?" No answer, not even one click. Using a hand-to-mouth gesture she mimicked eating, exaggerating the movements and making noises. Then she paused, looked around the tunnels, and saw lots of glowing eyes staring at her. Had they got the message? "A bit of food would be nice. Steak, medium rare, roasted potatoes and don't forget the gravy." Scooping out a seat for herself in the soft soil, she sat down. "A pizza maybe—with the works."

Once seated, she eyed the pool and decided to crawl over to it. Dipping her fingers in, she licked the tips. It tasted a bit musty. Her mouth was dry. She rubbed some of the water on her dry lips. Her tongue darted out. She may as well drink. Cupping her hands, she scooped more water into her mouth, and then drank deeply. It eased her hunger, lifted her mood slightly. She wasn't going to die today, which was a nice thought to have.

More clicks and then the sound of scampering feet echoed around her. She wondered what they were doing. Could they have understood her? Sophy was tired and her fear had lessened somewhat. Yet if she thought it through, there was not much hope. She was in a strange land, with barely any idea who she was or why she was there. These creatures had provided some shelter, or was it an early tomb? Without food she wouldn't last long. At least her headache had eased somewhat.

"Think, think, damn it. How long can you last on water alone?" She stared at the pool, wondering. Yet what point was there staying alive anyway? What was going to happen? What was she to do? A black wall of nothing in her mind was her only answer. Rufus was looking for her. He knew who she was and why she was there. Instinctively, she was afraid of him and memory was illusive, hiding the reasons for her fear. Yet, he seemed the only way she was going to find out about her life, about what she was doing there, unless she regained her memory spontaneously. Casting a look around the little hollow, she reminded herself of the world above. She wasn't going to last long in this place.

Curling herself up into a ball again, she tried to sleep, or at least nap. The sound of Rufus's voice tormented her as soon as she closed her eyes. The recollection of the trees shattering and crashing to the ground made her jump and twitch in her sleep. She groaned once or twice, trying to clear her head. Well rested, she might be able to deal with her new circumstances. Danger, she understood, but the loss of memory made things more difficult. There was something she should be doing, but for the life of her couldn't remember. Someone needed her but she didn't remember who or why.

Please note:
British/Australian spelling conventions are used in this book.

FOR EXAMPLE, WORDS LIKE COLOR ARE SPELLED COLOUR, RECOGNIZE ARE *recognise, traveling are traveling and so on*

DID YOU ENJOY OATHBOUND, THE SILVERLANDS BOOK TWO? Would you like to leave a review so that others can enjoy this series? *Leave a review*

GET YOUR COPY OF UNGIVEN LAND FROM AMAZON.COM NOW.

ACKNOWLEDGMENTS

Getting *Oathbound* ready for publication has been more of a challenge than I thought. It had been drafted for many years, but not revised and polished. No one had read it or commented on it.

I've learned a lot about writing since 2004, which is probably when I last looked at the manuscript. So, revising the book had its moments, to say the least.

Working on *Oathbound* has been a rewarding experience, despite the hard times. The novel required a name change—but the new title makes so much more sense. I hope you will agree.

I would like to thank Les Petersen for the awesome cover, and his patience as we went through a number of options. The new title of *Oathbound* helped with the design.

My lovely beta readers, Nicole and Aarjaun, who gave me some great feedback and advice. I couldn't address all their issues, but I did my best. Any lameness remaining in the story is all my own fault.

To my editor, Kaaren Sutcliffe, AE, thank you for your time and effort in bringing *Oathbound* up to speed. And thank you to Jason Nahrung for expert proofreading.

Many thanks also to my partner, Matthew Farrer, for his moral support, cups of tea and for getting it. He's a writer too, so when we are both involved in projects it's pizza or TV dinners and a very messy house.

I hope you are looking forwards to reading the conclusion to The Silverlands in *Ungiven Land*.

Donna Maree Hanson

ABOUT DONNA MAREE HANSON

Donna Maree Hanson is a Canberra-based writer of fantasy, science fiction, horror and, under the pseudonym of Dani Kristoff, paranormal romance. She has been writing creatively since November 2000 and has been a member of the Canberra Speculative Fiction Guild (CSFG) since 2001. She has had about 20 short stories published in various small press and ezines. In January 2013, her first longer work, *Rayessa & the Space Pirates*, was published with Harlequin's digital imprint, Escape. This was followed by *Rae and Essa's Space Adventures* in 2015. *Opi Battles the Space Pirates* was published in 2017. In September 2014, the first book in the dark fantasy Dragon Wine series, *Shatterwing*, was published by Momentum Books (Pan Macmillan Australia's digital imprint). The second book, *Skywatcher*, was published in October 2014. Two further instalments in the series will be published in 2017: *Deathwings* and *Bloodstorm*. In 2015, Donna was awarded the A. Bertram Chandler Award for services to science fiction in Australia.

Donna is currently a PhD candidate researching popular romance fiction.

Argenterra: Book One of the Silverlands, her epic fantasy series, was published in 2016. *Oathbound*: The Silverlands Book Two was published in early 2017. *Ungiven Land* was published in June 2017.

You can find out more about Donna on her blog and sign up to her newsletter Wing Dust.

http://donnamareehanson. com

Twitter @DonnaMHanson

Facebook https://www.facebook.com/DonnaMareeHanson/

www.ingramcontent.com/pod-product-compliance
Lightning Source LLC
Chambersburg PA
CBHW050502110726
47899CB00005B/1303